Her smile sucked the breath from him. "I've been hoping to hear ye say that fer quite some time now."

She was awakening parts of him that had been put to sleep long ago. Duty to God and to the throne came before selfish desire. Honor came before love. But not tonight.

Tonight he would give her what she wanted, and take what he needed. He'd promise her his heart amid the music and the spirits, and the laughter born from both.

"Ye've been staring at me like that all evening."

He raised an eyebrow. "Is that so?"

He gathered her in closer and kissed her as they came to the door. He kicked it open with his bare foot. He wanted to toss her on the bed and jump in after her.

"Tell me how I look then?" he asked, returning to the door to bolt it.

"Like a starving man."

He turned from the door to find her removing her kirtle. His lips curled when her dress fell to the floor.

"That," he told her while he unlaced his pants and moved toward her, "I am."

Also by Paula Quinn

The Scandalous Secret of Abigail MacGregor

PAULA QUINN

FOREVER

NEW YORK   BOSTON

Forever
Hachette Book Group
1290 Avenue of the Americas
New York, NY 10104

www.HachetteBookGroup.com

Printed in the United States of America

First Edition: March 2015
10 9 8 7 6 5 4 3 2 1

OPM

Forever is an imprint of Grand Central Publishing.
The Forever name and logo are trademarks of Hachette Book Group, Inc.

The Hachette Speakers Bureau provides a wide range of authors for speaking events. To find out more, go to www.hachettespeakersbureau.com or call (866) 376-6591.

The publisher is not responsible for websites (or their content) that are not owned by the publisher.

To my Savior King, You taught me how to dance again.

To my husband, my knight, I'll love you until the end of time.

To Daniel, Samantha, and Hayley, the three most thoughtful, caring, perfect beings in my world.

MacGregor/Grant
Family Tree

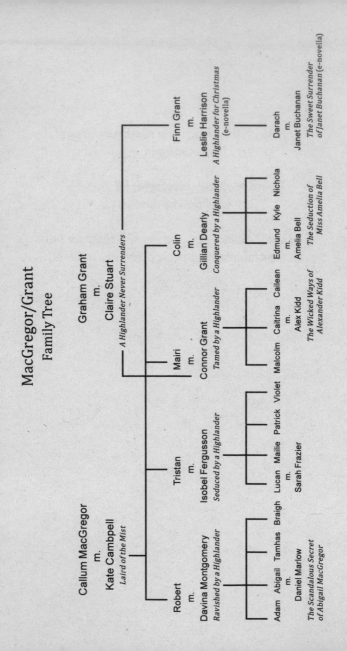

Callum MacGregor
m.
Kate Cambpell
Laird of the Mist

Graham Grant
m.
Claire Stuart
A Highlander Never Surrenders

Robert
m.
Davina Montgomery
Ravished by a Highlander

Tristan
m.
Isobel Fergusson
Seduced by a Highlander

Mairi
m.
Connor Grant
Tamed by a Highlander

Colin
m.
Gillian Dearly
Conquered by a Highlander

Finn Grant
m.
Leslie Harrison
*A Highlander for Christmas
(e-novella)*

Adam Abigail Tamhas Braigh
m.
Daniel Marlow
*The Scandalous Secret
of Abigail MacGregor*

Lucan Mailie Patrick Violet
m.
Sarah Frazier

Malcolm Caitrina Cailean
m.
Alex Kidd
*The Wicked Ways of
Alexander Kidd*

Edmund Kyle Nichola
m.
Amelia Bell
*The Seduction of
Miss Amelia Bell*

Darach
m.
Janet Buchanan
*The Sweet Surrender
of Janet Buchanan (e-novella)*

The Scandalous Secret of Abigail MacGregor

✠

Chapter One

*A*bigail MacGregor brushed her snowy tresses out of her eyes and watched her twin brothers, Tamhas and Braigh, cut across her father's private solar. "Faither!" they said almost in unison. "A letter was waitin' fer us in Broadford." Braigh, the oldest by four minutes, handed him a folded parchment. "'Tis from London!"

"Who is it from, Faither?" Abigail asked, rising from her chair. She smiled at her mother, convalescing in her settee by the window, and pulled her blanket up to her chin.

"Lads," Robert MacGregor said to his sons instead of answering her, "go fetch yer brother and yer uncles."

"Which uncles?" Braigh asked.

"All of them."

"Robbie, who is it from?" his wife, Davina, asked softly when the boys were gone. Bronwen, her giant hound, rested at the foot of the settee and raised her head to whine at the sound of her mistress's gentle voice.

"'Tis from... the queen."

Abby turned to her father. Her mother sat straight up.

Very few people in England knew Davina MacGregor was Davina Stuart, the true firstborn daughter of King James II of England and Anne Hyde. She'd been secluded in an abbey her whole life, unknown to her sisters or anyone else to ensure a Catholic successor should James II die without a son. Those who suspected her existence didn't know she lived with the MacGregors somewhere on Skye. So why was the queen, her mother's sister, penning them a letter?

"What does she say?" her mother asked, her voice shaken.

Her father read the letter silently. Abigail hadn't seen his face drain of so much color since his beloved wife came down with fever three months ago.

"She says..." He stopped and looked up from the parchment, his blue eyes startlingly vivid. "She says she knows of ye and she commands yer attendance in London."

Abby shook her head. Her mother couldn't leave Camlochlin. The exceptionally longer winter had struck her slight body like a plague. She was just beginning to recover and it was still brisk outside.

Her father shared her thoughts, proving it when he held up his palm to stop her mother from speaking. "Ye're not goin', Davina. My mind is set."

Thank God. Abby gave a soft sigh of relief. When her father set his mind one way, he rarely moved it again. Abby loved him and respected him as clan chief. She had grown up hearing tales of him from his bard, Finlay Grant, and also from their aunt Maggie, who favored her Rob above all others, save for her brother Callum, and from Abby's mother.

Her father was stubborn and steadfast in his duty. He

made certain that Camlochlin remained a safe haven for displaced Highlanders. With that responsibility came many challenges. She'd watched him face them with confidence and keep them all safe. Everything done was for the good of the clan and the land.

In the last few years, Scotland's independence had changed so much. Clans were changing, moving into burghs with Lowlanders as their neighbors.

Abby didn't want that kind of life. She was happy in Camlochlin. She hoped her father would always be there to make decisions that would protect the clan and their home, but when he grew weary of it all, who would take his place as chief? Her older brother, Adam? God help them all, no.

It was up to her.

She might bare more resemblance to her mother but it was her father's heart she followed.

"Robbie, my love," said his wife, "how do ye know I was going to suggest anything of the sort?"

He looked at the letter clutched in his hands and then at her. "Ye will when ye hear the rest. But wait a moment fer the others. 'Tis something everyone should hear."

Abby swallowed and sat down beside her mother. What was it? What was so important that everyone needed to hear? She worried that life here would change now that the monarchy knew of her mother's existence.

She and her mother didn't have to wait too long before her uncles arrived. Abby's brother, who was Robert's heir, wasn't with them.

"Where's Adam?" her father asked the twins.

"With Murron MacDonald," Tamhas answered.

"He said he'd be here shortly," Braigh added.

Her father didn't wait. When he told them who'd

penned the letter, Abby's uncle Tristan poured them all whisky from her father's decanter.

"She threatens to send her full army to Skye to come get her if Davina refuses to go to England." He stopped when his wife gasped and looked around at his brothers and his brother-in-law to gauge their reactions. He'd already decided Davina wasn't going. That meant the army would come. Their lives and their family's lives were at risk. Robert MacGregor was chief to his clan but he still discussed his decisions with them. If they all didn't agree with this one, what would he do? "She also commands," he continued without looking at the parchment again, "that my wife go with no Highlander to accompany her, but with the queen's personal guards only."

Everyone remained silent and still while his words settled on them.

"I must go." Her mother broke the silence and swept her blanket off. Abby held it in place in her lap while Bronwen sat up and plopped her huge paw in Davina's lap.

"Are ye mad to think we'd let ye go, Davina?" Abby's uncle Colin asked.

"Mayhap the fever has returned," said her uncle Connor Grant.

"Should I get Isobel?" her uncle Tristan asked, bringing more relief to Abby knowing that they agreed with her father.

"I can't let people I love die because of me. Not again."

"We need to alert the other clans."

"Aye, Tristan," her father agreed. "I dinna' think the queen knows where in Skye we are. She'll send her army throughout."

"Rob, my love," her mother pleaded woefully. "Please. I can make it to London and stop any fighting from taking place. Let me do it. I don't know how she found out about me but my sister simply wants reassurance that I am no threat."

Abby had heard tales of St. Christopher's Abbey, where her mother grew up, and how her royal family was responsible for hiring a madman to burn it down with more than twenty nuns who raised her inside. She would have died as well if Abby's father hadn't rescued her from the flames. Her mother didn't want to be responsible for more deaths.

"She knows ye're no threat," her father corrected. "No Catholic can ever claim the throne again."

"But she isn't certain I am Catholic," her mother argued. "She needs reassurance. I can give it."

How had Anne found out about her? Had she always known? Did she really just want assurances that the first-born heir to England's throne didn't want the seat?

"Davina," her father said softly. "My mind is set, my love."

"What of our kin?" her mother insisted. "Our bairns, Rob. What if they are killed?"

The thought of the queen's army coming down on Camlochlin turned Abby's stomach. Nae! She wouldn't let it happen. She stood up again. "I will go in her stead, Faither!"

Hell, she wasn't afraid to go to England. Even if she was, there wasn't a choice. She would go in her mother's stead and convince her aunt that the true heir was happy just where she was and that she was the last remaining Catholic novice from St. Christopher's. Davina Stuart wanted no part of the throne. Abby would make the queen see that. She would win the queen's favor for her mother's sake and try to guarantee some kind of protection for the

clan. Protection against the loss of their name and their
Highland way of life. She wasn't afraid. What was the
worst that could happen? Mayhap she might even meet
a handsome knight like the ones from her grandmother's
books. She'd be escorted by the queen's personal guards,
so nothing . . . She blinked at her father, who was staring at
her like she'd just sprouted a second head.

"Abigail, d'ye sincerely think I'd let ye go to England
alone?"

Her eyes glittered like the frost on the mountaintops
outside the castle, but there was nothing cold about her.
Like her mother, everyone at Camlochlin loved Abby.
She fit in with everyone—whether in the kitchen, in the
sewing chamber, or on the practice field. The chief's only
daughter won every heart, especially her father's.

"Ye dinna' have a choice, Faither. Our clan depends
on it. I will do whatever I must to keep us safe. The Royal
Army would do much damage and eventually they would
find us. I'm not going to sit back while my beloved faither
and uncles fight and possibly die in a battle. I'm going. My
mind is set."

Colin was the only uncle who smiled. It was slight, but
Abby caught it.

"Ye will go over my dead body, Abby," her mother told
her sternly.

"And 'twill be dead indeed if *ye* try to go, Mother."
She shook her head and turned to the men again. "Ye all
know that one day I want to be the chief. This clan needs
a dedicated leader when our chief steps down. Adam isn't
yer man and ye all know it. Though I'm a woman, I want
to prove to ye that I'm worthy of the title."

Colin raised his cup to her and smiled. "Ye're braw,
lass. Ye'll have my 'aye' when the time comes fer the

next chief to be chosen." He turned to her father and winked at him. "Not that I want that day to come any time soon, brother. I just think she's a better choice than Adam—"

"I dinna' give a damn about that," her father shouted. "Ye think my only daughter should go to meet our enemy alone?"

"Nae, of course not." Colin laughed. "Why the hell would ye think that? We'll stay a day behind her."

Tristan smiled. So did Connor. Abby loved them all. They were strong willed and fiercely protective yet tender enough to pick heather without breaking a stem. Each of them possessed traits she wanted in a husband and would wait for, no matter how long it took to find them.

"I canna' let her go." Her father turned to her. "Ye ask the impossible."

She knew she did. How could she expect her father to allow her to do such a perilous thing? She didn't expect it. She wasn't a fool. But it had to be done to save them. Her mind was made up. No one would change it.

She smiled softly and went to her father, taking his arm in hers. She'd learned it's easier to go around the mountain than to try to conquer it.

"Faither, I love ye with all my heart, but I didna' ask."

Abby penned her reply to the queen herself, and without waiting for her father's approval, she rode to Broadford and made arrangements to have the letter delivered to St. James's Palace. Afraid or not, she was going to England to see to the safety of her kin. The more she thought about it, the more she knew she wouldn't be stopped. No one in her mother's royal family knew of her existence. Or rather, they thought no one knew. Now the queen knew.

Abby wanted to use it to her advantage. Her blood ties to the queen could prove to be a blessing.

Upon her return to Camlochlin, she met up with her eldest brother, who was returning from Torrin.

"Where were ye earlier today, Adam?" she asked, riding her surefooted mount around his appropriately named dog, Goliath. There were many dogs at Camlochlin, but he was one of only five offspring of the late beloved wolfhound Grendel. "Faither sent fer ye and ye didna' come."

Adam exhaled a long breath and turned his eyes toward Camas Fhionnairigh. Abby knew where he'd been and what he'd been doing instead of seeing to his duty. She didn't blame Murron MacDonald. Adam was striking, with raven hair like their father's and pale skin like their mother's. It was a shocking contrast, and with even lighter blue-gray eyes than Abby's, his beauty was chilling and otherworldly. He was an indifferent danger to women everywhere he went.

"Aye, a letter from London. The twins told me." He swung his cool gaze to her. "Ye know I have nae interest in anything English."

"It seems ye have nae interest in anything that doesna' wear a skirt."

He smiled and Abby thought it a pity that he was so arrogant and flippant about his life.

"Ye are practically handing me yer birthright, Adam."

He shrugged. "Who says I want it?"

He didn't. He'd made it clear on more than one occasion. He didn't want to rule. He wanted to raid, women mostly. That was fine with her. Less opposition later. She smiled.

"Give it to me then." She waited for his answer. If he

handed his birthright over to her, no one would contest it. "Why wait? Find yerself a woman who can find a way to love ye, take her as a wife. I'm beginning to think that only Edmund and Lucan are fit to be faithers."

He laughed, infuriating her that he found his birthright a matter of jest.

"Why d'ye want the weight of our clan's survival on yer shoulders?" he asked her. "Ye're the one who should find a husband and have babes, sister."

Oh, she wanted to punch him in the face. She'd never wanted to punch anyone so badly. "Adam, ye—"

"I say that because I love ye," he cut her off. "I dinna' want to see ye carry such responsibility on yer back. Ye dinna' understand how crushing being chief will be."

"And ye do?"

"I've been groomed fer it my whole life. I have a better idea than ye have aboot it."

"That might be true, but the safety of the people in Camlochlin means more to me than it does to ye."

He cast her a wry smirk. "I dinna' think we should meddle in English things, but I would fight if an army came here, Abby."

"Well." Abby didn't smile back. "They might be doing just that. The difference between us is that I would stop them from coming in the first place. The letter, brother. 'Twas from the queen. She knows of Mother's existence." Ah finally, a reaction other than a glib quirk of his lips. "Queen Anne has commanded Mother to travel to London with English guards."

"She canna' go."

"She isna' going. I am."

He laughed again and she smiled with him but there was no humor in her eyes. Let them all think she was mad or foolish. She was willing to put herself in harm's way for them. Adam might not have been paying attention to his grooming, but she had been. She'd hung on every word, every lesson she'd watched from her place atop the barn with her cousin Caitrina.

Robert MacGregor's blood flowed through her veins. She wanted to be like him, and she was. Almost everyone had told her so. The passion to protect their clan drove her. She wasn't going to let harm come to them because of a queen's command.

"And Faither has agreed to this?" her brother asked.

"He will. If I dinna' go, the queen has promised to send an army here."

They discussed it more, with Adam finally taking the matter more seriously.

She was going to England to save her clan and to prove she was worthy of someday becoming chief. And nothing was going to stop her.

Chapter Two

Captain General Daniel Marlow, knight of the Most Noble Order of the Garter remained still while his valet, Albert, dressed him. Hell, he hated formal attire with all its pomposity and lace. His thick embroidered brocade waistcoat and justacorps made him feel heavier on his feet. He could barely move his damn head around the magnitude of heavy lace at his throat. His wrists too were shackled in it. And who in damnation decided to make shoes with high heels for feet the size of his? His squashed toes only added to his increasingly foul mood. He'd rather be wearing his uniform, though even that was a bit stiff and overdone.

"Think the queen would take offense to me arriving in my coat, breeches, and boots?"

"The queen," said she, herself, entering his chambers in her wheelchair, "takes no offense in anything you do."

He turned and offered Anne Stuart a half smile, reaching for her hand before she offered it. "You look radiant tonight, Ma'am."

A blush stole over her pale skin and her smile lingered

for a moment longer before disappearing back into the shadows.

He waited while she dismissed his valet and the servant who wheeled her around the palace. Her usually cheerless expression was hard and determined. Something serious was going on and he was about to become part of it. He hoped there was some form of trouble, some enemy that needed the justice of his sword. He welcomed fighting. He'd welcome anything that got him away from court, and from Charlotte Adler, the Duchess of Blackburn and the queen's close friend.

"Pour me a drink of wine, will you, Daniel?" she asked when they were alone.

He didn't ask her what her physicians said about her partaking of the vine. None of them knew what caused her to go lame. It could, they said, have been caused by anything from gout to a dozen different diseases. They were no help. Daniel believed it a culmination of many sorrows too difficult for any person to bear. She'd suffered miscarriages or stillborns twelve of the seventeen times she became pregnant. Four other children died before the age of two. Her fifth child lived for eleven years, and then he also died. Anne was utterly grief stricken and had never truly recovered.

If she wanted wine, she would have it. He poured some for himself, as well.

"Daniel," she spoke softly as he handed her the cup. "You know that I trust you more than anyone in my life, and that I favor you above all others."

Yes, he knew. Her favor had given him the title of Earl of Darlington. It had made him a knight of the Garter, the highest order of chivalry, and granted him the rank of captain general, the highest commander of her entire army. She didn't have to grant him such honor. He had pledged his loyalty to the throne, as his father and grandfather had done before him. Regardless of who sat there or what she gave or didn't give him, he would serve her. But he thanked God every day that he served Anne Stuart.

He'd known Princess Anne since he was a babe of two. His father, Edward Marlow, was a general in King William's army. He kept close to the royal family, moving his own family with Anne's from her residence in Whitchall Palace to St. James's Palace. He had wonderful memories of Anne, younger, newly married to her prince, happier. She loved Daniel from the start, keeping him close under her wing the way a mother might do to her child. They became close friends despite the difference of sixteen years, give or take, between them.

"There is an enormous thing I must ask of you, Daniel. You have never refused me, though you might decide to now."

Worry creased her brow. One thing he didn't want her to do was worry. His foul mood over his clothes forgotten, he flashed her a wide grin and fell into a chair by the hearth. "I'll do it if you excuse my presence at your ball tonight."

One side of her mouth tilted in a rare smile. "You will do it and you will attend."

She knew he would. He did what she asked. That was his duty. More of a privilege, because he loved her.

"What is she doing?"

"Who?"

"Charlotte," Anne said, the tilt of her fragile smile remaining. "What is she doing to you that makes you so desperate to avoid her tonight at the ball?" When he narrowed a skeptical gaze, she laughed softly. "Oh, come now, dearest, don't look surprised. Do you think I'm blind as well as lame? You are miserable. I just thank God you haven't taken her to your bed."

He set his cup down and let his gaze darken on her. She paid no attention to it.

"I asked her," she confessed, ignoring too his parting lips. "Knowing her, she would have taken enjoyment in telling me. But she reminded me, instead, that she is a lady."

Daniel caught the humor in her voice and if he wasn't so damned annoyed at her, he would have enjoyed her amusement. He tossed his head back to guzzle the rest of his wine and let the spirit soothe him.

Things had gotten bumpy between the queen and Lady Blackburn last year, after Anne's husband died and Charlotte was cruel to her about Anne's not wanting to remove his portrait from her chambers. Whatever bond they had formed before Daniel left for battle had been splintered by the time he'd returned. The wedge between them grew each day. Still, Daniel wasn't sure if Anne appreciated what a true viper Charlotte Adler was.

"Daniel, look at me."

He lifted his eyes from the inside of his cup and did as she asked.

"You're angry with me," she said quietly.

He hadn't realized his jaw had tightened until he relaxed it. "Not angry," he told her. "But I thought you would never interfere in my personal affairs."

She didn't back down. He didn't expect her to. "And I never shall again in any circumstance that does not have to do with you and Charlotte in bed."

He stood. He didn't want to talk about his intimacies, or lack of them, with her.

Her gaze followed him.

"Promise me you will never take her to your bed like my sniveling cousin Montagu has done."

"I've no intentions on taking her to my bed," he told her honestly. He wasn't a fool. "But why does it concern you so?"

She sipped her wine and shrugged her shoulder at him. "'Tis just wise counsel. The same I would give to my own son."

His anger faded. He didn't believe a word she said, but she hadn't meant to offend or insult him. Perhaps she was aware of Charlotte's true nature.

"She has done nothing to me," he assured her. "I keep her close to keep others safe. I know you don't care to hear this and that's why I rarely mention it anymore, but I don't trust her. She has secrets and I intend to learn them."

"Perhaps," the queen said, going pale and looking faint. Daniel went to her. "Perhaps 'tis best if you no longer associate with her, Daniel."

He cast her a confused look and felt her forehead. "What's going on, Anne? Do you know something about her or her husband that you're not telling me?"

"No, no, of course not! I simply don't want you to suffer her for my sake."

He bent a knee before her wheelchair and took her hands in his. Enough of her worrying. He would have no more of it. "I would do anything for you. You've no cause to worry about Lady Blackburn. Put her away from your thoughts, my dear Anne. I'm no fool." He kissed her hand and then smiled up at her. "Now, what is this enormous thing you must ask of me? You have only to speak it and I'll do it."

She set her dark, level gaze on his. "I need you to ride to the Highlands of Scotland in the morning."

No. Hell. Not that.

"There is a young woman whom I need you to escort back to me. She is very important. The daughter of a renowned Jacobite chief named MacGregor."

Daniel didn't know whether to laugh or have another drink. Or four. There was only one thing worse than Highlanders and that was Jacobites. They were those who pledged their lives to Anne's stepbrother James Francis Edward Stuart, allegedly born of King James and his second wife, Mary of Modena, and his claim for the throne. Daniel had fought enough Jacobites to know they were among the most fearsome men who lived. He also knew they hated Anne, and William and Mary before her. They were rebels with no loyalty to the throne or obedience to any law. They were everything he had been trained to despise. Traitors to their king, or in this case, queen. Such people deserved the noose. Why the hell would she want a Jacobite in her castle? He had to have heard her wrong. "You want me to ride to the Highlands of Scotland to bring the daughter of a Jacobite outlaw, whose name is proscribed, to St. James's Palace, and to your side. Is that correct?"

"Yes."

He straightened and poured himself another drink. After he tipped back his head, emptying his cup, he looked at her. "How can you ask me to put you in such danger?"

"The young woman is no danger to me. But because of her name, she is fair game to anyone who wants to bring her harm. I need you to see that none comes to her." She grabbed his wrist when he moved before her, shaking his head, against the idea. "I'm going to make her my hand-maiden, and she is going to help me secure the Jacobites' support."

"How?" he asked her. The Jacobites were her greatest enemy.

"Leave that to me. I'll explain everything to you later, but for now, you are the only one I trust to do this. Daniel, I know your feelings about the Jacobites, but I need you."

Yes, she needed him to babysit a Jacobite. No! He didn't have the stomach for it. "Anne," he tried one more time. "I don't think bringing a Jacobite here is wise."

"I know, dearest. But wise or not I want her here."

Daniel nodded and looked into the fire. What support could Anne hope to gain from a Highland chief's daughter? And why a MacGregor? Cameron MacPherson was the most dangerous Jacobite in Scotland. Why not seek an alliance with him? How could support from the MacGregors help Anne? "I'll do it, but she better know how to ride. I won't ride across Scotland with a Jacobite cradled in my arm. Give me the directions to her home."

"In the morning," she told him. "Tonight you'll dance." When he opened his mouth to speak, she stopped him. "You know how much joy it brings me to watch you."

Yes, he did know. She'd made certain he'd learned how to dance from a young age. He hadn't wanted to attend those lessons. He'd preferred his lessons on fighting, but he was glad now that he'd done it. He enjoyed moving to melody, and he did it well.

The queen left him a few minutes later and sent his valet back to him.

"You're brooding." Albert Carmichael had been in service to Daniel for the last nine years. He was more of a friend than a valet.

"I must go to the Highlands on an errand for the queen."

Albert snapped his tongue. "Lady Blackburn will be most upset."

Did Charlotte care for him? Like him, she'd been in service to the throne for many years, befriending Anne at a young age. As they grew older, Daniel saw less of her. She never showed interest in him until he returned almost a year ago from fighting Anne's enemies in Spain. Despite her being married, she confessed her love to Daniel on more than one occasion and brought her fury down on any woman who showed interest in him. Of course, Daniel didn't share her feelings. Over their long years of friendship, Anne had made Charlotte a woman of high influence. He could have his way with her if he desired it. She was dark and dangerously beautiful, and closer to his age than to Anne's. But he knew that once he became one of her lovers she would never let him go. Besides that, she had a husband.

"If you intend on giving her her way tonight," his valet pressed on boldly, "I wouldn't suggest a bed—"

"I don't," Daniel cut him off, "intend on giving her her way tonight. She's wed."

"How long can you deny her?" Albert put to him, leaving his side to reach for the powdered wig on Daniel's dresser.

"No." Daniel halted him from lifting it to his head. "I'll not wear that hideous thing. And I'll deny her as long as she has a husband and is mad in the head, which I'm inclined to think will be forever."

Daniel hooked his finger under the layers of lace at his neck and tugged. "Why couldn't it be Spain I was returning to in the morn?"

Albert bent to tie the bows on Daniel's shoes. "I'm inclined to think that's because the queen wants to take no more chances on your dying in battle."

"I'll tie the shoes. I'm not an invalid," Daniel said, taking him by the shoulders and straightening him.

"You insult me, Albert. You think my life can be so easily taken?"

Albert shrugged his frail shoulders, as stone-faced as he had been the day Daniel met him. Only now his skin was more weathered, his eyes, wiser. "You're getting older, my lord."

Daniel stopped tying his laces and stared up at him.

"I'm not yet a score and ten, Albert."

The valet nodded again. "You're close enough."

Daniel scowled at him, then ushered him out the door.

"If you succumb," the old valet pressed before he left, "shall I have your breakfast brought up at the usual time?"

"I shall not succumb!" Daniel swung the heavy door shut, then bent to finish tying his ridiculous shoes.

On the way out the door of his spacious chambers at St. James's Palace, he untied the colossal bow around his neck and let it hang open in lacy waves down his coat.

He descended the stairs and saw his valet again, waiting for him. He ignored Albert's disapproval at his less than formal appearance and passed the valet without a word on the way to the foyer.

Daniel stepped into the cavernous banqueting hall and looked around at the many familiar faces here for the queen's ball.

He was a decorated warrior, honored in battle on three separate continents. He'd fought for many causes over the last twelve years of his life. He'd never lost a battle or a brother on the field. Whatever he faced, he faced with firm conviction and without fear.

But the thought of Lady Blackburn clinging to his arm all night made him want to run for the doors.

✣

Chapter Three

The palace was brimming with every haughty nobleman in the kingdom. When Daniel stepped into the ballroom, their daughters and some of their wives turned their heads to watch him. Almost all of them smiled. He set his eyes on his queen at the end of the long chamber, seated on an elaborate throne, her smile going softer and more genuine when she spotted him.

He made his way toward her, giving her the honor of greeting her before he spoke to anyone else.

"Your Majesty." He bowed before her chair when he reached it.

"My lord?" Anne grazed her eyes down the length of him, then back up to his neck and bare head. "You appear before me in undress?"

"Hardly, Ma'am. I merely prefer comfort to propriety. Besides, I thought you might like this." He pulled the lace from around his neck and handed the pile to her. "I'm told it's imported from Spain. It would better serve you."

"You presume to know what I like, General?" She kept her eyes on his while she raised the fabric to her nose.

Everyone knew the queen loved him. Still, Anne did her best to appear austere toward him. She failed often.

"It's my duty to know everything about you, my queen."

Finally, she offered him an indulgent smile, handing her lace over to a servant at her side. "And your wig?" Her gaze rose to his deep auburn crown. "Do you refuse to wear it because you enjoy torturing my lady guests?"

He shook his head and raked his hand over his shorn waves. "You know I only enjoy torturing your enemies, Your Majesty."

His smile hardened when he turned away from the queen and spotted the Duchess of Blackburn. He didn't go to her. Instead, he cut a path to Jeremy Embry, Viscount Stockton, and his wife, Amanda, who were visiting the palace. He'd known them both for years and sought their friendship among his enemies.

"Tonight they'll dream of hacking off your bare head."

Daniel pivoted on his damned high-heeled shoes and raked his eyes over every eye that looked at him unkindly because of jealousy and resentment. He didn't give a rat's arse what they thought of him.

"Why must you provoke them to dislike you more by making the duchess and almost every other woman at court purr like a kitten?" Stockton asked him, handing him a drink.

"I don't provoke them," Daniel muttered wryly. "Their inadequacies do."

Amanda laughed and slipped her arm through his. "Dance with me tonight, Daniel."

"That wouldn't be wise, my lady."

She sighed and stomped her slippered foot beside his. "I don't care what the duchess thinks about it. You're the best dancer in England and my husband is the worst."

Daniel smiled. He loved Jeremy and his wife, and would go to any lengths to keep them safe. "Another time, perhaps."

"Dinner at our home next Sunday?" She grinned and tightened her hold on his arm. "We've missed you at the last two gatherings."

He glanced around at all the stately, powdered faces and high wigs. "You know how much I dislike all this, Amanda."

"How am I supposed to find you a wife if you never attend any gatherings?"

"I've no time for a wife."

"Oh, nonsense." She slapped his arm softly and looked up at him. "You choose to spend your nights alone rather than provoke her ire." She glared at Charlotte across the hall.

"What's wrong with that?" he asked with a wry quirk of his chiseled features.

"It leaves you with an empty bed and empty arms."

She might be correct but there was little he could do about it presently.

"His bed isn't always empty," Stockton told his wife quietly. "He's simply discreet about his affairs."

Daniel cut him a quick glare before offering a pretty raven-haired woman a slight smile. "As I wish you were, Stockton."

"Whom have you been with?"

Daniel laughed, moving his gaze to Stockton's wife. "Amanda, that's not a proper question to—"

"Lady Eleanor Hollister, for one," her husband confided.

Daniel stared at him while Amanda gasped and opened her eyes wider.

"She's pretty enough," Amanda decided, still holding

on to his arm. "But her father is a heavy gambler. He's known at all the tables and is slowly losing the family fortune."

"I don't plan on wedding her, Amanda."

"That's wise, dear." Stockton's wife smiled at him and then scowled at the man coming toward them with Charlotte on his arm.

Richard Montagu, the Earl of Manchester and one of Charlotte's present lovers, tipped his wide-brimmed hat and quirked his thin lips into a sneer when he reached Daniel and his friends. His salutation was brief but his eyes, as dark and dull as the thin mustache above his upper lip, lingered on Daniel long enough to make Amanda squirm beside him. Daniel's body, on the other hand, went stiff with the authority of his rank and confidence of his skill.

"What is this wise thing you've done, Darlington?" Montagu asked. "Tell us"—he glanced at Charlotte, then continued—"so that we may believe in the impossible."

The duchess deserted her escort, much to Montagu's indignation, and took Daniel's arm from Amanda's grasp. "Pay him no heed," she offered him, ignoring Montagu. "He is jealous of the favor I show you. Are you not, Richard?"

Montagu turned two different shades of crimson and glowered at Daniel's purposely ill-concealed smile. They were enemies. Daniel didn't care who knew it. "Of course not, I am merely—"

"Riddled with resentment, Richard," Charlotte cut him off. "Do not deny it."

"Of course, Your Grace." Montagu gave in with no further quarrel.

Daniel had offered him friendship over the years.

Montagu had refused, choosing instead to let his covetous heart rule him. He was the queen's cousin and only living relative, if one believed that James Stuart, the Pretender, was just that, a pretender. Montagu hated Daniel because he had the queen's favor and he constantly brought false accusations against Daniel before her, trying diligently to discredit him in Anne's eyes. Daniel had no use for him and preferred being away from his company.

"I shall see you later, Richard." Charlotte waved her hand at him, then turned to Daniel, dismissing her lover from her thoughts as well.

Montagu didn't want to go and remained in his spot casting his murderous glare on Daniel.

Daniel showed him no mercy and smiled in return. "That will be all then, Montagu."

Standing to his right, Stockton snickered.

"You're nothing but a guardsman's son," Montagu accused through clenched teeth. "You may have my dear Charlotte and the queen fooled, but I see right through you."

"Your dear Charlotte is the wife of the Duke of Blackburn, lest you forget. And what is it you see?" Daniel challenged him, keeping his cool behind the dangerous curl of his mouth.

Before Montagu replied, Charlotte held up her palm to stop him. Daniel didn't need her to defend him, but he enjoyed watching her berate her jealous lover—though it denied him the pleasure of doing it himself.

"In case you have forgotten, Richard, the general quelled a planned invasion by the queen's stepbrother, James, last year, ending a Jacobite uprising. Since then, he has subdued three other rebellions started by James's supporters, killing more of the traitorous Scotsmen than any single soldier before him."

Daniel never boasted his feats or accomplishments, for they often didn't feel like such things. But now, his hard gaze lowered on the Earl of Manchester and he allowed his smirk to sharpen when Montagu glared at him. Daniel hoped to provoke him. He wished his opponent had more confidence to actually oppose him...or even to oppose the duchess.

"Most important," Charlotte continued, "he is the queen's favorite. If you insist on continuing to insult him, you will force her to have you removed from court. Is that what you want?"

"No."

She didn't wait to hear him say anything else, but tugged Daniel toward the entrance, dismissing the rest of her escorts.

"I wish to have words with you in private, General Marlow." Her powdered face glowed against her dark periwig. Her full, rosy lips parted, exposing a glimpse of the slight, beguiling space between her teeth.

Charlotte Adler was an attractive woman. Daniel appreciated her allure, but she was like a feline predator on the prowl for food. Beautiful and deadly. He had no intention of being her next meal. Montagu was proof of the consequences of taking her to bed.

"Perhaps when I return to court, we can—"

"You're going somewhere?" Her dark eyes sharpened, but not on him.

"He's leaving on an errand for me." The queen waved over her shoulder, dismissing the servant who'd wheeled her close to Charlotte. She didn't look up at her friend but kept her eyes on Daniel. "He leaves in the morning."

Charlotte's glare at the queen was almost treasonous. Anne missed it. Had she missed it on purpose?

"Is he a boy that he should run errands?" Charlotte's voice was somehow sweet, sickeningly so.

"No, Charlotte." Finally Anne turned to look at her from her chair. "He's a man whose courage and loyalty I value above all others. That is why I would like a few moments with you in private. You may wheel me to the garden."

"Please excuse us, Daniel," Anne said as the Duchess of Blackburn took up her position behind the queen.

Daniel watched them, his legs aching to go before Charlotte had time to toss Anne and her chair over the side of the palace wall. The duchess looked angry enough to kill. She didn't like anyone stepping on her toes, including the queen, but she knew her place and wouldn't dare argue too much. He took off after them but stayed behind, far enough away to remain hidden. He followed them to the gardens and moved in the shadows behind them.

What did Anne want to speak to her about? Did it have to do with him? With the Highland Jacobite he was going to escort back here because he'd gone as mad as his queen?

"We are all friends, Charlotte."

He heard Anne's soft voice as he stepped around one of the queen's prized peach trees. "But when it comes to your affairs, please don't confuse my silence with my pardon toward them. I don't approve of your indiscretions, but they are yours to deal with, save when it comes to Daniel. Don't think I'll sit idly by while you try to seduce him."

Charlotte laughed and the sound rang empty against Daniel's ears. "Anne, dear, he was not born to you, despite how deeply you would have liked him to be."

Knowing Anne's past tragedies with the births of her children, it was a cruel thing Charlotte said to her.

"I know he isn't—"

"When are you going to tell him the truth, hmm, Anne?" Charlotte cut her off. "He should know, or do you like him playing the part of errand boy?"

"That's what I wanted to speak to you about."

A thread of panic in Anne's voice perked Daniel's ears. What truth? He moved a bit closer to them, still unseen, and inclined his ear to her.

"Has he been asking you things?"

"He asks me many things."

Daniel could hear the smirk in Charlotte's words.

"Things that we were just speaking about," Anne clarified.

"You mean his birth?"

His birth? Did he hear Charlotte right? Why would he ask her about his birth? He was Edward and Olivia Marlow's son. Born in—

"You must never tell him, Charlotte. Vow it to me again."

"He should know, Anne. What are you afraid of?"

Daniel's heart pounded. He wanted to go to them and demand to know what they were talking about. But they wouldn't tell him. Anne wouldn't tell him. His heart pummeled to his feet. What kind of secret was she keeping from him?

He remained hidden, certain they could hear his short, shallow breath.

"Are you afraid he will want to return to Denmark? Or do you want to keep him at your beck and call the way his father, Prince George, kept his serving girl until she died giving him the son you could never give him?"

Daniel leaned against the palace's west wall, trying and failing to take in what he'd just heard. Twice he almost threw his head back and laughed at the absurdity of it. His father was Prince George, younger brother of Christian VI, the king of Denmark?

Daniel's world spun on its axis. No. Of course, he wasn't. General Edward Marlow was his father. He was born and raised in England. He visited Denmark when he was a young child, but—

"Charlotte"—Anne cut off his thoughts—"Daniel is the only living son born to George. He is a royal bastard of Denmark and that must make him very appealing to you, but you must never tell him! Do you understand me? I told you about this because I trust you. Are you still worthy of that trust? Because if you are not..."

Anne. Daniel closed his eyes and did his best to remain in his spot. This all couldn't be true. It couldn't be. There had to be an explanation. Something that didn't involve Anne lying to him his whole life.

"Don't worry, Anne," Charlotte assured her. "I'll take your secret to my grave."

❈❧❦

Chapter Four

*A*bby stood with her kin and half a dozen bags on the coast of Kylerhea, overlooking the strait toward Glenelg on the mainland. She wasn't afraid of the journey she was about to take, but she'd never left Skye before. She'd never left her clan. Some of her kinsmen would travel a day behind her, but she wouldn't see them. The queen's men couldn't know they were there. She was to arrive in England with only the queen's men as escorts and that was exactly how it must appear to the queen.

The cup of whisky her uncles had given her before they all left Camlochlin afforded no comfort to her frazzled nerves. Instead, she reached for the comfort of a man's strong hand.

She looked up into his tender gaze and felt the sting of tears in her eyes. "I thought he would come, Grandpapa."

Callum MacGregor looked over his shoulder at the empty road they had traveled. Her father wasn't there. He wasn't coming to see her off, to wish her a safe journey. It almost stopped her from leaving.

"I remember the day I asked him to travel to England," her grandfather told her. "Our clan was invited to King James the Second's coronation. Rob didna' wish to go, believin' that the safety of the clan depended on us bein' here to protect them. The clan's safety always came first to him. Just like it does to ye, Abigail."

She smiled at him, loving him for the comfort he gave her in this moment.

"Was the trip to England when he met Mother?"

"Aye, 'twas." He smiled at her and for the life of her she couldn't imagine him slaughtering a regimen of men with his little sister tossed over his shoulders. "He'll come, love. Dinna' fear. Ye're his treasure."

"I know he loves me, Grandpapa. I hope he's not too late though."

She knew Queen Anne's men had to be close. It had been a fortnight since her aunt's reply arrived with her instructions to Abigail and an estimate of the day her escorts should arrive.

Today was the day. They were coming today and they knew nothing about her save for what Anne had told them, that she was to be one of the queen's handmaidens.

What would England be like? What if her aunt tried to have her killed? The thought had crossed Abby's mind. What if the queen didn't give a damn about assurances? What if she didn't care if she killed the true heir or the heir's daughter? She could go after the next one later. Abby had thought about it being a trap. But still, she had to go. There was no other choice. Of course, there was the chance that Abby's relative would be welcoming. Given the chance, Abby would win her over.

She felt the slight touch of strong, broad fingers against her arm and turned up to her father. He said nothing while he pulled her shoulder closer within the rippling power of his chest.

"I feared I missed ye, Abby."

She closed her eyes against his arm. "I'm glad ye didna' miss me, Faither."

When he swept her up in his embrace, she smiled over his shoulder at her grandsire, who winked a turquoise eye at her.

"I dinna' want ye to do this."

She knew. She knew what this was taking for her father. He was the protector, the guardian of the clan, as his father had been. But he could do nothing to assure his own daughter's safety against an entire kingdom.

"Remember," he warned, his powerful blue eyes wide with worry "We are proscribed. Tell no one yer name. Ye are Abigail Campbell if questioned."

"Aye, Faither," she obeyed. "Is Mother all right?"

"She weeps fer ye but yer aunts and grandmother are with her. She will be fine as long as ye are fine, as well."

"I will be. And ye will be close behind."

"Aye." He smiled, as handsome as any man had a right to be. "I'll be close behind."

"Rob." Colin came to stand beside his brother and pointed to the ferry coming in from the opposite shore.

Abby's heart clamored in her chest. Her thoughts turned to her mother weeping over her, her brothers and cousins, Mailie, Violet, and Nichola. When would she see them again? She felt responsible for them all. They needed her.

Determined to make it back for them, she conquered her sadness and her fear and stepped away from her father when the ferry dropped anchor and the queen's escorts gained their saddles and rode toward them.

She braced her legs, setting her boots firmly on the ground, and lifted her chin. She knew her defiance was born mainly from the sheer strength and power coming toward her. These men were escorts, nothing more. She didn't want their first impression of her to be that she was a sniveling woman afraid of them just because they were English. She was born of a long line of warriors. Her first instinct was to defend. She understood only too well that her country was being conquered slowly but surely by the English, perhaps even by the very men who trampled the delicate heather beneath the hooves of their stallions as they approached.

"The queen sends only four men to guard my daughter when she crosses the country," her father muttered angrily moments before the riders reached them.

Each wore a common man's dress of long coat and breeches, and a sheath dangling from his hip. Three of the riders held back, creating a line of brawn and steel as they drew their swords behind one whom Abby guessed was the leader. The four men were outnumbered at least five to one. If her kin attacked, the escorts' meager swords would offer them little aid.

For a moment, no one spoke a word while Abby tilted her head up to have a view of the mounted men. She could sense the thick tension emanating from her kin and she prayed none of them, especially her brothers, did anything foolish. When she turned to the lead rider, she was amazed to find only cool arrogance in eyes the vivid green of a glade on a summer day staring back down at her. A shiver, neither hot nor cold, trickled down her spine and quickened her breath. He was terribly beautiful, arrayed in strength and deep confidence. In fact, he looked positively fearless on his snorting black destrier with sunlight radiating off his broad shoulders and setting fire to his clipped auburn locks. She squinted up at him and scowled at herself for being moved by his appearance. He was no boy, but five to ten years older than her cousins. Experience and mistrust hardened his features. Taller in the saddle than his comrades, he radiated an air of authority of one who demanded instant obedience. She looked away before he did, sensing a power in this man that challenged her. Perhaps another day, she thought, biting her tongue. She was used to intimidating warriors and she wasn't afraid of him, but she wouldn't foolishly provoke him in front of her kin and get him killed.

"I am General Daniel Marlow of Her Majesty the Queen's Royal Army." His voice fell in deep, rich tones around her ears.

"And knight of the Most Noble Order of the Garter."

Her cousin Malcolm stepped forward. Malcolm had traveled to England on a number of occasions and must have heard of him.

"And also the Earl of Darlington, aye?" Adam added. Everyone there from her clan, including Abby, turned to offer Adam a surprised look that he would know such things.

So, her escort was a general, an earl, and a knight of the Most Noble Order of the Garter? Abby gave him another looking over, deciding as her eyes lingered on his booted legs and muscular thighs, his rigid posture in the saddle, the sun gleaming off his head, and the long broadsword dangling from his hip that he indeed resembled a knight.

"That's correct," he answered, sounding bored before he set his eyes on her again. "Miss Abigail MacGregor?"

Her blood heated her veins and rushed to her heart.

Her knees went weak beneath her and, not for the first time since Queen Anne's letter had reached them, she wished her kinsmen were escorting her.

Her father stepped forward. "I am clan chief Robert MacGregor of the MacGregors of Skye. Her father."

General Marlow turned his head and simply nodded at her father. Abby narrowed her eyes on him. She wasn't used to seeing anyone show her father so little respect.

"Is this the girl?" he asked, turning back to her, his expression darkening on her Highland attire. His distaste was obvious. He didn't like Highlanders, or mayhap it was Jacobites he had an aversion to. Either way, she didn't like him either. Knight or not.

This trip wasn't going to be pleasant.

"My father is the clan chief of one of the most fearsome clans in Scotland." She gritted her teeth as she spoke. "You should be off yer mount and on your knees thanking him fer not skinning ye alive."

The rider glanced down at her with eyes of fathomless, faceted green. "Lady," he said, his voice a compelling blend of elegance and cool undertones, "I serve God and Queen Anne. Since neither has decreed your father's royal status to me, I remain in my saddle."

He looked briefly to his right. "Hubert, unarm the lady of her sword."

Abby stepped back, placing her fingers on the hilt at her side. She raised her chin with an icy stare in the leader's direction. His expression changed in an instant from uninterested to threatening. He said nothing, and yet the raw challenge in his glare stilled her heart. She'd trained almost every day of her life but never actually fought an enemy. And she didn't want to fight one now, especially since her father would most likely kill the poor fool before she had time to fight, and then Queen Anne would send her forces to Skye for battle rather than diplomacy.

The brute called Hubert dismounted and held out his hand to receive Abby's weapon. She handed it over without comment, but managed a black glare to the general.

"I willna' have my daughter ride all the way to England withoot protection," her father growled.

"That's what I'm here for," Marlow said without taking his eyes off her. "She will—"

He didn't flinch when he felt the steel of her father's claymore between his legs. He merely looked from the chief's deadly eyes down to the tip of the blade and lifted an eyebrow.

"Before even one of yer men can move to save ye," the MacGregor chief warned him, his eyes burning fire into the arrogant rider, "I will have driven my blade into ye, riddin' England of any future heirs ye may have. The blade will then sever yer mount's spine. The beast will fall to the ground, and ye will find yerself on yer arse before me. I dinna' seek homage from ye, Englishman, only the respect due to my daughter."

The air went deadly still. Even the knight's own men dared not take a breath while their leader stared, seemingly unfazed, into the face of the man who threatened him. Then, to Abby's astonishment, the English knave had the audacity to curl his gloved fingers around her father's blade and lift it away from his precious nether region. He positioned it, instead, at his throat.

"I despise the senseless bloodshed of horses, especially that of a beast as fine as Vengeance. If you wish a display of why the queen sent me and not anyone else to escort your daughter to her, I would be happy to show you. But I will not kiss your arse, or hers, no matter how many men stand behind you." He looked over the chief's shoulder and spread his eyes over the rest of her kin.

Abby thought they looked damned fearsome. This knight was mad not to fear them. Either that, or the confidence he oozed from every nuance of movement was authentic.

In the next instant, he proved that it was.

Abby had to admit that lifting her father's blade to his throat had been risky, but now, as he moved, she saw the advantage.

No longer impeded by steel, the English knight swept his legs over the saddle in one fluid motion and was on his feet, his own sword positioned at the chief's neck.

Rob MacGregor smiled. Behind him, Abby squeezed her eyes shut. "All right then," her father said, "show me how ye will protect my daughter." He took a quick step back, his neck just out of reach of the other man's blade, and swept his fur cloak off his wide shoulders. "Ye'll begin with one man, me. Ye must work yer way up, if ye still can." He swung. He swung hard.

For an instant, his opponent blinked, then scowled as the MacGregor chief's shocking strength became apparent.

Abby gasped when the queen's man lifted both hands to stop her father's sword from descending upon his unprotected skull. He fought defensively for the next several moments, barely escaping the crushing weight of Rob MacGregor's sword arm. But he made the necessary adjustments fast, using his lithe, less bulky body to evade such power and find victory against it.

There was no doubt watching him. He intended to win. He moved very quickly and with precise intentions. His long coat snapped around his legs as he spun around and brought his sword up, almost slicing off the chief's arm when her father swung, barely an instant slower than the knight.

Abby watched with her heart in her throat. She would not gasp or even breathe loud enough to distract her father. She knew he was not fighting to the death, else he would have killed this General Marlow already. Still, she was loath to admit the knave was doing surprisingly well against her father.

They fought for another quarter of an hour before her uncle Colin stepped into the fray and let his sword dance under the stark sun. Hell, no one ever beat Uncle Colin.

It wouldn't be fair for any man to have to fight her father and Colin, but she wasn't usually placed in the care of any other man. If Marlow couldn't save her from a group of men, which was likely to be found in the forests leading toward England, then he wasn't fit to escort her. The fight was fair.

Amazingly, the general took them both on, slightly winded, but still quick enough on his feet to avoid most strikes. When the rest of her uncles joined the dance, Abby found her gaze fixed on the knight. Heaven help her, she hated to admit that he was astounding. Aye, his breath came hard and deep, the Highlanders had exhausted him by forcing him to defend himself against so many strong arms, but he didn't surrender and he didn't falter. His stamina and sheer determination moved her. When her brother moved to have a go at him next, Abby's grandsire stopped him.

"Ye need more time in the practice field, lad."

Adam didn't argue. Their grandsire commanded the respect of all his kin. They gave it gladly. Besides, he was fully correct about Adam. He didn't practice often and wasn't skilled enough for such a contest and would end up hurt.

Abby turned back to the fight. She watched for a moment, knowing that the only way to gain victory was to take out the chief. General Marlow knew it too, and with what looked to be his last ounce of strength, he feigned a right turn and came back left with lightning speed and brought his blade back to where it had begun. At her father's throat. The others all froze and then backed away. Her grandpapa smiled and nodded his head with approval.

With his spine stiff against the bracing Highland wind and the chill of steel against his pulse, Rob stared into Daniel's eyes. "Well done." And then he grinned and dropped his gaze to his own blade, carefully positioned exactly where it too had begun, between Marlow's legs.

The general straightened, the hint of a smile more dangerous than his sword. He withdrew his weapon and stepped back. "Word of your skill and strength are true, Chief. I thank you for acknowledging mine."

So, Abby thought, watching him, he'd asked about her father's strength and skill before coming here. He was prepared. A good trait in a warrior. And this man who'd just taken on her father *and* her uncles, including her uncle Colin, was a warrior indeed.

"My daughter's life will be in yer hands, General."

Her father went to her, took her hand, and kissed it. "Will ye no' change yer mind?"

"I canna' change it, Faither," she told him. She saw the helplessness on his face and felt sorry for him because she knew he didn't like feeling helpless. She knew what it was doing to him and wished there was another way.

He returned his attention to her escort. "General, will

ye fight fer her with the same passion and determination ye had whilst fightin' all of us?"

The general straightened his spine as if his words meant more to him than they realized. "You have my word that I will. She will arrive in England safely and return to you as she left with no mar or flaw." While he spoke, he looked over her father's shoulder at her cousins, who were carrying her bags to the horses. "What do you think you're going to do with those sacks?" he called out, stopping the lads.

"We're goin' to secure them to—"

The general shook his head and stepped around her father. "No. One bag. Our mounts won't be saddled down with useless trinkets and more gowns than the lady needs. One bag."

He turned his gaze on her, as did the rest of the men in her company. She could protest; being a woman, it would be expected. She believed she needed every item she'd packed, and she didn't know how she would do without them, but she would, damn it. For her kin, she would. She pointed at her brother, knowing what was inside the bag he carried. "Adam, just the bag ye carry then."

Marlow turned away without even thanking her for being so agreeable. She didn't like him.

Her father took her in his arms, looking miserable; Abby almost didn't want to go.

"Do I have yer word ye will remain with him throughout yer journey, no matter how he angers ye?"

"Aye, Faither, ye have my word."

After long, teary farewells to her kin, Abby tossed her escort a murderous glare when he spoke again.

"You can ride, I hope? I won't put my mount to the task of carrying us both all the way to England."

"If I didna' know how to ride, I would learn now. I'd rather walk than ride with an Englishman."

He didn't smile while he mounted his horse with a single leap.

After he gave the order to his men to ride out, he rode beside her toward the ferry, quiet and uninterested as she turned in her saddle, wiped the tears from her eyes, and waved farewell to her father and the rest of her kin one last time.

"That'll be enough crying, lady." He finally spoke to her. "This journey will be arduous enough. I don't want to hear that the whole way."

Abby glared at his back when he rode ahead of her. She didn't dislike him.

She hated him.

And she'd just given her father her word to remain with him no matter how he angered her.

"Let's strike a bargain between us, General. Ye dinna' speak to me and I will hold back my emotions and not smash a rock over yer head while ye sleep."

Damn it, was that a smirk half concealed on his face? She couldn't tell, because he moved forward and rode at her mount's shoulder. She should be afraid that the general had a temper and might strike her. But she was certain the queen had warned him not to let any harm come to her . . . at least not yet.

"Very well, Miss MacGregor, if you prefer to be bound while I sleep, I'll see it done."

Not if she killed him. But first, she had to get her sword back.

Chapter Five

While he rode, Daniel considered the cursed direction his life had taken in the last se'nnight. Considering that all he'd heard was true, and he had no reason to believe it wasn't, he was the bastard son of a prince, the result of a meaningless tryst with a serving wench, and not the son of men with a history of loyalty and dedication.

All that was enough to set his head into a tailspin, but it didn't end there. No. The worst part, the part that kept him awake at night during his journey to Skye, was Anne's deceit...her betrayal. He hadn't waited around the palace to question Anne the night he'd eavesdropped, but left the ball, then left for Scotland at dawn.

"I've never been to England before."

His hope for a smooth journey back to England shattered. Was he expected to carry on conversations with her the entire way?

"I said, I've never been to England before. Is it as bonny as Scotland?"

She wasn't going to give him a choice. He had to

answer her. "Some places are quite beautiful, yes," he said, keeping his eyes on the road. He hoped that mollified her.

"Why d'ye avert yer eyes from mine?" she boldly demanded. "Is it the MacGregors that ye hate, or all Highlanders?"

He avoided looking at her because never in all his travels had he ever seen a more beautiful woman than Miss Abigail MacGregor. Hair the color of pale, milky moonbeams illuminated her face... and damnation, her face—sweetly rounded with a slight dimple in her chin—made him forget to breathe. Her cheekbones were high and noble, her eyes, so vividly blue he doubted the good of his own vision. Not to mention how the disarming lilt of her voice wreaked havoc on him.

But it was more than that. It was the way she moved, with grace and command... like a queen... that gave him pause to look at her. Still, he found himself looking enough times to note the way her eyes glimmered like stars when she wept over her family earlier. Her pert nose had grown red, and he swore he'd never seen anyone more spellbinding. For a moment or two she was the only thing occupying his thoughts.

He swung his gaze to her, but only for a moment. "I don't give a damn about your name or your clan's proscription. You're a Jacobite, and that's enough."

Finally, she grew quiet. He was about to give thanks when her lily-soft voice, this time imbued with an icy edge, broke the silence.

"If ye'll excuse me, my lord, I'd rather ride with the geldings than with the arse." Without waiting for his approval, she yanked her reins to the left and rode back to his men.

He clenched his jaw, regretting his personal vow to

keep her safe. Still, damn him, he was committed to his duty and moved his horse beside her again, so close, in fact, their knees touched.

"My lord, I would prefer—"

"Don't be difficult," he cut her off.

Her mouth snapped shut but when he chanced another glance her way he knew by her clenched teeth and fists to match that her silence wasn't given out of obedience. She was going to be challenging.

"If ye hate Jacobites, then ye're a traitor to the throne and the true king, James the Third."

He chuckled. "The Pretender? He's not the true king. And it is you who is speaking treason."

"Will ye arrest me, then?" She didn't sound afraid of him. She sounded like she was mocking him. "Am I to hang?"

If he didn't strangle her first.

They reached the ferry and he paid the ferryman extra to leave early. He put Lieutenants Hubert and Ashley at her sides and Captain Andrews before her. He took her rear and watched both it and their surroundings as they boarded the vessel. Only after they began moving did Daniel give up his close proximity to her. Thankful for the blessing of distance, he let his thoughts return to matters at home. Home, with a father who taught him ideals and friends who were more valuable than all the gold in the kingdoms. It was all a lie. One that kept him from knowing his true father, Prince George, whom he saw each day.

Anne's warning to him about bringing Charlotte to his bed made sense now. Charlotte wanted to bed the prince and claim his child.

Hell, he was weary of life at court, so weary of all the deceit and games for power. He'd prefer a simple life, a good battle every now and then, but mostly quiet. Could he ever get it if his identity was discovered?

A thread of musical laughter reached his ears and he turned to see Miss MacGregor smiling at his men. Daniel didn't turn away. He couldn't. His body refused to deny him the pleasure of looking at her. How dangerous was it for any of his men to lose his heart to her? Should he keep them away from her? He strolled across the deck, coming up behind her, listening to what she said.

"Ye're verra' kind, Lieutenant Hubert."

Hubert's smile wasn't what worried Daniel. It was Hubert's reaction to hers. He raked his hand through his dark curls and blushed beneath his thick chestnut beard.

Damn. That, sure as hell, wasn't a good sign.

"Lieutenant," she chirped, ignoring Daniel when he stepped around her, revealing his presence. "Would ye be so kind as to tell me the names of the rest of my companions? I think 'tis dreadful to travel with people ye dinna' even know. Since yer general is too rude to introduce us, I was hoping ye would."

For a moment, Hubert looked about to be sick. No Jacobite insulted General Marlow and lived. Then the lieutenant coughed, since his officer didn't seem to take offense. "That there is Captain Andrews." Hubert continued on and pointed to the raven-haired man behind her. "Be wary of him, m'lady. He's a knave with the ladies at court."

That was true, Daniel thought, looking at him. Andrews went through women like fire in a dry forest. Daniel would have to keep an eye on him.

"That's Lieutenant Ashley with all the whiskers. He's a merciless bastard and will cut your throat while he hums his mother's favorite ditty.

"And you're already acquainted with General Marlow."

She cut Daniel a slightly interested glance. "What should I know aboot him?"

"He's known as the Jacobite killer," Andrews answered, passing them.

Damn him.

Daniel glared at his back. That was the last thing Miss MacGregor needed to know, especially since she was one, along with her entire family. He shouldn't care if she knew, but he did. He didn't like terrified women, and if she knew how many Jacobites he'd killed... "That's enough questions." Daniel spoke his command in quiet tones, but it was obeyed nonetheless. "Our guest, who from this moment on will be called Miss Campbell, doesn't wish to hear about such savageries."

"Jacobite killer," she said, favoring him with her coolest stare. "I've heard of ye."

Daniel inhaled a deep breath, not wanting to have this conversation with her.

"I expected the man who carried the weight of that title to be more savage, less clever and eloquently spoken and well-mannered. I would never have imagined a monster could be a knight of the Most Noble Order of the Garter."

She didn't sound terrified.

Hubert cleared his throat and cast her a dozen nervous looks in the space of a breath.

Daniel scattered the others with a steely glint in his glance, then crossed his hands behind his back when they were alone.

"You know the truth now. Whatever you wish to accuse me of or curse me with, release it from you this moment so the rest of the journey will be less torturous."

"Nothing I say now will ease the suffering I'll be forced to endure in yer company."

He slanted his gaze to her and damn him if he didn't smile a little, the first time in a little over a se'nnight.

"I've heard it all before, lady. I won't be swayed."

She looked like she wanted to fling herself at him and wrap her hands around his throat until he was dead.

"I have nothing to say to ye, General."

That was it? He rather liked her strength to control her tongue. He could handle quiet. Perhaps the journey wouldn't be so bad after all.

"One more thing," he added before leaving her alone. "I won't have you seducing my men. Nor—"

"Seducing yer men?" An octave higher and she would be shouting at him. Her temper was boiling. "How dare ye even suggest that?"

"Quite easily, when I see it with my own eyes."

She was tempted to take a swing at him. He could see it in her eyes, iced over and sharp as swords. He was tempted to take a step back. No strike came, though she gazed at his auburn whiskers and the cut of his jaw like she was thinking about hitting him good.

When the captain of the ferry came over to share words with her, Daniel studied her silently. Apparently, the ferryman knew her family. Daniel watched her. She wasn't intimidated by his command, or his savage reputation. He dipped his eyes to her throat and found the pulse that beat there. Beguiling. He thought about bending his mouth to it, running his tongue over her milky skin. He felt her eyes on him and leisurely lifted his gaze from her throat. Her cheeks blazed as if she could read his thoughts. He looked away. What the hell was he doing thinking about taking her in his arms? Kissing her?

They were alone once again.

"Do I need protection from ye, General?" she asked him quietly.

He returned his gaze to her. Damn. Did he just entertain a thought of seducing a Jacobite? "No, Miss Campbell. Not at all."

She quirked her brow. "Truly? Because when *the* Jacobite killer looks at the throat of a Jacobite lass like he's thinking of devouring her, she usually needs protection from him."

She was correct.

"Give me back my sword," she demanded, "so that I can protect myself from ye, murderer."

So much for her having nothing to say. He let his expression soften a bit, amused that this veil of a woman thought she could protect herself from him. If he were a different kind of man he would toss her blade to her and let her have a go at him. But he didn't fight women and none ever needed protection from him. Moreover, none ever wanted protection from him. He would be more careful with this one. She was more appealing, bolder, and cleverer than the others.

What the hell did Anne want with her? Despite what the queen had done to him, he wouldn't walk away from her until he heard her reasons for lying to him his whole life.

God help him. He wasn't who he'd thought he was. He had been born out of wedlock. The prince may have forced his servant to his bed, or he may not have—and now Daniel would never know. So much for honor, loyalty, and dedication. It was a difficult truth to accept.

"You have nothing to fear from me, Miss Campbell," he told her as the ferry prepared to dock. "I've never killed or harmed a woman. I admit to allowing myself a brief moment to admire you, but I would never act on emotion."

Damn him, but the scarlet blush drifting over the bridge of her nose was glorious.

"Good," she said, her eyes like ice-tipped landscapes. "I'll be certain to tell yer queen that ye were a gentleman."

Daniel moved past her, glad that they seemed to have come to an agreement. Whether she hated him or not, he'd keep her safe, as promised, from thieves or anyone who brought danger to her, including himself or Charlotte. "Yes, lady, you do that."

They left the ferry and rode into Glenelg without sharing words. Daniel didn't mind. He enjoyed the quiet.

Apparently, the queen's new handmaiden did not. She chatted with his men like they'd been friends for years. During the early part of their journey he learned much about her. More than he cared to know, in fact. Why did he have to be privy to knowing that her favorite flowers were bluebells, or the names of all her relatives and their dogs? What good would any of it do him? He was a soldier and he was a bit more interested in her conversation with Hubert about the men of Camlochlin and their service to the throne. So, two of her uncles fought for the queen's father, King James, in the Royal Army, one a general and the other a captain. The queen must hope that if the MacGregor chief's daughter was in her care, the Jacobites wouldn't attack. But Daniel was unsure if her assumption was correct. This clan, the MacGregors, had a history of bloodshed the likes of which frightened kings enough to proscribe them. The lady's "kin," as she called them, had fought through the ages to keep what was theirs. He doubted they would stop now, with a queen who threatened more of their rights. It was a mistake bringing

Abigail MacGregor to the palace. She was a Jacobite, and a beautiful one at that. It was only a matter of time before harm came to her. When it did, the men from her clan would attack. He didn't doubt his army could defeat them, but he would likely lose good men in the fray. He'd been sent to escort her. Now he had to become her protector for the throne's sake…and because he promised her father she would return without mar or flaw.

He shouldn't have vowed such a thing. Not *to* a Jacobite. Not *about* a Jacobite.

"General Marlow?" she called out, riding up on his left flank.

"What is it, Miss Campbell?"

"Tell me of yer life." She slowed her mount to a canter at his side. "What drove ye to make such terrible choices in yer life to give you this reputation? The men and I have exchanged stories, but ye have remained quiet. Now 'tis yer turn to speak. Begin, please."

He turned his head to look at her. His gaze was dark and razor sharp. Clearly, she suffered some foolish notion that she could command him about. "I prefer not to." He turned forward again and set his eyes on the distance and off her.

It wasn't safe to let his gaze linger on her. He might be tempted to ponder the shape of her lips and a plan of action to see them smile. He might also be tempted to compare her to moonlight and stars—light in an otherwise black void.

"Let us pretend, fer yer sake, that I care aboot yer preferences, General Marlow. I am bored and will go along with it."

Curious at her boldness, he turned to her again. She took her time letting the glacial stare she'd been aiming at him change into something more curious.

"Ye're deadly enough to have earned such a loathsome title, ye fought my kin with great skill and stamina, but ye avoid me as if I were a dreaded foe who frightens ye oot of yer boots. Why is that?"

He wanted to inhale the sight of her standing up to him, draped in her plaids, her wheaten tresses windblown and pulled free of her thick braid. He wanted to blink or swallow, just to see if he still could. There seemed to be much more to Abigail MacGregor than he suspected.

More wasn't necessarily a good thing.

He should keep his distance.

"Miss Campbell, each one of us fears something. Let me assure you, you are not my something." He almost doubted his declaration for an instant when she set her unblinking gaze on him. "Let us direct our questions toward less self-indulgent avenues."

Her eyes sparked like lightning striking ice. Was she smiling or biting her lip? "Of course, my lord. I misspoke." And then, possessing more courage than many of his men, she looked him square in the eye when he didn't move right away. "But why else do ye avoid me?" she boldly continued. "Or allow yer eyes to roam over me like I gave ye permission to do so, when I have not?" She stared at him, challenging him to look away first. He didn't. How was he supposed to tell her the truth, that he was afraid if he looked at her for too long now, she'd likely haunt his sleep for a while later.

"I'll be certain to stay oot of yer way then." She slowed her mount and let him pass her.

She rode behind him in silence, which Daniel fully enjoyed, until it became a deafening accusation that he was a cad.

Chapter Six

*H*er escort was the hated Jacobite killer, the queen's most fearsome warrior, quelling uprisings quickly and without mercy. Abby had heard of him. Everyone had.

Why had Anne sent him of all people to bring her to England? Was it all a trap? The thought of it frightened her. She'd never done anything like this before, without her kin there with her. But this was what she wanted. This real responsibility, this vital need to see her duty through no matter what.

She watched the knight struggle with pride and something else that brought him back to her with a softer edge to his expression. Had he changed his mind about talking with her? What would she ask a man with his reputation? For a few moments he said nothing at all. Abby let him have his silence. Then,

"Lady, my life has been a violent, bloody one and would play hard against your ears."

"Harder than hearing that ye're the barbarian who has likely killed some of my relatives?"

She found it a bit insulting that he thought her so

frail-spirited that he couldn't even mention certain things in her presence. She hadn't fallen to pieces when she found out who he was, had she? She was a MacGregor. She'd heard plenty of bloody stories around the supper tables in Camlochlin. She could take whatever he wanted to tell her.

"General," she said, cantering her horse closer to his. "Have ye ever helped bring a babe into the world? Or cut the balls off a sheep? *That's* violent and bloody."

She caught the movement of his hand reaching for his groin as if to protect it.

"I imagine it is," he conceded.

"Hubert tells me"—she turned to his first lieutenant and smiled, setting light to Hubert's heart—"that ye fought many battles against James Stuart's supporters and that's how ye earned yer title."

"Lady, let's drop this topic before you hear things that will make our journey together even more difficult to endure."

"I doubt anything could make it worse." She tilted her chin at him when he caught the insult and cast her a hard gaze. "How many have ye killed?"

"Eight hundred," he said, sparing her no more mercy. "Perhaps more."

Abby stared at his profile for a moment, wondering how many of her relatives had lost their lives to him last year in the Stirling rebellion.

"Ye enjoy killin' Scotland's patriots, then?"

He shook his head, keeping his eyes on the road. It infuriated her that he barely looked at her. It was as if she wasn't important enough to acknowledge. Who was he to make such an assumption? It pricked at her pride, but she decided to be the better person and ignore it.

"I don't enjoy it," he said. "It's my duty to protect the throne."

"I see. So if James Francis Stuart took his rightful place on the throne, ye would defend him?"

He squinted up at the sun and then finally turned to her. "If he could prove that the throne was his rightful place, I might be forced to consider it."

Abby took a good look at him full on and thought about how foolish she was to want him to pay her any attention. His eyes penetrated her, tearing away her layers as if she had no defense at all, making her a bit weak in the knees. This time, she looked away first. What could he tempt her to tell him? That she could prove it? She could prove James's claim was genuine. He was, after all, her uncle on her mother's side.

She would never do it, especially not to him. She would never tell anyone that her mother was King James II's firstborn daughter, his Catholic heir. A month wouldn't pass before the throne, Parliament, and God only knew who else had people trying to kill Davina MacGregor. Of course, the queen wouldn't tell a soul. As long as Abby could convince her that her mother didn't want her throne, the queen might never tell the kingdom that she had another older sister.

Damn it, though, Abby thought, eyeing the general, she would take such pleasure in telling him that the true queen was married to an outlawed MacGregor, and that she, the Jacobite he hated, was a princess.

"Only fools believe that drivel about Mary of Modena's babe being stillborn and another babe being smuggled into her chambers that she and the king would claim was theirs."

The general shrugged his broad shoulders. "James was desperate for a Catholic successor."

Not true, Abby thought. He had one in her mother and he hadn't forced her to take the throne.

"Did ye know King James personally?" she asked him. "That ye would believe such tales about him?"

"I knew of him. I was a boy when he was king."

She cut him a disapproving side glare. "My kin actually knew him. 'Tis dishonorable to take action against a man ye know nothin' more about than what ye've heard."

He made a sound like a chuckle...or a snort. She turned to look at him head-on as sunlight splashed across his coppery features. "What do you know of honor?" he asked her.

Pity he was so gloriously handsome, Abby thought, looking at him. She knew it was wrong to kill a man simply because she hated him. If he kept making these constant assumptions about her, she might just claw out his eyes. She'd hate to do it, for they were the color of the lush verdant vale of Camlochlin in summer.

"Tell me," she said, doing nothing to conceal the frost in her eyes and in the curve of her lips, "why d'ye assume I dinna' know of honor? Is it because I'm a woman, or because I'm a Highland Jacobite?"

"A Highland Jacobite of an outlawed clan," he continued smoothly, then looked away.

"Ye dinna' know our history," she told him, trying to keep her voice from shaking because of her anger. "I've read the *Prose Tristan*, *Le Morte d'Arthur*, *Historia Regum Britanniae*, and Gildas's *De Excidio et Conquestu Britanniae*, just to name a few. Before I learned to read, my grandmother read her books to my cousins and me. But more than that, General, I grew up learning about honor from men who live it. My grandsire, my faither, and my uncles paid whatever it cost to do what they believed was right. I learned of honor firsthand."

There was no trace of his smile when he set his eyes on her again. "I stand corrected."

"Yet again," she pointed out, trying not to sound too smug.

She was pleased to see that he didn't scowl at her correction. Mayhap he wasn't a complete wretch. There was, however, still the issue of his honor...or lack of it.

"Did ye serve William after he invaded yer country?" she asked him.

"You mean, after King James deserted the throne?"

She yawned and patted her mouth, refusing to let him goad her. "Whether or not James fled doesna' change the fact that he has a son. Even the kings of France and Spain dinna' deny that the Prince of Wales is the true king."

"I don't serve the kings of France or Spain."

Abby was silent for a moment while she studied him. Was there more to the knight's devout faithfulness to the throne than anyone knew?

She moved her horse closer to his until she leaned up to his ear. "Do ye love her?"

"Who?"

Lord, but up close she could see flecks of sapphire in the depths of his green eyes. They would be mesmerizing if she wasn't careful. "The queen."

"My feelings toward our queen don't concern you." He returned his attention to the road.

Blast him, but he was stubborn! "Is it a matter of honor then?" she asked him, pressing boldly. He'd asked her what she knew of it. Now it was her turn to ask him. "Ye called yerself a knight but what d'ye truly know of it?"

He swung his gaze back to her and quirked a corner of his mouth. "Those Jacobites were a threat to the woman I swore fealty to. Killing them was indeed a matter of honor for me. Honor isn't easy, but knowing the difference between right and wrong, and choosing right at any cost, never is."

He spoke with the passion and conviction of a true knight, like the ones in her grandmother's books. For an instant, with the setting sun behind him, he looked like the kind of man she dreamed of, held tall by honor, loyal to his convictions, gleaming like a bronze statue upon his steed. A knight in shining armor.

Jacobite killer. He killed for the queen. He'd just said as much. What would stop him from killing her mother once he found out that she was a threat to the queen?

Good lord, what was wrong with her? What was she thinking? She was tempted to slap her own cheek. Letting her mind take off in this direction about a soldier who'd killed many of her kinsmen, betrayed their memory. General Marlow was her escort and her enemy. She didn't need to get to know him. She needed to remain focused on what she was going to England to do. Win the queen's favor. Keep her mother and the rest of her kin safe from the throne. She couldn't fail, not when she could possibly stop a war and General Marlow from ever returning to Skye.

When she turned her horse away from his, he didn't move to stop her.

Just as well.

Daniel let her move her mount off to the right and didn't follow. His charge was safe with Hubert and the others. She didn't need him riding attached to her hip. He preferred not speaking to her, not looking at her. He wondered if everyone else found her so easy to read, or if that was a privilege exclusive to him. Why would it be?

For now though, he pondered an even bigger quandary: What did she have to do with the queen? Anne's story about taking her in as a handmaiden to gain favor with the Jacobites didn't make sense, since the outlaw Cameron MacPherson was the most powerful Jacobite in Scotland. What else was Anne hiding from him? How could he ever trust her again? The thought of it sickened him, as it had the other day when he found out the truth of his lineage. And if he couldn't trust Anne, who was left?

Certainly not a woman who believed that Anne's alleged half brother was the true king. Abigail MacGregor and her entire family were guilty of treason against the throne. He should be carting her off to prison, not to St. James's Palace.

And what about Charlotte Adler? Of course she knew of his illegitimate birth. She and Anne had been friends for a long time. The queen would have confided in her. Charlotte had lied to him too. How long had the Duchess of Blackburn known the truth? Her attention made sense to him now. She knew the blood of a childless prince flowed through his veins. She knew what he stood to inherit and she wanted to secure a place in his life.

He thought about his life over the past year. He hadn't been home a month when the duchess proclaimed her love for him. It was all very sudden and Daniel didn't know what to make of this woman he'd known for years, who'd never shown him any interest at all. He'd told Anne about their friend's sudden attention, but Anne was reluctant to get involved. Charlotte's heart was fickle, the queen had said. The duchess would find interest in someone else soon enough.

But she hadn't.

Charlotte's attention had only intensified. She made

veiled threats toward any woman he showed interest in and when she began making good on some of them, she proved that she would remove any opposition that stood between them.

He glanced at his charge and knew that Charlotte would hate her. She hated any woman who was considered beautiful. To contend with them she powdered her face and stained her cheeks and lips ruby. And here was Miss MacGregor, whose skin was naturally as white as freshly fallen snow. Her cheeks and lips were not painted, but softly enhanced in shades of pink and coral. He looked away from her and set his mind on other things, like his true mother. A nameless servant.

But she had a face. Tucking him into bed when he was a babe, kissing his scraped hands, and telling him to mind his father. No matter who gave birth to him, in his mind she had Anne's face.

When they finally stopped for the night and made camp, Daniel watched in silence while Miss MacGregor and Captain Andrews spoke and got to know each other. He didn't protest when Hubert offered to sleep closer to her so she'd feel safer. He didn't care about these things and turned in early, closing his eyes to go to sleep.

An hour later, and an hour after that, Daniel remained awake, a slave to recollections, not of his life, but of the last twenty hours. The image of the MacGregors of Skye, standing beside their horses waiting for him, would be forever emblazoned in his memory.

He forgot them the moment he saw her, braced against the wind, her shoulders squared, her chin high. She looked ready for anything. The damn sight of her alone had rattled his breath and caused him to miss her father's bold move.

Ah, it had been a good fight. He'd earned the Mac-Gregors' respect and they'd earned his. But now was the time for sleep. He turned to his right side and commanded himself to the task. But a moment later, his eyes opened and fixed on his ward. Miss MacGregor lay sleeping close to the fire, her pale complexion flushed from the heat of the flames. He stared at the curve of her nose and the slant of her brow. Firelight infused her hair with shades of gold and strands of pearly silver. Her lilting, defiant voice invaded his thoughts next until he finally sat up and leaned his back against the tree he was lying under. What the hell was wrong with him? So what if he found so many things appealing about her? What did it matter? It wasn't as if he could ever care for her—even if she wasn't a Jacobite. He wasn't going to get any sleep with her fitfully turning, trying to sleep. He turned his gaze away from her while he remembered her saucy demeanor and how she made him feel like a fool when he presumed to know her, twice. He'd controlled his desire to look at her on their journey, but he couldn't do it now.

A twig snapped and he looked in her direction. She was gone. He blinked, doubting his tired eyes, but when he looked again his heart ceased to beat while he leaped to his feet. She was gone.

❖

Chapter Seven

$\mathcal{A}$bby came awake abruptly with a yank of her hair and a hand over her mouth. She had no time to cry out before another hand fell over her throat and dragged her into the shadows.

She'd trained often with her cousins, male and female. She could wield a sword with skill, shoot an arrow, and fire a pistol with good accuracy, but she had never been abducted by men who meant her harm before, and this had happened so quickly. How many were there? She tried to think through her fear but then a fist made contact with her face and almost knocked her out.

She managed to hold on while the world went out of focus and voices around her sounded warbled. Something pinched her breast and caused her pain. She cried out. At least, she thought she did. She still wasn't sure if any of this was real. If it was, then let her faint and never wake from it.

Nae. It wasn't in her nature to give up. She had to conquer her fear and think.

"I'm takin' her first. I carried her!"

Who the hell was that? She didn't recognize the deep, menacing voice close to her ear.

Something pinched her again. This time on her thigh. "Hurry with her," said another male voice, hot along her throat. "Me and the boys are hard to burstin'."

Her heart crashed hard against her ribs. How many were there? How would she fight them all? Her father was at least a day behind. Where was Daniel? She tried to scream his name but her mouth was stuffed with a rag. The more aware she became, the more she realized how dire her situation truly was. Two men on either side of her held her wrists while another pressed his body against her. A fourth man, dark, even in the moonlight, grinned and pointed a pistol at her head.

Abby closed her eyes and fought to think clearly. She'd never been so afraid in all her life. This was real. These men were talking about raping her. With her wrists bound, she couldn't get to any of their weapons. She struggled but was finally victorious over her chattering teeth.

She opened her eyes again. She didn't want to but she had to in order to see what was happening. The man who pressed her to him came closer to lick her face. She waited with stilled breath until he withdrew enough for her to smash her forehead into his.

The other men shouted when their comrade fell limp in the leaves. The two holding her wrists let her go to aid their companion.

She needed only an instant to free a dagger from one of the men. She managed to ram it into its owner's back and then yank it back out. If she was going down, she'd go down fighting.

The cock of a pistol halted her movements. She turned her eyes toward the dark man with the pistol. As he took a step forward Abby was certain he could hear her heart thrashing wildly in her chest. He swung his hand over his shoulder, preparing to strike her.

She stared at him. She was a MacGregor and she would die proud like one. She wouldn't cower or close her eyes.

That's why she saw the sword come out of his belly. He looked as stunned as she, and then fell to the earth, dead. Abby looked up at the knight standing in his place and had never been so happy, so utterly grateful and relieved, to see anyone in her life. He finished her first victim with a blade to the neck and a kick to his shoulder, knocking the man off his knees, where he slumped over dead like his friend.

Her rescuer didn't wait while Lieutenant Hubert, Captain Andrews, and Lieutenant Ashley made an end to the last two.

He tugged her away a few feet, then stopped and smoothed his palm over her hair, swiping it away so he could examine her face more closely. Judging from the rage darkening his eyes, she suspected she had a black eye.

"It's not as bad as it likely looks." She tried to smile but her cheekbone hurt.

His eyes softened on her for a brief moment, then he shook his head. "It's bad. Don't try to make light of it."

She might have scowled at the way he tossed orders around, but he was correct, it was bad, and she wouldn't argue. "I think I was knocked oot fer a wee bit," she told him, reaching her hand to her cheek. She'd never been struck so by a man before. She swiped away the tear about to fall from her eye and looked up to find General Marlow's warm gaze there to meet her.

"Forgive me," he said roughly.

He sounded utterly repentant, but for what Abby had no idea. What could he possibly be asking her forgiveness for? He saved her life!

"I won't let you out of my sight again," he vowed.

"Ye won't?" She asked faintly, torn between enjoying the concern in his voice and terrified that being with him constantly would destroy her and her plans. What if she began to like him, an English general who hated and killed Jacobites? What would her kin think? What if she strangled him for being a stubborn oaf and the queen hated her for it?

"Did they hurt any part of you that I cannot see?"

She shook her head. "I'm all right, truly."

He didn't look convinced. In fact, he frowned at her. But at least he quit asking her. Silent while they walked back to their camp, about a half mile away, she thought about the violence of what had happened to her and what might have happened to her had General Marlow not arrived in time. She'd never been so frightened in her life. No practice could ever prepare her for the real, raw danger of the world outside Camlochlin. Her father had been correct when he'd warned them all that Camlochlin gave them a false sense of safety. Outside their nest in the mountains, folks were capable of doing terrifying things. Until tonight she'd never understood true fear and what it could do to a soul. Or what being saved from such terrors was capable of doing to the heart.

When they reached camp he set her beside him against the tree. She didn't protest. Her muscles were still trembling and her teeth chattered freely when she thanked him.

"I heard them talking," she told him when he draped his blanket around her shoulder. "They were going to rape me." She squeezed her eyes shut to stop the flow of tears burning to be free. She couldn't forget it. How would she ever forget it?

"But you stopped them." He reminded her in a whisper against her cheek.

"I didna' stop them," she insisted, leaning her lips up to his ear so he would hear her. "Ye did. Thank ye fer finding me."

"I would have gone mad if I hadn't."

She lifted her head to look at him, wondering what he meant. His expression went soft. "Thank God, I did."

"Why?" she asked softly, looking into his fire-lit eyes. "I'm a Jacobite. Why thank God that you found me?" She didn't know why she was asking him such a bold question. Mayhap she wanted to break through the shield he seemed to wear around himself. Had killing so many men created it? Or was it there to guard him from something else?

"Because I vowed to my queen and to your father that I would protect you."

She looked away, unsure of why his words stung a little.

"And because"—he cleared his throat but his voice sounded even deeper when he continued—"I've come to . . . you're not at all what I thought you might be . . . what I mean is . . ."

She smiled at him, thinking how handsome he was dressed in humility. She'd seen it worn by some of the men at Camlochlin, but she hadn't expected General Marlow to wear it. He was her clan's enemy. She didn't want to thank God for him tonight because if he hadn't found her when he did . . . She didn't want to like him. It felt too much like betrayal.

He didn't have a chance to continue, since his men rushed to her side. After patiently answering their queries regarding her well-being, she thanked them for coming to her aid and bid them good night when Daniel ordered them to sleep. He would keep watch until the morning.

When they were alone again, Abby glanced at him, then looked away. She'd never felt so vulnerable in her life. She hated it, but she was glad she was with him during it. What was he trying to tell her before his men interrupted them?

"You've been through much tonight." His heavy voice filled her ears. "Try to get some sleep. You have about four more hours until daylight."

"Ye sound angry with me."

He shook his head. "Not you. With myself. Now sleep."

She couldn't. She didn't like sleeping outdoors in the first place. Now, after being attacked in the dark, she doubted she'd ever sleep again. "And what about ye? Will ye sleep too?"

"No, I'll keep watch."

She nodded and leaned against the trunk, thankful for his blanket, and closed her eyes. Voices invaded her thoughts almost immediately. Men, fighting over who would have her first.

She sat up again. "I'm not sleepy. I think I'll keep watch with ye."

He didn't argue with her and she was thankful for that too.

"Tomorrow," he said instead, staring into the flames, "we will begin training."

"Fer what?"

"Staying alive."

She'd thought she already knew how to do that, but

she'd been wrong. "I know the principles, so I hope to be a quick student."

"I share your hope. I'm your escort, not your teacher."

"Of course." That was all she wanted him to be—her escort. She didn't expect him to like her and she certainly didn't like him. He'd saved her life and she was in his debt, but that was all.

"Besides," he added a moment later, "we'll be back in England in a little over a se'nnight. You don't have time to be slow."

"Why can ye not continue to teach me when we get there? Are female warriors frowned upon at court?"

He didn't answer her for so long she assumed the answer was yes and he didn't wish to tell her. She wouldn't push the issue. Not tonight. She would learn what he wanted to teach her quickly.

"I was verra afraid," she admitted, needing to get it out of her. "I know I'm unharmed, but I canna'..." She laughed at herself. "I canna' seem to shake it off."

She felt foolish for saying it, but she didn't know what else to do. This fear was new and unfamiliar to her. She didn't know how to harness it. Or if she even should. Aye, she needed to control it. Home was far away and her father might as well have been in France. She couldn't ask his advice. Daniel would have to do. She didn't know General Marlow well, but she found that she actually didn't mind showing herself to him a bit. He'd already seen her scared out of her wits and he hadn't laughed at all her claims of protecting herself. Hell, but he'd raked down those men with a heavy, merciless arm. What could her sword ever do against him? He was a wee bit haughty and arrogant, but he hadn't been brash or crude with her. He'd proven he would and could protect her. He made her feel safe.

"I'm afraid I will have to live with fear for the rest of my life."

"Learning to protect yourself will help, I vow it."

His voice was like a blanket, covering her. The warmth of his body close to hers made her nerves feel raw and sensitive. She smiled, even though she knew he couldn't see it.

"Ye dinna' mind a lass knowin' how to fight, then?"

So close to him, she could feel his every elongated breath. "I'd prefer she not only knew but could keep herself alive."

Goodness, she was thankful he couldn't see her grinning at him like a fool. She was sure she would hate herself in the morning, but she wanted to thank him with a kiss.

"D'ye think I'll ever know enough to stop four men from killing me?" she asked him instead.

He turned to look at her, his breath warm along her brow. "Yes, you'll know enough. I'll make sure of it."

She moved an inch closer to him. She was no stranger to freezing nights. Body heat was the best way to keep warm. When he stiffened beside her, she almost moved away.

"Fergive me, General," she said, turning to the fire, mortified by her own boldness. "I was only trying to get warm."

"Miss Campbell," he responded in his clipped, English accent. "Regardless of how I feel about my enemies, I'm not some proper gentleman you have to put on airs to impress." While he spoke he took up his blanket from around her shoulders and placed it around his, as well. "Tell me about your mother."

"My mother?" Abby's heart went from finally slowing

to racing once again. Why would he want to know anything about her mother...the true queen of England? As he'd said, they were enemies.

"If you're keeping watch with me," he explained, his voice as smooth as the nearby flames, "talking will help you stay awake. Now, tell me why your mother wasn't present at your departure. Does she live?"

Does she live? It was the question any one of her enemies wanted to know. Was he Davina Stuart's enemy? She thought about it for a moment. Nae, he couldn't be. It would mean he knew the truth about Davina's identity. In order for him to know, Anne would have had to tell him. Abby doubted the queen would entrust the name of the true heir to anyone. Nae, he knew nothing.

She let her herself relax a little and snuggled closer into his blanket.

"She was verra' ill last winter and it took its measure on her slight frame. She is still recovering."

"That's good news," he said. "Her illness must have been very difficult for your father. Being the kind of warrior he is and not being able to help her..."

She knew what he was doing. He was averting her thoughts from the new fears that enveloped her and moving them toward the love of her kin. But how did he know how hard her mother's sickness was for her father?

"He feared losing her," she told him, wanting him to know he was right. "He paced before the door to their bedchamber hour after hour, day after day, while priests and physicians came and went. He prayed by their bedside every night and held her and whispered things to her during her fevered deliriums. He chased away her nurses and fed her tea and soup and kept her head cool with wet rags. Ye may laugh and mock such tender care and unshakable dedication to keeping her alive, but I believe that he did help her, General. I believe he fought for her and brought her back."

His eyes lingered on her for a moment, reading her, taking in the depth of her words and snatching her breath away. "It would seem so," he replied without the mockery she expected.

He remained quiet for a moment, seeming to ponder something in his mind. "That's a mighty difficult memory to compete with."

"Aye." She smiled at him, liking that he understood. What could compete with watching her big, brawny bear of a father carrying her fevered mother up and down the hall and whispering close to her ear how much he adored her and needed her in his life? "'Twould be difficult."

"You must resemble her."

"Pardon?"

"Your mother. You must look like her. I saw your father and you don't have his face or his coloring."

She laughed. "My mother is beautiful."

"Hell," he said, "you don't think you're beautiful?"

She was glad for the shadows cast by the trees. They prevented him from seeing the flush burning up her cheeks. She also liked how the loss of vision honed her other senses. His scent of leather and metal and a hint of pleasant sandalwood went straight to her head like fine wine. The silken cadence of his voice that only she could hear. The width and strength of his shoulder against hers as they huddled beneath his blanket.

She knew she wasn't homely. But out of all her cousins, she was the least attractive. Caitrina, stunning with her mischievous dimples; Mailie, with her fiery red waves; and Nichola, with her breathtaking golden, green eyes turned many heads. She was white like snow. Plain and drab.

"I dinna' often think about my appearance," she told him.

She was certain he moved a little nearer. "What do you think about then?"

She shrugged and liked the feel of his body so close. "I think about my clan and the best ways to protect and take care of them."

"Isn't that your father's duty as clan chief?"

She could hear the smile in his voice above her. She wanted to see it. She looked up at him but it was too dark beneath the blanket.

"Aye, 'tis, but someday, 'twill be my duty as well."

"You plan on becoming chief?"

She nodded and told him about her brother Adam and her plans, and her kin, careful not to tell him anything about her royal blood. He was easy to talk to, and soon she forgot all about other men and their dangerous ways.

"What are you doing serving the queen as a hand-maiden if you intend on becoming your clan's chief?" he asked her.

He didn't know the true purpose of her visit to England. She wondered what her aunt had told him.

"She requested I come and to keep peace with her, I accepted." It wasn't a lie.

"Why d'ye scowl so much, General?" she asked him before he had time to ask her anything else.

He was silent for a moment, his breath falling faintly on her jaw. "I hadn't realized that I did."

"Ye never smile," she assured him.

"Is that so?" The playful dip in his voice set her flesh on fire. "I'm smiling at this precise moment."

"Prove it."

He took her hand, and covering her fingers in his, he carried them to his mouth. "Do you feel it?"

"Aye." She barely breathed while he traced her finger-tips over his curved lips. "I feel it."

"You can always trust my word, my lady."

He wasn't supposed to make her feel weak, and breathless, and he especially wasn't supposed to make her feel like a fevered maiden anxious for his touch.

Why, oh why, did he have to be the damned Jacobite killer? Why did the most chivalrous stranger she'd ever met have to be the deadliest man alive when it came to her kin?

She couldn't trust him, even if he'd just saved her life. Not ever.

✣

Chapter Eight

They headed out early the next morning, with Abigail MacGregor taking her usual place between Hubert and Andrews, with Ashley just behind. She had them wrapped around her delicate little finger, Daniel decided, listening to her voice behind him while they crossed bridges and rode across heather-lined glens. He was as bad as the rest, perhaps worse. Sometime during the night he'd promised to train her to fight better and to see her safely back to her home on Skye when her service to the queen was over. What if the queen didn't want her to go home? He shouldn't have promised her father that he would protect her. But even as he thought about it, he knew he would have protected her even if no vow had been made. Why? He hated Jacobites. She was no different from, no better than, any other treasonous outlaw. But he'd saved her.

Hell. He would never forget finding her bound by the men surrounding her, ready to hurt her. The fury that welled over him surprised him afterward. He'd leaped toward the bastard who was pointing the barrel of his pistol at her. Daniel couldn't kill him fast enough. He didn't remember his men killing the others. His only thought had been to get to her.

Finding her alive was such a great relief to him, he'd felt drunk with it. Drunk enough to say things to her he likely should not have said. Something about his going mad if he hadn't found her?

He wasn't even supposed to like her. But he did like her. He liked her courage to stand up to him and to fight off her attackers, despite her guaranteed defeat. Spending an entire night talking with her was the most pleasant thing he'd done in more years than he could remember. He liked how her voice sounded to his ears when she spoke of her family, and worst of all, he liked how she felt pressed close to him. He needed to get her to England before she stirred anything else in him.

When about an hour had passed, he noticed the pauses in her responses were growing longer. He turned in his saddle to look at her just as she began to slip from her horse. She'd fallen asleep! He whirled his horse around and reached her before anyone else did, though they were closer to her, and caught her in his arms before she hit the ground. She woke with a jolt and clung to him while he pulled her into his saddle and onto his lap, a place he'd sworn he wouldn't put her.

"Ye didna' have to do that, my lord," she protested, her eyes bloodshot in the sunlight.

"Shh," he muttered gruffly. "Don't argue."

He was glad she didn't. He wasn't sure how he felt when he heard her snore a little while later. How did she manage to snuggle so comfortably against him that he almost smiled like a fool? It had been years since he'd held a woman while she slept. He didn't remember how many years. As a soldier, he never lingered in brothels, even though sometimes he was so damned tired he ached to stay in bed, but his damsel for the night had other suitors waiting for her.

After he returned home he didn't share his nights often. When he did, he made certain that his guests left while it was still dark, so there was less chance for the duchess or her cohorts to find out about his dalliances. He'd certainly never stayed up all night talking with any of them.

Being his friend could be a dangerous thing for Abigail.

He wasn't wrong about Charlotte's obsession with him. He knew firsthand what she was capable of. It was no coincidence that Lady Margaret Byron went missing the night after she slept with him. She was found a few days later in an alley behind a brothel, naked and beaten. There was also Lady Victoria Everly's demise to consider. After a very brief courtship with Daniel, her family name was ruined by rumors of her father's gambling debts. The Everlys left England in shame. He believed both of these incidents were messages from the duchess. Anne wanted proof. He didn't have any, so he kept his bed empty and his eyes and ears open for proof against her. He'd warned Charlotte that if she ever hurt another woman because of him, he would personally see her hanged for her crime. She'd only laughed and denied his charges.

He looked down at the top of Abigail's hooded head. It wasn't just because of Charlotte that he wanted nothing to do with his charge. He'd fought his whole life against people like her and her family. Enemies of the throne. How could he ever reconcile loving a Jacobite? He wasn't sure it was possible. There was also the question of why was she truly being brought to England.

He dipped his nose to her head. She smelled like clean misty air with a hint of a flowery scent he couldn't place.

Why had he let her stay awake with him? He felt closer to her, drawn by more than her beauty, and despite the power of her beliefs. He envisioned her father sick with worry over his wife. He imagined he would have felt the same way. He couldn't help but smile when he remembered her declaration about being the next clan chief, a high aspiration and one that required dedication and duty. Was she simply the overindulged only daughter of a powerful chief? He had a difficult time imagining why she would want to take on such an enormous role as leader.

If he had to take a guess about her now, he would say she could do it. She could be a leader if she could fight a little better.

There it was again, his foolishness taking over, letting himself forget, even for a moment, that he could get her killed, or she could get the queen killed, if he wasn't careful. He shouldn't let her sleep on him like he was her favored pillow. It tempted him to lose himself in the intimacy of it.

She moved and he closed his arm around her—to keep her from falling. That's what he told himself and what he told Ashley when his lieutenant rode at his side.

"You know—"

"I know, Lieutenant."

"I just meant to say—"

"You don't have to."

He watched Ashley leave without another word. He didn't need his men telling him not to get attached to Miss MacGregor. He was still reeling from the betrayal of his queen and closest friend. He didn't want to believe his heart could betray him, as well.

When they reached the Great Glen, he scouted out a suitable campsite, eager to separate from her. She shouldn't be sleeping on him all soft and nestled close.

What kind of general held his enemy so tenderly in the crook of his arm?

He shook her gently awake as they stopped. "Wake up, Miss Campbell. We are stopping to eat."

She roused herself and stretched her arms over her head, hitting him in the eye. "Oh, I'm so sorry!" She covered her mouth with her hands and gaped at him for a moment. "I wasna' expecting to wake in yer...yer... ehm...arms."

"You almost slipped from your horse. I had no choice but to catch you."

"In that case, ye have my thanks yet again." She smiled at him. He did not smile back.

He nodded, then leaped from his saddle. Just another moment he told himself. He held his arms up to her and she fell into them.

He looked into her eyes while he transferred her from the saddle to her feet. In the early mist, they appeared cool, like the color of a November sky over snow-capped peaks. And yet they contained the warmth of a passionate woman. Recklessly, he allowed his gaze to survey the rest of her countenance, her soft contours and strong curves. He pulled back, forbidding himself to wonder what things she was passionate about. Why did he have to be curious about her in particular? Damn it! He was torn between wanting to shake her out of his arms and pulling her closer into them.

What the hell was he thinking last night, smiling at her like a smitten stable hand? He needed to stop doing that.

But according to her, he already had.

Putting her down, he smoothed his coat, stepped away, and turned to his men. "Hubert, see to the horses. I'm going to take a rinse. Miss Campbell, come with me."

She resisted and gave a little laugh. "Ye're going fer a rinse, my lord. I'll be safe here with Hubert and—"

He gave her hand a tug and pulled her along.

"General Marlow!" She resisted again. "I willna' be—"

He glanced down at his fingers clamped around her wrist. "Forgive me." He loosened his hold. "My men can protect themselves. I can protect you and myself. You'll stay in my care."

She nodded. "Still, ye dinna' need to be a brute aboot it."

He lifted his gaze to hers and knew right away that it was a poor judgment. She didn't say anything and still he had the urge to smile. What in blazes was happening to him? Every ounce of logic in him demanded that he turn away from her, consider her nothing but his Jacobite ward. But he didn't want to turn away.

"Every knight battles a darker *brute* within," he told her, turning her wrist over in his fingers and bringing it to his lips. "I'll keep him away. You have my word. You've nothing to fear from me, my lady." He smiled again. Very slightly. Damn it!

Moving along, he looked around, remembering the path.

He chose this place because it was close to the River Garry, which flowed into a clear, secluded loch surrounded on almost every side by lush foliage, wet rock, and sunshine. He remembered it for its raw beauty and he thought about it on balmy summer days in England.

He would take his rinse and then teach her some defense. Until then, he would speak to her as little as possible and think of her even less. And tonight he would insist she sleep away from him.

He followed the path he remembered, eager to wash away the past few days of grime.

"'Tis verra' bonny, here," she said, keeping up with him.

"Give me your hand."

After a quick scowl at him, she ducked with him beneath an array of low branches, stepped over hundreds of thick roots growing about the dirt, and climbed small boulders.

When they reached their destination, he smiled over the sun-splashed surface of the stream and threw off his coat.

"Wait right here. I will not be long." He unclasped the belts at his waist and tossed them, along with his sword and hers, to the grass. He pulled his shirt over his head, then yanked off his boots. When he unbuttoned his pants and began to lower them over his hips, she stopped him.

"General! Ye dinna' intend to—"

"You're free to turn your head, Miss Campbell." He turned away from her and stepped out of the remainder of his garments. His back was to her but he didn't need to see her to know she hadn't taken his suggestion. He could feel her eyes burning into him. He wanted to turn and look at her.

He dove, headfirst and naked, into the water instead, barely creating a splash.

It was just as he remembered, warmed by the sun and gloriously refreshing. He kept his eyes on his charge while he scrubbed with leaves and thin twigs. She sat on the grass, her back against a tree, napping perhaps.

Away from the rest of the world, he swam and basked in the sunshine like a lazy merman and pondered what to do when he returned to the palace. He intended to confront Anne about his birth and her reasons for not telling him. The queen was a large part of his life. He loved her, but he wasn't sure he could forgive her.

He'd stay away from Abigail MacGregor and put her in no danger with Charlotte. He turned back to check on his charge and found her untying the laces of her kirtle.

"What are you doing?" he called out. Surely she wasn't thinking of undressing and entering the water with him. He didn't trust himself with her, buoyant and weightless and naked.

"I smell," she called back. "I need to bathe and since I'm here—"

"No." He held up his palm. "You smell quite nice. You don't need to bathe."

"I see." She folded her arms across her chest and sent him a frosty glare as he swam closer to the shore.

At least she'd stopped undressing.

"This is how 'tis going to be with us? You barking orders at me?"

Her lovely eyes widened on him as he stepped out of the water, then darted away and looked at everything but him.

"I would enjoy it even more if you obeyed them," he said, bending to his clothes. He looked at his belt and noted that hers was still there. Why hadn't she taken it back when she had the chance?

"I do obey ye!" she argued. "I'm astoundingly agreeable."

"Then cease arguing with me."

"I dinna' argue with ye!"

"What are you doing right now?" he asked, pulling his shirt over his head.

She looked like she wanted to pick up a rock and fling it at him, but she lowered her gaze instead.

"Abigail," he called out, bringing her eyes back to him. He bent to retrieve his belt and tossed her sword to her.

"What's this?" she asked.

"Come at me."

She paused for a moment, then jabbed her blade at him before he put his belt back on. He deflected the blow with ease, swinging around on one bare foot and coming to rest with his arms around her, her back to his chest, her sword useless in her captured hand.

"Try again." He pushed her back toward her starting position.

She came at him slower, with a bit more caution but with the same result. He captured and subdued her in the blink of an eye, holding her securely, her back to his chest. When she tried to pound her heel into his shin, he avoided harm once again and then disabled her feet with one of his legs wrapped around both of hers.

She felt so damn perfect pressed against him. He never wanted to move again. He dipped his nose and lips to her neck and inhaled the alluring scent of her. "What will you do now?"

Her breath came hard and heavy, tempting him beyond reason. He spun her around so that she faced him and dragged her up against him. For a moment, nothing existed in the world but her. He looked into her eyes and thought about kissing her. He feared it would be the only thing he thought about for the next month.

"Now is your chance to use your knee, my lady."

"Nae! I couldna' do—"

"Then you're dead." He released her and turned for his coat.

Chapter Nine

$\mathcal{A}$ bby attacked him before he had a chance to get to his coat. She couldn't let him think she was giving up. He was taking her lessons seriously. She was thankful for it and promised to hurt him if she could.

If she was being truthful, as she'd been taught to be, she didn't want the practice to end. She doubted she'd ever forget how it felt to be crushed up against him, held in his arms while his desire for her flashed across his eyes.

He'd fought whatever it was he wanted to do and made certain she learned how to attack without getting caught. He showed her many effective defense moves and made her feel safer. Not because of what he could do, but because of what she would become able to do.

But a thought nagged at her while her lesson continued. What good would any of it do against him, should he try to have his way with her?

It would be a miracle if she ever managed to get his naked body out of her memory. Heaven help her, he was a masterpiece sculpted in lean, tight sinew, honed to perfection by years of battle. He'd glistened under the sun like some fire god come to haunt her dreams and mock any mortal man who dared enter. His hair gleamed like a crown beneath the sun in all the colors of autumn. His steady breath and unruffled regard attracted her in ways that made her ache somewhere deep in her groin. She wanted to ruffle him, to see him pant. Never had she felt this way before, so drawn to a man that if she didn't stay focused she would end up smiling at him all day like a damned fool.

He was dangerous to his enemies, and she must not forget that her kin was his enemy.

"Drive your heel here." His thick voice rolled over her ears while he motioned to his foot. "The hilt of your blade or your elbow here." He pointed to his belly.

They practiced more defense and he let her strike him to make it feel more real to her. He reminded her of her promise.

The first time she rammed her elbow into his guts, she felt a twinge of guilt, but he barely doubled over. She might have thought he was carved in leather armor beneath his flowing shirt, but she knew he wore nothing underneath his damp clothes. This hardness was all him. And damn her to Hades, but he'd looked hard while she watched him leave the loch. She'd seen naked men before. Well, they were mostly half-naked, wrapped in nothing but belted plaids. Highlanders in summer. She'd never seen anyone who looked like Daniel Marlow. He was built like one of her grandsire's prized horses. Strong, fast, almost regal.

"You're not paying attention, Miss Campbell." He slapped away her sword and clasped his fingers around her throat. "What will you do now?" he asked her, tightening his grip and cutting off her air. She couldn't panic. She had to think. If this were really happening, her attacker wouldn't show her mercy.

She did the thing she'd been taught to do since she was a little girl. She pulled back her leg and drove her knee straight into his groin.

He almost blocked the blow but he must not have expected her to do it, even though it was his suggestion. He went down like a lightning-blasted tree, clutching himself and squeezing his eyes shut.

No! She felt awful! "General, fergive me!" She bent to her knees beside him and bit her lip when he writhed on the ground.

Should she run? For a moment, she panicked, not knowing what to do. What did she know of the man lying on his side, helpless because of her? Nothing but that he killed Jacobites. Would he strike her? She didn't run, but clutched the hilt of her sword tighter and prepared to defend herself against him.

"'Twas yer idea to—"

He held up his palm to stop her. "No." He groaned and tried to sit up. "You did the perfect thing. As you can see, I'm debilitated enough for you to finish me."

She smiled at him, grateful for his kind response. "Still," she said, touching her fingers to his arm. He glanced down at her touch. "Fergive me for causing ye such pain. If 'tis any consolation, 'twas a verra' good lesson."

Honestly, how was she not supposed to like him when he set those large, piercing eyes on her? He might hate Jacobites, but when he spread his wide, dashing grin on her, she wasn't sure he hated her.

Or perhaps she didn't want to believe he did.

"Ye have a verra' handsome smile, General."

"I'm glad to see it has returned."

If she had more courage, she would lean over and kiss him. Aye, she looked at the sensuous curve of his lips and wondered how they would feel molded to hers.

She looked away from him, trying to pull herself together. What in blazes was wrong with her? She'd been attracted to men before. None of them had ever made her feel so helpless against her own emotions. It frightened her. She had to use more caution, be more aware of his effect on her and guard against it more efficiently. She could never trust him with her mother's secret, and because of that, there could never be anything between them.

As if sensing her mood, he moved away from her and rose slowly to his feet.

"We'll resume tonight."

"In the dark?" she asked him while he pulled his boot over his foot.

"Yes. Don't be afraid," he commanded, pulling on his other boot. "I won't hurt you, nor will you hurt me again."

It wasn't that. Her trust in him was growing. She didn't doubt what he said. She wasn't afraid of his hurting her.

"What if it reminds me of what happened last night?" she asked him honestly. Hell, she hated herself for letting it worry her, but it did. "What if I remember how afraid I was and I canna' move?"

He stopped securing his belt to his waist and turned to look at her. His lids appeared heavy as his gaze on her softened. "You *should* remember and not hide from your fears. But remember this also." He moved closer to her on his way to retrieve his sword. "It will be me with you, not them."

"All right." She smiled as he passed her, feeling better. If he thought she could do it, then she would. "General?"

"Yes?"

"Will ye no' change yer mind aboot me having a quick rinse? Like ye, I feel grimy. Please, my lord," she added quickly when he looked unsure. "I will be but a moment."

He ground his jaw. "Very well. But be quick."

She nodded and then waited until he turned his back on her. "Is it verra' cold?"

She heard him swear under his breath before he answered her. "Yes, Miss Campbell, it's cold."

Heavens, but he was irritable, she thought, untying the laces of her kirtle. "I dinna' like it when ye call me Miss Campbell," she called out. "I'm a MacGregor and proud to be one. We are alone. Ye can speak my true name."

"MacGregors are proscribed," he reminded her. "And if we fall out of habit, it could bring you trouble."

He was correct. She couldn't argue. She could curse him, though, for not letting her take a few more of her bags. Thanks to him, she didn't have a change of dress, save for the gown she would wear when she met the queen.

She peeked a glance over her shoulder to make certain he wasn't looking before she slipped out of her earasaid, then her kirtle, and finally the shift underneath. She waded into the water and disappeared in its depths. The cold was shocking to her flesh but she was used to it after swimming in the lochs around Camlochlin. She came up and set her eyes on him where he stood with his back to her.

He was a knight of the Most Noble Order of the Garter. Thanks to her grandmother's lessons, Abby knew all about knights. The Most Noble Order of the Garter was the highest order of chivalry and the most prestigious honor in Great Britain. What had he done to earn such a title? Why did he have to be a slayer of her people? What was between him and Anne? There was definitely something. Every time they spoke of her he wore an almost pained expression. He loved the queen. Even more reason never to trust him.

What if he weren't her enemy?

Abby tread water and examined the flare of the knight's shoulders, his muscular thighs, and the snug fit of his breeches.

"Why are ye dressed like a commoner instead of a solider or a nobleman?"

"My uniform would draw attention to you and make men more curious. There are only four of us and while I've no doubt we could take on a small army, I'd prefer not to have to prove it in every town or village we enter."

Confident, wasn't he.

"Finer garments—and six bags tied to our horses—would also attract unwanted attention," he told her as if he could read her previous thoughts about her clothes. His decision to leave her bags behind was the right one.

She smiled behind him, grateful to him for considering her safety even before he'd promised it to her father.

She scrubbed quickly and swam to the edge. "I'm leaving the water."

He shifted on his feet and balled one hand into a loose fist at his side.

She reached her clothes and dressed in a hurry. "Thank ye fer not looking," she said, reaching him, fully dressed.

"There's no need to thank me for that," he grumbled. "Can we go now?"

She nodded. "Should I ride with you again tonight or can I be trusted on my own steed?"

"Your own steed." He reached for his long coat, slung it over his shoulder, and began walking.

She followed, keeping a steady pace at his side. She

realized he was walking slower deliberately so that she didn't have to rush to keep up.

She glanced up at his profile a number of times while they walked in silence. She lived among many handsome men, but none were more beautiful than him. His strong, unbroken nose added to his perfection. His chin and jaw were defiant, confident, and shadowed in glistening golds and fiery reds.

On the way back to camp she pondered how his mind worked. Last night while they stayed awake together, she'd shared intimate details of her life with him. He'd listened and hadn't told her she was a fool to want to be chief. They'd shared space and laughter and this morning he kept her from falling off her horse when she fell asleep and let her sleep in his arms. Blazes, he smiled at her like he might actually be fond of her even after she kicked him between the legs.

And then whatever they shared was gone. She knew why she had turned from him. She was afraid. Who in her right mind would want to fall in love with her enemy? He had turned away from her also. Was he afraid as well?

She thought about it for a moment longer, remembering how well he fought against her kinsmen.

What the hell could frighten him?

Chapter Ten

The Duchess of Blackburn stood at the window overlooking the rolling hills of Carlisle. The view would have captured her breath, but she longed for another—a view with him in it. Four Lawns Manor was the most beautiful of all her and her husband John's estates. Yet even here she could not forget Daniel Marlow. She saw his eyes in the dancing treetops, his fiery locks in the rising sun.

She didn't love the general. That is to say, she'd never loved him in the past. Finding out that he was the bastard son of Prince George had helped open her eyes to what an irresistible man Daniel was. She wished Anne would have told her who he was earlier, before he'd gone off to fight. Well, it had given her plenty of time to plan. If she could make him fall in love with her, she could figure out a way to get rid of her husband and secure an even better position for herself in the kingdom... and in Denmark as well.

She had a number of lovers. Daniel wouldn't be her first. That is, if he would give in to her. Damn him and his code of honor. The others didn't care if she was a married woman. Why did it make such a damn difference to him? She knew she was beautiful, for enough men had told her so. Was it just her husband that kept her knight away? If so, there was an easy remedy. But Charlotte didn't want to give up her duke if she couldn't have the prince. She needed to know how Daniel felt about her first. She was almost certain he did care for her, since he didn't entertain many women.

And then there was Anne. Poor, pitiful Anne. Always another tragedy. Daniel loved her like a mother, and though Anne had kept the truth from him—that she was, in fact, his stepmother—her favor for him trumpeted loud and clear. Anne adored him enough to recently make it clear to Charlotte that she would not, in any way, ever be considered as a future wife for him.

Charlotte's eyes hardened on the landscape and the image of the queen in her mind. How dare Anne say such a thing to her? Her! The only person, other than Daniel, who put up with her misery day after day, year after year. What was wrong with a widow as the prince of Denmark's bride? Anne would pay for saying that. She'd pay for never letting Charlotte forget that she was once a servant under Anne's sister, Mary. Charlotte had already begun to slice her down to size. She didn't care if she was sometimes cruel or that Anne saw it. If taking Daniel to her bed upset Anne, then Charlotte was doubly determined to do it.

She wanted him, his body hot and ready in her hands. She daydreamed often about the different ways she wanted him. Poised above her, like a conquering general about to lay siege to her body. Subservient beneath her, because that's where he belonged, whether a general or an earl. Because she held the power and she'd enjoy putting a man like him in his place. The more she thought about having him, the stronger her desire became, until she was ready to risk getting caught in plain sight with him.

Someone knocked at the door. She wiped the beads of moisture from her brow that thinking about Daniel produced and moved away from the window. Who the hell was it? She wasn't in the mood for having servants scurrying around her. But she did have to get dressed. "Enter!"

When Richard Montagu did as he was told, she rolled her eyes toward the heavens. He'd arrived in Carlisle with her yesterday. He would have ruined everything had Daniel been here. But Daniel wasn't here. It put her in a foul temper.

"What do you want, Richard? I haven't even broken fast yet."

He came toward her, arms outstretched to take her in. She stopped him with a palm to his chest. "None of that now," she told her lover, a man very close to becoming her past lover.

He ducked his chin to his chest and reminded her of a worm. Poor, pathetic Richard. He claimed his hopes involved usurping Daniel and taking over leadership of the queen's military. It was never going to happen. Anne might be bloated and sickly, but she wasn't a fool.

"My darling," he said, making a dramatic recovery, "I've been called away. I know I just arrived yest—"

"Go then, Richard." She flicked her wrist at him. "What does your business have to do with me?"

He smiled beneath that ridiculous mustache, bowed, and left the room without another word.

Dolt.

She threw herself on her bed and thought of her general. Was it his dedication to Anne that made him the ultimate prize to win? Or the way he laughed with her and danced with her around the ballroom, like he owned her? Or because someday he would wear a crown?

She smiled. A crown.

Captain Nathaniel Andrews's smile made Daniel clench his jaw.

They'd left camp and were continuing southward with Miss MacGregor riding her own steed beside him. Andrews kept pace on the other side of her while Hubert and Ashley brought up the rear. For the last hour Daniel had listened to most of his captain and the lady's conversation. Of course, Andrews did most of the talking, and most of it was about himself. Daniel guessed he had much to say. Women adored Nate, with his dark good looks and winsome smiles. Miss MacGregor didn't appear to be any different, exchanging dozens of smiles with him.

Daniel didn't care what the men did with their time, but they were forbidden to take pleasure with women while they were on a campaign or fulfilling their duties to the queen. Miss MacGregor was the queen's lady and it was their duty to see her arrive in England safely. He sure as hell wasn't about to let the scoundrel of Hallingford Hall seduce her.

"Captain."

Andrews looked past her shoulder, his wicked grin still intact. "Yes, General?"

"A word." Daniel didn't wait for him to follow but tugged his reins and rode off a short distance away.

He waited while his captain said one last thing to her, then took off after him.

"Whatever you're doing with her stops now," he commanded when Andrews reached him. "Understood?"

"General?" Andrews wore a different kind of smile now. This one wasn't anywhere near as friendly as his last.

"Captain." Daniel's mount grew anxious immediately and moved closer to Andrews's horse. "Do you understand?"

The captain nodded his raven head. "Of course. Is that all?"

Daniel nodded and watched him ride off, back to the others. When he reached Miss MacGregor he didn't stop or pause, but rode by her and stayed behind her.

When Daniel moved his gaze back to her, he found her staring at him. She looked angry ... or curious. Damn it. He turned back to the road and trotted away.

"What was that all about?" She caught up with him and cantered beside him. "Why does Captain Andrews look angry with me? What did ye say to him?"

Hell, she was direct and bold. "He's angry with me. Not you," he told her.

"Why?"

He cut her a sharp glance. "It doesn't concern you."

She laughed, but after hearing her laugh all afternoon with Captain Andrews, this time it didn't sound genuine. "Really, knight? Since when is lying a virtue?"

"Since honor dictates that a mistruth is sometimes more beneficial."

"Fer whom?"

He clenched his jaw, irritated that she wouldn't let up. "Very well, lady. You don't know him. Captain Andrews is—"

"A knave with the ladies at court?" She quirked her brow at him. "The scoundrel of Hallingford Hall? Aye, I know. Hubert told me."

She knew and she still laughed at his disingenuous flattery? Was it too late? Had she already lost her heart to Andrews? The captain was closer to her age, and he was considered the most handsome man in London.

"My duty is to keep you safe. If that means keeping Andrews away from you, I'll do it."

"Thank ye, but I dinna' need yer help with him. I—"

"Whether you need my help or not is not important, lady. It's expected of me to see to your safety. I won't send you home to your father with one of Andrews's babes in your womb."

She gasped. "General Marlow!" The command in her voice drew his attention to her. "Dismount so that I can slap yer face and hopefully take oot yer eye. How dare ye suggest that my mind is so weakly crafted that I would fall fer the tedious boasts of Narcissus himself! To suggest that I would toss myself into his bed just because he's handsome is such a great insult I dinna' know if I can ferget it."

Before he could say a word, she yanked her reins and took off ahead of him.

He wanted to go after her. Hell, it wasn't supposed to happen this way. The queen had sent him because she trusted him to remain detached and see to his duty—not lose his ground after a few days. He wasn't supposed to care about honor now. Miss MacGregor wasn't supposed to expect it of him. And there was a very good chance the queen didn't deserve his loyalty.

He decided not to go after her right away. He wanted to give her time to be angry. She had every right to be. He had indeed insulted her, whether he meant to or not. He didn't think she was weakly crafted at all. He should have realized she wouldn't melt at Andrews's empty compliments.

He would apologize after she'd had a chance to cool down.

When they stopped several hours later to make camp for the night, she still hadn't spoken a word to him, save to refuse to practice with him. He granted her wish because he had caused her such an insult and he understood her anger. But he wouldn't let her refuse tomorrow. She needed to learn to protect herself better.

They all ate in silence, with Andrews saying nothing, the lady keeping silent, Daniel following their lead, and Hubert and Ashley staring at their food while they ate.

"Men," Daniel said, rising to his feet when he finished his meal. "I'll keep first watch. Then Ashley, Andrews, and then Hubert."

The men agreed and Daniel left the fire. He stopped just before the shadows, at the nearest tree, and sat against it. He didn't mind sleeping out of doors. He was used to it. A soldier didn't sleep in a bed when he was fighting battles. And in England there were many battles to be fought.

The absence of a soft mattress beneath him didn't bother him. Of course his body longed for such pleasure but his duty came before his comfort.

His eyes roamed the fire-lit camp until he found her laying out her Highland plaid close to the fire. He remembered her moving closer to him last night because she was cold. He was used to sleeping on the cold, hard ground, but she wasn't. She hadn't complained—not once since they left Skye.

He watched Hubert lay his blanket out close to her and speak to her in the firelight. He realized almost instantly that what he was feeling was jealousy. Was it jealousy also that prompted him to warn Andrews to leave her alone?

He looked away from her delicate frame wrapped in wool. This was bad. He was the general of the queen's entire army. He couldn't let himself make rash or overly harsh decisions because of his emotions. He had no claim on her, nor did he want one. If one of his high-ranking officers did—and she agreed to it—then it was her father's concern, and not his.

His eyes found Andrews going down for the night on the opposite side of the camp, farthest away from Miss MacGregor. The captain had resisted but in the end he was obeying orders. Daniel respected him for it.

Slipping his gaze over the camp once again, his eyes settled on his lady guest. She'd turned in her plaid and was now lying on her belly, her face in his direction. The problem was, he couldn't see her face with the flames and the moon behind her. Was she awake, watching him watching her? He looked the other way for as long as he could before the temptation to return to her became too strong.

She hadn't moved. She could still be watching him, or she could be sleeping, dreaming of a day when she became ruler of her clan. He wasn't sure if she should mention to the queen her plans to become chief. The bigger worry, though, was why the hell did he care about any of it? He looked away again.

He hated what she and the rest of her kin stood for. They were all guilty of treason and were worthy of the noose, and why? Because their sovereign had different religious beliefs than they did. Foolish, prideful people, loyal only to what benefited them, rather than what benefited the kingdom.

He didn't realize his gaze had returned to her again until he found himself watching her rise up and, taking her plaid with her, stride toward him. He wanted to scowl at her. This was the last thing he wanted. Another night pressed into her, keeping her warm, listening to her captivating voice. He smiled instead, damn him.

He remained still and silent while she dropped to her knees right beside him.

Cloaked in the shadows with her, he could barely see her face. It made her breath falling softly on his chin that much more sensuous.

"Are ye going to watch me all night, General?" she whispered. "Because I must tell ye, I'm finding it verra' difficult to sleep with yer eyes on me."

His smile remained and he didn't care if she could see him or not.

"Well?" she insisted.

"Will I be criticized for my honesty?"

"That depends on what ye say."

She certainly had no trouble saying the first thing that came to her. He found it quite refreshing. Annoying and frustrating as well, but refreshing.

"Yes, I will most likely be watching you. You'll forgive me if I fear losing you again." He wanted to stop there, at the most open, honest part of his response, but it was foolish, and he was not a fool. It was childish, and he was not a boy. "It's my duty to deliver you safely to the queen and then back to your father."

She didn't reply right away and he counted her breaths. Sixteen. He hadn't wanted to say it to her, and when he did, it made him feel ill. But it was best if she knew she was his duty and nothing more. It wasn't a lie. Was it? It couldn't be. She couldn't be anything more to him. He was a damned general. He controlled his emotions when other men faltered. He needed to get a hold of himself.

"Ye have my gratitude fer doing such a fine job then."

"As I said, it's my duty."

"Aye, ye did say that," she murmured. "Well, since we're both awake, we might as well spend the night together again."

The innocence in her voice struck him in the gut. She wanted nothing more from him than someone to be with outside in the night.

He, on the other hand, was not innocent at all. Her choice of words sent a little spark of heat to his groin. The way she turned on the pads of her feet and ended up pressed against his side and tucked neatly under his shoulder tilted him on his axis a little.

"I'm cold," she whispered, her teeth chattering.

He put up no fight when she lifted his arm around her shoulder, then covered them both with her plaid. The desire to protect her overwhelmed him and sent tremors through his muscles. He knew little of her. Was she an innocent daughter of a Jacobite chief, or part of some secret scheme Anne was devising?

Hell. Anne didn't devise schemes.

"I wasn't certain if you were ever going to speak to me again," he said, when what he *should* have said was, *You should go sleep somewhere, lady, and not on me.*

"I was verra' angry with ye. But I've forgiven ye." He heard the smile in her voice and made a mental note of how well it pleased him that she was no longer angry. He would decide what to do about his unwanted concerns for her tomorrow. Right now, he only wanted to sit just like this, with her beneath his arm and pressed snuggly into his side. Warmth swept over him like fine wine until he felt drunk on it.

How was it that she fit so neatly into him, now and

earlier when she slept in his lap, like she belonged there, close to him?

Close to his heart.

Hell, it scared him, and after fighting for over a decade, not much scared him anymore.

"D'ye have a wife, General Marlow?" came her sweet voice against his chest.

"No, lady."

"Are ye betrothed?"

"I am not."

"Is there a lass somewhere who has yer heart?"

"No."

"Well"—she laughed softly—"are all the ladies in England fools?"

"They're the opposite," he told her. "They're wise to set their interests in another direction."

She shook her head, then tilted her face up to his. In the filtered light of the moon, he could make her out enough to fall victim to the alluring curves of her mouth, her soft, sweet breath against his chin. "Nae, they are fools not to try to win yer affections."

He knew every reason there was to stop what he was thinking, what he was feeling, and what he was about to do. But reason was a puny opponent compared to desire.

Slipping one hand behind her nape and the other to her throat, he tilted her chin another half inch, then covered her mouth with his. The instant after he did it, he regretted it, but then she coiled her arms around his neck and drew him closer, and he couldn't stop. He never wanted to. She didn't resist him; in fact, she melted in his arms. She groaned softly when he drew his tongue across the seam of her mouth. She bit his lip and ignited his blood to liquid fire. He swept his tongue in and out of her, holding her close to him while they kissed, wanting nothing more from her than what she was giving him now. Making love to her could be dangerous if Charlotte found out. He'd have to make sure she didn't find out, at least until he had proof of other crimes and could arrest her. If she hurt Abigail before that he'd hang her himself.

He wondered, as he held her in his arms and kissed her long into the night, how he could be so content with one he was supposed to hate.

Chapter Eleven

$\mathcal{A}$ bigail rode her own horse and remained awake and in her saddle every day after that for the next two days, though she was damned exhausted! After the night that she and Daniel kissed for three hours, she'd been careful to keep her distance with him at night. She slept little and was frozen half to death in the morning, but that was better than the warmth of his embrace. She hadn't fought to get here to find a husband, or to destroy her clan over a lover.

Anne was in love with him. That's why the ladies in England were wise not to set their interests on him. That had to be it. That's what he was afraid of, and what she was afraid of too. He was wise. She had to be wise, as well.

It was especially difficult to remain unaffected by him while they practiced in the morning and in the early twilight. She was glad that he looked as pained by their forced separation as she did.

"Tell me about her," she asked him on the third morning after their kiss. They were practicing, and he had just shown her how to break his nose with the pad of her palm. "Tell me about the queen."

He grabbed her wrist and twisted her arm behind her back. "She's a lady of steadfast resolve."

Heavens, Abby thought while she rammed her heel into his shin, not hard enough to cause him injury, but enough to make him double over, was that good news for her clan, or bad?

"Her body suffers the effects of all her sadness."

Abby knew the queen was lame. Camlochlin might be lost somewhere in the mists, but when her mother wanted news of her sister, she got it. They knew Anne was ill, as did the rest of the kingdom, but they didn't know anything personal about her.

Abby stopped fighting him and looked at him. "What is she so sad about?"

He told her and Abby felt a surge of compassion rise up in her. She knew women in Camlochlin who had suffered the loss of pregnancy. Anne had suffered that and more, even losing her husband more than a year ago. But where did Daniel fit in?

"And she's jealous when it comes to you?" Abby asked him.

"No." He cast her curious smirk. "Why would she be— Oh, you thought..."

Abby swung at him and nearly struck him. He reached for her, but she ducked and slipped away. "Then, if not the queen, who?"

"Her name is Charlotte."

"I see." Abby let him deliver a fatal wound. At least, it would have been fatal had it been real.

He scowled at her as if he truly cared about her being killed. Who was this Charlotte? Did he love her? No, he'd told her he had no lady love.

"Is she dangerous, yer Charlotte?"

"She isn't mine, but she is dangerous," he told her honestly. "She would be to you."

"Why?"

"To punish me for losing my heart to someone else."

Was he telling her that he could lose his heart to her? Abby looked away. She didn't want to see what was in his eyes. Damn it to Hades that out of all the knights left in the world, this one had to belong to a madwoman. But his deadly lover was of little consequence. He was the sworn enemy of Jacobites—and he would never ever allow one to take the throne.

She should hate him.

She tried to but about thirty breaths in, she gave in, knowing there was no hatred for him in her. She also tried to keep herself from speaking to him for the rest of the day. She succeeded until they ended their evening practice and were on their way back to where they'd set up camp for the night. "Ye said ye hated Jacobites," she said, looking up at his profile in the twilight. "How passionate are ye about that?"

He didn't answer her right away, and she suspected he was getting ready to tell her. Then he spoke, and suddenly she realized she'd returned to him to hear his voice. Silken decadence dipped deep in integrity. She missed the sound of it.

"About as passionate as one can get."

She was afraid of that. But it was for the best. "Well," she said with a sigh, "we can hate each other but remain civil. Can we not?"

"I'm not certain we can."

She moved a bit closer to him while they walked. His scent was growing more familiar, more pleasant every day. She inhaled and power filled her nostrils. He'd saved her, and though she'd always believed she could save herself should danger arise, she'd panicked and those men who took her would have eventually killed her if not for the knight. She couldn't hate him. It was impossible.

"Will ye do something fer me, General?"

"What is it?"

"Tell me what ye know of James the Third's supporters."

"Miss MacGregor." He glanced at her beside him and filtered sunlight illuminated the different shades of green in his eyes. "I really don't—"

"'Tis just that ye strike me as an intelligent man." She stopped him before he ended the conversation. "I simply want to ensure that the decisions ye're making are based on the truth."

He looked at her again and smiled. "And what is the truth, lady?"

"Ye mock me, my lord."

"No, but I've heard many 'truths' about the movement. Everyone has his own defense about why he committed treason. I've heard the Catholics' side and the Protestants'. I don't think the Almighty gives a care about whose religion is the 'correct' one, as long as they both center around Him. So, please, don't blame God for your defiance."

Now it was her turn to smile. Just as she suspected, he didn't know much...about her clan anyway. "Ye're correct that many of James's supporters do so because he is Catholic and will not strip them of their religious customs. While I cannot support subjugation of any kind, even of one's right to worship the way he or she wants, that's not why I support the king."

"Then why do you?"

"A large part of it has to do with his sympathetic support of Highland clans. Previous monarchs have been opposed to the Highland way of life. Our support for James is rooted in resisting hostile government...or worse, the Campbells' invasion into our territories."

"I see," he said pensively, and Abby wondered if he truly did, or if he was indulging her. "What does the other part have to do with?"

"Pardon me?" she asked.

"You said a large part of your support has to do with his sympathetic support of Highland clans. Why does the other part of you support him?"

She blinked. She said that? She wanted to tell him, if only to have him stop hating her.

"Because he's the true king." She wanted to tell him everything. But she didn't dare.

"How can you be certain?"

"I simply am."

He smiled, and she wondered how many times in her life she would dream of the indulgent spread of his lips. She never knew if he mocked her with those wide, almost carefree smiles that came more frequently now, or if he genuinely found her humorous. She suspected it was a little bit of both.

"I wish that was a good enough reason, lady."

"So do I, General."

He looked away for a moment, following the path ahead. "You would have me stop fighting for Anne and take up the Jacobite cause based on your word alone?"

Her gaze dipped to the path, as well. He asked a fair question. How should she answer it? "Based on my character, mayhap, my lord. If I can recognize honor, 'twould stand to reason that I understand it. And if so, then I, too, would follow it. If I tell ye that I'm absolutely certain about a thing, I am."

"You never lie, then?"

"Not if a lie is more beneficial than the truth."

He laughed, and heavens, but she could watch him do it all day. She liked the tiny lines at the corners of his eyes, like he laughed often. Did he? When she met him, he barely smiled. In fact, he'd looked quite miserable. She imagined he hated his duty, having to ride to the Highlands, in the middle of enemy territory.

"How long have ye served the throne?" She wanted to know.

His smile faded and he looked away into the darkness. "A long time. I was brought up to serve the throne."

He looked miserable again. Mayhap it wasn't Highlanders who evoked such a dismal mood but something or someone in England. Was it the queen? Charlotte, whoever she was? She wanted to ask him but she doubted he'd tell her. Still, mayhap she could help.

"Have I said something to upset ye?"

He angled his chin and looked at her from beneath his lids. "No."

He wasn't telling her the truth. Something pained him, drew shadows over his clear green eyes and tightened his jaw. She waited a moment for him to say something else. He didn't.

She wanted to soothe him, run the pad of her thumb over his brow to ease it. She remembered the night of her attack and the way Daniel had asked her about her mother to distract her. "Tell me about yer father. My mother once told me that ye can tell much aboot a man by knowing a wee bit aboot his father."

He blinked at her and appeared even more melancholy than before. "I would rather not discuss him if you don't mind," he said after a moment.

"Of course." She smiled at him because she wanted him to know that she hadn't meant to tread into his private life and she respected his privacy and the desire to keep it private. She had secrets of her own.

When he seemed to forget everything on his mind and smiled back at her, she couldn't help but wonder what would become of them. What kind of future could there ever be for them? How broken would she allow her heart to become? She couldn't let herself fall for him. She had to stop it now, before the thought of any kind of life without him in it would be too torturous to endure. The folks in her family had a history of doing illogical things to keep the ones they loved by their sides.

The thought of love and Daniel flashed across her mind as they entered the camp. It was empty. The men were not there. Daniel called out their names, but only silence returned.

Abby looked around. The fire was still lit, and the men's pallets were laid out for the evening. "Would they have just wandered off?"

"No," he answered her. "They would not." He looked down at the footprints scattered about. "I need more light."

"There's a small lantern tied to my saddlebag."

He grinned at her and she came undone. His brief kiss to her knuckles after she retrieved the lantern and handed it to him left her in ruins.

"Come," he whispered after he lit the lantern. He took her hand and led her away, following one set of tracks over the others.

She would ask him about his choice later. Now, she needed to stay alert and keep her head in the right place.

She didn't like this kind of life, with danger at every

turn. There were a few of her cousins who craved such adventure. But not Abby. She wanted continued peace in Camlochlin, not war for her kin.

"If we fall upon them"—Daniel stopped leading her and turned to look at her, holding the lantern between them—"if there's danger, I want you to give me your word that you will stay where I put you."

Abby could see the determination in his eyes and nodded. If it meant that much to him, she would obey him. She didn't want to admit it so soon, but she trusted this knight with her life. How could she? She had a bit of time to ponder her thoughts while they crept through the foliage. She knew it was foolish to trust anyone. Why, her mother had been betrayed by her closest friend, and almost burned to ashes. She didn't consider Daniel Marlow her enemy. But he wasn't her friend either.

Still, she followed him and did as he said.

When they turned the next bend, she was glad she did.

Chapter Twelve

A shaft of pale moonlight broke through the clouds and shone down on the small clearing in the distance like the finger of God.

Daniel made a choking sound when he saw what the shaft of light revealed. It looked like Lieutenant Ashley sprawled in the grass, his tunic stained red with blood from a wound to his belly. Another body had fallen beside him. Hubert.

Abby covered her mouth with both hands and turned away. This was real. This was not practice in the lush, peaceful vale outside her parents' castle.

"Stay here, Abigail," Daniel warned her and started to leave.

She grabbed his arm, stopping him. "I have a poor feeling about this! Ye must not go!"

Oddly, he offered her what seemed to be his most tender look and touched his finger to her cheek. "You have good instincts. You're correct. It's a trap, but I'll return. Just stay here."

"Should I run?" She hurried after him when he turned to go for the second time.

"No, lady." He stopped her and turned her back. "I'll return."

Heavens, how could he be so sure? She wanted to go after him. What if his men were dead and whoever killed them was about to kill Daniel? She should help him. Or run for her life. But she'd given her word.

She looked toward the clearing but couldn't see much. She surveyed her surroundings and then ran for a certain tree a few feet away, perfect for climbing.

She'd climbed many trees with her cousins when they were children. She hiked up her skirts, tied a knot between her legs, and then set her hands to bark.

When she reached the branch that gave her the best visibility and the best place to rest, she looked for Daniel. She found him just as he reached the clearing.

Her heart beat madly in her chest while he moved forward into the light and knelt beside one of his men. The men. Hubert. Dear God, who did this?

She caught movement out of the corner of her eye and set her gaze in that direction without blinking. She waited, certain she'd seen something. She wished she had a bow and arrow. There it was again! Her heart skipped and she almost fell out of the tree. The foliage was moving. Someone was approaching Daniel. She wanted to shout out, but another movement on the other side of her caught her eye, and then another. Soon, everywhere around the clearing, the forest moved. Daniel was surrounded on every side.

She watched, terrified and then mesmerized, as the knight drew his sword in one hand and a pistol in the other as the light came alive with movement.

More than a dozen men came at him from every direction. Some brandished pistols of their own. Daniel took them down first.

From her vantage point high up in a tree, Daniel appeared like a lithe, limber wraith fashioned to kill. He moved with chilling grace and brutal precision, killing four others. Still more appeared from the shadows but he took care of them all, just like he'd fought her father and her uncles and kept himself unharmed and alive.

A few moments later, he stood bathed in streaks of blood beneath the moonlight. The sight of him should have terrified her. He'd just killed fourteen men with a sword and a pistol. He knew how to fight. Of that, there was no doubt. He stepped around the dead and made his way back to his fallen lieutenants. After another moment or two, he appeared again with one of his men under his arm.

Hubert! Hubert was alive! But for how long? Daniel would need her help with his fallen comrade. She scrambled down the tree and ran to meet him.

"Does he live?" she asked him, her teary eyes fixed on Hubert, dangling from Daniel's shoulders.

"Barely," he breathed out, exhausted but not pausing as he passed her. "We need to get him back to camp."

She nodded and ran beside him, made speechless by his dedication and stamina to carry his comrade after fighting more than a dozen men.

She would ask him who the dead men were after he rested and cleaned himself of the evidence of his victory. Why were there so many? Thieves didn't travel in such large groups. Did someone send them? If so, who? Her questions would wait. They needed their energy to see to Hubert.

They moved quickly and came upon the camp without any sound but that of their breath. Their sudden appearance stilled the men ransacking it.

Before he said or did anything else, Daniel stepped in

front of her, shielding her from what she wanted to see. She stole a look around his arm at the half dozen or so men picking at their camp. She noticed one in particular, a man as tall as Daniel, with dark, shoulder-length waves and even darker eyes peeking from beneath his leather tricorn hat. He seemed to go as pale as moonlight for an instant when he set his eyes on them. "Easy, friend," he said. He held up his hands, also covered in leather. "We thought"—he craned his neck around Daniel's arm to see her while she did the same—"this camp was abandoned." His mouth crooked into a half smile an instant before Daniel lowered Hubert to the ground and drew his sword.

He couldn't fight again! Was he mad to take such a stance?

"We're not here to fight ye," said the man in the hat. "We thought this was the camp of the men who were killed."

"It was," Daniel told him in a low, menacing voice.

"Ah, yer comrades." The man shook his head as understanding dawned on him. "We saw what happened to them and understandably believed ye all dead." He spoke like a Highlander, but he was dressed like a common English citizen, like Daniel, save Daniel wore no hat.

"We're only here to do what anyone else would," the man continued, slowly and cautiously, glancing at Daniel's bloodstained sword. He smiled above the low flames of the campfire.

"Yes," Daniel said. "Rob what you could find."

"Aye, though there isn't much here." The man scratched his dark whiskered face, then set his steely eyes on Abby. "Yer wife?"

Abby wished she had a handful of pistol balls in her pocket. She looked around at the faces of the other thieves. They were all staring back at her and Daniel, some with wary, hooded eyes and hands ready to draw swords, others sneering like they knew her fate and it wasn't going to be pleasant.

"One touch," Daniel warned the leader in a deep, confident growl made all the more terrifying by the blood drying on his face. "One touch upon her by you or anyone else and I'll kill every one of you, beginning with you." He pointed his sword at the leader. "I may do that anyway if I suspect you had anything to do with the deaths of my friends."

"My men and I had nothing to do with the deaths of yer friends. We would be covered in blood if we'd been there."

Daniel didn't lower his sword. "Tell me who you are."

The man plucked his hat off his head and held it to his chest. "Cameron MacPherson of Badenoch."

Abby peeked her head around Daniel again. She had heard of Cam MacPherson. Everyone in the Highlands knew his name. A hero in the Jacobite cause. He'd led thirteen rebellions against the throne since William had been king. He'd killed many to see James's son take his rightful place as king. He was not an inexperienced lad who could be easily defeated by a weary warrior.

"We want nae fight with ye." MacPherson looked at the men standing around him for agreement. "Especially when ye single-handedly slaughtered more men than I have in my company. Are ye an army man?"

"Cameron MacPherson," Daniel repeated his name, his voice going hard. "I've heard of you. You're deep in treason, defying the throne and waging wars on the queen for the last four years."

MacPherson grinned and dropped his hat back on

his head. "Normally, ye would be correct about that. But there are bigger problems for both of us brewing in England."

"What happened to my friends?" Daniel demanded.

"They were cut doun within the trees and thick foliage, I'm afraid they never saw their demise coming."

Daniel listened without a change in his expression. He stood with his shoulders straight and his blade pointed at the Jacobite leader. "You saw the attack? Why didn't you offer yer blades to help them? Three men against fourteen sounds even to you?"

"Two men," MacPherson corrected him. "There were only two against fourteen and by the time we got close they were already half dead."

Daniel closed his eyes as if the images the Highlander created were too much. Suddenly though, his eyes opened again. "Two men?"

"Aye, were there three then?" the Jacobite asked without judgment staining his voice. "Did one abandon his friends?"

Abby remembered seeing poor Lieutenant Ashley's body, and Hubert was here with them. It was Captain Andrews who had run.

"Yer friend looks bad," MacPherson noted and stepped around him.

Was he being genuine? Was he innocent? Abby knew they wouldn't find out by standing here in the forest.

"Let me offer my physician, Alfred, to yer service. He can help. Alfred!" MacPherson shouted over his shoulder and waited a moment while a short, bald man hurried to his side, adjusting his spectacles.

"The doc fixed me up good after my last fight," MacPherson informed them. "He took three arrows oot of me. One from my leg and two from my back. Let him have a look, aye? See if anything can be done fer the lad."

Daniel nodded, weary and looking needful of a little help. He kept his eyes on Alfred while the doc examined Hubert.

"D'ye have a name?" the Highlander asked. His smile was amiable enough, but Daniel didn't answer him. He kept his eyes on Hubert and Alfred.

"Will he live?" Daniel asked him.

The doctor held up his finger and examined Hubert in silence for another ten minutes. Finally, he looked up at Daniel first, and then at MacPherson. "It's difficult to say. He's suffered many knife wounds. He might have a chance if we get him to camp in the next few days. I've got some herbs and ingredients with me, but much more at camp."

Daniel raised his gaze from Hubert and set his eyes on Abby. She nodded her head, understanding his silent message. He couldn't refuse to go with them, not when it meant Hubert's life. Abby wouldn't have agreed to continue on toward England without trying to save Hubert.

There was the question of her kin, likely less than a day behind her. They were going to catch up with her if her group sidetracked. Should she tell Daniel about them?

"How far is your camp?" Daniel asked him.

"'Tis about two leagues west of here," MacPherson told him. "Ye're welcome to come."

Daniel nodded. What choice did he have? For Hubert's sake, they had to go. Abby knew Daniel's concerns: Who were these men? Did they have anything to do with what happened in the clearing? Could they be trusted? She wouldn't get any answers, at least not now.

She watched Alfred quickly apply salve to Hubert's wounds and then they were off. Two of MacPherson's men picked Hubert up and carried him to his horse. He was secured carefully under Daniel's close supervision.

They rode for more than an hour and stopped only to let Daniel take a quick rinse in a loch to wash the blood from his body. The rest of the journey was made with little conversation. After MacPherson found out that he was traveling with General Daniel Marlow, slayer of Jacobites, he had little to say.

When they finally slowed their pace, Abby had no idea where they were or how far behind her kin were. When she rounded the next bend, she hoped they weren't far.

When MacPherson invited them to his camp, she had no idea that his camp was a keep, complete with a court-yard and a garrison of at least seventy armed men. If this was some sort of trap, she, Daniel, and Hubert didn't stand a chance.

There was nothing they could do about it now. They waited while Hubert was lowered from the saddle and carried across the small courtyard.

"Stay close to me," Daniel ordered her, clasping her wrist as he picked up his steps to follow Hubert.

"My lord," MacPherson called, stopping them with a hand on Daniel's arm. "Join me fer a drink while the lady refreshes herself. There's something I wish to discuss with ye."

"No," Daniel refused. "I—"

"Here is my sister now." MacPherson smiled at a lass descending the courtyard stairs. She was a bonny thing with long, dark waves spilling down her back and over her petite frame like a cloak. She was shorter than Abby, but she carried herself like a demure queen. When she reached them, she looked up at Daniel with gloriously huge, coal-colored eyes. "Nora, see to our lovely guest…"

MacPherson paused and turned a softened gaze on Abby. "Fergive me, lass, I didna' ask what ye're called."

Abby cut her eyes from Nora and set them on the Jacobite warrior. Both brother and sister were equally beautiful, equally breathtaking to look at. "I am Abigail Campbell, my lord."

"Ye brought a Campbell to our camp, Cameron?" his sister asked, her dark eyes matching her expression. Unlike Abby's father's side of the family, the Campbells were loyal to the Protestant Anne Stuart.

"Aye, and General Marlow of the Queen's Royal Army with her. They needed my aid."

Her eyes opened wide. "You brought the Jacobite killer here because now ye're a saint?"

"Saint?" He laughed and swept his hat off his head with a flourish. "I'm afraid even hell will turn me away."

Nora didn't share his humor and, as she led Abby away and into the keep, she glanced at their unwelcome guest and spoke to Miss Campbell directly for the first and last time that day. "He appears to jest, but he speaks the truth. Even hell will turn him away. Ye'll do well to remember that, Campbell."

Chapter Thirteen

Daniel had been in a place like this before, many times, in fact. A dark place, where sins festered and the haunting voices of his fallen men convicted him. He didn't like it here, where images of a fiery-haired demon hacked at bodies until he dripped with his victim's blood.

"D'ye like whisky?"

Daniel blinked out of his darkness and looked at the cup MacPherson offered him. "Anything will do."

They sat in the Great Hall of Tarveness Keep, a rundown, sorely neglected fortress in the middle of nowhere. A perfect hideaway for a small army of derelict outlaws. He doubted MacPherson would let him live to find and arrest him another day.

He took the cup the Jacobite held for himself and left MacPherson with his. He swigged the whisky, shook for an instant at the hot potency of the spirit, then set the cup on the table.

"What did you want to discuss with me?"

MacPherson swiped his hand across his mouth and set

his cup down as well. "I want reassurance that if I help ye with something, ye willna' come against me in the future."

Daniel smirked. Honestly, the Highlander didn't think he was that naïve, did he? "I don't need anything else from you. You're helping my lieutenant and for that I'll let you slip from my grasp if we meet up in the next three months. After that, if I'm ordered to battle you, I will obey."

"I think I know the men who attacked yer friends."

Daniel looked at him and shook his head when his host offered him more whisky.

"I'll tell ye if ye swear to ride away from me and my men should we meet on the field. Ye're the damned Jacobite killer and ye live up to the whispers about yer skill and the merciless heart ye possess when ye use it. I dinna' want to lose my men to ye."

"Who were the men?"

"Do I have yer word?"

Daniel gritted his teeth. He didn't make deals with his enemies. What could MacPherson possibly know that was important enough to agree to turn his face from his duty?

"'Twill benefit ye greatly to know what ye're up against, General." MacPherson baited when Daniel didn't agree.

"I won't turn a blind eye if you come against the throne, MacPherson. Not for any amount of information you may or may not have."

MacPherson downed two more cups of whisky, then shook his head. "Very well," he finally said, "I'll tell ye what I know and then ye can decide its value."

That sounded better. Daniel nodded.

"I've seen some of those men before. The men who attacked yer friends."

Daniel looked up. "Where have ye seen them?"

"In England. In the service of a certain nobleman very close to the queen herself."

Richard Montagu, the Earl of Manchester? No. Montagu wouldn't be foolish enough to lure Daniel's men to a slaughter. "Who is the nobleman?"

"My price, General," the Jacobite insisted. "Will ye leave us alone should ye come upon us in battle?"

Daniel didn't need to ponder it for long. Losing his men was among the worst things that could happen. He never took it easily. Hubert and Ashley...Dear God, they were good men. They fought well but an ambush of fourteen men was difficult to survive. It was a cowardly attack and because of that, Montagu was a prime suspect. Daniel felt sick to his stomach at the memory of Ashley's fallen body. He would never forget the sight of his friend lying bloody and lifeless in the grass, his face a macabre mask beneath the moonlight. Hubert lived, and if this man before him now could be credited with the recovery, Daniel owed him much.

But he couldn't betray the throne.

"I'll find out myself." And he would, he vowed to himself as he stood from his chair. "You have my gratitude, not my allegiance."

He walked away, then stopped and turned back to his host. "Which way was the lady taken?"

MacPherson pointed west and didn't say another word. While he made his way to his charge, Daniel considered how easily MacPherson had given up. He thought the Scotsman would plead a little longer. MacPherson's clue led him to believe who might be responsible for the death of his men. But why would Montagu do this? What would he gain? Daniel would find out, and if the earl was guilty, Daniel would make it his personal mission to bring his enemy to his knees.

But for now, he needed to focus on Miss MacGregor and keeping her safe. But after he rounded another curve and wandered down the corridor, he admitted he was lost. He also became aware that he wasn't alone.

"If you find the courage to reveal yourself and help me, I will reciprocate the favor someday."

He wasn't surprised when Nora MacPherson stepped out of the shadows. The trace of honeysuckle lingered about him, just as it had earlier when she escorted Abigail away.

"Where is Miss Campbell?"

"Are ye truly General Daniel Marlow?" she asked as she reached him, her dark tresses flowing around her like a remnant of the shadows she'd just left.

He nodded and didn't stop while she continued, coming nearer until she stood toe-to-toe with him.

She looked up at him with dark eyes of deep smoky onyx. The kind of eyes that if one peered too closely into, he could find himself lost forever in a web of all kinds of sticky things. "The famous Jacobite killer?"

"I am he." He wouldn't lie. "You can hate me later. Right now, I need you to bring me to Miss Campbell."

"I've hated ye fer three years, General. I—"

"Miss MacPherson," he cut her off with the finality of a sharpened guillotine. "You're not the first Jacobite to feel this way about me, and you won't be the last. I'm not here seeking redemption." And he wasn't. Not with her and not with Abigail. He was a soldier, loyal to the throne despite the betrayal of his queen. Any other time, he'd be arresting these people or killing the men in battle. Now he was charging around a keep to protect one and arguing with another. "Just Miss Campbell," he continued, done wasting time. "If you don't tell me where she is, I'll cut through every room and find her myself. I won't leave one undone."

They stared at each other and Daniel was reminded of a wild mare snorting and ready to bite. When he turned away to leave, she stopped him with three words.

"She's this way."

He followed her down the opposite staircase to a dimly lit alcove with a door in the center.

"Who's there?" Abigail's voice rang out from inside when Nora knocked.

"It's General Marlow, Miss Campbell," he called out, stepping around Nora and reaching for the door. "I've come to check on you."

She unbolted the door without hesitation and let him in. He wasn't sure if it was the overwhelming sense of relief coursing through his veins, or the way her visage lit the room like the bright of day piercing the gloom, that made him pause his steps and scramble for something to say. Every time he tried to consider her unworthy of praise, her grace tempted him to bow before her, as if he stood before royalty.

"Wait for me outside," he requested of Nora, and then closed the door to the room, separating them before the MacPherson woman could protest.

He turned back to Abigail and was arrested by the sight of her. She looked like she'd been weeping. He shouldn't let it affect him so, but he couldn't stop it. "How do you fare?" he asked, moving toward her. "Were you harmed in some way?"

Until that moment, he hadn't realized how protective of her he'd become. He'd slaughter an army for her and not because of some duty to the queen or a promise to her father. She was becoming someone meaningful in his life. He liked her and it terrified him. He'd almost forgotten what such fear tasted like. How could he betray all his convictions and the queen by losing his heart to her enemy? His heart was abandoning him and he had to try to hold on to it.

She shook her head, then slanted her wintry gaze downward. "I worry about Hubert." She sniffed, not seeing the battle playing out in his eyes.

Daniel thought it was kind of her to worry about his friend. He stopped himself from taking her hand and offering her physical comfort. Fighting the temptation cost him much though.

"He'll be fine," he reassured her with a step back and a short, deep breath. "And then we'll leave this place and deliver you safely to England." *And somehow, even if it kills me, safely through your time at the palace.*

She nodded. "That's good. I dinna' like it here. There are too many of them and not enough of us. Even with ye on our side, I'm not sure we would gain a victory."

He smiled, liking that she had confidence in him. But she was right, there were too many of them. Even for him. He didn't want her to worry herself over it though. He was no fool. What the hell would he do with Hubert if he killed the physician? "Taking them on isn't an option, I know," he told her. "But trust me, I can keep us safe."

"Safe from who?" she asked him soberly.

"That's what I'm going to find out."

She lifted her gaze to his and offered him a faint but heart-twisting smile. "Ye speak to me in riddles, my lord. How can I trust ye to keep us safe when I dinna' know what ye're keepin' us safe from?"

He wanted her to trust him, to trust him with her life. It had nothing to do with his heart or hers, only with her trust and the peace it gave her.

"MacPherson claims to know the men who killed

Lieutenant Ashley," he told her, giving her the truth to gain what he sought. "He insinuates that they were the men of a nobleman very close to the queen. Someone I might know."

He didn't back away when she moved toward him. He should have.

"Would these men not recognize a captain and two lieutenants?" she asked him, proving to possess a sharp mind.

"Yes," he told her, breathing in the soft, heathery scent of her. "They would."

"D'ye have many enemies in England, General?"

"Likely more than I imagine." His smile drew her closer. He should have taken his eyes off her and broken the spell. But to hell with it. He wanted to take hold of her and press her body close while he kissed her mouth. He hadn't forgotten the last time he kissed her or how she tasted. He didn't want to think; he just wanted her.

He reached his hand out for her.

"One who does the queen's bidding?"

His hand dipped back to his side. "The queen wasn't behind this."

"How d'ye know that? What if she had a reason to want me dead?"

"What reason could that be?" he argued. "She's having you brought to her in the interest of peace. Or is there another reason—"

"Nae, there is no other reason," she said quickly. "She wants peace, and since that is the truth 'twould seem to me that ye no longer have a reason to hate me."

Hate her? He moved closer to her and smiled, looking deep into her eyes. "You don't truly believe that I do, Miss MacGregor."

"What has changed then?"

"Nothing," he told her, lifting his gaze from her mouth.

Indeed, what had changed in him? When had he put his doubts about trusting her aside? Each day he believed more and more that there was something else to her story. Was she just a pawn for peace? He didn't trust her—and trust had become a major concern for him lately—but madly enough, he didn't care. "I never hated you to begin with."

She tossed him a mocking smile and stepped away. His arm looping around her waist stopped her. He pulled her close and cradled her cheek in his weathered palm. "At the risk of being hanged for treason, I don't hate you now."

She went weak in the crook of his arm and he pulled her closer. She wouldn't think him very chivalrous if she knew how he wanted to strip her naked, lay her down, and sink deep into her. He curled his free hand around her nape and steadied her when he took her mouth deeply, and with meaning. He wanted to taste her, every inch of her, mold her delicate, yielding body to his while he ran his hands down the back of her. He rolled his tongue over hers, wanting to possess her. She parried each stroke, letting him know that no victory over her would come without a fight. He liked it. It made him want her more.

He was a fool and a danger to her.

He withdrew his tongue—slowly, reluctantly, and then withdrew the rest of himself.

"I don't hate you, my lady," he promised, as breathless as she. "Of that, you can be certain. If I did though"— he stepped away, moving for the door—"it would make everything easier."

She didn't call him back, either too prideful or too wise.

Damn it all to hell, Daniel thought, leaving her room and stepping into the hall. Was there nothing he didn't like about her?

Chapter Fourteen

*A*bby didn't expect the knock on her door so soon after Daniel left. Was it him? Had he returned to apologize for kissing her? Saints, she hoped he wasn't sorry. Her body still tingled everywhere, especially her lips. Consumed in his embrace, set aflame by his tongue and the play of his mouth. Heavens, his hungry mouth...it drove her mad. When had she become so reckless? Could she keep her heart guarded from him much longer? There was another knock, interrupting her thoughts.

She opened the door, unsure if she would scold him for coming back or fling herself into his arms.

But the man standing across the threshold wasn't Daniel. His smile, darker than the deepest shadows, spread over her. The absence of his leather hat did nothing to lessen his dangerous appeal.

"Mr. MacPherson, may I help ye?"

"Aye, Miss Campbell, ye may." He moved the arm she was using to block the entryway of her room and stepped inside. "Ye may tell me why ye speak like a Highlander and why ye're traveling with one of the queen's most infamous generals."

Abby looked down both corners of the hall. Daniel was gone, and so was Nora. Damn it, she couldn't tell MacPherson the truth. But this man was no fool. He'd see right through her story.

It didn't matter what he thought of her. She was sticking with the plan her father and uncles had agreed was best. To say as little as possible.

"I was adopted into a Highland clan and General Marlow is delivering me to the queen."

"Fer what purpose?" he asked her, leaning his rump on her windowsill and keeping his careful eyes on her, as if he were watching for any telltale signs of deceit.

Her kin's safety was at stake. No one could ever know about her mother. She slowed her inhalations and, leaving the door open, faced her uninvited host full on without re-entering the room completely. "Fer peace with the Jacobites."

He smiled, revealing a silver tooth that sparked as brightly as the moonlit gleam in his eyes. "Ah, then ye are one of us."

She nodded, unsure if it was wise to tell him even that.

"Ye'll be close on the inside," he pointed out, his gaze darkening. "Will ye try to kill her?"

"The queen?" She gaped at him like his nose had just melted off his face. "Are ye mad? She wants peace. Why would I jeopardize that?"

"Lass." He drew out a long sigh, as if having to point out the obvious to her was the low point of his day. "If the queen truly wanted peace, she would have come to *me* fer a deal. I am her greatest enemy. Instead, she sends her fiercest soldier to escort a Highlander's adopted daughter to England." His smile grew into a grin and he shrugged his shoulders. "Ye see why I find ye a wee bit humorous? Ye think I would believe such a tale."

Abby had to admit he was correct. To a world that didn't know about Davina Stuart MacGregor, Cameron MacPherson would be considered the queen's greatest enemy. If Anne wanted to ensure peace with the Jacobites, she would have taken Nora in as her handmaiden.

"Now," he said, pushing himself off the window and coming closer to her, "why dinna' we not cease this pretense. Who are ye?"

Her heart pounded against her ribs. Was her story that flimsy, or was he that clever? She wasn't sure which was worse. She only knew that she wanted to kick him in the kneecaps. "I told ye who I am, Mr. MacPherson. I willna be called a liar, so if ye will, please leave."

He eyed the door when she stepped aside to clear a path for his departure, then he looked at her. "Fergive me fer insulting ye," he amended, moving to leave. When he reached the door, he grasped her hand and brought it to his lips. "Accept my apology by sitting at my side tonight at the table."

"Nae, I—"

"I insist." His eyes dug into hers over her knuckles, dark, piercing, reminding Abby of a predator. "I willna take no for an answer." He smiled, but there was nothing humorous or soft in it.

Cameron MacPherson was a striking man, but he frightened Abby. What would he do if she refused him? Would he have his physician cease helping Hubert? Would he have his men try to kill her and Daniel while they slept? How far away were her kin? She wasn't worried about the MacGregors and Grants taking on MacPherson's men.

Even though her kin were outnumbered by at least ten to one, depending on who rode with her father, she had no doubt of her kin's victory—and with Daniel fighting on their side . . . Hell, he could likely take down twenty men on his own.

"Ye'll honor me then, Miss Campbell."

It wasn't a question, and a sinuous curl of his lips accompanied the pause before he spoke her name, just to let her know he was indulging her.

She succeeded in keeping her breath even and in hiding the effect he had on her. She didn't care who he thought she was. She was a MacGregor—from a great line of MacGregors—and she'd be damned if he saw fear in her.

With a bow of her head that dropped tendrils of her hair over her face, she offered him a gracious smile. "How can I refuse?"

MacPherson's voice, along with his gaze, went helplessly soft. "My wish would be that ye refuse me nothing, lass. I would give ye the world in return."

"MacPherson."

Abby's heart nearly stopped altogether at the sound of Daniel's low snarl behind her. She whirled around to look at him, torn between being so relieved by his presence that she thought she might faint and wishing he'd stayed away. They called him the Jacobite killer, but he couldn't fight them all.

"General Marlow," the Jacobite warrior said, stepping around her to meet Daniel at the entrance of her room. "Look at her and tell me ye dinna' want to tell her the same thing."

As if he couldn't stop himself, Daniel shifted his eyes to her.

The touch of his gaze felt like a physical caress as it traversed over her unkempt braid and the contours of her face. Here was the man who made her feel flush, not with fear, but with something else entirely. She suspected she was gazing at him the same way MacPherson was gazing at her when Daniel arrived.

Would he ever kiss her again? Could she stop him if he tried? Did she want to? Lord help her, to be in his arms again, to feel the rhythm of his breath on her face, her mouth, her throat . . . just one more time.

His expression hardened, along with his gaze when he returned it to MacPherson.

"Perhaps you misunderstood me at the campsite, Jacobite. This lady is in my care. If you should ever want my favor, and trust me, you should want it, then you will not enter her room unchaperoned again. Trying to seduce her will gain you nothing but my anger."

"My lord." MacPherson laughed and held up his hands. "I'll do as ye ask. I dinna' deny yer charges. I simply ask that ye understand my reasons. She is glorious, is she not?"

Both men looked at her again, but both men did so very differently. It wasn't MacPherson's dark, mysterious edge that attracted her, but Daniel's inability to keep his heart out of his eyes.

"Dinna' hold me in contempt fer being a man who can see," their host said with a half bow. "I meant nae harm to the lass and nae dishonor to yer duty."

Abby watched Cameron MacPherson transform from a mysterious and dangerous leader to a cautious and humble ally.

But he wasn't Daniel's ally, and the knight wasn't moved by the Jacobite's attempt to share a common bond between men.

"Put away your desires," Daniel warned him. "Or you will find the eyes that offend removed from your head. Do you understand me clearly?"

MacPherson grinned and moved his fingers to the hilt of his claymore. "Ye do realize what ye come against if ye come against me."

Abby's heart smashed against her chest. She thought she might collapse with worry about a war breaking out against them.

When Daniel smiled back, she closed her eyes to keep from losing feeling in her knees.

"How many do you think I can take down before I'm killed?" Daniel's silky voice cut through the air like a sharpened blade. "*If* I'm killed? And who do you think will die by my blade first?"

MacPherson thought about it for a moment, then bowed. "I value my eyes, and my men. Consider yer request done, General."

With nothing else to say, Daniel nodded, then stepped aside to let MacPherson leave the room.

"Don't trust him, Abigail," he said when they were alone.

There was something in the intimacy of his command, in the way he spoke her name, that made her want to hear him speak it forever.

"Why did ye come back?" she asked him softly.

"I forgot to tell you earlier that I will be sleeping in here tonight."

She blinked, certain that she should say something other than, "Ye will?"

"I will." Finally, his gaze slid to hers. "And now I know it is the only thing I can do."

She should refuse. It was foolish to spend the night

with him with a locked door between them and the rest of the keep... and a bed in the room. She didn't trust herself spending another night with him.

"I'll sleep on the floor," he continued. "By the door."

She should have refused him. But she nodded her head and smiled like a witless milkmaid. Damnation, how could she not be attracted to him? He was everything she'd ever dreamed about in a man. "By the door." She cast him a teasing smile. She couldn't help it. "To protect me."

"Yes." His green eyes glittered at her. "And what, may I ask, is objectionable about that?"

Her smile remained. There were many women in Camlochlin who would resent his resolute chivalry. She wasn't one of them. She needed protection from a hundred men and she didn't mind admitting it.

"Nothing," she told him. "I make nae objection at all, knight."

※

Chapter Fifteen

Daniel looked over the supper table at Tarveness Keep and wondered how a Jacobite leader, living off the land with a price on his head, could afford such luxuries as roasted lamb and tender ducks stuffed with rich puddings. They lived like outlaws in a broken-down keep, but they dined like dukes and earls.

Wine and whisky flowed freely into cups, keeping the inhabitants warm, satisfied, and happy. Daniel partook of the merriment, but not of the spirits. There was too much at stake to get drunk. That didn't mean Miss MacGregor couldn't enjoy a drink or two, which was exactly what she had, seated between him and Cameron MacPherson.

He kept close to her the entire night and steadied her against his shoulder twice when MacPherson addressed her. The Jacobite wanted her. He'd promised her the world and admitted aloud to finding her glorious. And oh, but she was. Daniel wished he'd had the freedom to speak it to her first. He didn't—because of his promise to the MacGregors, and because of the code ingrained on his bones, fueling his blood. The code of honor.

He could never love an enemy. He cared about Miss MacGregor's welfare and she wasn't altogether terrible to be around but she wasn't his. And she likely would never be. And yet, he'd already decided that if their host tried to have his way with her, Daniel would kill him.

"Miss Campbell." Nora leaned forward on the other side of her brother and addressed Abigail. "I dinna' know of any Jacobite Campbells in the Highlands. Ye told my brother ye were adopted into a Jacobite clan. Which clan is that?"

Daniel looked at Abigail, wanting to give her reassurance that he was here and not to be afraid of answering whatever questions were put to her. He'd agreed with her father that none should know she was the daughter of a powerful, outlawed clan. They could arrest her and hang her without trial.

"The MacLeods of Skye," she answered calmly.

MacPherson turned his piercing dark eyes, and a smile to match, on her. "MacLeods? Why did ye not say so? Now the queen's actions make more sense. In ye, she has the daughter of two powerful clans. The Campbells and the MacLeods."

"That's correct," she told him. "Ye also see now why I dinna' go aboot telling everyone who I am. There are many who dinna' want peace."

He grinned at her when she stared, unblinking, at him.

"I want peace, lass. But ye know as well as I that we'll have it only when James Francis Stuart takes his rightful place on the throne."

"James will never take the throne," Daniel said, his voice serene, but with undercurrents of warning. "The longer he continues to pursue the throne, the longer Great Britain will be divided."

"Thanks to ye," Nora said, her dark eyes sparking on him like embers in a furnace. "Ye've stopped him three times now."

Unfazed by her temper, Daniel graced her with a slow smile. "Alas, I cannot take all the credit. The queen has many skilled soldiers at her service."

"Ye're despicable," the dark-haired beauty snapped at him.

Her brother opened his mouth to admonish her but Daniel stopped him. "Am I to apologize for doing my duty, Miss MacPherson?"

"I doubt ye apologize fer verra' much, General." She stood up from her chair, appearing taller than her slight frame of five feet. From behind a tumble of raven hair, her hard gaze shifted to Abigail. "Am I correct? Has he asked yer fergiveness fer swayin' yer Jacobite heart?"

Daniel's gaze on Miss MacPherson darkened while he concluded that he didn't care for her. His gaze then darted to Abigail. The hint of a smile graced her face. Was it so preposterous that he could sway her heart?

"If he has swayed my heart in any way," she said in her dulcet burr, her soft mouth yielding into a full, gracious smile that held him captive, "'tis I who allowed it. Fergiveness is not needed."

He wanted to smile.

"But ye—"

"Nora." Now her brother did stop her. "Ye may go."

"I'll go when I please, Cam. I—"

Her words were cut off by her brother leaving his chair and hauling her over his shoulder all in the space of a breath. "Excuse me while I bring her to her room," he said and then left with her without waiting for his guests' reply.

Daniel watched them leave the hall, then turned to Abigail again and smiled.

His damned heart accelerated when she smiled back at him.

"Are ye trying to sway my Jacobite heart right now, sir?"

He moved closer to her in her chair. From their first night together, he'd wanted her closer, safer. Denouncing her allegiance to the imposter would end most of his concerns. "Could I truly sway you if I tried?" He would count it a victory to win her to his side. It would also please the queen to send Abigail back to Skye with a seed that could possibly yield a good harvest.

"Ye have a better chance of trying to convert Nora than ye have with me."

He raised one eyebrow at her, studying her before he spoke. "You don't seem to hate me as passionately as she does. Am I incorrect in my judgment?"

"Nae." She shook her head and didn't move her leg back when it brushed against his under the table. "I dinna' hate ye at all, General Marlow. But that doesna' change the fact that I know fer certain that James belongs on the throne, in Anne's place."

Damn it, even if he could allow his heart to give in a little without making her a threat to Anne, there was still this enormous dragon between them.

"You would have to have proof," he told her. "And no one does. Mary of Modena lost her first two babes. Her third died as well. Your James the Pretender was smuggled into the chamber and pronounced the king's son. He cannot prove his identity."

She looked like she wanted to say something and it was costing her much to keep from saying it. "Ye are correct," she finally said with a soft smile and a sigh. "There's nae proof... but I still believe him."

She looked into his eyes and snatched away his every thought, save one.

"Does that anger ye?" she asked him.

"No. Your loyalty is a virtue I admire. Your honesty is quite refreshing, as well."

She nodded and sipped from her cup. "I canna' imagine the back-biting and deceit that goes on at court."

"No," he agreed quietly. "You cannot imagine."

The secrets about his birth, for instance. His royal birth. Hell, he was the sole heir of George of Denmark, an unclaimed prince. What in damnation was he going to do about that when he returned to England, or about Anne, or Charlotte?

Who else knew the truth, besides Charlotte? Did he want to be claimed, to someday take his title? He would never be king, nor would he ever want to be. Would he remain loyal only to the English throne?

"There's no place in my life for you." He breathed out—lucky to breathe at all. His emotions never ruled him. But now, suddenly, he was afraid, afraid that his heart was being swayed by her. "Our country," he told her, "is divided by our two different beliefs. There will be war if the rebellion continues. Many more lives will be lost. We stand at opposite ends of the battlefield. There's no hope of you in my life, but I cannot find the will to keep you out of it."

He reached in and tilted his face to hers. He wanted to relish her, taste her with his tongue, tease her with his teeth. He moved in close enough to share her sweet breath. Then, cupping her cheek in his hand, he kissed her slowly and with purpose.

He wondered if her blood blazed through her veins, scorching like wildfire, like his. If her limp body against him didn't convince him that it did, then her short, hot breaths against his chin when she withdrew should.

"We canna' continue on with this kissing each other all the time. 'Tis too dangerous and there will be no happy ending fer us."

He knew that. He knew she was right. "Let's retire, Abigail," he said quietly against her cheek. "I want to hear all about this happy ending of yours."

"I grew up with more books than dolls," Abby told the ceiling in her chamber while she lay in bed, her hands canted behind her head. Saints, but she'd never lain in anything so comfortable in her life. It felt wonderful to be indoors and she wished there were a bed for Daniel too.

"My cousins and I all read, or were read to. But most of them enjoyed other pursuits, like swordplay and archery, finding ways into a lass's bed. I preferred quiet afternoons with an old volume and the smell of stale pages making my nose itch."

"What is your favorite?" Daniel asked from his blankets on the floor beside her.

Abby sighed and smiled at the ceiling. She was growing to love her nights spent with him, talking, listening... kissing. She couldn't kiss him now unless she leaned over the side of the bed.

"*Le Morte d'Arthur* is my favorite. I love Sir Gareth's tale. His love for Lady Lynette is verra' courtly, and the death of Arthur always makes me weep."

"Sir Gareth's death caused the war between Arthur and Lancelot," Daniel said, proving that he, too, knew a thing or two about Thomas Malory's work.

"Aye." She smiled, recalling the beloved tale. "Lancelot never meant to kill Gareth. He loved him like his son…"

They talked of knights, honor, and glory for another hour. Abby told him about her family. He would like her cousin Lucan. And mayhap Uncle Tristan, Lucan's father. They knew much about chivalry and courtly manners and the codes by which all men should live.

She didn't care about such things tonight.

She leaned over the bed and dangled her head above him. "But I didna' learn aboot happy endings from any of my grandmother's books. I lived them. I saw them remain consistent and steady in the lives of my mother and faither, my aunts and uncles, my grandparents. I want the same."

Candlelight spilled over the hills and valleys of his bare chest, setting her soul on fire. When had he undressed? With a swift glance she determined that he was still wearing pants. Her gaze returned to his chest and tight, sculpted torso. She wanted to run her fingers, her tongue, down his body.

"You strike me as the kind of woman who will get one. A happy ending, I mean."

"Do I?" She smiled, loving his face in the golden glow of candlelight.

He nodded. "Yes. If I were your husband I would make certain you got one."

Boldly, she ran her fingers over the rough angles of his chin and jaw. She basked in him for a moment of pure bliss, tracing her thumb over his lips, until he clasped her fingers and kissed each one.

When he pulled her down off the bed and into his arms, she didn't protest. She doubted she would ever try to stop him again. She wanted this—to be here with him, clutched in his arms, his warm skin and hard muscles beneath her.

His hands on her face, drawing her mouth closer to his, made it difficult not to hurry to his waiting lips.

"We should stop." Though she was the one who whispered it against his teeth, she had no intention of stopping anything. It appeared he didn't either.

He kissed her, but he didn't just kiss her with his mouth. He used his breath, the curious strokes of his fingers. He moved in harmony with her, holding her, laying claim to her thoughts and emotions. He made her insides twist and burn, her heart accelerate. She was falling for him. The Jacobite killer! Dear Lord, if her father ever knew! Her clan would likely disown her. She'd never be chief. Still, she didn't want to stop kissing him.

They barely heard the knock at the door, so when it swung open, Abby bolted up and struggled back to the bed.

Cameron MacPherson stood at the entrance, staring at the scene before him. He cleared his throat and then opened his mouth.

"We have visitors," he told them. "A rowdy bunch with a reputation fer bein' ruthless. They want beds fer the night. Ye might want to bolt yer door."

"Who are the visitors?" Daniel asked, less fazed by MacPherson's discovery.

"MacGregors," MacPherson told him and walked away from the door. "The bloody MacGregors are here."

The MacGregors? What the hell were they doing here? Were they following him and the chief's daughter? Did they not understand the queen's instructions that no Highlander accompany Abigail? Daniel looked at her. Had she known?

<figure>✣</figure>

Chapter Sixteen

Abby threw on her earasaid and beat Daniel out of the room before he could ask her any questions. Her kin were here. They weren't supposed to be and Daniel, the queen's general, likely wouldn't be pleased that they'd disobeyed his sovereign's commands. She would protect them from Daniel. After all, they'd come to find her and make certain she wasn't harmed.

She slowed when MacPherson appeared in the hall as the great doors were unlocked. She moved aside so that she wouldn't be the first one her kin saw. The less reaction they all had to one another, the better. She felt someone move along her back and turned to see Daniel behind her.

"What d'ye suppose they want here, Miss Campbell?" MacPherson asked her.

"Ye mentioned beds fer the night, Mr. MacPherson. I assume since that's what they asked fer, that's what they want."

Her host grinned and then turned toward the doors as they were opened.

Abby's heart raced and her mouth went dry when she

saw her father standing just outside the entrance, his plaid belted low on his waist and hooded over his head.

"My lords!" MacPherson called out. "Enter! Enter! Welcome to Tarveness Keep." He stepped back as the group of Highlanders accepted his invitation.

From somewhere to Abby's right, she heard Nora enter the hall and gasp at the sight of them. Aye, they were a sight to behold, in their pelts and plaids, commanding and fearsome with four large, gangly mongrel dogs at their boots.

It was hard for Abby to keep her eyes from meeting her father's, her brother's, her uncle's, as they filled the Grand Hall. She missed them. She wanted to bask in their presence. But another time. She needed to keep her true identity hidden for now. She couldn't keep such a secret if she gave in to running into her father's arms. She wanted to be chief and she would do whatever it took to keep her clan safe.

But once, when her strength wore thin, she looked up to find her father's eyes on Daniel behind her.

No. She didn't want her kin to think he'd been careless with her. His men had been ambushed, massacred, and he had the chance to save one of them. He'd made the correct decision in coming here. She would tell them the first chance she got.

"Cameron MacPherson at yer service, most honored guests."

Abby wondered if his reverence was genuine. These men before him were more than Jacobites. They were fighting wars long before King James and Mary of Modena had their first living son.

"Allow me to present Miss Abigail Campbell—"

MacPherson's introduction drew all eyes to her. Abby

grazed her eyes over each of them and somehow managed to appear subservient and ladylike. She noted her brother's smirk and vowed to hit him for it later. She flicked her gaze to Gaza, her cousin Edmund's dog, and then to Gaza's offspring, almost twice Gaza's size.

"—and her escort, General Marlow, Earl of Darlington."

Abby looked up at her father again and this time his gaze met hers, but just briefly before it returned to MacPherson. "Word reached us aboot an attack," Rob MacGregor told them. "We were just checkin' to see if all was well with ye."

She smiled ever so slightly to prove that she was indeed well and then returned her gaze to the ground while he fixed his eyes on MacPherson.

No wonder her father looked so relieved. They'd heard about the attack in the woods. Perhaps they'd stumbled upon all the dead soldiers, including one of Abby's escorts.

"We need beds fer a night," her father announced to his host without giving her any further notice. "But I dinna' know if I can stand sleepin' under the same roof as General Marlow."

"The stables," Daniel said in a steady voice, still standing behind her, "are large enough to fit you and your companions, and, I'd imagine, are more suited to what you're accustomed to."

Abby's heart felt like it was echoing throughout her chest. For an instant its frantic pounding was all she heard. Would her father lop off his head for his insult? No, Daniel was merely keeping to the plan of her being a Campbell. The insult was clever, if not a bit dangerous. MacGregors and Grants didn't like being insulted, even if it was only for show. Her cousin Will looked like he wanted to punch Daniel's face back to London.

Hands moved to hilts and shoulders squared with pride. MacPherson paled in his boots just a bit. Insulting Highlanders was a risky endeavor.

Abby kept her expression serious when her uncle Tristan stepped forward with his hound, Ettarre, at his side.

"General," he said with his soft, swaying voice, one hand resting on the top of his dog's large head. If anyone could get them out of a fight, or a pretend one, it was Tristan. "'Tis true, many of us have slept in stables once or twice. Darach there"—he motioned to Abby's cousin, standing at the far end of the hall, his sharp green gaze on MacPherson's men—"was a prisoner in one, chained to a stall while he recovered from a vicious beating by the Buchanans."

Abby knew that only Darach would have the boldness to marry one of the Lowlanders. But Abby was fond of his wife, Janet, and Darach looked happy enough, save for right now.

"While it might be true," Tristan continued, making a good enough show of pretending to know neither Daniel nor Abby, "that the smell of horse manure and moldy hay may be preferable to yer presence, I came here fer a bed, and a bed I shall have." He turned to MacPherson when he finished the sentence and waited to be shown to their rooms. Ettarre, sitting patiently at her master's side, growled from someplace deep in her throat.

Their host didn't hesitate. "Right this way, my lords."

Abby watched her kinsmen follow MacPherson upstairs, her heart still racing at how close they'd come to a fight. She thanked God for Tristan's intercession and her eyes softened on her kin, loving them for risking life and limb in coming here, not knowing what kind of men or how many awaited them at MacPherson's keep.

"How long have they been following us?" Daniel's cool voice grazed her ear as he came to stand at her side as everyone emptied the hall.

"Since we left Skye," she admitted. "They've stayed a day behind. The queen doesna' know them, nor will she see them anywhere near me once we get to England. No one will be more careful to keep me safe than my faither. They followed because they love me, sir."

For a moment, he simply stared at her; those big, beautiful, piercing green eyes made her want to fall into his arms or run for her life.

"I don't like being deceived," he said with steely steadiness in his voice.

"I'm under nae obligation to tell ye everything, General. Besides, I wouldna' endanger them by telling ye."

"What did you think I would do to them?" All at once, his gaze on her went soft and warm, searing her blood, melting her bones.

"I dinna' know," she managed. "I dinna' want ye to fight with them again. Even fer show."

"You fear for their lives. I understand."

"I fear fer all yer lives." She moved away from him before she ended up in his arms, in his bed. Wherever he wanted her. "'Tis all verra' distressing to me," she told him and started up the stairs.

"Very well." He followed her, making her feel giddy and ridiculous with titillating tremors that shook her belly. "I will not fight with them."

"Even fer show?" she pressed, offering him a repentant smile.

He smiled in return. "Even for show. We do have a slight dilemma, though."

"And what is that, my lord?" Was he going to confess

that he had lost his heart to her? That he still wanted to kiss her senseless even though thirteen of her deadly Highland kin had just arrived? Was he mad? Was she?

"We must sleep in separate quarters tonight."

Aye, he was correct. If he was discovered in her bedchamber...

"I will miss your company, Miss MacGregor."

Her muscles went weak. Her cheeks blazed red, like she'd been caught in a blizzard. His declaration took her by complete surprise, as did her reaction to it. "Elation" was a fair word.

It wasn't because she was unfamiliar with fond, eloquent confessions. She'd had many suitors over the last few years. There were many men who sought her hand in marriage, but at her sweet mother's request, her father was allowing her to decide her own fate. Not one of those suitors had made her feel the way Daniel did—safe, and yet terrified of falling over a precipice and dying for everything she held dear. Daniel hunted people with her beliefs and killed them as traitors to the throne. What would stop him from turning his blade on her father? He said he wouldn't. Could she trust him?

"Daniel." She stopped on a step and turned to him. She wanted to know now instead of staying awake all night with the burden of it. "Would ye harm my faither? He is a Jacobite, lest ye ferget." And my mother, she ached to add but didn't dare. Would he kill her mother if he found out who Davina MacGregor truly was?

The last remnant of his smile disappeared as he looked down into her eyes and shook his head. "Would you have me vow it?"

"Aye," she said softy. Heaven help her, if they were any other two people with two different lives, she would fling her arms around him and drag him in for a kiss. But she was a Jacobite and, moreover, the niece of King James III. Perhaps if she could tell him the truth, he would leave Anne and fight for the true king. But she couldn't tell him her secret without putting her mother's life in more jeopardy.

"Give me yer word and I will trust it without question."

His smile returned. Slightly, but enough to make his eyes grow more vivid. "You honor me." He bowed his head to her and made her breath quicken. "You have my word, then. No harm will I bring to your father."

"Or the others."

He closed his eyes and tilted his head toward heaven. "Or the others," he agreed with a sigh.

She thanked him and continued on up the stairs. There was no use in regretting what could never be, but that's just what Abby did while she ascended with him. She was sorry she wouldn't get to feel his mouth on hers again. It was just too dangerous. She wanted to kick something at the thought of returning to Camlochlin and someday marrying a man she didn't love. A man who would never measure up to her knight.

When they reached her chamber door, her father was waiting for her.

"Faither." She looked around the hall nervously. "If MacPherson—"

"I dinna' give a damn aboot him or anyone else, Abby. I would have more assurances that ye're unharmed. We saw the clearin'." His eyes shifted to Daniel. "What happened?"

Daniel told him everything quickly and then answered the queries her father put to him.

When the chief seemed satisfied with all he'd heard, he drew his daughter into his crushing embrace and bid her good night.

"We will speak more in the mornin'," her father prom-ised Daniel before turning to leave. "Ye have questions nae doubt aboot what we're doin' here." He paused, as if something just occurred to him, and turned back to Daniel. "Are ye no' comin'?"

Daniel shook his head. "I'll be sleeping outside her door."

Her father set his piercing eyes on her and seemed to see beyond her flesh, mayhap to the little girl sitting at her grandmother's knee, listening to tales of King Arthur. "A true knight then?"

"'Twould seem so, Faither," she answered softly, then lowered her gaze to the floor. He knew her too well. "He's kept me safe and has treated me with integrity."

The clan chief of the MacGregors nodded his head and grunted in Daniel's direction. "He'd better."

After another brief kiss good night, her father left her alone again with Daniel. Abby looked at him against the soft glow of the candlelight that lit the hall. Her knight. She was mad, but she didn't care. Shadows danced over the strong cut of his jaw while he tightened it, seeming suddenly awkward in her presence.

"It'll be morning soon. You'd best get to bed." His voice fell like luxurious silk across her ears, quickening her heart, making her wish he would speak other, more intimate words to her.

"Aye." She nodded, not wanting to leave him. If only they were different people. "I'll bring ye yer blanket."

She needed to go before she couldn't. "Sleep well, my lord."

He smiled at her, bowed elegantly, and then brought her hand to his lips. "And you, my lady."

Later that night, while Abby sat propped against her

chamber door, lost in the sounds of her English escort on the other side, she knew things had gone very awry. She was in trouble, deep, deep trouble. The kind of trouble that makes a heart groan with the hopelessness of it all. It would have been better for her entire clan if she had never come.

She feared she was losing her heart to an English enemy. She fought it as best she could, but her attempts failed. It made her weep softly into the night knowing that masking her emotions would be even more difficult... more necessary. She had come on this journey to save her mother, her entire clan, to do what any chief would.

She pushed the sadness and regret out of her voice as they talked, sharing their lives through the cold slab of wood, and fell asleep as the sun came up.

Chapter Seventeen

The room reeked of pungent herbs and other medicinal concoctions that burned Daniel's eyes and clouded his judgment. Why else would he imagine that he was losing his heart to a Jacobite? How was it possible? He almost laughed at himself. How quickly his defenses had fallen. How maddeningly complete was his defeat. Hell, he couldn't even remain angry with her for not telling him about the group of Highlanders following them.

The rhythm of his friend's hollow breath dragged his thoughts back where they belonged. He was responsible for his men. Hubert's condition, whether or not Abigail MacGregor agreed with him, was his fault.

"Whoever is behind the attack dies, Hubert. You have my word."

But she had agreed with him last night when he told her. He was thankful that she hadn't seen his face behind her door. She agreed, understanding the responsibilities of being a leader.

She would make a fine chief. She was strong, confident,

but not overbearing or brooding. A perfect queen of the Highlands. He'd like to serve her, and then...

"General."

Daniel drove the thought of Abby from his head as he turned to watch Rob MacGregor enter the room with another man, equally as big, behind him. A wolfhound, whose enormous head reached the Highlander's waist, looked at Daniel and licked its chops. "Easy, Ula." The Highlander smirked. "He's scrawny, but he's no' supper."

"I thought I might find ye here," the chief said, ignoring his friend and crossing the room to the bed. His companion moved about, examining tables and holding up various bottles to the light. "This is Will MacGregor, my cousin. Ye parried a few of his swings in Skye, but ye were no' properly introduced."

Daniel nodded, then scowled at the dog when she came to sit near him. He wished the men would both take a seat, as well. They were daunting to look up to.

"I hadna' meant fer ye to discover us." Abby's father dragged a chair away from the hearth and set it by the bed. Will did not sit, but remained standing. "I'll tell ye now. We're no' goin' back. I love my daughter and there's no way in hell I'm lettin' her go to England, as hostile as 'tis to us, alone."

"She isn't alone," Daniel reminded him, then ran his hand down his face. He'd promised her... "If the queen discovers ye, all hope for peace will end."

"Then let's no' let the queen discover us, aye?"

Daniel nodded. What damn choice did he have?

"Any improvement in this one?"

"He remains as I found him."

They were quiet for a moment, then the chief looked at him. "Ye dinna' believe the attack was random?"

"It has been suggested to me that it was not."

"Who suggested it?"

"MacPherson, the Jacobite," Daniel told him with a distasteful sneer. "So you understand if I weigh other possibilities."

MacGregor shrugged. "The only possibility that concerns me is the one of harm befalling my daughter. She has only one man protecting her now instead of four."

Daniel wanted to tell him that one man was enough— if that man was him. But he kept quiet while Abby's father spoke.

"I would like to bring her home and ferget aboot meetin' the queen. But it willna' be an easy task. My daughter is stubborn like me. Aye, Will?" he called over his shoulder to his cousin.

"She's worse," Will agreed, stepping close to the bed and appraising Hubert's wrappings.

"She seems fond of ye," her father continued. "Mayhap she might even listen to ye if ye agree when I tell her that 'tis safest fer her to return home."

And just like that, Daniel would never see her again? "I can keep her safe," he said before he could stop himself. He only wanted to stop himself after looking at Hubert and remembering that keeping people safe wasn't always possible. That didn't mean he wanted to send her away. He couldn't, not without disobeying the queen. But there was more to it than that. He was a mad fool. He wanted to stay with Abigail MacGregor, by her side, in her bed. But he wasn't the same man he used to be. He was a prince of Denmark. "I'm afraid I cannot agree to sending her back. I have my orders."

Her father scowled, and Daniel recalled the sweet tales Abby had told him about the chief. Those images of the

hulking Highlander playing with his wife and young children in the water, laughing at their antics and protecting
them from the waves, sharply contrasted with the man
Daniel had fought in Skye, the one who nearly took off
Daniel's head, and then his arm.

"Besides," he continued, "your daughter is quite determined to meet the queen and do her part toward peace.
I don't think you will be able to convince her to give it
all up."

"Aye," the Highland chief agreed. "A few days with
her and ye already appreciate how stubborn she is."

Daniel wondered what spending many more days with
her would be like. What would he do with the knowledge
of what makes her happy or anxious? How would it make
him feel to fall asleep with her in his arms and wake to
her dreamy gaze?

"May I ask why you think my opinion will matter
to her?"

"Because," MacGregor told him, "ye're a knight…
and one, it would appear, who keeps his word. And
because I know my daughter. Yer word will carry much
weight. Once she's away from ye she'll ferget ye, fear not.
She'll remember who ye are and what ye've done to our
people and she'll come back to her senses."

There it was, in no uncertain terms. Abby's father didn't
want them together, and rightly so. They didn't belong
together. But knowing it didn't make losing his wits any
easier.

Damnation, he had most definitely gone mad.

"Your daughter isn't smitten," Daniel assured him,
clinging to his logic. "There is nothing between us."

"Good—"

"And even if there were," Daniel forged on ahead, not

knowing why the hell he opened his mouth or why he couldn't shut it, "we are not foolish children led from our duty toward desire."

"That's comfortin' to know." The chief stood to his feet and put his hand on Daniel's shoulder before he left. "'Tis no' that I dinna' find ye likable, Marlow, but ye are a general in the queen's army. If that wasna' bad enough, ye're English. But worst of all, ye're Protestant. Ye'd have to be familiar with my wife to understand why she would never approve of ye."

"No need to explain," Daniel told him, then listened while the two Highlanders and their dog left the room.

Why was his heart so heavy within him? Why did he care about what some outlawed Jacobites thought of him? He hated what was happening to him. He hated that, so far, he was helpless against it. It would only get worse the longer she stayed with him. It was best that the choice was out of his hands. Perhaps he should go along with sending her back to Skye. He'd figure out something to tell Anne. She'd be angry with him at first, but he'd help her understand. Abigail wasn't the only Jacobite handmaiden the queen could use for peace.

He looked up when Nora entered the room and went to a table without a word.

Nora.

Wasn't she more valuable to the queen than MacGregor's daughter? Hell, how much of a threat was Abby's family to the throne anyway? They rarely left Skye, keeping to themselves and their own laws.

Cameron MacPherson was a much bigger danger to the throne. Why couldn't he escort Nora to England instead of Abby? Surely Anne would agree that she could get more from Nora MacPherson than from the daughter of an outlawed chief who rarely left his clan. By doing this, by agreeing to MacGregor's plan, he'd be saving their arses too by keeping them out of England.

He watched Nora move about the room preparing more herbs and the next round of dressing changes Hubert needed.

Daniel owed the MacPhersons much.

Damn it.

"Ye'll have to leave when Alfred returns," Nora advised him as she swept past him and moved around to the other side of the room. "He doesna' like folks in his way."

"I'll go," Daniel assured her, looking her way and catching a glimpse of her shadowy eyes and faint smile on him.

Besides the obvious difference in likeness, Nora was nothing like Abby. This one had secrets kept carefully hidden behind her nimbus veil. Whatever they were, they were her future husband's worry. He preferred Abby's open, honest elegance to childish games of cat and mouse.

"Ye dinna' have to go just yet," she told him with a pink blush spreading across her cheeks.

So, she didn't hate him after all—or was it just part of her game? He wouldn't want to travel the rest of the way to England with her.

"I've heard of ye."

He raised an eyebrow. "What have you heard?"

She stepped around the bed and almost into Daniel's lap. "Ye're the queen's favorite. The apple of her eye."

And now he knew why.

Daniel remained quiet while Nora knelt between his knees and continued revealing facts he didn't like hearing coming from her lips. Why did she know so much about him?

"In fact, ye have the hearts of two of the kingdom's

most powerful women. The queen and the Duchess of Blackburn." She looked toward the door and then back at him. "And countless others, I'm sure."

"Anything else?"

She smiled and nodded. "Ye dance verra well."

He couldn't help but smile back. He *did* dance damn well. He moved quickly too, pushing back his chair and rising to his feet. "How does the lady of a rebel Jacobite keep know these things?"

"She has ears to listen. If she's wise, she hears much."

They spoke of him here, then. It was telling to be considered at the table of an enemy. It meant you were deemed worthy to warrant concern and observation. Why did Cameron MacPherson, infamous Jacobite warrior, not kill him the first chance he had, or the hundred that followed? Why had his sister Nora change her mind about him? She'd hated him passionately just yesterday.

"What are your ambitions, Miss MacPherson?"

"I have many."

He was sure she did. That's what convinced him that his plan was foolish. Besides his disobeying his queen, which he'd never done before and wouldn't begin doing now, he didn't want Nora anywhere near Anne. It would be like putting another Charlotte in Anne's life.

Her smile deepened and Daniel thought she truly was lovely. "I'd love to meet the queen."

He quirked his brow at her, wondering if she'd been reading his thoughts all this time.

"Why is that, my lady?" he asked, knowing full well why Nora MacPherson, sister of the Jacobite hero, would want to meet the queen. "What would you do if you met her?"

"I heard she is kind and benevolent. I would thank her for not being like her sister, before her."

Daniel almost believed her. He smiled and was about to tell her that he hoped he never saw her in England when she bowed her head and swiped her nose with a kerchief she pulled from her sleeve.

"Ye're verra' kind to offer to bring me, General Marlow. I know escorting two women to court will be a challenge. Mayhap ye could return here fer Miss Campbell at a later date."

"Mayhap the general had better do his duty."

Daniel's heart paused at the sound of Abby's voice. She sounded angry, and a bit betrayed. He didn't want to turn around, but he was no coward.

She stood at the entrance of the room. Her velvety cheeks burned with a healthy glow—or leashed rage. Either way, all at once it became difficult to breathe. He had the urge to bow in reverence. Her pale tresses were plaited into a long, loose braid that hung over her breast. Gone was her Scottish earasaid, replaced by gown of soft indigo wool. The fit was slightly snug, accentuating her alluring, feminine curves. As he took in the sight of her, he forgot everything else, every threat, every alarm, his name . . . to inhale.

"Would ye grant us a moment to speak privately, Miss MacPherson?"

She wanted to speak to him. He wasn't sure if he was up to it. It was difficult enough looking at her. Every time he did, he saw a queen. He was mad, he knew. For she was the daughter of an outlawed, Jacobite Highlander—the furthest thing from royalty. And still, he ached for a few moments alone with her.

He turned to Nora and waited for her reply.

"I need to stay," she told Abby, "to assist the doc."

Daniel didn't wait but stepped around Abby, to the

door, and held his arm out before him. "Then you'll excuse Miss Campbell and me." He only had to wait an instant before Abby turned on her heel and left the room.

"Why are ye so eager to be rid of me, General?" she demanded when he shut the door behind him.

He didn't answer, but continued leading her away from the door and onward, down the corridor.

"Ye gave yer word to escort me to the queen," she said, stopping to face him when they reached the stairs. "Would ye disobey her now? Fer Nora?"

"No, I have no intention of bringing her anywhere," he told her. "Did you hear me promise her anything?"

"No," she admitted. He smiled, but a moment later she looked up at him. "But I believe ye would do anything to be oot of my presence."

His gaze on her intensified, but instead of taking her into his arms and kissing her senseless like he wanted, he took her hand in his.

"I'm not sure if being out of your presence is better than this, but I know my duty and I will do it." He would work things out with Anne when Abby returned home. He prayed Anne had good reasons for keeping him from his true father. "I will take you to England, Abigail," he continued. "Perhaps I'll even learn what you're hiding behind your ice-tipped gaze."

She looked away. "Ye're better off not knowing."

Was he? Is that what Anne believed and why she'd never told him the truth?

He followed Abby into the shadowy stairwell and took her wrist, stopping her from going any farther without him.

"I don't like secrets that involve the queen, or worse, me," he warned her. "If there are things I should know, you need to tell me."

Her breath sounded short, tight, but her voice remained soft. "What secrets could I be keeping? If ye mean my faither and the others following us, I thought..."

Hell, when had she gotten so close and why did he let her distract him? He was glad he couldn't see her clearly while she spoke. But after a moment of listening to her breathing, intoxicated by her scent, he realized feeling her was far more dangerous. He couldn't think straight, couldn't recall what they'd been talking about.

"I want to keep you safe," he said before he could stop himself.

"From who, Daniel?"

How was resisting her in the dark any easier than in the light? It wasn't. Somehow though, he found the strength to step away from her.

"From me, my lady."

He moved out of the shadows and bumped into Nora on the other side.

"General," she said, taking the hand that Abby had just been holding. "Yer friend is dead."

Chapter Eighteen

Abby's heart broke for Daniel while she stood beside him over his friend's bed.

Hubert was dead, along with Lieutenant Ashley. Only God knew what had happened to Captain Andrews. She understood the weight Daniel bore on his shoulders for his men. She felt it for her kin. Losing even one would devastate her.

She waited quietly while he confirmed what Nora had told him. Hubert had left them. She watched Daniel's features shift with emotion, mostly anger—but everything else made her throat burn.

She wanted to comfort him, but listened instead while he spoke to Cam MacPherson about burying Hubert before he left.

"Of course, General, ye're welcome to stay as long as ye wish. Ye'll have whatever ye need."

If MacPherson was lying, Daniel didn't seem to care.

When all the arrangements were made, Daniel left the room, with Abby close behind. When he saw her, he looked so pained she nearly choked on her tears. He'd lost two friends and the third was missing.

"Daniel, I'm so—"

"Your father wants you to return to Skye," he said abruptly, interrupting her without looking into her eyes. "I think he may be correct. The dangers to your life are too great to ignore. I'll deal with the queen."

Then he *had been* considering it. When she'd heard him with Nora earlier, she suspected that he was rethinking his duty. It had frightened her, but he'd convinced her that she was wrong. But now...

"She will send an army to Skye if I dinna' go to her," she told him, risking much. "I canna' let ye stop me."

He stared at her, looking for the truth. "Why you? Why not..."

"Nora?" she provided. It was a logical question and she hadn't thought of a believable answer. None of her kin had anticipated General Marlow. How much truth could she tell him without his guessing the rest on his own? Did she dare risk it? If she didn't, he wouldn't take her to England and the queen would send her army anyway.

"My faither knows someone close to the queen." A truth. "Making peace with my clan first almost guarantees her success with MacPherson." Did that sound believable? Damn it, there was nothing she could do about it now. She decided quickly that changing the topic was best.

"Ye mentioned wanting to keep me safe from yerself. I would like to know what ye meant and how ye think ye're going to hand me over to my faither, yer duty undone."

"Your father wants to keep you safe, as well."

"What aboot what I want?"

"You want peace for the Jacobites. We can accomplish that feat with Nora."

She closed her eyes and prayed for a direction to take. She wanted to tell him the truth. She wanted to make him understand what this meant to her. What it really meant. Of course, she wanted peace between the throne and the Jacobites, but she wasn't a fool. She knew what Cameron had said was true. There would be no peace until James Francis took the throne. But none of that mattered anymore because Anne knew about her sister, Davina. The stakes had changed. Everything was personal now. Whatever danger she was in was worth the risk. She wasn't giving up and going back now. "I want more than that, Daniel. I want... I want time to convince the queen to... to lift the proscription from my clan." She felt ill suddenly, not telling him everything. It wasn't that she didn't trust him... "My motives are selfish, I admit." She tried to stop the moisture from pooling in her lids, but her words, though they were not about her mother's true identity, were sincere. "I'm doing this fer my kin more than my country. It needs to be me, Daniel. If ye stop me it could cost the lives of those I love when they are arrested and hanged without trial simply because of their name."

"You're on a crusade for your name." He lifted one corner of his mouth into a smile that made her kneecaps burn. "I recall hearing tales about a MacGregor chief who went to war with the Campbells because of his name."

"Aye, my grandsire. Take me with ye and I'll tell ye about him. Please, Daniel. Miss MacPherson will likely try to kill Queen Anne an hour after she arrives."

He stared into her eyes, tearing away her defenses. But his seemed to desert him as well. "It will be just me and you. Your father worries that you—"

She took a step back. "My father will see it my way. Come, let's find him."

She hurried ahead of him down the stairs to find her relatives. She believed that her father had voiced his concerns about her safety because Daniel was escorting her alone now. She was no longer a babe. She was going to be chief one day—it was time she made her own decisions.

She found her kin in the Great Hall and sat at the table with them. She didn't care what anyone made of it. She had to speak to her father now. She wouldn't wait.

"Alas, Hubert has died in his sickbed"—she waited while the Highlanders lifted their cups to Hubert and gave honor to his memory—"therefore we have no more reason to remain here. General Marlow and I will be leaving tomorrow, after Hubert is properly buried."

"Abigail." Her father took her hand and pulled her down gently to sit beside him.

"Aye, Faither?"

She watched his sapphire eyes rise to Daniel. "General Marlow and I have decided that 'tis safer fer ye to return to Skye. Is that no' correct, General?"

Both men avoided her gaze and missed her blazing cheeks.

"It's correct," Daniel admitted, his large green eyes finally settling on her. "But your daughter has put your clan's safety above her own."

"Och! Stop!" Abby sprang from her seat and glared at both of them. "I'm not going back to Skye. I'm continuing on the course I set fer myself and neither of ye will stop me!"

"What good will yer course be," her father asked her softly, "if ye're dead?"

She knew he was talking about her quest to win over the queen and convince her that her mother didn't want the throne.

"The same good 'twill be when an army comes barreling

over the hills of our home," she replied, folding her arms across her chest. "Besides, I willna' be killed with him guarding me." She darted a glance at Daniel. "He took down fifteen men and could have easily taken fifteen more. Ye must stop worrying and let me do what I have to do. Fer I will do so with or without yer approval."

Sitting in a chair next to her father, her uncle Colin laughed and patted his oldest brother's back. "At least she's not off on some bloody pirate ship, like my son and Connor's only daughter."

Hell, it was true, Abby thought. She was going to England, not the West Indies like her cousin Caitrina for goodness sakes!

"As I was saying, Faither. I'm continuing on to England with General Marlow. We are leaving tomorrow, after Hubert is buried. I wish fer ye to go on ahead, rather than make ye wait fer us in the forest. We will meet ye in England twenty-three hours after ye arrive. But we must stick with the plan." She set her gaze on her uncles, then looked back at her father. "We cannot alert the queen to yer presence in England. Doing so will put General Marlow in a verra' precarious position."

"Abigail—" Her father lifted his palm to refuse her.

"Faither," she cut him off gently, lovingly. "This needs to be done fer the good of our kin. I will not be stopped."

He looked as if he wanted to say something, but he stayed his words with a quiet laugh and said, instead, "My blood runs through ye, daughter."

He turned to his brothers and stood up. They followed. "We do as she asks and leave today. Gather the others."

She couldn't fling her arms around her father's neck without drawing attention. She smiled at him instead and whispered her thanks as he prepared to leave her.

He trusted her and it meant more to her than any of them knew. She swiped a tear from her eye and turned to Daniel.

"They're leaving without me," she stated, looking up into his eyes. "Now ye have nae choice to bring me with ye."

She moved to pass him and return to her room, but he caught her and pulled her back just close enough to say into her ear, "I already had no choice, my lady." He leaned into her and pressed his mouth against her lobe before he moved away again. "My lord MacGregor!" he shouted across the Great Hall, stopping her father, who was about to leave.

"Nae! Please, I beg ye!" Abby clutched his arm. "Please take me, else I'll have to find someone else who will. And ye are the only one I trust."

His breath slowed and deepened and he swore softly enough that only she could hear. Then he called out to her father, "My previous promise stands."

Her father nodded, looked at her, and then looked around and left.

"Thank ye," she managed and rested her forehead on his chest when her kin left the hall.

"Don't thank me yet," he told her.

"I will handle whatever difficulties arise," Abby said, sitting down at the table.

He sat next to her and didn't return her smile. "And what about whoever just lured my men away from camp and slaughtered them without going back to loot the camp."

"But someone was looting the camp when we got there," Abby reminded him. "Then again, just because MacPherson was robbing the camp doesna' mean he led the attack."

"I know." He nodded, agreeing with her. "There's one other man who might have done it. But that Jacobite still tried to rob me."

Abby looked away as their supper was placed before them. He hated Jacobites. How could she let herself forget that? How could she ever bring him to Camlochlin and anywhere near her mother?

"Why must you risk all and go?" he asked her, lifting his cup to his lips. "And what is this plan you spoke of with your father?"

She wasn't prepared for his query. Weren't they just talking about who might have attacked them?

"'Tis my duty to my clan to do all I can to keep them safe." She truly believed that. "I have something to prove to the men, men, I remind ye, who have fought one battle or another." She didn't believe that. She had to deceive him. She had no choice.

He took her hand under the table and set her nerve-endings ablaze. "I'll do what I can to help you."

She smiled faintly. She didn't want him to help her too much, but at least he believed her. For now.

Just then, MacPherson entered the hall, found them sitting where the MacGregors had been, and headed straight for Daniel. He held in his hand a folded parchment. Its broken seal revealed that he'd already read its contents. "General, a letter was just delivered into my hands from England. 'Twas penned by someone you know." The leader of the Jacobite rebellion smiled and held the parchment away when Daniel reached for it. "I would insist first on ye agreeing to my request."

"As I've already said," Daniel told him, "for trying to help Hubert, you will have three months without me on your tail. I will extend to you another three months for this information. If you refuse my proposal and keep the letter to yourself, the first three months will stand, but after that I'll find you and bring an end to your cause once and for all."

Abby paled. MacPherson's cause was hers as well. She was falling in love with a man who would always be a danger to her kin... to her.

MacPherson handed the letter to him and looked at Abby. "Verra' well, then. 'Tis from Richard Montagu, Earl of Manchester."

Chapter Nineteen

I will keep this brief,'" Daniel read aloud from the letter signed and sealed by the queen's cousin. Every now and then, since he'd entered MacPherson's private solar with his host and Abby, a cool draft clenched his heart. Things were going to change for him in England after he killed Richard Montagu. He'd give up whatever he needed to, but Hubert's and Ashley's killer was going to die by his sword.

"'I've penned this correspondence to yourself and twelve others,'" he continued reading, "'to inform you that the Earl of Darlington, or as your people know him, the Jacobite killer, is dead.'"

It was Montagu who'd had his men killed. Who had intended to kill him as well. He'd failed and he didn't know it. That would work to Daniel's advantage. He went back to reading the letter.

"'His army will soon be transferred into the capable hands of a new leader.'"

Covetous snake. Daniel would chop off his head.

"'After the queen grieves over the death of her beloved

knight, she will make me captain general of her army,'"
he continued. "'I will hold in my hands the power to
allow you to attack who and where you want. And for
but a meager donation, I will grant you such pleasure. I,
unlike your previous general, don't give a damn who sits
on the throne."

Evidence to show the queen proving why he'd slaughtered her cousin.

"'Therefore, it will be to your benefit to meet with me
in Edinburgh—'"

Someone knocked at the door.

"Aye?" MacPherson called out. "Enter," he granted
when he heard who was on the other side.

The MacGregor chief stepped inside, filling the room
with his presence. His eyes fell to his daughter first, then
to Daniel and the letter in his hands, and then to their host.
"We'll be on our way, MacPherson. Thank ye fer the beds."
Before he turned away, his eyes caught Abby's again.

Only because Daniel knew the nature of their relationship did he notice the tenderness in the chief's expression
when he bowed slightly to her. "Miss Campbell." In perfect form, he didn't spare Daniel a second glance as he
moved to leave.

"My laird," MacPherson's voice stopped him. "Are ye
one of the twelve? Did ye get a letter?"

Abby's father turned to face them again. He looked at
the letter and nodded.

"What d'ye think?" their host asked him, keeping him
longer.

Daniel blinked, waiting for MacGregor to answer.

"If the Earl of Manchester ordered me to Edinburgh,"
Abby broke the silence, saving, it would seem to Daniel,
her father from saying something wrong, "I would not

trust him. I hope none of ye are so foolish to do so. He could not have penned these letters to twelve Jacobite leaders less than a se'nnight ago, informing them of General Marlow's death, when the attack occurred only yesterday."

Daniel stared at her. What the hell was that all about? Why did she need to tell her father the entire contents of the letter? He was one of the twelve, wasn't he? An important one, correct? That's why Daniel was about this duty of escorting his daughter to the queen.

"What do we care aboot the life of the Jacobite killer?" the chief growled at her. "If Manchester wants to make an alliance with us, then we want to hear it."

"Well, then?" MacPherson pressed. "Is that where ye're headed?"

"Aye," her father answered and then set his diamond-hard eyes back on Daniel. "I wouldna' bring the lass near the city. The earl thinks ye're dead. Best to keep it that way fer the safety of yer charge."

"Good thinking, Chief," MacPherson complimented him, agreeing.

"I'll tell my faither of yer kindness to me, my laird," Abby called out, next to stop the chief from leaving. "Let me repay ye," she offered when their eyes met, "since we are both Jacobites, after all."

"Be aboot it then, lass."

"Dinna' trust him."

With a nod and without another word, her father left the solar.

When the three of them were alone again, MacPherson turned to Abby with a pout. "I thought I'd done enough to gain yer trust when I shared Montagu's letter with ye."

She smiled, keeping her composure, shining in Daniel's eyes like a star. He could have watched her all day.

"Mr. MacPherson," her soft voice rang out, "I was referring to the earl. Why would ye think I meant ye?"

He dazzled her eyes with a handsome grin that Daniel wanted to punch off his face. Then, in a show of defeat to the pale goddess, MacPherson turned to Daniel without another word to her. "MacGregor's correct," he said. "Yer best weapon is that ye're dead."

No. Daniel's best weapon was that he knew Montagu's secrets. The earl had tried to have him killed. He held no allegiance to his cousin, the queen.

"My men will help ye bury yer friend."

His friends, dead by Montagu's order.

"Nora will assist ye if there is anything else ye need." MacPherson turned his bright grin to Abby. He went further and reached for her hand and kissed it. "It was my great pleasure meeting ye, lass." He didn't wait to see her reaction, but Daniel did. She didn't blush or giggle like a child. She purposely turned and looked at Daniel and did something to his insides, twisting them until he ached, robbing him of everything he possessed.

Could she tell by looking at him that he was losing his battle against her? Could she see in his pitiful gaze that he would overlook anything for her, even his new suspicions about why a MacGregor, in particular, had been summoned to the palace? He would think about it all later.

MacPherson winked at him and smacked him on the shoulder as he left the room. "Ye're a stronger man than I, General. Ye'll need to be."

"Did he just insult me?" Abby turned to him when they were alone.

Daniel couldn't help but smile. She was intelligent and courageous, and yet naïve about subtleties.

"No, my lady. He praised you, as you deserve."

Her lips, so decadently full and inviting, slanted into a curious grin. "As I deserve, my lord? Remember who I am."

He did. He wanted to forget tomorrow and the throne and take her in his arms. He wanted to carry her to bed and praise her while he made love to her until the morning.

"General Marlow?" someone said from the door.

Daniel turned to see Charles, one of MacPherson's men, waiting at the entrance.

"I've come to help ye dig yer friend's hole."

Charles's words hit Daniel like a kick to the gut. He did all he could to resist groaning and straightened his shoulders instead.

"Thank you, Charles. I'll be right along."

He turned back to Abigail before he left to begin his task. "If you are asleep by the time I'm done, I'll not wake you. We'll leave for England in the morn."

"I'll be awake," she promised him. "I'll wait up fer ye, to offer ye comfort."

He looked into her eyes and reached out his hand to stroke her alabaster cheek with his fingertips. "Thank you, fair Abigail." He swept his hand down her arm, circling her wrist when he reached it and drawing his fingers over the pulse beat throbbing beneath her skin. He took her hand and brought her knuckles to his mouth. "Until later."

Abby put the finishing touches on the small table she had set up in her chamber. She made certain to get the best cut of meat from Tarveness Keep's cook for Daniel's dinner and enough whisky to help him not care that he was hours late and the food was cold. She hoped he didn't mind eating in her room. She considered that after burying his friend, he would want to be away from all the men in the Great Hall.

She repositioned the candle so that it would shine more directly on his face when he sat down to eat. She loved his face, lined with decisions, marked by maturity. The cut of his jaw made her want to sigh and shiver in her boots. He was the male embodiment of elegance and arrogance perfectly blended together. He moved with the grace of a supremely skillful hunter and spoke like one of the knights in her legends.

She was quickly growing mad about him…sinking deep in reckless, rapturous love with him. She couldn't decide if she should collapse in a heap and cry at her weakness or laugh out loud and spin in circles. What would the queen do if she found out? How could Abby allow Daniel to ruin her plans to gain the queen's favor? Even worse, how could she continue keeping her secret from him?

He was more than a knight. He was a general, and according to everyone who knew him or of him, he was a relentless assassin. She'd seen firsthand, while watching him kill all those men in the clearing, that beneath the graceful nobleman was something more raw, more intent. When he'd read from the Earl of Manchester's letter, she'd heard the leashed fury shaking his voice. Abby felt sorry for the earl.

She had to convince him somehow, sometime, that her kin wasn't his enemy. She had to find a way to do it. And what if this Montagu managed another attack when he discovered that Daniel was alive? What if he succeeded next time? What would she do if Daniel was killed? Every day it was getting more difficult to think of being without him. But what if an order came from the throne to march on Camlochlin and kill her kin? Would he do it? She was glad her kin had left Tarveness Keep. The less Daniel was around them, the better.

She considered the bath she'd prepared for him and wondered if she'd gone utterly mad to want to see him, to comfort him, to do whatever he wanted.

His arrival in the chamber stilled her thoughts and chased away her fears. He stood beneath her door frame, his chest bare, his belly flat and tight as harp stings. Where was his shirt? She hoped never to see it again. His muscles were sleek and beautiful. She found herself wanting to touch them, feel them under her tongue. What the hell had come over her?

His gaze finished taking in the elegant little candlelit table in the middle of the room, and then it fell softly on her and it gave her heart pause.

"How did you know this was exactly what I needed?" he asked her, rubbing his shoulder.

She had a better question. Why did the resplendent curl of his smile make her so willing to give up anything for him?

But "Are ye in pain?" is what she asked him.

"Yes," he admitted. "I still feel as if there's a shovel in my hands and I'm hunched over." He flashed his grin at her again and she giggled.

Och, hell, she giggled!

"I'm afraid I need to rinse before I sit at the table, Abigail."

She loved how her name sounded coming off his tongue, his lips.

"Wait!" She stopped him when he turned to leave the room again. When he returned his gaze to her, she hurried to a wooden partition beyond the bed. "A bath awaits ye here, my lord. Though I'm afraid the water has cooled by now."

He looked at the partition, and then at her. Were his eyes always so green, like large, lush vales that tempted her to run through them? She could tell by his patience with her that he liked her. But he fought it every time. She was glad, for his wide, bold smiles would only seal her heart sooner.

"I don't mind cool water," he said, offering her a softer, more intimate smile that pulled her breath.

Hell, she could benefit from some cool water in the face. Especially when she caught a glimpse of his tight lower abdomen before he began unbuckling the belt. His sword and two holstered pistols fell to the floor. When he reached her and the partition, his grin widened and he bowed.

When he disappeared behind the partition, she shut her eyes and took a deep breath. Lord, help her, she would never forget the flare of his shoulders, the lithe cut of his back and waist when he stepped around her.

She jumped when his pants fell over the divider next. She listened breathlessly as he stepped into the bath, naked, and purred like a satisfied lion.

As she pulled his pants free from the partition, she imagined his bottom half, as shapely as his top.

"You have my endless devotion for this, my dear lady."

She opened her eyes and bit her bottom lip. "Careful what ye promise me, knight. Fer I may hold ye to yer word."

"I'm counting on you doing just that."

She smiled on the other side of the partition, then disappeared out of the room to have his clothes cleaned.

When she returned, Daniel had finished his bath and

was sitting at the candlelit table, bare-chested and wet, his lower half draped in her earasaid. He looked up when she entered and stood up.

"I'm feeling better already," he told her, moving behind her chair. He looked better, wonderful, magnificent.

"I'm pleased to hear it." She moved toward him as if he pulled her by a tether. She didn't want to fight it anymore. She didn't want to deny what she felt for him. She allowed herself a moment to bask in the glory of his sculpted, virile physique as he pulled out her chair and waited for her in the candlelight. She accepted the seat and waited while he bent to her ear. "I'm glad to be here with you, Miss MacGregor."

She closed her eyes in front of him and shivered as his warm breath trickled down her nape to the valley between her breasts. He didn't hate her, or even dislike her, and she was glad because she wanted to know him, to touch him and learn his body. She wanted to possess him and be possessed by him. She wanted to kiss him and stroke all his hard planes with her tongue. And she wanted to do it all without fear of letting him in.

"Forgive my appearance," he said, coming around her to his chair.

He didn't look repentant at all; in fact, she was certain she saw the dazzle of a flame in his emerald gaze.

"I left my shirt outdoors and I couldn't find my pants when I left the bath."

"They are being cleaned."

His smile widened into a knee-buckling grin that made her thankful she was sitting. "You're quite thoughtful, my lady. I'm in your debt yet again. Ask anything of me, within reason, and I'll grant it."

Did he mean it? She believed that if he said it, he would

do it. She wanted to ask him to vow never to kill her or harm her mother. But if she did, she would only draw attention to Davina. She thought of the closest threat to his queen after her mother.

"Dinna' kill James Francis Stuart if you have the chance."

He looked up from his dish and studied her for a moment or two. Abby thought his hesitation alone was a good sign.

When he spoke again, she smiled, feeling slain and reborn together. "As you wish. I shall not kill him."

Abby watched him begin to eat and couldn't help but grin like the mad fool she was. "And what if ye are ordered to kill him? What would ye do then?"

"I'll stay true to my word and remind the queen of something we share. She won't order me to do something I'm passionate about not doing."

She looked him over and didn't care what he saw in her eyes. She cared for him. She wanted him to know. "And ye would do this fer me, General?"

"Yes," he told her, taking her hand across the table. "I'd do many things for you."

Abby wanted to smile at how worried he looked saying it, but she didn't because she felt the same way, and it worried her too.

Chapter Twenty

Abby looked down at the golden slabs beneath her fingers and wondered how she came to be standing behind Daniel's chair, massaging his sleek, bare muscles. She wasn't suffering some kind of loss of memory. Nae, blacking out would have been easier to explain.

In truth, she remembered well enough. She just wasn't sure how she had let such madness come over her. The night was foggy, like she was under a spell. Or a wee bit drunk on whisky. They'd spoken of Hubert while Daniel ate and then Abby had asked him if his muscles still ached.

They did, and here she was, kneading his hard sinew in her hands. She'd never done anything like it before but she had seen her mother massaging her father's shoulders many times after a hunt or a long day's practice.

Abby had almost changed her mind about touching Daniel, but he groaned at her closeness and she was lost.

"It's odd, you know?"

"What is, my lord?"

When she dug her knuckles into his shoulders, he moaned like a lazy cat and rattled Abby's bones.

"I've traveled to many destinations and met many women." He rolled his neck and tilted his head back to smile at her. "But no one like you."

She didn't care if it was whisky or her reckless heart that moved her. She took his face in her hands and stared into the fathomless depths staring back at her. "Are ye trying to butter me up fer breakfast?"

He laughed, a deep, throaty, sensual sound that drew her lips to his chin, his jaw, and then his mouth. She held him in her palms and pressed sweetly wanton, open kisses to his lips until she dragged a sound from him, like the pain of his restraint being defeated.

She smiled like a full-blooded wench against his mouth as he closed his fingers around one of her wrists. In one fluid movement he pushed his chair away from the table and pulled her around and into his lap.

There she lay, cradled in the arms of a man who should be her enemy. Did it make her a traitor? Did she care enough to move? She remained still, enraptured by the sight, the feel of him descending to kiss her.

Abigail knew in that precise moment that if a hundred men kissed her in the future, not one kiss would come close to this one. Her knight wove a spell over her with the mastery of his tongue and the intoxicating demands of his lips. She answered his demands by helping him unlace her kirtle. Tonight all restraints were off and it was the raw, honest desire in Daniel's every touch, not just the touch of his lips, that swept her away.

She was afraid of what was to come, but she didn't stop him when he ran his rough-skinned palm over her creamy thigh. She didn't protest, but rejoiced, when he stood up and carried her to the bed.

"Take off your dress," he commanded in a low growl, then turned for the door.

Abby stepped off the bed and reached her hands behind her back for the laces that would loosen her skirts. She kept her eyes fastened on him while he approached the door. The earasaid that covered him had slipped farther down, revealing two dimples just above his arse.

Her heart skipped at the sound of him bolting the lock. It raced, making her lightheaded when he turned, giving her a front view and a devilish grin at the trouble she was having getting out of her own clothes.

"Let me help." He came toward her and with a gentle grasp, turned her around so that her back was facing him.

She felt the heat of him behind her and was overcome with a wave of foreign, primitive desires. He moved his fingers across her throat, sweeping away her hair to kiss her neck. Her flesh grew hot with a need she didn't fully understand, never having felt it before. It didn't frighten her, though. She wanted to explore it.

His fingers worked with deft precision to free her of her laces in the back, while she worked to get out of the front. Her skirts fell around her ankles and his fingers rose to where his mouth had been. Her blood sped through her veins while he touched the pulse beating in her neck. He could break her in two if he wanted to.

How could she stop him when her mettle was giving out? But this man of honor meant her no harm. She didn't want to think of consequences. She let the fire he'd ignited in the pit of her belly burn when he slipped his hands over her breasts. With one tug he freed her from her binds and caught her breasts in his hands.

She trembled when he lifted her in his arms to lay her down on the bed. He stepped away from the edge and stared at her for a few moments, taking her in from head to toe. She'd never been viewed in such a way before, had never been so vulnerable to the hunger in a man's eyes. She followed her instincts and crossed her arms over her most intimate areas.

She revealed her breasts to cover her mouth when he tugged at the earasaid and it crumbled in a heap near her clothes. Her eyes fell immediately to the heavy arousal between his thighs. She'd never seen a man half erect before. Was that why it appeared so big? Would she be able to take it?

"I've never done this before," she told him truthfully, giving him a chance to change his mind and seek a more experienced woman to set beneath him.

"Do you think I would hurt you, Abigail?" he asked, moving over her on the bed.

Abby looked up into his powerful gaze and watched it grow warm on her. Her heart raced and her breath grew more shallow. "Nae," she whispered, feeling his breath on her. She wanted him to kiss her, to speak her name again. "I know ye willna' cause me harm."

Suddenly he looked pained and turned away. "But I could, if we do this."

"Daniel!" She closed her fingers around his arms to stop him from leaving her bed. "I want this moment with ye and I will have it." She pulled him down to her waiting lips and then rolled him over to his back.

Atop him, she shackled his wrists in her hands and quirked her mouth like a conquering empress.

"I'll have ye, General. After that, ye will likely be the only man I'll ever have."

He stared into her eyes and smiled, easily able to break free of her hold if he wanted to. He didn't, and she felt the proof of it in his fully stiff erection against her rump. She swallowed, suddenly unsure of her claim. It was more likely that he was going to have her.

"Come here, lady."

She happily obliged, pulling on his wrists and squirming her way up his hard body. She knew she was arousing him by his unsteady breath and the tightening of his muscles under her. She knew by the way he took her mouth, with utter mastery and possession, drinking her breath and devouring her soul. She was his. She would always be his. She would never tell her father or anyone else that she loved the enemy of everything they believed in. She just wanted this night with him. She would remember it always. As long as she wasn't taking him from the queen, what did she care about some insane past lover of his?

He withdrew from his siege upon her mouth and looked up at her with scalding, hooded eyes. Fearful that he would see her whole heart in her eyes, she almost looked away. But she was no coward. Let him see what he'd done to her. Let him understand that she would not surrender to a man she didn't love.

She didn't know what he saw but with a flick of his wrists, he freed his arms and slid them around her. He lavished her face and neck with kisses and scooped her buttocks up in one of his hands. He cupped one of her breasts in the other.

When he grasped her nipple between his teeth, she cried out, arching her back. He caught her around her slim waist and kept her close while he suckled and kissed each nipple in turn and made her wiggle atop him, hot and moist against his abdomen. His mouth on her breasts drove her mad. His hands stroking her back and squeezing her bum made her ache from somewhere deep for more of him.

Instinctively, she rubbed herself against him. He suckled her more deeply, then released her nipple with a lick and tossed back his head to groan at her gyrations.

When he held her buttocks in his palms and clenched his hands around them, she tried to move off, not really sure of what to do and not convinced that it wasn't going to hurt like hell. His hands slipped to her hips and he held her, but not still. He guided her slowly, sensually, against his warm, hard length.

She sucked in a breath as titillating sparks scorched her most private part. Up and down and down and up he dragged her, teasing her until she wanted to eat him alive. She moved to take him into her, trying to fulfill some unknown, ancient desire to have him inside her. He stopped her with a low growl and a slow smile, then he pushed her up so that she straddled him, his huge cock nestled between her thighs. She looked down at it and bit her lip and then, from behind her pale locks, she cast him a smile as sinful as his own and began to move over him.

She wasn't sure how long she watched him basking in the throes of ecstasy. She would have watched him for ten lifetimes if she could. Oh, if she could. He was sex incarnate, tilting back his head, licking his lips, grinding his jaw. When he met her lusty gaze and smiled at her, she almost came undone.

Mercilessly, he gyrated his hips and held her down to feel every raging inch of him gliding, not inside her, but against her. She whimpered, lifting her hands to her mouth to keep from bringing anyone to the door.

He swore and caught a handful of her hair in his fist.

He moved sensually under her, tugging her hair, clasping her breast when she arched her back.

He groaned her name twice while he came all over his belly, but Abby barely heard him as she matched his passion and found her sweet, painless release in the arms of a knight.

A little while later, she cleaned him with his bathwater and a rag and then lay with him in the bed.

"That was verra' nice," she purred, satisfied, against his chest.

"Yes, it was."

She didn't want to admit to him that his size, fully erect, stunned her. He had been kind and she appreciated his consideration of not fully taking her on their first night together.

She leaned up on one elbow and told him, "Ye possess true honor, my lord Daniel."

He smiled at her and then closed his eyes. "Well, I won't have a child raised without his father."

Abby blinked. He did it to keep his seed from her? She was thankful. He was using logic, staying rational—as she should be doing. She knew they had no future, and yet she felt a little stung. She knew it was foolish, but she was already daft over him, wasn't she? This was to be expected. She would have preferred not to be reminded that they no had hope together just after being intimate with him, but what was done, was done.

"Yer verra' thoughtful," she told him, then left the bed.

He opened his eyes and watched her step into her dress and reach for the laces. "Where are you going?"

"To get more whisky." She offered him a smile that almost made her choke. She was in love with him, despite all the danger, all the hopelessness, of it. What was wrong with her heart? It worried her, and madly enough, it hurt that he didn't feel the same way. He said he'd do many things for her, possibly defy the queen. He just wouldn't give up his lifestyle for her… and it would be selfish to ask him to.

She wanted to be chief someday and that meant not responding to things emotionally. She had to think and she couldn't do that in bed with him. She had a task to perform, a duty to fulfill, once she arrived in England; she couldn't be distracted. Win over the queen, keep England out of Skye. The safety of her mother and her entire clan rested on her shoulders. She couldn't let them down because of one man. "I'll return shortly," she lied and left the chamber.

✤

Chapter Twenty-One

$\mathscr{D}$aniel ignored his painful erection as he rose up in bed. He hadn't been this hard in…hell, he couldn't recall.

He looked down at himself and then at the empty space beside him. Where was Abby? It wasn't yet dawn. Why was she not in bed? He called out her name and then left the bed when no answer came. Was she roaming the keep alone? Damn it, he had no clothes!

While he yanked a blanket from the bed and wrapped it around his waist the memory of her thick hair spilling onto his chest like endless sighs invaded him. He thought he couldn't find her any more beautiful than he found her every damn day, but at the end of each night she proved him painfully wrong. What they'd shared wasn't an error in judgment, at this point, at least. He didn't regret it. But if he had to do it over again, he would have left her alone. How would he forget the way she looked poised above him, her face contorted in ecstasy, convincing him once and for all that no woman on all the earth, in all its civilizations, was more enchanting than she?

He wished the start of the new day would clear his thoughts. For they remained filled with only her. How would he keep what he felt for her masked until he made certain she was safe from Charlotte? He was certain a mere look her way would convince everyone at the palace that his heart was lost to her. What if Charlotte found out that Abby was a MacGregor? A Jacobite? How much trouble would she make for Anne by going after Rob MacGregor's daughter?

Abby would be in danger because of him. But he could keep her safe. Nothing could stop him. Nothing but Abby. She had to do what he said at the palace, behave the way he told her to behave.

The door to the chamber opened and Abby entered carrying a bundle he recognized as his clothes.

She needed to begin practicing now.

"Abigail," he said, sounding hard to his own ears, "from now on you won't take off and roam about on your own. Do you understand?"

She handed him his clothes and stepped back, folding her arms across her chest. "Is that a command, General?"

He knew she wouldn't like it. But if he was going to keep her—

"D'ye think I'm one of yer men?"

He smiled because he knew she was being coy. "After the night we shared, you answer that."

He noted the sparking flames in her eyes just an instant before she swung at him. He caught her wrist before her palm reached his face.

"You'll start obeying me. It's for your own safety," he warned.

She cocked a corner of her mouth at him. There was no humor or affection in her tight smirk. "Fer my safety.

Of course." She tried to free herself from his grip. "Are ye going to keep me captive then?"

"Not if you agree to stop being a fool and finally begin using your head."

He should have seen it coming. One didn't order a woman about who had aspirations of being her clan's chief. He should have expected her to fight back. He was treating her like he was a general and she was his underling. But in truth, her lips distracted him. Her bosom, rising and falling beneath her laced kirtle, made him forget the world and his duties and everything but the sound of her breath.

He should have noted the slight change in its rhythm when he bent down to sit next to her.

He wasn't sure what she hit him with, but he knew he was losing consciousness and he was fairly certain he heard her voice as she left the room again.

"But I am a fool and I would much prefer to use yer head, General."

He wanted to say something, but he was falling deeper into the chasm. Damn it...

Daniel woke sometime later. He opened his eyes, then closed them quickly again at the early morning sunlight streaming in through the window. He reached his hands to his head to feel for the knife rammed through his temple. There was some dried blood but no knife. He was on the floor beside the bed. Was she in the bed? He'd have to pull himself up to find out.

When he rested his palm on the floor, he hit something cool that rolled away. A metal vase. Was she mad to strike him with a metal vase? They needed to talk.

"Abigail?"

He pushed himself up, gritting his teeth. He should throttle her, but as his memories returned to him, he knew he'd deserved the blow. He should have used more tenderness with her. But really, what did he know of women? He'd slept with a few of them in the past, but he'd never cared about any long enough to learn about her.

He looked toward the door and cursed under his breath. She'd run away again. The keep was dangerous, filled with a hundred Jacobite men. He fought back the urgent desire to protect her. He would find her and make certain she'd come to no harm.

He retrieved his clean clothes from the bed and changed into them, including his boots. They were leaving today. The faster he got her in and out of England, the better. He still had Montagu to deal with. Hubert and Ashley were dead; only one of them buried. And Andrews. What had become of him?

And what the hell would he do if the MacGregors were discovered and he was ordered to arrest them?

He cleaned the blood off his temple and left the room. He looked down the hall. He wished he'd never been sent to escort Abigail to the queen. He wished he'd never met her. He had enough trouble; he didn't need her and her kin adding to it.

As he stood there contemplating his troubles, the door to a chamber opened and Abigail and Nora stepped out. The sight of his charge, safe and well, banished every one of his silent declarations against her. He was the fool, abandoning his good sense, forgetting why he was angry with her when he left the room.

Before he spoke and made a damn fool of himself, he turned on his heel and began walking the other way, toward the stairs.

"Do we have time to eat before we go, General?" she called out, hurrying to catch up with him.

General. He cursed under his breath. What in blazes was she so formal about? He was the one who should be angry. He was angry!

"Do whatever you like," he said without stopping. "I'll be saddling the horses."

"I would like to eat."

He paused and turned to look at her as she reached his side. "Well rested and hungry are you, lady?"

She nodded. He arched his brow and wondered if it was too late to strangle her. "You smashed a vase into my skull. I'm glad you slept well and didn't burden yourself with thoughts that you might have killed me."

She blinked, giving reprieve from the cold frost of her eyes, but only for a moment. "Ye were treating me like a misbehaving child. Be thankful ye're still alive."

He wanted to strangle her and toss her out the nearest window.

"Do ye wish to apologize?" she had the boldness to ask him.

He smiled, refusing to show her how she affected him. "Forgive me."

"Nae." She quickened her steps and began to pass him. When she did, she tossed him another frosty look over her shoulder. "Knight."

❖

Chapter Twenty-Two

*R*ichard Montagu looked out across the many faces filling Edinburgh Castle's cavernous Great Hall. He recognized a few of the faces, like James Robertson and Amish Ogilvy. It was Robertson who'd helped him acquire the names of the Jacobite leaders on his invitation—the ones who had been arriving since noon. For the most part, his guests were behaving civilly. That, of course, could be attributed to the fact that there were so few Highland chiefs in attendance. You just couldn't trust a Scot, especially the high mountain clans who all sided with the Pretender.

He'd invited some, but he didn't like the sight of them draped in their warrior plaids and long, unkempt hair. Highlanders were unpredictable and dangerous. He was glad there were so few in the growing crowd. They didn't all have to be in attendance for word to reach them of agreements made between their countrymen and the new captain general of the queen's army.

Many wouldn't trust him. They would wonder why he would agree to look in the other direction when the Jacobites struck, even threatening the queen's seat. Some of the more devoted kind would hate him for selling her sovereignty for a price. But he didn't care. If he could benefit from whoever sat on the throne, why shouldn't he?

"My lord"—one of his servants approached—"the sun has been down for an hour. 'Tis time to make yer nightly introduction."

Montagu rolled his eyes. Did the idiot think he'd forgotten what to do an hour after the sun went down? Must he put up with these unfortunate people much longer? He missed England. "I'm ready. Begin."

He stepped back as the servant, Roddie or Robbie or Roger, or whatever the hell the servant was called, moved forward and cleared his throat.

"My lords, may I have yer consideration while I introduce yer honored host." Roddie glanced toward him and Montagu nodded his approval, as he had given the previous two nights.

He listened to the introduction, deciding that in the future a bit of a pause needed to be set before his name was finally spoken.

He waited until all his guests were seated around the grand table and then he stepped forward.

"We are making history at this moment, my friends. It is only fitting that decisions that will shape the kingdom be made here, where your Parliament once sat."

"What decisions are those?" someone asked.

Montagu hated being interrupted. He turned to cast his smile on the arrogant bastard who had spoken, seated at the table. "I'm coming to that, good sir."

"Come to it quickly," the man warned boldly. "This whole thing stinks of a trap." He turned to the others for their agreement. They gave it.

Jacobite vermin, Montagu thought. None of them

could be trusted. "This is no trap," he assured his guests with a sneer beneath his mustache. "If I wanted—"

"Ye could have gathered us all here to kill us," the man went on.

Two of the other guests laughed as if it were the most preposterous thing they'd ever heard.

Montagu's smile remained intact, his dark eyes fastened on the man who had spoken. "I believe I will gain more with you as my allies. How can you pledge your donations if you're all dead? I'm no fool. I will tell you of my plans shortly. Perhaps you'll grant me your name in the meantime?" *So I can send my army to annihilate, at least, you and your entire family.*

"William Buchanan, clan chief of the Buchanans of Aberfeldy."

"Buchanan." Montagu locked his eyes on the young loudmouth. "As the queen's right, I will have her ear. I would be willing to plant seeds in favor of her granting you ownership of Ravenglade Castle in Perth."

He tilted his mouth higher until his teeth flashed. That's correct, he wasn't some lackwit but equal in tactical cleverness to the previous captain general. He hadn't planned this takeover in a week, or even a month. For more than a year he looked into every chief and leader he'd invited and made himself familiar with their circumstances. He knew their strengths and their weaknesses.

The bold rogue's gaze slipped for an instant to a man sitting to his left. Montagu watched to see what passed between them. Nothing did. The other, older man didn't flick an eyelash.

Who was he? Montagu wondered, then decided he must be a bodyguard to one of his guests. He looked to have been in a good battle or two. It wasn't anything in his appearance that warned Montagu to be wary of him, for he was dressed like the rest of them. But the merciless depths of his gold-green eyes convinced Montagu this opponent would be a fierce one. And to back away.

Montagu shone his wide, more amiable smile on them all. "Gentlemen, my men don't want to die any more than yours do. Let's conduct affairs more civilly."

"How?" another man called out from his place at the table.

"I'll let you attack twice a year, anywhere you please. Do anything in your James Stuart's name. After that, I'll dispatch my army."

"And what d'ye want in return?" someone else called out.

Montagu spread his eyes over his guests as he took his seat at the head of the table. "I want your allegiance that you will stand behind me should I fight against an enemy. When that time arrives I pay my army well. But until then, I'll need your generous purses to help me build an army."

"Ye speak more of a personal battle," Buchanan's companion with the wolf-colored eyes speculated from his seat.

Montagu picked up his dinner knife and twirled the hilt in his fingers. Yes, the shorn-headed rogue was correct, he would need them for a more personal battle. "What makes you suggest such a thing, Mr. . . . ?"

"Campbell," the man said. His eyes were like arrows forged in gold, piercing deep. "Colin Campbell of Breadalbane. I am also kin to a Highland clan or two. I have the ears of all of them and could promise ye their allegiance."

The Campbells? Oh, to have the Campbells behind him! What did he care who was a Jacobite and who was not? This Colin Campbell seemed earnest enough.

"Let us strike a bargain here and now," Montagu offered. "I will allow—"

"Fer guaranteeing so much favor toward ye…" Colin Campbell continued as if Richard hadn't spoken, "I think ye should throw something a bit more valuable into the pot."

"Such as?" Montagu knew he should have stayed away. Campbell was no child. If the Scot made demands and he refused them, there would be fighting. Montagu hated him but he was born of royal blood. He didn't let lesser men get the best of him. Marlow had tried. How he had tried. The thought of finally killing him bought a smile to Montagu's face. He wished he could have seen Marlow's body. But who would have shown it to him? The men he sent were dead. Captain Andrews was the only one who'd survived and that whimpering worthless scum couldn't tell him a damn thing.

He made a mental note to have Andrews killed tomorrow.

"We want information from ye about the queen; where she is and when. Things of that nature."

"You want me to spy for you so you can kill the queen?"

"Ye speak of killing her, not I. Ye wish us to make room for ye to claim the title of king. That's what ye desire, is it not?"

Montagu chuckled into his gloved hand. "You're a very amusing man, Campbell."

"So are ye, my lord, if ye believe we would trust ye. Ye want to claim the title of king, and with the queen out of the way, yer only other enemy is James Stuart. We will be trapped by our own vow to fight on yer side and against our true king, thereby committing treason."

Montagu narrowed his eyes on him. Had he underestimated the Scots? Were they all this clever, or was Colin

Campbell an exception? He sighed a little with relief, deciding that the latter was true. Still, one clever man was one too many. These men were loyal mongrels. If they believed he was the enemy of their precious Pretender, they would not only refuse his offer but they'd likely kill him.

He was going to have to win them, convince them that he sought military power, not the throne. The stars help him, Montagu thought, closing his eyes. It was exhausting work, but he had set things in motion and he would follow through. He would gain their trust by whatever means necessary. And he would begin right where he was looking.

"My good Mr. Campbell, I empathize with your concerns, but let us not make any rash decisions. Enjoy my hospitality. Rest and eat. You'll see that I've spared no expense for my finest guests." He had to stop himself from grinning at the ridiculous things flowing off his tongue. He was good at deception.

He lifted his cup to his guests. "Drink of my finest wine and let's discuss minor details later."

Yes—he nodded slightly to himself—all it took was drink to bring these heretics to heel. He would keep their cups full, their plates piled high, and their laps warmed by buxom young wenches.

His gaze returned to Colin Campbell throughout the night. He was too clever to be a simple ruffian. When asked earlier, he claimed to travel with the Buchanans, but why didn't Montagu know of him? After two hours, Campbell had barely touched his first cup of wine and he refused every wench who offered him something more than food or drink.

"I'm wed," he told his host when Montagu watched him refuse another.

Loyal mongrels.

"How would she ever find out?" Montagu asked him.

"She would find out when I returned to her leaden with guilt and heavy-heartedness, no longer worthy of her love."

Montagu barely kept himself from laughing. Was this what they taught young *lads* in the hills and glens of Scotland? Why, it was positively nauseating. There was nothing a man could ever do to be deemed worthy of a woman's love. They were all bitches.

"I admire such steadfast loyalty in marriage," he admitted to his guest. "I tried it for three years and failed. I had to send her back to her father. The shame it brought me left me a bit bitter."

"How tragic fer ye," Campbell said, but there wasn't even a hint of pity in his voice.

Montagu smiled. "I'm fully recovered."

"Tell me." Campbell's gaze locked on him. "Did ye admire the previous captain general's loyalty to yer queen? He was known fer his dedication to keeping her enemies, the Jacobites, from becoming a serious threat."

"General Marlow was unbendable. Loyalty is a trait I respect from anyone, but when it makes you sacrifice the good of all for the good of one—even if she's the queen— if you are willing to let your own loyal men continue to die for a tyrannical ruler, then perhaps it's time to be taken down."

"So 'twas ye who had him killed?"

"With him out of the way, she's easier to get to," Montagu answered instead. "If your people desire to kill her, I've done you a favor."

Campbell smiled at him for the first time that night and raised his cup to him. "We shall see."

Chapter Twenty-Three

*A*bby didn't care if she ate another thing. It didn't matter what she'd put into her belly over the last two days, nothing satisfied her. The pain in her gut remained, right along with her memories of Daniel's mouth and body on her, the glide of his long, hot shaft against her. She'd been fighting the desire for him for the last pair of days. It made her hurt and she wanted it to end. She hadn't had a full night's sleep since she left Camlochlin. She was exhausted.

She ate to survive, but with no inns around in which to eat and spend the night, they slept on the cold hard ground and ate the remainder of their dry food. Sooner than she had hoped, the lack of food and sleep began to take its toll on her. When her escort insisted on getting them something fresh to eat, and taking her with him on the hunt, she didn't refuse. Better to be with him, even if he tempted her to cast all to the winds, than be alone in the forest. She was glad he took her without her having to ask.

A brisk, northern chill washed over her and reminded her of home. She was lovesick for it. Even if Daniel did share her foolish fancies and considered a future with her, it could never be. She could never leave home. And he... She preferred not to, but she looked at him while he waited patiently for his prey in the gray-blue mist of predawn... He could never go home with her.

Was that what she wanted? To take this man home as her husband? He certainly had the fortitude and the skill to be wed to the MacGregor chief. He didn't have to be as brawny as some of her kin; he was fast on his feet and quicker of mind.

But he was more than an experienced soldier, more than the right-looking kind of husband to have on her arm.

He was always kind to her, even when he first brought her from Camlochlin and considered her an enemy. He'd been valiant since the beginning.

He'd explained to her why he'd demanded her obedience. He worried for her because of his Charlotte. She understood and promised to do her best to do as he *suggested*. If he barked orders at her, she couldn't make any promises.

Saints, she did want him. She wanted him for the rest of her life. Her revelation didn't offer her any peace. What was she going to do? He'd drawn her in with his deep melancholy and then seduced her with the slow graze of his eyes over her and the wide, confident grins only she could pull from him. He lured her away from her responsibilities and made her careless of moments beyond the ones spent with him. But he hadn't done it with any malice or insincerity.

He favored her. It was plain to see. She'd been foolish to doubt it. He hadn't withheld his seed because he didn't care for her. He did it to protect her. Always to protect her. She had won this knight's favor.

Favor that could get her killed, according to him.

She was thankful that at least one of them was level-headed and didn't waste time imagining a future together.

He motioned to her that he'd spotted a grouse and for her to take the shot, and then the next. She realized quickly that he was making her practice. He didn't mind that she caught their dinner. In fact, he smiled at her, pleased with her aim.

She didn't smile back. She couldn't. She felt too miserable. How could she have let this happen? How could she lose her heart to him? Could she save herself? Was it too late?

"Abigail." He carried her name on a cloud of cool breath as they walked back to camp, their supper in his hand.

She tried to remain strong against his charms.

"Will you be angry with me forever?" He stepped in front of her to block her path, then bent his head to catch her gaze and hold it.

She saw something in the sea-green depths of his eyes that stilled her breath—a glimpse of his heart through a hole in the wall he'd built to protect it.

She'd broken through, and it frightened him.

"I thought you'd forgiven me. How long will you withhold from me even your slightest smile?"

Look away from him, she commanded herself, but that thread of desperation in his voice and the way his second breath descended on her made her defy reason.

"I'm not angry with ye, Daniel," she promised softly. "I…have allowed my heart"—she paused for a deep breath—"to rule me and have acted foolishly."

"Abby, I—"

She shook her head and held a finger to his lips. "Let's

never speak of it again, aye?" she begged. "I have too much to lose to be a fool. Ye may have as well."

He nodded, withdrawing his gaze and his body from her path with reluctance. "Yes, of course."

Was that regret she saw in his forced smile? Resignation?

"Do I not still represent all that ye hold in contempt?" she called out as he moved past her.

"Apparently not all," he replied, glancing over his shoulder at her. "If you did, I wouldn't let you trouble me the way you do."

She gave his back a dark scowl. She'd tried not to be any trouble at all and it was impolite of him to say so. But now that he brought it up, she wanted an explanation.

"How do I trouble ye?" she asked him.

He stopped, turned, and tilted his brow at her like some curious aristocrat.

The memory of his teeth along her breasts, and his hungry tongue in her mouth, flashed across her thoughts.

He might fool his peers, but she knew better what he was.

"You trouble me by staying inside my thoughts. You trouble me when I find myself willing to do whatever you ask in exchange for a smile."

Och, that kind of trouble. He did care for her.

The thought of it tickled her belly and made her want to smile for him right now, but he wasn't enjoying his self-professed obsession. His feelings for her troubled his mind and his heart.

Why did knowing that twist her insides in a painful knot? How did she make the ache of giving up her heart to him go away? How did she get it back?

"We'll come to the next inn tomorrow night when we reach the border," he told her a little later while he fed the last stick of wood to the flames of their campfire. "You will sleep better on something soft."

She looked up from plucking one of the grouse as he came around the fire and sat next to her. He picked up the other carcass and joined her work.

"I made no complaint."

"I know," he said, stilling her breath as his eyes left the flames and settled on her.

Her heart pounded hard in her chest. She needed some kind of defense against him, against even his most casual smile.

Home. She thought of home. Only Camlochlin could turn her from her personal desires.

"I'm quite used to sleeping on the ground. I've often done so with my kin on hunts. Dinna' make exceptions fer my benefit; I'm perfectly fine with sleeping beneath the stars." Who cared that she was lying through her eyeballs? She hated sleeping outside. Her back was killing her and she was sure a critter or two had tried to make a nest in her hair last night while she slept. If she didn't sleep in a bed soon she'd go mad. But her pride prevented her from grumbling. She watched him while he prepared the grouse for the spit. They didn't speak. What was there to say? Odd, that the silence wasn't awkward, though. They weren't angry at each other. They were ... resigned.

It made Abby want to cry all the more.

They practiced swords while their dinner cooked. Their glances lingered and he even brought several smiles to her lips, but that was all they shared.

He finally spoke to her while they ate. "Tell me about these hunts you've been on where you had to sleep on the ground."

She smiled, remembering them, and realized that Daniel knew exactly how to draw her out and pull her closer. He did it slowly and with supreme patience.

She had no defense against him.

She happily told him about some of her hunting expeditions with her cousins. It wasn't as dangerous as it might sound, she explained. They all knew the terrain like the backs of their hands, even in the dark.

Somewhere within, a small voice warned her to pull back. What was she doing? Why was she telling him so much about her kin when she knew nothing of him? If he was her enemy, she should keep him close, shouldn't she?

"I've told ye enough aboot me, my lord. Now tell me of ye. Nora told me that ye're renowned fer yer skill on the ballroom dance floor."

He raised an eyebrow at her. "Did she? She mentioned it to me. I've wondered how she knows."

"Then 'tis true?" She offered him a smile that made his gaze soak her in all the more. "Will ye dance with me at the palace?"

He didn't answer her immediately, but then shrugged. "We shall see."

"What aboot yer upbringing? I know nothing aboot it." She wanted to know about the other thing Nora had told her when she'd run into her in the hall after she hit Daniel over the head.

He looked into the flames. Would he tell her the truth? When he told her about his father and his childhood, she knew—not by anything Nora had told her—that he wasn't telling her everything.

"I was taught at a young age to be loyal to the crown. My family was quite rich and sent me off to Whitehall

Palace, where I spent much of my life. I also spent many years at Kensington, and St. James's Palace with Anne."

All wrapped up neat and tidy.

"Where did ye learn to fight?"

"Everywhere. I had different tutors at different palaces. How about you?"

He didn't want to continue talking about himself and she let it go, hoping she could earn his trust one day, if they knew each other long enough.

"I know that judging by my skill, ye wouldna' think I practiced as much as the other lasses," she was happy to tell him. "But I did. I just never fought real enemies before. A chief must be able to fight, Daniel, so I intend to learn everything I can. My brother is a master with a bow, but he doesna' know how to properly fight because he always had other interests to see to when we practiced. He doesn't have an ounce of interest in taking over after my father. Who knows who the council will choose as chief? It worries me. Why are you grinning?" she asked him. "Are my concerns humorous to ye?"

"Not at all. I find you completely wonderful and altogether beautiful, Abigail MacGregor. I don't know much about Highland clans, but I'm sure being chief of one requires many skills, strength, and determination. The fact that you want to follow in your father's footsteps says much about you that a warrior would find very attractive."

She returned his smile and blushed. Goodness, she blushed! She also thought about how thankful they should all be that she wasn't trying to follow in the footsteps of anyone on her mother's side of the family.

"There are still some things I need to learn, General."

His teeth flashed as his grin brightened. "Leave that to me."

Chapter Twenty-Four

Daniel turned his reins over to the stable hand and surveyed the outside of the inn. It was the first time he and Abby would be sleeping in a bed in almost a se'nnight. He would pay the innkeeper whatever the man asked for his most comfortable bed for Abby. He didn't care what his bed was like, but he knew he would be paying for two rooms. He had his own coin, and plenty of it, to see to all her comforts. She'd told the truth when she'd said she never complained about the harsh conditions of traveling all day and sleeping outdoors. She hadn't said a word. But it showed in her pallid complexion and droopy lids. She wasn't sleeping and her appetite was minimal. She was suffering and she hadn't said a word. It made her all the more regal in his eyes. It made his desire to protect her outweigh everything else.

"If anyone asks, you're my sister."

"Why yer sister?" she asked him as they walked toward the inn together.

"Because men don't travel on horseback with their wives. If I'm escorting you, then that means you're likely someone important whom they can hold for ransom. You're my sister and I'm bringing you home to our mother."

She nodded as they stepped inside the crowded downstairs tavern. She moved closer to him when a man, struck by another, sailed by her head, but she didn't seem anything more than slightly distracted.

It took less time than Daniel had anticipated before one of the patrons, a tall, bleary-eyed drunk, grabbed hold of her.

"And who is this?" the patron slurred his words and stumbled a bit to the right.

"His sister," Abby informed him with a smile that was likely going to get Daniel killed one of these days.

The drunk found his balance and looked at Daniel. His smile faded at the promise of violence in the knight's gaze. A flick of his emerald hard eyes to the drunk's fingers curled around her wrist was enough to set her free.

Watching him leave, Daniel realized how difficult it was going to be with her around other men. She was too beautiful, too bright, with her pearly hair and snowy complexion. It didn't matter that her skin had turned pasty or how dark the circles were beneath her eyes. She was like a star in the darkest night.

Men noticed her.

They sought out the innkeeper and quickly found him settling an argument between two of his patrons. For a man of more than a few too many pounds, he moved quickly when the first punch was thrown.

"Pardon me," Daniel interrupted the scuffle, catching another flying fist. The troublemaker sank to one knee while Daniel bent his fingers back. "If you throw that fist again, I'll break all your fingers." When the man nodded, Daniel released him and turned to the innkeeper. "I need a pair of rooms. Make one of them your finest and I'll pay you handsomely."

The innkeeper's lips joggled when he shook his head. "There are no rooms. We're full."

Daniel stared at him. They couldn't be full. Abby needed a bed. They couldn't sleep outside again. He looked at her and she smiled at him. Damn it!

"I'll pay you double."

"Well," the innkeeper considered it, rubbing his chubby chin. "I suppose I could put out old Kevin Fullerton and Cal McNeil."

"Nae." Abby stepped forward. "I willna' put anyone oot. Our horses were taken to a stable; we can sleep there."

The innkeeper nodded and called over a young boy with dirty cheeks and unkempt curls as black as coal. "My son Reggie will take you to yer…ehm…beds."

"In the stable?" Daniel asked Abby, stunned that she would even suggest such a thing.

"That'll cost ye twenty silver."

"Twenty silver!" Daniel swung around and stared at the proprietor like the man had just sprouted another head. Were they all mad? Was he? When had he lost control of the evening? "I wouldn't let you pay *me* for sleeping in a—"

"That will be fine," Abby interrupted him, accepting graciously.

"Abigail," he said as she pulled him away. "I'm not sleeping in the stable."

"And why not?" she demanded softly, pausing at the door and fisting her hand on her hip. "Are the stables only fer Jacobite Highlanders then?"

Hell, he remembered what he'd said to her family the night they'd arrived at Tarveness.

He didn't think he was like the rest of the stuffy nobles at court, but in truth, he was. He did believe he was too good to sleep in hay and Highlanders weren't. Damnation. He didn't want to think of them as devoted husbands and fathers. They were easier to kill when he thought he hated everything about them.

It turned out he was wrong.

Not the first time since he met her, panic settled over him. What the hell was he getting himself into? Falling for one of them and betraying everything the men of his past stood for.

"Tell me, Daniel, are ye truly that haughty?"

Damnation, he was. What would she think of him if or when she found out that he was a prince? She'd probably go back to hating him.

"I don't...I simply..." He looked down at her and scowled. Then he scowled even harder when she waited for him to continue. "Very well then. We'll sleep in the hay. I was simply concerned for you, Abigail. You don't sleep well outdoors."

One side of her mouth hooked into a smile that he found more and more appealing each day he spent with her. "Is that so?"

"Yes, it is," he said, following her outside. "You've been doing it without complaint, but anyone can look at you and see that you're exhausted. I was hoping to see you a bit more comfortable."

She remained quiet for a few moments while they followed Reggie in the twilight. Then, her soft, husky voice permeated the crisp air like a kiss to his ears.

He was lost. He was in trouble.

"That's thoughtful of ye, Daniel," she said. "I dinna' mind the hay, though."

"You wouldn't tell me if you did."

He caught her smile in the starlight and was thankful that she forgave him for being vain and arrogant. He smiled back.

"Would ye prefer it if I whined throughout the journey?" she teased him.

"No." He laughed. "I wouldn't change a thing about you."

"Not a thing?" She raised her brow in doubt. "Not even the fact that I support King James the Third and not your Anne?"

He loved her loyalty to the throne, despite it being given to the wrong person. She wasn't afraid to remind him that she was his professed enemy. He would do best to remember it. "We'll work on that."

"Aye." Her smile widened slightly as she turned away from him. "We will."

He wasn't sure what that little spark in her eyes meant. Did she think she could change his mind? He smiled, and damnation but he didn't know why. She did that to him. Often.

When their guide opened the door to the stable, a great whiff of manure and something else just as foul assailed his nostrils. For a moment, he seriously considered turning around and sleeping under the stars without Abby. He slanted his gaze to her. She was watching him and shook her head at him when he coughed into his hand.

"You don't smell that?"

"'Tis a stable, Daniel," she said, accepting a folded blanket from Reggie. "Have ye not slept in a stable before?"

"I prefer the outdoors," he growled, frightening poor Reggie. When the boy ran for the doors, Daniel called him back and gave the child a coin for his trouble. He caught the curl of Abby's lips and exhaled as she walked past him to one of the empty stalls. He heard Reggie leave and the door slamming shut against the wind. His eyes remained on her while she disappeared behind the wall. He followed her but was stopped at the entrance by a flying bundle of moldy hay.

He stepped back in time to avoid getting hit in the face, then sneezed, twice. For a moment, he watched her dispose of the old hay, then he looked around, found a fork of his own, and helped her replace it with fresh.

When cleaning their nest was complete, he lit two lanterns and hung them from the low walls of the stall. He waited until she set down their own blankets, rather than Reggie's moldy offering. He sat down after her.

He felt like hell that this was no more comfortable for her than sleeping outside. He had wanted to sit at a table and order her a fresh bowl of something warm. Instead, here she was, unwrapping dry, bland meat and stale bread for them to eat. Hell, every other woman he knew would have soaked his shirt with tears and complained until he couldn't take another instant of her company. But not Abigail. This woman, this Jacobite woman, beside him possessed every quality he admired. She would make an excellent wife to some extremely fortunate Highlander.

He felt his blood rush to his veins, making him feel ill and murderously angry at the same time.

There was a thought he never wanted to consider again.

Looking at him, she caught his gaze and smiled in the golden light. Only she could change the entire atmosphere of the stall in a single instant, transforming the place with her presence into a cozy, private alcove with a soft ground beneath his arse.

"Is the smell as bad?" she asked him.

"No. It's better."

Hell. Was he cursed with the inability of controlling his mouth not to smile or grin at her every fifty breaths?

"Ye get used to it," she said, handing him his food.

"We have a large barn at Cam—" She paused, catching herself: "—my home. Some of my fondest memories are of sleeping in it with my brothers and my cousins."

She smiled into some far off place he couldn't see. Her home. Her sanctuary. He didn't know where it was in Skye, but thanks to her stories during their late nights awake together, he knew what it was like to live there. He knew there was honor among her relatives and he knew how much she loved it and that she would never leave it.

"I always find myself talking aboot my life." She laughed. "Tell me more of yers."

It was true. He knew much about her life and about her family and he enjoyed hearing all of it. Not because it was information about his enemy, but because he liked watching her share her life with him.

It had also taken the light off him to talk about his upbringing. But now he would share with her. He didn't normally open up to many people. Not even his closest friends at court. Hell, there were things Anne didn't even know, like how he sometimes found himself sitting with his men before a heavy battle, encouraging the new young soldiers in his regiment who were afraid to meet death. There were some things that could be shared only with a few.

Daniel wasn't sure why he wanted to share details of his life with Abby. Was it the warmth in her eyes when she looked at him, the authenticity of her smile, the openness and trust in her voice that made him want to tell her everything? But he knew he couldn't. How does one tell someone else that he's a royal bastard prince of Denmark?

"Who hurt ye?" she asked him, dragging his gaze to hers beneath the lantern. "I see it in ye like darkness settling across yer features. Was it the woman ye told me aboot, Charlotte?"

He shook his head. "No, it wasn't Charlotte," he told her. "It was someone else."

It felt good to say it, to get it out of him. He already knew she was one of the few who would ever hear him speak this way, but he wasn't sure why or how far he wanted to go. She had secrets she hadn't shared with him yet.

"Anne?" Abby asked, then shook her head and patted his knee. "Fergive me fer imposing. I—"

"I recently discovered that she's been hiding something from me."

A few stalls down, a horse snorted. He smiled first. She quickly followed.

"I will admit, it was a bit of a blow," he continued, feeling oddly at ease telling her these things. "I acted rashly when I learned of it and left the palace without speaking to her about it."

"'Tis true then?" she asked him. This was the other thing Nora had told her, the thing she'd been waiting for him to admit openly and then tell her why it was so. "Ye are Anne's favorite?"

"Yes. My family..." He paused and cleared his throat before starting again. "My father moved me in with the royal family when I was two. Anne was newly married to Prince George and had already suffered a stillborn child. She took me into her fold and raised me like one of her own. So, yes, we are close."

"Och, Daniel," Abby said quietly, "I didna' know. Was this thing she hid from ye something personal?"

He nodded, then exhaled and smiled. "It was, and it will likely be difficult to forgive her deceit, but I will."

After they ate, they lay down together on a surprisingly pleasurable pallet. Beneath the soft lantern light they talked for many more hours—as they had done on other nights, nights he missed with her. She traced his lips while he spoke and he held her in his arms when she began to yawn. He wanted her more than he'd ever wanted anything in his life. But he was stronger than his desires. He had to be. Even if Charlotte were not an issue, or if he weren't Prince George's son, Abby would never give up her home or her desire to be chief of her clan. Hell, why did her clan have to live in the Highlands and be outlaws? How could he ever live among them knowing they wanted to depose his queen?

His duty was to Anne.

Still, something was happening to his heart when it came to the woman in his arms.

Lying with her, he considered his surroundings. The horses were quiet. The mice were not. If he breathed deep enough, he could still smell manure and mold coming from the other stalls. He didn't breathe deeply.

He was sleeping in a barn for her—and it wasn't so bad. He would do anything for her—and *that* was. She was coming first before everything else that mattered to him. How far would he go for her? What if her family threatened the queen?

He listened to the rhythm of her breath deepen, then he kissed her head. "Queens," he whispered, captive of his own heart, "should sleep in enormous beds carved in the finest wood and cloaked in the most beautiful silks.

They should eat every night at banqueting tables and have servants at their every beck and call."

He didn't expect her to move, or to answer him. He thought she was asleep. By the slur of her words, she almost was

"Nae, my mother docsna' want to be queen."

Daniel smiled, unsure if he heard her right. Her mother? He lifted his head and looked down at her so close to slumber. What did her mother have to do with it?

He wasn't about to wake her up to ask.

❖

Chapter Twenty-Five

Abby didn't remember mentioning her mother in response to Daniel's whispers about queens and their beds. She remembered only falling asleep in his arms, drawn close to the languid beat within his chest.

She woke from her dreams to find him beside her, asleep in their small haystack. Careful not to wake him with the fierce ache of her heart, she let her gaze rove over his features, taking him in like a starving waif.

Soon, their nightly talks would end, along with his kisses. Why did it have to be?

She sighed, waking him to her gaze.

He smiled, taking her in like a glorious sunrise.

"You slept well," he said, after a moment when he seemed to struggle to breathe.

"I feel better," she told him, failing to keep her worshipful grin off him, especially when he leaned up and kissed every part of her face, including her mouth.

"I'm pleased to hear that."

She watched him rise up over her, and proving once again his supreme control, he left her arms and stood.

"Come." He extended his hand to her, then closed his fingers around hers when she accepted his chivalrous offering. "Lying around here will get us nothing."

She agreed, but she could have done without his haste to be away from her. They folded their blankets in silence and left the stable without looking back. Mayhap it was the stable and not her that he hurried away from. If it was, it didn't make her feel any better. She'd hoped sleeping with animals had humbled him a wee bit.

They stepped outside together. The sun had barely come up, but it was light enough for Abby to note the color returning to Daniel's face as he drew in a deep breath. He turned to her and smiled, then took her hand and fit it into the crook of his arm. She didn't refuse him, of course, but walked at his side back to the inn.

When they stepped inside, there were only a few patrons littering the seats and no men standing but Daniel and one other.

"How was yer night?" The innkeeper grinned when they reached him.

Daniel glared at him.

"'Twas lovely," Abby answered, before her knight swiped off the proprietor's head.

But when she tossed him a warning look, she saw that Daniel had already forgotten about him and was looking for a suitable table.

"Two of everything you have warming in your kitchen," he ordered, then tugged her away.

He led her to a table in the right corner, away from most of the sleeping bodies, and as she looked around, she realized what Daniel's hurry had been. When he offered her a chair, she let her fingers graze over his.

"I see the wisdom now in yer decision to leap from yer

blanket," she said as he took the seat opposite her. "By arriving before anyone else is awake ye're guaranteed getting the freshest portions of what the inn is serving."

He smiled. "You deserve a hot meal at a table, like a lady." He moved back in his chair when a serving girl swept her body over the table to clean it. "Did you think my haste meant something else?"

Abby blinked out of the spell he cast over her by being so considerate of her needs. He certainly was charming. "Something else? Nae. Of course not. I just meant . . ." She couldn't tell him her fears without sounding like a child. She wouldn't. "I only meant that—"

He had mercy and saved her from any further stammering. "A fresh, hot meal will do much for you."

"I believe 'twill," she told him softly. "Ye're verra' gallant, sir."

Firelight from the hearth reflected like emerald facets in his eyes when he leaned forward in his chair and said in a low voice, "Before you form such an opinion of me, I must be honest and tell you that it was extremely difficult to leave the warmth of your body."

She blushed at the passionate thoughts he provoked. She wanted to go back to the hay and to hell with breakfast.

"My hope is that your breakfast pleases you."

The spell he cast was a powerful one. She didn't want to give him up. She wasn't sure if she could. "Every meal I partake of with ye pleases me."

The playful intimacy of his smile coaxed a flip from her heart. "Who taught you how to charm a man, even one who is supposed to be your enemy, so artfully?"

"Who says I ever bothered charming anyone before I met my first knight?" she replied.

"I don't know if it's a blessing or a curse to be so

favored," he told her while the servers set their bowls down before them. "You make it difficult to deny you."

Abby blinked, looking into his eyes. "And ye tempt me to win ye."

His grin widened, along with his glorious eyes. "What would you do with me after you won me?"

She shrugged and felt heat smudge her milky complexion. Did he expect her to be so bold as to tell him? Butterflies fluttered in her belly, making her want to laugh. She wanted to tell him that she loved him beyond endurance and she wanted to return to their haystack, but what if he reminded her that they had no future together?

"We should be heading out before the crowd awakens," he said, possibly reading the emotion in her eyes and ending it before it erupted into speech.

She nodded and swallowed back a rush of disappointment. She couldn't win him. Abby wondered if any woman could.

But his detachment made sense to her. Letting himself care for her was a betrayal to everything he stood for, fought for. He wisely held back. He also believed his affection for Abby would put her in danger from this Charlotte lass. He rejected her to keep her safe. It was a noble cause. One that every legend of honor would applaud. Normally, she would agree and applaud along with them in her books and in her dreams. But this was real. Daniel was real and she wanted to spend all her days with him.

He'd promised not to harm any of her kin, no matter what. He'd given his word. Did she trust it? Could she ever bring him to Camlochlin? How she would break the news to her father, her grandfather? Her mother? She wanted to hold Daniel in her bed and sit at his side while she made decisions for her clan. She wanted to tell him about her uncle James Francis Stuart, the king, and turn him to the Jacobites' side. How wonderful would it be to love him without secrets?

But he would never leave his service, and she couldn't leave hers. So, again, he was wise to rebuke her. Their future was over before it began.

They shared breakfast over light talk and scant smiles. Daniel had ordered too much food, but it was hot and fresh and it tasted quite decent. They ate what they could and would take the rest with them.

She watched the way sunlight finally streamed through the windows and bathed him in flames when he stood up. For an indulgent moment she basked in his profile, in the cut of his jaw—straight, strong, determined—in his classically carved nose, and in the almond flare of his eyes. Truly, his babes would be beautiful. She wondered what it would feel like to be heavy with his child.

"Come then."

She blushed, coming out of the trance she'd fallen into, and looked at his hand, offering her aid from her seat. She accepted and walked with him while they returned to the innkeeper and paid him what was due.

They were about to leave and travel onward toward part of her destiny. She was thankful that Daniel was thoughtful of her safety and immune to her flirtations. A little hurt, as well. But thankful.

A hefty man bumped his shoulder into Daniel's and turned to him. "Pardon me."

Daniel let go of her hand, alarming her, as his eyes widened and he turned both hands to his side, where the hilt of a dagger protruded from his flesh. At the same time, the larger man stepped around him and grabbed Abby by the waist.

His muddy eyes dipped to her breasts and his hands followed. "I've been watchin' ye while ye ate. I'm going to—"

He grunted and stared at her as he slipped to the floor, almost taking her with him. His eyes went blank, distant, and finally cold. Daniel stood behind him. The knife the assailant had plunged into him was now jammed and twisted in its original owner's back while he lay twitching on the floor.

Abby ignored the fallen attacker and rushed to Daniel's side as he clutched the table nearest him and reached for his bloody wound. "Daniel! Daniel!" she cried, catching him before he folded to the floor. She examined him with shaking fingers and a racing heart. All the blood frightened her because it was his. What if he died? Not being with him was one thing, knowing he no longer breathed on the earth was different. Thankfully, the stranger had stabbed him in the fleshy part of his side, a few inches from his lung. Daniel would live. She kissed his forehead, then held her mouth to him. "I'll fix ye up, my lord. I'm quite good with a needle."

"Somebody get this flea-bitten pile of rat shyt out of my inn!" The innkeeper kicked the dying man and then bent to Daniel. "No one gets stabbed from behind at my inn without a free night's accommodations. Ye'll get two of my finest rooms, meals, and—"

Abby stopped him with a hand on his arm, a bit short of breath. "One room will be enough, kind sir." She had to keep her wits about her while the man she loved bled in her arms. She did. "I'll also need some water and clean rags. Some garlic will do, and cinnamon, mayhap clove. I need a number of mints: thyme, sage, and basil." She patted his beefy shoulder when he offered her a lost look. "Just bring me what you have."

"I'm fine," Daniel assured her.

She ignored him and so did the innkeeper when he nodded and sent two of his daughters to the task, then helped her and Daniel up the stairs and into a spacious room.

Abby looked around while another young lass, mayhap a few years younger than herself, scooted around her and hurried into the chamber first. Abby guessed she was the innkeeper's daughter, but didn't ask while the girl prepared the bed to receive Daniel. The room was brightly lit with wall sconces and candles. A huge hearth on the eastern wall promised even more light and heat when its embers were stoked. Which the lass rushed to do next.

Two small windows were unshuttered, allowing streams of light to spill over a cushioned chair and the bed.

She and the innkeeper set him in the bed, despite his objections. She began unbuttoning his shirt, then saw the futility of it in her trembling, useless fingers. She pushed him down on the bed and tore the rest of the woolen obstruction away and set about examining the gaping wound at a closer angle.

"Abigail."

"Ye had to rip his blade from yer flesh?" she asked him, glancing up briefly from her exam. "If ye had left his dagger where it landed, I could have removed it more neatly."

She caught the slant of his mouth before he spoke and she lowered her gaze again.

"I needed a weapon and didn't want to lose one of my finer blades in his thick flesh and then have to ask you to remove it for me. Had I known that you had no aversion to yanking blades out of men's bodies, I would have made what you're about to do for me much easier. As it is, I'm in your debt."

Lord help her, but he mesmerized her. His breath on her head and the raw cadence of his voice stilled her heart and drew her eyes to his. In the harsh sunlight, his skin was pale beneath his dust of auburn facial hair. His eyes were like pools of shallow water dappled in light and shadows. They opened to his soul and sought out hers at the same time in a trade-off of emotions. She loved him, and everything about him, including the way he looked. Was there any returning from this? God help her.

"I'm not in jeopardy, Abby, and that was my last clean shirt."

"I know ye're not in jeopardy," she told him, a willing captive of his slow, seductive smile. "But I want to help ye avoid infection. Would ye deny yerself a woman's touch?"

"I would," he told her. "But I can deny you nothing." He gave her leave to do whatever she needed to do. He drank her bitter teas without quarrel, though she knew he despised her thinking he needed any kind of pain reducer. He remained silent and stoic most of the time while she tended to him, but when she moved him to clean inside the gash, he cursed under his breath.

She kept her touches light and as tender as she could while she stitched him up, then wrapped him in bandages. She did her best not to let seeing his honed, warrior's body splattered in scars or touching them affect her. She soon realized, though, that the short, shallow breaths filling the room were hers and not his. She also noted that the innkeeper and his brood had gone away sometime during her ministrations, leaving her alone with her knight.

She rinsed his blood from her hands in a basin of fresh water.

"You've saved me," Daniel said, sitting up and testing

his mobility by turning left and then right. "I owe you my life."

She laughed, drying her hands. "Infection can kill ye."

"Which is why I'm so grateful that you were here to save me from it."

She knew he was teasing her but she didn't care. "'Tis the least I can do," she told him, "after all ye've done fer me."

"What," he asked, "have I done but only my duty?"

His duty. She was his duty. She tried not to feel anything and she failed. She felt like smashing him over the head with another vase and then running to find a quiet place to cry her eyes out.

"Lay back, Daniel." She pushed him down, perhaps a bit harder than needed. "I mixed an herb in yer tea to help ye sleep and ye're already halfway there. Ye need to rest and not disturb the wound."

He tried to fight it but finally fell back on the bed, asleep. She hoped, as she walked out the door, that she hadn't given him too much. Good thing the herb wasn't too potent. Even better that he couldn't speak to dash her already frail fancies to pieces.

She was his duty.

Chapter Twenty-Six

Thirteen hours later, Daniel stumbled out of bed and then onto his knees. The herb and his long hours of sleep had weakened him. What the hell had she given him? His wound felt quite well, though, just a bit stiff. He gave himself a few more minutes before he attempted to regain his footing.

Successful this time, he noted the fresh, ivory linen shirt thrown across the chair and put it on. He didn't remember Abby removing his boots, but they were on the floor next to the bed. Bending to retrieve them, his wound ached a little and he cursed his attacker. Was this what it would be like everywhere he brought Abigail Mac-Gregor? Would men always want her enough to kill or be killed for her? Which of the two was he willing to do? Both?

The room spun him in a circle when he thought of Abby below stairs now, alone and unprotected for all these hours. How many hours? Daniel felt the color drain from his face and his heart leap to life. He hurried to the door in one boot and left the room with blood on his mind. One of them had gotten her. He gritted his teeth and clutched the hilt of his blade in the hand with the stronger arm. He wasn't naturally left-handed, but he'd make do and kill anyone who harmed her.

He half-clicked all the way down the stairs, drawing attention to his bare foot.

"Daniel!"

He heard her voice and turned to find her rising from the innkeeper's table. She looked unharmed, to his great relief.

"What are ye doing oot of bed? Are ye hungry?" She reached up and cupped his forehead and then his cheek in her palm. "No fever. Come, sit."

He wanted to look her over a moment longer to make certain she'd suffered no harm in his absence.

He followed her to the table and he wondered if he would follow her to her death.

He looked around at the faces of men going back to their supper. None seemed overly interested in her. With the wind blown from his sails, he relaxed and slipped his dagger into his pants at the waist and accepted a seat at the table. He answered the half dozen questions she put to him and asked her a few of his own . . . mainly about the tea she had given him. As his usually good fortune would have it, he was just in time for supper. Hot stew and not so fresh bread. He was starving.

"Are ye not going to thank Ferguson for all his aid?" Abby asked him in a half whisper while he ate.

He looked up vaguely, "Who?"

"Ferguson Hampton, the innkeeper."

Daniel eyed him and then tossed their chubby host a smile. "You have my thanks."

Everyone at the table, including Ferguson's wife and

three daughters, smiled. It left Daniel feeling like he'd just signed his name in blood, to terms he didn't remember agreeing to.

He kept his attention on Abby throughout the night, though the wine and watered-down whisky made it difficult to concentrate on much.

Laughter flowed more easily than Daniel would have expected from sitting with an innkeeper. Abby seemed to get along well with Lorraine, one of Ferguson's daughters. Watching her interact with another woman distracted him from thoughts of protecting her to thoughts of devouring her.

When tables were cleared for dancing, he thought about asking her. He'd likely open his wound, but he wanted to hold her hands, draw her close, move around her to the sound of merry music. He hesitated until a young traveler left his chair and began walking toward them. Daniel kicked off his boot, clasped Abby's hand, and drew her to her feet. His wound still ached but he could bear it. He turned her hand in his with an elegant flick of his wrist he'd learned from all his years around royalty and kissed the inside, where her pulse beat. "Dance with me, my lady."

She nodded and moved away with him toward the center of the hall. She didn't spare the man who'd been about to ask her to the floor another thought. Neither did Daniel.

"Ye dinna' look to be the type who dances," she said while they took position with the three other pairs and waited for the music to begin.

At the first note, he bowed, left arm and leg extended, right leg bent, tipping his body slightly forward, while he kept his right arm close to his wound. "What does the type who dances look like?"

She blinked and, moving closer, smiled at him, unknowingly making him forget the next step.

"Like ye, I presume." Her voice fell across his ears like a soft kiss. She pulled away but was stopped by his gentle tug. He drew her under his arm and met her half turn with a smile. She let him lead her around the floor, sweeping her in wide circles or twirling her in his arm.

He liked dancing and didn't get to do it often anymore, not like this. His boots were already off. Unrestraint beckoned him, just this once, to let go, to enjoy himself.

The most beautiful woman in Great Britain was in his arms and he'd withheld his affection long enough. He wanted to feel her naked in his arms again, aroused and wet enough to take him. He intended to sweep her up, make her laugh, and shower her with everything she deserved.

"Tonight"—he pulled her in close and dropped his gaze to hers—"I don't give a damn about tomorrow."

Her lips curled in a smile that sucked the breath from him. "Nor do I."

He wanted to snatch her off her feet, right here and now, and race up the stairs to their bed. She was awakening parts of him that had been put to sleep long ago. Duty to God and to the throne came before selfish desire. Honor came before love. But not tonight.

Tonight, he wanted to kiss her and waltz with her with equal abandon. He would give her what she wanted, and take what he needed. He'd promise her his heart amid the music and the spirits, and the laughter born from both.

By the end of the night, he'd danced with her and every other female at the inn. He met Abby on the dance floor four times and then once again with the innkeeper on her arm. They drank too much wine and they danced too closely when they came together. Or were they doomed before this?

Daniel didn't think about anything but Abby while he finally followed her up the stairs. Not Charlotte, or the queen, or Skye, or what they had just done, or what they were going to do. He thought of only one thing. He loved her. He loved her with his entire being. There wasn't a single iota of him that wasn't madly, deeply in love with her—a proscribed MacGregor Jacobite. He sighed as he brought her to their room. What else could he do but sigh?

"Ye've been staring at me like that all evening."

He smiled, pulling her into his arms. "How do you know how I looked when you were in front of me?"

She gazed up at him; her lids were heavy and shafts of diamond blue stilled his breath. "I can feel it."

He raised an eyebrow. "Is that so?"

"Aye." She nodded her head and quirked her mouth at him.

He gathered her in closer and kissed her as they came to the door. He kicked it open with his bare foot. He wanted to toss her on the bed and jump in after her. Hell, why did he have to be wounded tonight?

"Tell me how I look then?" he asked, returning to the door to bolt it.

"Like a starving man."

He turned from the door to find her removing her kirtle. His lips curled when her dress fell to the floor. "That," he told her while he unlaced his pants and moved toward her, "I am."

Somewhere deep in Abby's muddy thoughts, she heard a small voice, warning her about trusting him so quickly. She denied it and clasped his shirt in both fists when he got close enough. Dancing with him, watching him dance with others, and laugh, and make friends—it all left her very enthralled and...excited.

She'd danced before, at home in Camlochlin, but none of her partners had ever danced like him. Daniel moved with fluidity of grace in every step, undeniable masculinity oozing from his pores. Every lass present wanted to dance with him, and he obliged them while she watched, laughing and clapping and knowing where he was sleeping tonight.

It probably should mortify her, but she had drunk too much to care. He sparked fires in her all evening and she felt like she would combust if she didn't have him. She didn't know exactly what it was that her body craved. Him. More of him. All of him. She began by tugging at his shirt. When he helped, tearing it over his head and casting it over his shoulder, she bit her lip and ran her fingertips down his chest. His smile, so intimate and deep with desire, emboldened her to slip her fingers down the front of his pants and tug.

His arm coiled around her back and pulled her up close against his hard, rigid body. She tilted her face to him and parted her lips, waiting...waiting.

His mouth, hot and hungry on hers, unglued her and drew long, lusty groans from her. She fell to pieces in his arms as they landed on the bed in passion's embrace. His tongue explored the inside of her mouth with slow, sensuous strokes that set her nerves aflame. He tasted her, delighted in her, while he cupped her breasts and pinched her stiff nipples. As if waiting until the precise moment when she was ripe for the picking, he dipped his head and took her in with a tight growl that made her insides burn and her legs spread beneath him. His tongue burned like a flame skipping across her nipple, then down the valley between her breasts. She spoke his name. "Daniel." She wanted to say it. "Whether ye mean to or not, ye're emblazoning yerself into me. 'Twill be verra' difficult trying to ferget ye when the time comes."

She didn't know what it was that she said exactly, but it made him look up from his kisses, a troubling thought marring his brow. When she smiled, he stretched out his body beside her on the bed.

"If we both know the outcome, why do we do this?"

She leaned up on her elbow and stared at him above her. "Because if we dinna' do it, I fear I will go mad."

The depths of his eyes tempted her to expose all to him, not just her body, and then explore everything about him. She pulled him back down and stole a kiss from his decadently shaped mouth. "But even if nothing changes," she whispered, "ye'll always be mine, and I'll always be yers."

When he smiled again, she pushed him off her and mounted him all in one swift movement, careful of his wound. Her bold advance made her head spin, thanks to all the whisky she'd consumed. Setting her palms on his chest, she pushed herself up. A flick of her hair to get it off her face made her dizzy again and she gave it a moment to pass.

His hands went from holding her steady to cupping her, kneading her, caressing every curve. His eyes basked in her while she set herself down on the thick bulge under his pants. She wanted to release him and feel his flesh against hers, but in a moment. His body felt so good beneath her right now, she almost didn't want to move. But she did. She rubbed and wriggled until he nearly snapped. She wanted him and if she had to tear off his pants herself, she would.

She straightened her back and he followed. When he moved to kiss her, she backed away. "Ye seem to have brought oot a side of me I didna' know existed."

"I like it," he said in deep rasp riddled with desire.

Aye, so did she, she thought, leaping off him. "Take off yer pants," she demanded with a playful smile.

His breath came hard and heavy as he rose off the bed and shook his head. She knew why.

"While ye were dancing with Eileen Hampton I took the opportunity to mix a few herbs I know to stop pregnancy from occurring and steeped it in my drinks."

"A trusted concoction?" he asked, his voice covering her from the other side of the room.

"I wouldna' risk so much if 'twasna' trusted."

His mouth hooked into a dark smile that made her want to run. She watched him undress and then stand fully naked before her. He was a long, lean masterpiece with a huge cock reaching toward the heavens.

She hadn't seen it before in all its glory. She'd felt it, but that was different. Seeing the size of it, and the intent in his eyes of what he was going to do to her with it, frightened her a little. But Abigail MacGregor prided herself on not scaring easily. A chief should be brave.

When he moved toward her, she held her ground. It wasn't easy, but it was she, after all, who'd demanded he remove his pants. Now wasn't the time to second-guess her decision. He was coming to take what he wanted, and she wanted to give it all. Her breath stalled as he neared, spreading his warmth over her. When he caught her up in his arms, she was certain she was going to faint in them. She'd come to feel safe in them, and she'd come to ache for them. She never wanted to leave his embrace. She remembered to breathe and looked up into his smoldering gaze, and then forgot again as his mouth descended on hers.

He snatched away her air and left her gasping with the passion of his kiss. His flirty lips parted to let his tongue invade her with sensual, teasing licks that deepened quickly into something more like complete possession. Things were about to change and she didn't want to stop it. She didn't resist him but tossed back her head in surrender when he hoisted her over his naked body and wrapped her legs around his hips.

She held on tight while he kissed her and moved them back toward the bed. His hands beneath her rump supported her, and it also gave him control of her movements. What he did was rather sinful. The way he rubbed her all over him, up and down his fiery lance, until she thought she might combust.

She wanted more, something instinctual and feral, something he gave to no other woman before her or after her. More than his body, she wanted the wild heart beneath all the armor. If he wanted to give her more, who was she to argue? She would take it all. Every scintillatingly slick, steel inch.

He guided her over him one last time before she took control of her own movements. Tightening her thighs around his waist, she leaned up and out of his hands and paused at his swollen tip. She held herself up for a moment, pressed snugly against him, her breasts pushed against his chin. She closed her eyes, preparing herself to be cleaved in half. It couldn't be that bad or other women would never do it.

While she was still pondering it, he snatched her back, dragged her over his steel once, and then again, and then dropped her onto the bed.

He stood over her, heavy cock in hand, and without taking his eyes off her, gave himself two pumps and erupted poised between her legs. He soaked her and smiled like pure temptation come in the flesh.

She couldn't deny that the sight of him thrilled her senseless, and that she could have watched his passion all night long. But that was the problem. "'Twas over rather quickly fer ye," she told him, "and I told ye that I drank a mixture of herbs—"

He leaned over her and bit her right lobe before he whispered against her ear, "We're not close to being done."

Chapter Twenty-Seven

The candles had burned down three hours later but there was enough candlelight left for Daniel to watch Abby while she slept. He admired the delicate silhouette of her form curled up beside him, facing him pillow to pillow.

The inn was quiet, their room dead silent but for the sound of Abby's breath. He let the slow rhythm of it soothe him. It was too late to think about consequences now. He'd made love to her until he'd exhausted her. Hell, the mere thought of her milky thighs coiled around him made him hard again. He didn't want to think about England. He had until morning at least.

Her lips were like something out of a dream, delectably full and shaped like a finely cut wooden bow. He was tempted to wake her up so he could kiss her some more.

He let his eyes drift over the pale tresses draping her bare shoulder. He followed the softly illuminated line of her body, down the valley of her waist and back up with the swell of her hip.

He reached out to touch her, his hand shaking a bit.

Hell, he never shook.

He coiled a strand of her hair around his finger and watched it shine in the soft light of the moon filtering through the windows. Was that silver he saw? No wonder all the men of Skye had followed them. What man in his right mind wouldn't kill to keep her safe?

When she opened her eyes, he could do nothing else but smile at her.

"I had a pleasant dream," she told him in a voice husky with sleep. The cadence of it scalded his blood.

"Did you?" he asked.

She nodded and when she stretched, he used the opportunity to scoop her up in his arms.

"Tell me of it."

When she smiled at him, he doubted the good of his senses, the strength of his resolve. If Charlotte saw how much he loved this handmaiden—

"'Twas aboot my home." She interrupted his thoughts. "'Twould dull yer ears."

He shook his head and drew her closer, coiling their legs together. "Tell me of it. I want to know more of this place that brings you such happiness and contentment. Like you want for nothing."

He didn't expect her to reach up and touch his face. She stared into his eyes, telling him what her lips didn't. They were doomed. Hell, they were so doomed.

"'Twas a clear summer day. I could almost feel the refreshing breeze coming off the lochs. Heather danced on the hill and the sound of children laughing filled the vale. I was chief, and behind me stood my grandfaither, who built the foundation of Camlochlin, and my faither, who protected it."

"Is Camlochlin a castle?"

She blinked away from her dream and looked at him, anxious and afraid. "Pardon?"

"Camlochlin?" he repeated. "What is it?"

"Och, Daniel." He could feel her heart pounding against him. "I didna' mean to— Mayhap I cannot be trusted to protect my clan."

"What, my love? What is it?"

She leaned up in the bed. "If ye care fer me…If ye care fer me in the smallest way, please never use what I've said against my clan. Swear to me."

"Abigail, I—"

"Swear it, Daniel."

Of course he would swear it. He'd promise her anything. Why would the name of her home be such a dangerous thing to know anyway? It upset her greatly that she'd said it. He wanted to ease her mind and tell her what she needed to hear. "I will never use anything you tell me against your family, Abby, I vow it."

That, at least, earned him a smile. He knew by now that talking about her family brought her happiness. He loved the way she smiled. He wanted her to do it often. Even more, he wanted to be one who made her happy. "What about your mother's father?" he asked, wanting her to relax again in his arms. "You never speak of him."

She went stiff in his arms. So stiff, he couldn't feel her breathing. If he didn't know he loved her already, his actions now convinced him. He laid his instincts aside for her—instincts that had brought him victories on the field more than a dozen times in the past. She was hiding something from him—not only the name of her home, but a secret concerning her family. She'd told him so much about her upbringing and the people in it that he wondered how she'd managed to keep her secret safe in the midst of it all. His instincts told him to get the truth from her, but he didn't care about truth, or even honor. Love was lord of everything else, and he let have her secret.

Holding her close, he spoke in a quiet voice into her hair. "My love, take heart. I've promised not to harm your family, have I not?"

Would he have to remind her about his vow to her the night her father and the rest of the MacGregors arrived at Tarveness? Did she think he wouldn't keep his word?

Her muscles softened in his arms. "Aye, my love," she found her breath and whispered, "ye have promised not to harm them. Any of them."

He thought she might confess her secret now, but she chose to kiss him instead. He didn't resist her but enjoyed every inch of her mouth with long, silken strokes of his tongue. How would he ever live without her? How could he be with her while the queen lived?

He would think on it when the sun rose, not now. He pushed the thoughts out of his head and pulled her body up over his.

"D'ye intend to leave me lame for the next day or two?" she asked, gazing down at him with a sexy tilt of her mouth.

"Now that you put it that way"—he rubbed her hot center over the length of his cock—"I just might, unless you would have us wait." He stopped, unwilling to force her if she was in pain.

She giggled like a siren against his ear and then spread her thighs wider and flattened herself atop him. She drove him to the brink of madness, but it was she who moaned with the terrible rapture of his return. He broke through again and again, grinding beneath her, lifting his hips and giving her more of him. She took every inch, raking her nails across his chest and her tongue over his throat. He squeezed her buttocks and guided her up and down while he kissed her, then took her bottom lip between his teeth. Tightening his thighs, he drove himself in deeper until he thought he might split her in two. He groaned and closed his eyes as ecstasy filled his veins and his body prepared to pull out and shoot another stream of his source across the room. He didn't intend on giving her a child, no matter what offense she took to it. Part of him still clung to reality, for both their sakes. This time though, she took no offense.

Normally, there would be nothing left in him, but she mounted him again and managed to pump every drop from his body. In a burst of abandon, he sat up, pushing her up with her in his lap, attached to him. He took hold of her round breast dangling before his face and suckled her until she panted above him. He curled his arms down her back and, cupping her rump in his hands, guided her to her release and then came with a torrent of thrusts that sapped the last ounce of strength from his body.

He did it inside her, but there was nothing left, and she wouldn't let him go.

They slept soundly until the break of dawn, when Daniel rose quietly from their bed. He dressed without a sound and left to bring her breakfast while it was still hot.

He found Ferguson in the same place he'd found him the morning before. This time though, Daniel approached him differently. They'd shared drink and laughter last night. It didn't make them friends, but Daniel wasn't opposed to smiling at him. After he ordered their meals, he and Ferguson shared one last drink before the innkeeper left to see to the food in the kitchen.

He heard the inn door open and turned at the sound of many men entering. His men. He watched them file inside, filling the tavern. He left his stool and stood.

"Captain Lewis, what are you doing here?"

"He's escorting me."

Daniel knew her voice. He watched in disbelief while Charlotte, the Duchess of Blackburn, cut a path through his men and looked up at him when she reached him. He wasn't happy to see her.

"What are you doing here?" What would take her from the luxuries of the palace and put her in the saddle? "Is it the queen?"

She set her dark eyes toward the stairs. "All is well with Anne," she told him. "I'm here because I dreamed that you were gone from me for good." Her gaze fell back to him. "I've been searching for you for weeks."

He couldn't think clearly. Hell! Charlotte was here! Had Anne told her about Abigail?

He didn't look toward the stairs. He hoped Abby wasn't standing at the top. He hoped that when she did appear, she would remember Charlotte's possessiveness of him and follow his lead.

"You must have dreamed of your lover, Montagu, also then."

She arched her brow. "Why him?"

"If your dream was prophetic, Your Grace, you would have known about the Earl of Manchester planning my murder. Did you know that he arranged an ambush and killed my men? He thinks me dead, as well."

As he hoped, she forgot all about the stairs. She clasped his forearm, careless of what anyone standing around them thought. "Richard tried to have you killed?"

"Yes," he told her. "Did you know of his plans? I would have the truth."

"Of course I didn't know, you fool! I would make certain he was lashed and thrown into prison. Why, I could kill him myself right now. But how do you know it was him who planned the ambush? Tell me everything."

He told her what happened and about the letter Montagu had penned to a dozen Jacobite leaders, beckoning them to Edinburgh. While he finished his tale, he sensed Abby's presence. She'd awoken and left their room. He didn't look toward the stairs even after most of the men packing the inn had.

"...and that's where Hubert died. I stayed to bury him..."

He lost Charlotte's attention next when she turned toward the stairs. Only then did Daniel look up. It didn't bode well that Abby illuminated the hall, like moonbeams spilling down the stairs.

He was lost...doomed. He should be hanged for treason.

"Miss Campbell." He moved to the bottom of the stairs and hoped Abby caught on to who this was facing her. "May I present Her Grace, Charlotte Adler, Duchess of Blackburn."

Abby paused and darted her eyes to Daniel as she realized who it was. Daniel watched her, holding his breath. What would he do if Charlotte tried to hurt her? "Yer Grace," she said, her expression colorless. "Daniel has spoken of ye. I didna' know ye were joining us."

"Campbell?" Charlotte echoed, turning to fix him with a pointed look. "Does the queen know about this?"

Daniel nodded. "She is to be the queen's new handmaiden."

Charlotte lifted a raven brow. "The queen sent *you* to escort a new handmaiden to the palace? A tad overdone, don't you think, General?"

Yes. He did. But he'd get to the bottom of it later. He wanted a moment with Abby to warn her about Charlotte. He should have told Abby the duchess claimed to be in love with him. He wished he'd told her the lengths to which Charlotte had gone to make certain he remained available. If she suspected that Abigail had claimed his heart, he didn't know what she would do.

"My lady," Abby spoke up.

Seeing the proud tilt of her chin and the now familiar flames in her eyes, Daniel wanted to stop her, to protect her from this viperous woman.

"My kin hail from Argyll and Breadalbane. I also have kin on the isles of Islay and Mull."

"Ah." Charlotte's green eyes twinkled like facets in emeralds as a coy smile played at her lips. "A touch of Scottish pride. How sweet.

"Miss Campbell," the duchess said softly, while her eyes hardened. "In the future you will refrain from bursting out when the mood strikes you. I don't care who your relatives are, you are to be the queen's handmaiden and will be expected to behave with some decorum."

She returned her attention to Daniel, leaving Abby to boil in her spot. "She's quite lovely."

He didn't answer and watched with as little interest as he could force when Captain Lewis moved slowly toward Abby.

"We've much to discuss and I'd rather do it on the road where there are fewer ears to hear." The duchess touched her fingers to his arm and let them linger there. "Do you owe the innkeeper for one room or two?"

"One," Daniel told her, still not looking at Abby. He wasn't afraid for himself but for her. "For her. I stored my things with her and slept down here."

After Charlotte confirmed his answer with Ferguson Hampton, she beckoned Abby to follow her back to their horses.

Daniel watched them leave, then bid Ferguson farewell. He left the inn and saw Charlotte directing Abby to ride with Captain Lewis near the front of the line.

When Charlotte saw him, she called him to her side in the middle of the line, where it was safest.

No, Daniel thought, reaching her. This wouldn't do.

"Charlotte," he said. "Anne obviously has intentions of forming some sort of alliance with Miss Campbell's family. I'm not about to jeopardize that by leaving my charge in the hands of soldiers. My duty is to protect Miss Campbell. I will ride with her."

Charlotte didn't bother masking her anger. She drew her lips tight over her spacey teeth. "Bring her to this position then. I want time with you and I won't have that brat steal it from me."

"She's is stealing nothing, Duchess," he assured her with a bland smirk. "And you'll watch how you speak to her. If calamity befalls her, we could have more than a thousand men at the palace doors."

Her soulless eyes widened and she placed her hand at her chest. "The palace?"

"Yes. I met a group of them—her family. They are quite"—he let his gaze skim over her breasts—"uncouth."

It was difficult to tell if Charlotte paled as his innuendo became clear to her. Her skin was naturally milky white, not pure as snow like Abby's complexion, but rather bloodless.

"I will do my best to conceal my displeasure of her," she conceded. "Go on then, get her and hurry back."

Daniel obliged and as he rode toward the front of the line, he was relieved that at least Charlotte wouldn't push Abby into a battle. He saw her a few feet away, her flaxen tendrils blowing behind her. What was his fighting

Highland lass thinking? Thrust into Charlotte's company after a night of ... She hadn't looked at him—at least not when he risked a glance or two to her.

When he reached her, he dismissed Captain Lewis, then moved his mount closer to hers. "We need to speak."

"The Duchess of Blackburn is yer Charlotte," Abby said hollowly. "She is the queen's dearest friend."

"No."

"All she has to do is talk Anne into refusing all my requests, or punishing me ... Or you and the queen will—"

Daniel shook his head. "I, not the duchess, have the queen's ear, Abby. She will bring you no harm. But the duchess will. I have no proof or I would have arrested her long before this, but she has already destroyed the lives of a pair of women I took interest in. Do you understand what I'm saying? If she discovers that we were intimate, she will try to get rid of you."

Abby raised her cool gaze to his and he felt the finality in it. "Then, General, ye had best return to her and leave me in Captain Lewis's hands from today on, fer I fear I could never mask my feelings fer ye."

"Miss Campbell," he said sternly, cantering his horse in front of hers, then turning to block her progress. "If you want to make it back to Skye alive and have a chance to lead your clan, you will."

※

Chapter Twenty-Eight

Stationed at Daniel's side, whether she liked it or not, Abby brooded the entire way to Carlisle. Her foul mood was the result of two things: One being that the Duchess of Blackburn was Daniel's "mad Charlotte," the queen's good friend, despite Daniel's objections. The second reason being that the duchess's laughter was the most annoying sound Abby had ever heard. And the duchess made certain to find everything Daniel said quite amusing.

She didn't offer her attention to Abby once. Abby found her enormously rude. A few times she felt Daniel's eyes on her but she didn't look at him. Better that way.

Och, who would have ever thought the day would be so sour after such an amazing night?

She had awakened from her sleep this morning wearing a smile on her face as memories of the night she spent with Daniel flooded her thoughts. They'd made love, and lots of it, catching an hour or two of sleep here and there. Daniel's sexual appetite was insatiable, and his stamina, as she suspected, was endless. When she had come awake and found him gone, she thought about staying in bed for the rest of the day. She was exhausted and sore. But being alone in their bed made her consider her actions. And she didn't want to consider them.

She wanted to find him and speak to him in the cold light of dawn about what they should do. She didn't want just one night with him. She wanted forever.

But she never got the chance to talk to him. She'd nearly fainted when she saw the regal-looking woman standing at Daniel's side with a dozen soldiers at her back, thinking it was her aunt. She felt like she was descending into hell, for the duchess's eyes burned hotter than the fires between Abby's legs. On her way down, Abby had cursed Daniel for his stamina and prayed she wouldn't tumble down the stairs. After cool introductions, Lady Blackburn had them all moving.

Of all the people in the kingdom—why Charlotte Adler? All of Great Britain knew of the close friendship between the queen and the Duchess of Blackburn. Hell, there was a building being erected for Anne's dearest friend and the duchess's husband not far from the palace. What if the duchess begged the queen to take revenge on the Mac-Gregors for her stealing Daniel away? What would Anne do for her closest friend? How far would she go? If Anne sent her army, possibly led by General Daniel Marlow, to Skye, all would be lost, including her mother, her family.

Their night had come to an end. They'd both known it would. Lord, what was wrong with her? She loved an English general, a Jacobite killer. What would she tell her father? He wouldn't give a rat's arse about her reasons. He'd never let her lead the clan now. How could she be entrusted to guide and protect them, as he did, when she couldn't control her own heart or her body? She could have ruined everything by sleeping with Daniel.

They rode the entire day and reached Pall Mall in London just before nightfall. Daniel helped her dismount, letting his gaze linger on hers as he set her on her feet.

"General," Charlotte called out to him, interrupting Abby's thoughts of how she wished they were different people. "Captain Lewis will escort her from here. Unless," she added when he looked about to protest, "there is another reason you wish to stay so close to her side that you have not shared with me?"

Abby watched him smile—as if he hadn't just given his heart away—and the duchess warming to it.

"What are you implying, my lady?" he asked mildly. "That I would keep things from you? You know how I feel about deceit."

He waited, watching her with a gaze powerful enough to make the duchess squirm. After a moment or two, he took pity on her and turned to Captain Lewis. "Guard her with your life, Captain," he warned Lewis quietly. "If harm comes to her, it will go poorly for you."

Was it wise to appear so concerned in front of the duchess?

"Her death would bring war to our doors."

"Yes, General," Lewis swore, then turned to her, a little colorless. "This way, my lady."

Abby took a step forward, then stopped as a burning pain between her legs gripped her.

"Are you ill, Miss Campbell?" Lewis asked and reached for her when she stumbled a bit to the right.

"I'm fine, Captain." She righted herself. "'Tis just been a long day in the saddle." Her eyes darted to Daniel a few feet away. He was watching with dark, hooded eyes. Then the duchess reached him and coiled her arm through his.

Abby tortured herself watching, and then returned to Captain Lewis.

He showed her into the palace while the duchess went another way with Daniel and some others. Abby craned her neck, watching them, but Captain Lewis patted her shoulder.

"The queen will no doubt send for you soon," he informed her. "She offers you a chance to refresh yourself."

Abby turned to him. "She already knows I'm here?"

"Her majesty knows everything that goes on in her palace."

That wasn't good. Would she see right through Abby's detached veneer to her feelings for Daniel? If so, would she take offense for her best friend, Charlotte?

Captain Lewis seemed nice enough. Dare she question him about the duchess's relationship with Daniel... or with the queen? Probably best not to speak of Daniel at all. She didn't know the people here, and it was wise not to trust anyone either.

"Come, I'll show you to your room."

Abby followed him through the kitchen, looking around as they went. It was much like the kitchen in Camlochlin, save for the flash of silver and bronze cooking utensils hanging up... and the smell of meat cooking. They moved through a series of corridors, all breaking up to lead to different rooms. She followed Captain Lewis to a door set into an alcove at the end of one of the dimly lit halls. She waited a few moments while her escort lit the four wall sconces, two inside the alcove and two on the outer walls.

The entryway brightened considerably, enough for Abby to notice a lock on the outside of the door.

Her heart lurched in her chest. She fought the panic rising up inside her. Would she be locked inside? Was she to be a prisoner? She hadn't allowed herself to think it could be true. Wanting to lead her clan was one thing, actually living it was another. Fear coursed through her and she wondered where her father was. Did her aunt send for her to hold her for ransom against her mother?

She felt ill. Had she been a fool all along to think that her aunt simply wanted assurances that the true heir had no interest in the throne?

"Are you certain you're not ill, lady? You're quite pale."

"She's always pale."

She looked up to find Daniel leaving the shadows of the corridor. Relief flooded through her. She trusted him. What was he doing here? How had he gotten away from the duchess so fast?

He didn't say a word to her but stepped passed her, pressing against her slightly in order to push open the door.

He met and captured her gaze an instant before he moved away from her and into the room. But in that instant she saw his heart in his eyes. He cared for her. And he would keep her safe.

"A grand chamber for a handmaiden," Captain Lewis noted, looking around the room.

He was correct. It was bigger than any room she'd ever slept in before. Everything in it was crafted in the finest wood. Beautiful paintings hung on the paneled walls. The hearth was the only thing not made of wood. It appeared to be set in stone and carved into the busts of horses on either side.

"The queen has indeed been generous to her new handmaiden," Daniel agreed, glancing at her. He seemed, for an instant, to look through her, as if he were looking for secrets.

Two lasses, servants, most likely, hurried into the chamber, apologizing to Daniel and Captain Lewis for not having the room more prepared. Without waiting for any responses, they set about lighting the hearth fire and pouring fresh water into the basin.

Abby looked at the carved four-poster set against the western corner wall. Three steps led up to the elevated mattress, draped in fine linens. It was a fine room. Mayhap a gesture from the queen to gain Abby's trust.

"Do you have everything you need, Miss Campbell?"

She let her eyes drift to Daniel after he spoke. He sounded cool, detached. His eyes, and och, she knew them well, were anything but.

"Aye, General. Fer now."

"Very well then," he said, flicking his gaze away from her. "I'll be close by." He motioned for Captain Lewis to follow him. They left the chamber without another word.

"Captain Lewis smiled at ye!" One of the serving gels giggled to the other. Her friend, set aflame in crimson cheeks and strawberry blond hair, smiled more subtly and slanted her gaze to Abby.

"He was smiling at her, not me."

"No, Jane!" her friend objected.

"I, too, saw him smiling at ye, Jane." Abby climbed up the steps and sat on the bed. "He was being courteous to me, but when ye entered the room, his eyes followed ye only."

Captain Lewis had, in fact, watched Jane while she went about her duties. He watched her friend, as well. Though their resemblance suggested that they might be sisters. Abby didn't mention it, though. She didn't want these gels hating her for no reason other than that Captain Lewis was being nice to her.

"His eyes followed me?" Jane asked rather meekly.

"Aye, they did," Abby said, and Jane's friend agreed. "Is yer heart lost to him? Or are ye simply taken in by his appearance?"

Captain Lewis was a handsome man. He was tall, with gold hair and eyes to match. Aye, he had a nice face, but if the gels giggled over him, what must they think of Daniel? Did she want to know?

"My heart is lost," Jane confessed.

Abby smiled, reminded of her cousin Violet when the lass thought she'd lost her fourteen-year-old heart to Bruce MacDonnell of Glengarry.

"Come." She patted the mattress beside her. "Tell me of him and his ways, and let me see if there is anything I can do to help."

Jane and her friend both cast her a doubtful look.

"How can ye help? What do ye know of men and their ways?" Jane's friend asked.

"Judith, don't be unkind," Jane chastised her gently. "Fergive my sister," she said, climbing the steps to join Abby on the bed. "She's only trying protect me."

"That's a verra' noble trait." Abby turned her kindest smile on Judith and invited her to sit with them.

She listened to an hour-long description of Captain Lewis's best attributes. She learned the subtle nuances of his facial expressions, all memorized and seared into Jane's brain. Throughout the gel's narrative, Abby also discovered that Daniel's captain was a bit of a fox, charming and clever and most likely not in love with Jane.

She didn't lead the poor lass on but she also didn't tell her what she truly thought. She agreed that he likely found her a wee bit young. She being sixteen summers and he, twenty-six.

"Well, Abigail, what should I do?"

"Let me see if I can find oot a bit more, then we shall discuss it further."

The sisters agreed and returned to their duties. But Abby wasn't done listening to what they could tell her.

"And what of General Marlow?" she asked, helping them unpack her bag. "What do ye both think of him?"

"He belongs to the duchess."

He belonged to her. What precisely did that mean?

"He has nae admirers then?" Abby asked them.

"He has many," Judith told her. "But he's Lady Blackburn's and they all know it."

He had told her about this. He was telling her the truth. The women were afraid of her. She should be too.

An hour later, Abby was washed, dried, and dressed, assisted by Jane and Judith, which she found a bit unnerving. She didn't have servants at home and preferred doing things by herself.

"What's she like, the queen?" she asked her new friends.

"She's…" Jane looked at her sister.

"Reserved," Judith finished for her.

"Aye, reserved," Jane echoed. "She's not unpleasant like the duchess, but she's doesn't smile much."

Abby recalled what Daniel had told her about all the queen's lost pregnancies and her son dying at such a tender age. Truly, it was heartbreaking, and despite the power she had over the fate of Abby's mother, Abby felt sorry for her.

"Thank God she has General Marlow," Jane said. "He's like a son to her."

"Aye," Judith agreed. "She loves him above all else."

Chapter Twenty-Nine

She loved him above all else.

Abby tried not to think about Daniel's favor with the queen a little later while he escorted her up a grand, ornately carved staircase leading to the queen's private chamber.

She'd been summoned.

She took a few moments from her anxious thoughts to take in the sight of the palace around her. The walls were painted white with carved gold molding and smaller wrought iron balconies above the staircase. A giant chandelier, crafted in finely ground, high-karat gold over bronze, provided light in the spacious foyer.

"General?" She paused her steps and waited for him to stop. She was glad it was Daniel escorting her. She trusted him.

He turned to look at her and told her everything her heart wanted to know without speaking a single word. Och, how would he hide the expressiveness of his beautiful eyes from the wrong company? And who the hell *was* the wrong company?

Good lord, why did he have to look so extraordinarily handsome—and dangerous—dressed in full army regalia, including his red coat, lined in rich indigo and turned out at the lapels, cuffs, and collar. His lean legs were clad in snug black pants with polished boots reaching to his knees.

"I have a question, which if ye answer truthfully, will give me the courage I need to meet her."

He moved a touch closer to her so she could hear his whisper. "You have the courage it takes to meet ten of her, Miss Campbell."

Courageous enough to tell him she was in love him?

"What is your question, then, my lady, that I might answer it truthfully and convince you?"

She smiled at him. She couldn't help it! They were doomed! Her family was doomed! Unless there was a chance of getting the queen on her side. Anne's favor toward Daniel didn't matter. Daniel's favor toward the queen did. Abby trusted his judgment of character—despite the name he'd earned. He was an honorable man. A true knight of the Garter.

"Is the queen someone ye hold close in yer heart?"

He could have asked her what that had to do with anything, but he didn't. He simply answered her. "Yes, I hold her close."

A difficult spot to earn—close in his heart. Abby knew he didn't give it lightly. It told her much about her aunt. Her smile widened while the rest of her relaxed.

She took the arm he offered and they passed through two other grand halls carpeted in lush crimson to match the velvet-curtained windows and upholstered benches. Huge paintings set in painted gold frames lined the walls. Images of stately men and women whom Abby suspected were her relatives stared back at her as she walked beneath them. Everything was done in grand design, from the thick, round wooden tables, carved and polished to a mirror finish, to the beautifully crafted blue and white vases sitting atop them.

All this could have been her mother's. Hers, someday, if King James hadn't hidden his firstborn in a Catholic abbey after her birth. If Abigail's father hadn't rescued her mother from the abbey as it burned down around her. But what was this beautifully chilling isolation compared to the warm, inviting arms of Camlochlin?

She didn't want any of this, and neither did her mother. She stopped upon coming to two great, wooden doors as something occurred to her.

"Every time anyone speaks of your relationship with Anne, they mention her loving ye like a son. Ye yerself said it. I ask ye now, are ye her son?"

He glanced down at the space between them and then drew in a deep breath. "Are you still expecting truthfulness?"

She resisted the urge to smile at him and nodded.

"Very well then, but I'd like to remind you that I just recently discovered the truth of my birth."

"The truth?" she echoed quietly.

He nodded and knocked on the door. "My father was not who I thought."

"Who was?" Abby asked him.

A woman's voice called from the other side of the door bidding them entry.

Her escort pushed the doors open, then stepped aside, making room for Abby to enter.

"Miss Campbell, Your Majesty."

Och, she would kill him! How could he begin to tell her his secret and usher her into the presence of the queen of Great Britain at the same time? What was he telling her? She couldn't think clearly. Not when she'd just stepped into the same room as the queen.

Drawing in a deep breath, Abby looked up from the marble floor at the queen, who was sitting in a heavily cushioned chair of deep emerald and dark wood. She moved closer and curtsied like a supplicant angel when she reached the queen. Anne looked pleased even while she took in Abby's crown of pale silver.

"Miss MacGregor."

The queen's voice snapped Abby out of the dreamlike state that had come over her, unable to believe that she was truly here, at Anne's feet. She blinked, still staring at the queen. She had been taking in her aunt's melancholy features and didn't find any trace of her mother in them.

"You will need to learn how to behave in public. Let me start you in the right direction. You will not look at me so boldly."

Abby blinked and worried that she'd already found disfavor with the queen. "Fergive—"

"I know you Highlanders are a defiant bunch, but if I'm correct, your mother was raised in an abbey. I know she has taught you deference as well as defiance. Am I mistaken?"

"Nae, Yer Majesty."

"Good. Because we don't want anyone discovering who you truly are, do we?"

Did she mean a possible heir, or a Jacobite outlaw?

"Nae, Yer Majesty."

The queen smiled at her, stilling Abigail with the fathomless shadows in her dark eyes. "Lovely, that's better. Now come, sit with us." She motioned to another chair by the hearth fire. "You know General Marlow, of course. He escorted you to England and insists on escorting you still."

Her narrowed gaze settled on Daniel and he answered

with a slow, subtle smile no woman with blood in her veins could resist. "I'm the only one she's truly safe with. You said it yourself."

"So I did," Anne agreed without the slightest trace of humor and returned her attention to Abby.

"The general was telling me of your journey together," the queen went on. "There were quite a lot of interesting moments between your family and my knight."

Abby looked to Daniel for guidance. His slight smile was a beacon of light in the shadows of the court.

"He proved himself well, Yer Majesty."

Anne smiled ever so slightly and Abby thought she saw the tiniest resemblance to her mother.

"May I ask ye a question?"

The queen nodded and glanced at Daniel while he sat opposite her.

"Do all the doors have locks on them, or just mine?"

Anne laughed softly, but there was nothing delicate in her dark gaze. At least, not unless one looked closer. "All, dear. A widowed queen, especially one with such relentless enemies as the Jacobites, can trust very few."

After that, they spoke of everything, including finding Daniel's soldiers dead and his getting stabbed at the inn. The queen asked her about her feelings for her stepbrother, James Stuart, and what she thought of the palace. The small talk was enjoyable, with her and Daniel almost answering together twice.

Abby discovered her aunt to be a pleasant woman, who found her pleasure in reading and playing chess with General Marlow.

The evening was going well, so it was even more shocking to Daniel when the queen dismissed him, wishing to speak to Abigail alone.

The chamber was silent save for a resounding snap of wood burning in the hearth. Then Daniel moved a step away from the queen's chair. "I'll be outside, Ma'am."

"Now, do tell me," the queen of Great Britain said, turning to Abby the instant Daniel was gone. "Tell me of your mother. Is she a Catholic?"

"Aye, she is."

Anne looked relieved to hear it. Thanks to a law called the Act of Settlement, no Catholic heir could succeed to the throne. There were exceptions, though. Still, so far things were going very well. It seemed that Abby's mother was correct in assuming that all the queen wanted was reassurances.

"Do you resemble her?"

"Some say I do," Abby told her, truthfully.

The queen pinched her lips at her and arched her brow. "Well, it's clear she got the looks in the family."

"Ye're verra' bonny, Yer Majesty."

Anne's faint smile widened a bit as she drifted off into a more pleasant place and time. "I was. A long time ago." She looked up, her smile intact but fading. "Enough about me. Tell me about Davina."

Abby had some questions of her own before she answered. "Why do ye believe she is yer sister?"

Anne eyed her, then shrugged her shoulders, as if coming to a silent conclusion about her niece. "I heard my father speak of her to one of your uncles the night of his coronation. I wasn't sure if she lived. It took me twenty years but I found her. I know I did."

She was correct, Abby admitted to herself. Anne had found her sister.

"To what purpose?"

"You are bold, niece."

"We speak of my mother, Yer Majesty. Let me assure ye, she doesna' want the throne."

"That's nonsense, child." The queen laughed without humor. "Who wouldn't want this life?"

She was indeed rather bonny, Abby thought, looking at her, with chestnut locks coiled about her head and her alabaster skin, free of any powder. There was something about her expression when she wasn't brooding that reminded Abby of her mother—the beautiful curve of her cheekbone and jaw, mayhap, and the confident tilt of her lips.

"My mother wouldna' want it."

"Do you expect me to believe that your mother would prefer the life of an outlaw, who is likely living in a hovel at the cold edge of the world, over all this?"

Abby kept her hands folded in her lap and nodded her head. "'Tis the truth. If ye knew my faither—all my kin— ye would believe me. She is happy with her life."

"She is loved?" the queen asked, sounding a bit distant, like she was somewhere else in the palace.

Abby wondered where. "Aye, she's loved verra' much, and by many."

The queen didn't speak for a moment, and then, still looking off but now with a creased brow, she said in a soft, stifled voice, as if what she was about to say crushed her heart, her soul, "My husband, George, died more than a year ago. Of his love, I was certain. He is greatly missed. There were times when I believed my sister Mary loved me."

Abby smiled and swiped moisture away from her eyes when the queen returned her attention to her.

"I would like some time to get to know you and learn more about my sister in Scotland."

"Whatever Yer Majesty wishes." Abby curtsied.

"You will act as my handmaiden during your stay. It is

the story I told General Marlow, and I wouldn't have him think me dishonest."

Aye, Abby remembered him telling her that the queen had deceived him. She'd seen the result of that deceit. How would he take it when she told her who she really was? *If* she told him?

"Do you understand the duties of a handmaiden, Abigail?"

"Aye, Yer Majesty. I am to remain at yer side as yer companion."

"Correct." Anne examined her from foot to crown, then smiled. "You're not dimwitted, as I was told Highlanders were."

Abby gritted her teeth but managed a smirk and bowed her head to show her thanks. "I'm sure whoever told ye that has never met a Highlander."

"General Marlow has met many. He's killed many too. The Jacobite ones, I mean. Are you aware of this?"

Abby felt sick. "Aye, Yer Majesty. Why do ye bring it up?"

"Your affection for him is apparent."

Abby's heart halted in her chest. No! "Yer Majesty, I—"

The queen held up her hand to stop her. "I understand that he is a good, honorable man, and handsome as well. Desirable to many. But it will end today. If Lady Blackburn discovers these feelings, she'll be quite jealous."

"Then why dinna' ye toss her out and strip her of her title? Why do ye allow her to make Daniel's life miserable? Why, the poor man denies himself love because he too fears Lady Blackburn will take action against any woman in his life."

"Miss MacGregor, you forget yourself," the queen warned.

Abby lowered her eyes and cursed herself for letting her emotions rule her. "Fergive me, Yer Majesty."

Her aunt was quiet for another moment or two, giving Abby enough time to realize she'd just implied that Anne feared Lady Blackburn.

"I see that he shared much with you, Abigail," the queen said, her dark eyes sharp and fathomless in the lamplight.

Abby immediately recognized her error. Before she could think of how to react, Anne continued.

"Does he deny his love for you?"

Abby's heart pounded in her chest. She somehow sensed that much rode on her reply. Anne favored him above all others. She'd heard it from everyone.

Dear God, Abby thought suddenly, feeling sick to her stomach, the queen couldn't know. She couldn't. Abby had to do better here or she'd ruin everything. "He has nae love fer me, dear Aunt. I am a Jacobite. We traveled fer many days with no one else to speak to but each other. So aye, he told me much."

Anne sized her up and then gave her a resigned nod. "I don't know why he continues to even speak to Lady Blackburn."

"Mayhap," Abby offered boldly, "he suspects that pushing her away while continuing his loyalty to ye might put ye in danger from her jealousy."

The queen shook her head. "Lady Blackburn can sometimes be a vindictive wretch, but she wouldn't bring harm to me."

Abby hoped it was true. Anne was her kin. She might be queen, but she didn't seem so bad. Of course, Abby still believed that James Francis should be king, but that didn't mean she wanted her aunt dead to usher him in.

She wasn't a fool to think the danger of her task was

over because her aunt appeared civil. She was in England, in a palace far from home. It didn't matter where her father was. He couldn't do anything to help her without starting a war.

"I'll have you escorted to the Banqueting Hall," the queen told her. "But after we do something about that gown."

Abby blushed. "I didna' have time to get the wrinkles out."

"I'm sure it's lovely without the wrinkles," her aunt said, kindly not mentioning that its style and cut were no longer in fashion. She called for Daniel to fetch Jane and Judith and then see himself to the hall without them.

The queen of Great Britain was going to help dress her. She should be hopping on both feet at the thought of fine silks and satins against her skin.

Instead, she couldn't stop thinking about what the queen would do if she lost the man she considered like a son to her niece.

She was here, representing her clan, her mother. She would honor them and not bring them trouble.

Daniel didn't belong to Charlotte Adler. He belonged to the queen. And that was worse.

Charlotte strode through the halls without an escort. Daniel should have been here but Anne had called him away. Oh, how she hated when Anne stole Daniel from her. Despite her hands wringing her handkerchief at her chest, her gait wasn't hurried or frantic, but always determined wherever she went, whether inside the palace or out.

She tried not to let too many things rattle her. But what was she to think of Anne's new handmaiden? What in damnation did Anne want with a Highlander? Charlotte had seen a few of them before. Guarded, brooding, terrifying men, with whom she never wanted any part. But the girl, Abigail Campbell, was more like a radiant star than a dark threat. She hardly seemed important enough to warrant Daniel's protection, so who was she that the queen would bring her into the palace? The girl could bring danger to Anne, so why had Daniel agreed to bring her here? Heaven forbid any danger should come to his queen. Why, he'd even warned her on a few occasions to watch her step with Anne. Charlotte had merely laughed, but he was serious. He was always serious when it came to Anne.

She wondered what Daniel would do when he discovered that his dear queen had lied to him all his life? Oh, she'd see that he found out the truth. But the timing had to be flawless. And then, while grieving the loss of his father and the trust of his friend, she would comfort him in her bed.

She scanned the faces in the large Banqueting Hall when she reached it. Where was Daniel? Where was Miss Campbell? Were they together? They'd been together for many days, and dear lord, Abigail Campbell was beautiful enough to tempt any man. Even one who swore to hate her.

No. Not Daniel. Miss Campbell might enchant other men, but not Daniel. He was a rock. A man of solid strength and honor and integrity. He couldn't be moved. She knew firsthand, after months of failing to move him. Of course, she hadn't suspected the damned queen to be the one warning him not to sleep with her.

She took her seat, two chairs to the right of the queen's, who would sit at the head, and looked around. When she finally spotted him talking to his friends, the Embrys, she waved her hand to him like one stricken, arrested by the sight of him standing at the entrance, dressed in his high-ranking attire. She hated that he embodied the very essence of masculinity, for it weakened her, and that was not only a pathetic flaw, but a dangerous one as well.

She watched him while he moved toward his chair, the first at Anne's right, a seat of honor; the first at her left was the other. The queen didn't hide her favor toward him, the son she did not bear.

"Where were you?" Charlotte asked him, trying to sound unfazed and unshaken by his absence. "Had I known you were going for a walk, I would have joined you."

He barely looked at her, but reached for his cup. "I was not alone."

"Oh?" She tried not to let him hear the tremor in her voice. "Miss Campbell?"

He shook his head. "I had many questions to put to Captain Lewis about Montagu and Captain Andrews."

"Oh." She let her smile fall on him full force. "You should have asked me about Montagu. I knew he was in Edinburgh. Instead I sat here worried that you had abandoned me for that little trollop."

Daniel flicked his gaze to hers and something scalding hot passed over her. "I thought my lady might be safer without me near."

She blushed. "Feeling amorous General?"

"You could say that," he answered in a low murmur, almost a growl.

He smiled at her and she caught her breath. She understood why Anne didn't hide her feelings. Charlotte was having a hard time concealing hers. He wove a spell with his large, soulful eyes and dashing grin.

"But passionate is a better way to put it."

A tight spell. She didn't intend to let go. Ever.

❊

Chapter Thirty

The last person in the world Daniel wanted to be sitting next to tonight was the Duchess of Blackburn. It was his place, but he didn't want to be here.

With any of them, save Abigail.

Instead of asking Anne about his true father, he'd given her opportunities all day to tell him the truth. She hadn't.

As they had all day, his thoughts returned to Abby. Hell, she was bold and courageous, if not a bit reckless, questioning Anne about locks on her door. Daniel could tell that Anne liked her. He had thought she might. Abigail was open and honest and Anne admired those qualities, as he did.

He'd almost told her about the prince. He'd tell her tonight. He trusted her enough. He loved her more than a lie or a truth.

"Tell me about her."

"Who?" He sipped his wine, then raised his cup to one of his lieutenant friends.

"Miss Campbell," Charlotte said. "Does Anne plan to marry her to someone here? What's her tale?"

He slipped a side glance to her. "Knowing her tale wasn't part of my duty."

"Weren't you curious?"

"No."

"Did she defy you often on your journey?" She glanced at him. "It will tell much about her."

"No," he told her, knowing what she wanted to hear. "And even if she had, what concern would it have been to me? Defiant or not, she was coming with me."

Charlotte smiled and shook her head at him. "Sometimes I wonder if you have a heart, and if you don't, then are you merely charming your way into my decisions, perhaps even into Anne's?"

He laughed. "You put too much in my abilities, Your Grace." He didn't skip a beat, well practiced in the art of directing the path of her thoughts. "If I were heartless, I would have broken either one of your hearts already." He lifted his gaze to the entrance, to Anne being brought in first, pushed in her chair by her new handmaiden.

Charlotte made a sound beside him and Daniel suspected it had something to do with Abby's transformation.

Daniel had known Anne would help with her wrinkled gown, but she hadn't said anything about turning Abby into a princess.

She wore a deep blue sack-back gown made of fine velvet with pleats flowing from the shoulders stitched in cream silk. Her hair was gathered atop her head like a crown of radiant light. Every man in attendance stared at her. Daniel didn't blame them for looking, but he didn't like it. There wasn't anything he could do about it.

Charlotte watched her push Anne to the head of the table and then take her place at the queen's left, opposite Daniel.

"Lady Blackburn," Anne leaned forward in her chair and addressed her friend. "I'm told you met Miss Campbell, my new handmaiden, already when you joined General Marlow on the road after a dream?"

"That's correct," Charlotte told her stiffly "After a prophetic dream. I'm sure he has told you about your cousin trying to kill him."

"Ah, yes, Richard." Anne reclined and waited while her plate was set before her. "What shall I do with him?"

"Let me ride to Edinburgh and kill him," Daniel muttered. "He thinks me dead. He'll never see me coming."

Anne gave him a slight smile and patted his hand. Charlotte watched, pinched lipped. "By the time you get there, he'll be back here. I received a letter from him a short while ago telling me he's returning in the morning. We will discuss what is to be done later, in my private chambers." She gave his hand a loving pat, then asked Abby if she wanted more wine.

"Tell me, Miss Campbell," Charlotte said, looking across the table at her. "How was your journey here from the mountains?"

Daniel looked up and glanced at Abby. He couldn't worry about her. She would do fine with Charlotte, just as long as she kept her feelings for him hidden.

Abby smiled. "Argyll isna' verra' mountainous, Yer Grace. But as fer the journey, 'twas mostly unpleasant and at times, harrowing. I am glad to be here, safe and sound."

Daniel caught his breath again at her grace and beauty and wondered if Anne saw the true elegance of her. None of them had expected to see it in a Highlander. But here she was, as refined and polished as any royal.

"Oh, but that's General Marlow's duty," Charlotte

insisted. "Did he fail at making you feel safe and sound then?"

"Nae, he did not," Abby told her. "He saved my life, but I dinna' like sleeping outdoors. It makes me feel vulnerable."

Against his will, Daniel's eyes found Abby and settled on her. He missed just looking at her, basking in her features and little nuances of emotions like one who revels in a painting by his favorite artist. The outlawed MacGregor's daughter straightened her back and didn't flinch at the duchess's scrutiny.

"He kept me alive on our trek," Abby continued. "He succeeded, though I think there were days when he would have preferred to toss me over the nearest cliff."

There was only one time, Daniel wanted to tell her. He wanted to smile at her and promise her a thousand services, but he didn't. He reached for more wine and kept his gaze off all of them.

"If there is any talk of the general subduing his true opinion of me, let me inform ye here and now that he showed little kindness and even less mercy, complaining when I wept as I left my kin."

The duchess liked what she was hearing. She knew Daniel wouldn't compromise his beliefs completely.

"Yes." She shuddered, touching his biceps, then let it slide down to his hand. "General Marlow is indeed heartless. I was telling him that before you arrived, wasn't I, General?"

"You were," he agreed, his tone, dull and weary.

"Ye were quite correct, Yer Grace," Abby continued, not only stroking Charlotte's pride but waking him from the tedium. "If he is a representative fer knights, then I say that they are the savages."

Daniel tossed her an icy look, then leaned in toward

the duchess. "This is how the entire journey went with her. She complained about everything without ceasing."

"I simply questioned yer decisions," Abby said curtly. "Some of them seemed poorly considered."

"Poorly consid—" She went too far in their little game to say such a thing, even in jest. All right then, if she wanted it real... "Lady," he said, just as crisply. "I very seriously considered leaving you in the last three villages in which we stopped. I didn't do it."

Her pale blue eyes shone on him like frost beneath the full moon. She didn't back down. "Times like now, I wish ye had."

The duchess grinned, happy to see them at each other's throats. Anne's reaction was different. She slapped the table with her palm. "That will be all, both of you! I'll not have bickering at my table. Miss Campbell, General Marlow is a well-respected warrior and servant to the throne. You will not speak so willfully to him again. Do you understand?"

Abby unlocked her gaze from his and he felt the void of her separation, like a drop into a black abyss.

"Aye, Yer Majesty," she surrendered quickly.

"And you, General." Anne turned to him. "Like her or not, you will respect her in my court as my handmaiden and faithful companion."

"How can you say she's faithful, Anne?" Charlotte asked, sounding offended for Daniel's sake. "You don't—"

"Lady Blackburn." Daniel cut her off. "You forget your place. The queen's decisions are hers to make—without question or quarrel from you. Do you not agree?"

To say anything but yes was treason, and he was the highest-ranking officer in the queen's army.

"Of course, General." She relented finally and said

very little the rest of the night. When she finally grew bored enough to leave, Daniel rejoiced at seeing her go.

So, it appeared, did Anne.

The queen covered his hand with hers and smiled at him and then at Abby. "I loved your display. I almost believed it. I certainly enjoyed going along with it."

"What do you mean, you almost believed it?"

"Come now, Daniel." She tossed him an indulgent look. "You forget I know you well. You may have spoken to her with cool detachment, but your eyes said something else. Fear not, Lady Blackburn couldn't see from her position. But I warn you, take care."

"I thought I was," he told her. He wasn't sure if admitting his heart to the queen was wise, since Abby was a Jacobite. He hoped she wouldn't ask about what he felt for the Highlander. He doubted he could deny her. "I'll practice more caution in the future."

Anne didn't question him further, and he was grateful.

"Caution with Lady Blackburn is imperative," she told Abby. "She's a venomous snake who seems to be charmed by Daniel alone."

"Where I grew up," Abby told her, "we cut the heads off venomous snakes."

Daniel reveled in the glorious woman sitting across from him, so bold, so proud. Anne saw her inner strength also and leaned closer in her chair.

"What if the snake has been your friend for many, many years? What if you don't know how cut off her head?"

"Ye're the daughter of kings. Royal blood from William the Conqueror and King Richard the Lionheart flows in yer veins. What is a snake to that?"

Anne's laughter was faint and brief but he heard it. He saw it.

"Not very much when you put it that way, Miss Campbell. I will retire to my chamber and think on it for a bit before I sleep."

She excused herself and left the two of them in the Banqueting Hall with his men and a warning not to tarry for too long.

"Forgive me for not preparing you for this," Daniel said, turning to her.

"I think I did rather well. 'Twas difficult not looking at you," she told him. "I wanted to so many times. I was a coward."

"No." He shook his head at her. "You're wise, and clever, and courageous. I believe the duchess may have had at least one woman I knew murdered."

He hated frightening her, but she needed to know what she was up against.

"I don't have the proof I need to arrest her, and even after everything, the queen wants proof."

Abby smiled. "She's fair."

"Yes." Daniel was tempted to leave his chair and kiss her senseless for seeing it as he did. "She is."

Chapter Thirty-One

Abby and Daniel obeyed the queen's quiet command and didn't remain at the table too long. She'd agreed with Daniel that for now, for all their sakes, they needed to keep their hearts in their chests and not on their sleeves. She could do it. She just wasn't sure how long she could keep it up.

She also didn't know why she'd been called to the queen's private rooms this morning, or why Daniel was here looking especially dangerous, hanging back in the shadows with an older man at his side. Judith was here, as well, tending to the queen, along with a male servant waiting to wheel the queen's chair if she wanted to be moved.

Another beautiful gown had been waiting for her this morning, neatly arranged on her bed when she woke up. Abby had simply stared at it for a while before lifting it into her arms. She'd never seen such fine fabrics, such delicate stitching, as on the gowns worn here at the palace. This one was crafted of embroidered damask silk, dyed robin's egg blue and shot through with gold thread. Thank heavens for Judith and Jane, else she never would have been able to wear it. It took both lasses to help her dress. An over-gown was pinned over the stiff corset to show the stomacher and gathered back at the hips to show the embroidered petticoat. Lace frills on the shift flirted at her neck and wrists.

"You won't kill him, Daniel," the queen said in a soft voice rather than a commanding one, pulling Abby's thoughts back to the present.

"Not unless he put your lives in danger."

Abby surmised that Richard Montagu must have returned from Edinburgh and he was about to discover that his plans had failed.

"If he is guilty, he will hang for treason. But he is my cousin."

Abby felt sorry for her, thinking that the queen's own blood relative would betray her. Davina MacGregor was fortunate indeed to have escaped this life.

Soon, they all heard the sound of Montagu's arrival outside.

Daniel didn't move but remained still where he was. Abby never wanted to be his enemy.

"Just let me question him, Daniel."

"He will not confess and hang," Daniel disagreed from the shadows.

They waited to see if he was correct. But the queen's cousin never arrived at her chamber door. He'd returned to the palace and then left again for no apparent reason.

Save one. Charlotte Adler told him that Daniel was alive and waiting for him in the queen's rooms. It had to have been Charlotte!

"She warned him," Abby thought out loud.

Anne eyed her, considering it, then said, "Judith,

Albert." She waved her servant and Daniel's valet over and commissioned them to find out where the Earl of Manchester was.

While they waited, Daniel left the shadows and came toward them. Abby felt her blood go warm, along with her skin. He was tall, lithe, and perfectly capable of protecting them against Montagu, or anyone else, but Abby didn't want him to be in any danger. She didn't want him to risk a musket ball to his heart or a dagger to his lung. What was she going to do without him when she returned home and he remained here to serve his queen?

"Miss Campbell is correct," he told the queen. "Someone warned him. I'm not certain, though, if it was Lady Blackburn. That would mean she was behind him in all of this, and I don't believe she would sit idly by and let him murder me."

"I agree," the queen said. "Besides, we don't even know where he went. Let us get all the facts."

She didn't want to believe her own cousin would betray her. Abby understood, but her aunt had to maintain her mettle. She could and should listen to her heart, but she shouldn't follow it blindly.

Later, when the facts came in that Richard Montagu had run off, Anne could no longer deny his guilt and issued a decree for his arrest and capture.

Daniel led the charge but Montagu seemed to have left the kingdom entirely. They knew he was hiding, but where and what were his plans?

"Charlotte told me years ago to keep him out of court," the queen told Abby that night while they rested together in Anne's private solar after supper. "I didn't want to think he was dangerous, but now I see she was correct. But to go after Daniel, my dearest, most trusted friend.

How could Richard claim to care for me and then try to take the one person I haven't lost away from me?"

Abby listened, as was her duty as the queen's handmaiden to do. But she felt terrible. She was as bad as Montagu. Didn't she too, want to take Daniel from Anne? Didn't she want him to give up all for her and come to Camlochlin to be with her forever?

"It makes me wonder what else Charlotte was correct about."

No. Abby may have thought they were still friends, but after seeing Charlotte Adler's blatant animosity toward Anne over the last two days, Abby no longer entertained that notion. "I dinna' think Lady Blackburn has yer best interests at heart."

"Oh, I know that, dear," the queen said softly, making Abby loathe the thought of hurting her even more. "I just don't know what she wants—besides Daniel, I mean. Richard likely wants the throne. He must never find out about your mother."

Abby shook her head. Never! "My father would kill him and then likely start a war with all of England if she were harmed."

Anne smiled for the first time that day. "Tell me of your father, this man who took a princess from the king and lives to tell of it."

"He tells no one, Yer Majesty. Och, but I do wish you could meet him. Then ye would understand why my mother wants to remain where she is. She never wanted this life. When we were children, she used to tell us about her life at the abbey and how she would pray fer her faither to come to her. She didn't understand why her parents left her to be raised with nuns. She never saw the outside of the abbey until she was a woman, but she had a good life; until her enemies came for her and burned doun the abbey. My faither saved her life and pulled her from the ashes."

"Did he know who she was?"

"Nae, she didna' tell him the truth until they were almost home."

"I remember my father weeping over the fire at St. Christopher's Abbey," the queen told her, reminiscing about that night. "Do you know if my father knew that his firstborn daughter didn't perish in the fire?"

"He knew," Abby told her. "He visited her a number of times."

Anne smiled retrospectively. "He never told us of her. He kept her well protected."

"There was no reason to tell anyone of her. She never wanted the throne. She wasna' raised fer it. She chose to stay with my faither and to be loved beyond measure by him and her new family."

"But, Abigail, you are young. You don't understand. This is her birthright. You said yourself she never saw the outside of the abbey until she was a woman. She went from one seclusion to another. If she came here, she might want to stay."

Abby shook her head. This was why she came to England. This was her chance to convince her aunt that her claim to the throne was safe, at least from Davina MacGregor. "There is nothing here she would want, save mayhap to know ye."

"To know me?" her aunt echoed, sounding almost wistful. Abby suspected she was quite lonely. "Does she have no one else to share her life with besides her husband and children? You mentioned your uncles. Do they not have wives?"

"They do, and they all love my mother verra' much. But you are her sister by blood. She wanted to come here to meet you, but my faither was afraid to let her come. We didna' know what her reception would be like."

Anne nodded. "You said in your letter that she was ill."

"We almost lost her," Abby told her. "But my faither wouldn't let death take her either."

"He sounds like an amazing man," the queen finally admitted.

Abby opened her mouth to agree that he was when Daniel entered the solar like a whirlwind and made her forget everything else. He had been out all day searching for Montagu. It was clear by the storm brewing in his eyes that he hadn't found him.

"Someone is hiding him." He moved about the chamber like a plague, dark and dangerous. "I should have been waiting for him at the entrance to the palace this morning, not hiding in the shadows."

"Did any of the men speak to him?" the queen asked him while he paced.

"No. I questioned all of them. Whoever warned him did so away from any witnesses. Of course, some of them could be lying."

"Have ye questioned Lady Blackburn?" Abby asked him, then hated herself for letting her thoughts take her to his bed. She missed his mouth on her, passionate and hungry for her. She missed his gaze studying her in the firelight. Hell, she missed sleeping outdoors with him. He hardly smiled at all since returning to England. He seemed more haunted, more troubled here. And why shouldn't he be? He had an enemy at court...an enemy who was getting aid from someone close to him.

"She claims to know nothing."

"And ye believe her?"

He looked up from pouring himself a drink. "I've no reason not to. She doesn't want me dead."

No, but she did want him in her bed.

Abby knew she was terrible for thinking it, but she wished Lady Blackburn were behind everything so the queen could toss her in prison and they could all be done with her.

"It isn't that I trust her," Daniel explained to her while he fell into a chair close to both women. "I know she wouldn't do anything to cause me harm."

"What about the queen?" Abby asked him. "Would she do anything to cause the queen harm?"

Daniel stared at her for a moment, boldly too, as if he hadn't considered every possibility.

The queen answered before he did. "I've known Charlotte for many years. She was a servant in my sister's house when Mary and William ruled. She has become more antagonistic toward me over the years, it's true, but she would never cause me physical harm."

Abby sighed. Mayhap they were correct. They did, after, all, know the duchess better than she did.

"I'll question her again later." Daniel finished off his drink in two swigs, then stared into the flames of the hearth. "Perhaps there's something I've missed."

Later? Later when? Was he planning on spending more of the evening with Lady Blackburn? Abby didn't like it, and she liked it even less that there was nothing she could do about it. He still hadn't explained to her what he meant about his father. And what did it have to do with Anne loving him like a mother? Was he suggesting that Anne was his stepmother? If so, that would make him the son of Prince George. Had Anne kept it from him all his life? Poor Daniel. Most of what he did, he did for Anne. He was dedicated to the throne, to Anne herself. Her deceit must have nearly destroyed him. She remembered how somber he was when they first met.

He didn't seem to be angry with Anne and Abby admired him for seeing that the queen might be powerful but she was also heartbroken and lonely. Abby loved Daniel even more for the way it affected him.

She studied him in the firelight illuminating the solar. His glorious eyes, usually so vivid and fiery, were cast in shadows. He'd avoided eye contact with her all day and it was driving Abby mad. She knew he barely spoke to her in obedience of the queen's request, and to keep Abby safe, but knowing it didn't make it any easier.

"Let us forget Charlotte for now—and Richard, as well," Anne suggested. "It's been a very taxing day and I wish for some peace."

Daniel nodded, but he didn't look any less frustrated. His enemy had escaped him and it was eating away at him.

"Abigail." The queen turned to her. "Pour me a drink, will you? There's something I'd like to say." She smiled faintly when Abby rose to her task. "Daniel," Anne said to him next. "Did you know that Miss MacGregor's mother is recovering from an illness that almost took her from the world?"

"Yes," he said, finally looking at Abby. "Miss MacGregor has told me much about her family."

"Oh?" Anne raised an eyebrow at him.

"It was a long journey," he explained. His regard, though brief, was as palpable as a touch. "Miss MacGregor shared much of her life with me."

"Yes." The queen accepted the cup Abby handed her and surprisingly downed its contents. "So I was already told."

On the way back to her seat, Abby paused at the queen's words.

"I wish you had met her, Daniel. There's so much I still want to know about her."

"Who?" Daniel asked her.

"Miss MacGregor's mother," the queen told him as Abby turned around, a sick, sinking feeling washing over her. What was Anne doing? Why did she bring up her mother to Daniel? What would he do? What would he think of her for deceiving him? Abby wanted to speak but her throat felt as if it were closing up on her, suffocating her. She took a step back to the queen's chair, her hand outstretched as if that alone could silence the queen of England.

"Or, as we would know her if circumstances had been different, Davina Stuart—my eldest sister."

Chapter Thirty-Two

This wasn't really happening. Daniel looked at both women and ran his hand down his face. Davina MacGregor was a Stuart? Anne's eldest sister... Hell, no, this wasn't happening. It couldn't be. It meant that he'd been deceived by a woman yet again. And not about anything minor. No, falling in love with an enemy was one thing, with an heir to the British throne was quite another.

"You're not the true queen?"

"Aye, aye! She is!" Abby answered for her. "My mother wants nothing to do with—"

"Enough!" he shouted, quieting her. He needed to leave. To think. First Anne. Now Abby.

He left the room and walked the halls of St. James's Palace not really knowing where he was going. How could everything change in one moment? More lies! God help him, he'd known Abby wasn't telling him something. But this? Her mother was Anne's sister? He shook his head, hoping the movement would jar him awake from this dream. It had to be a dream. James II didn't have three living daughters. He had two, Mary and Anne. Davina

MacGregor was a Highland Jacobite, not the true queen of Great Britain! This was madness!

He stormed down the stairs. Someone was deceiving them. He was going to find out who. What if it was Abby? Dear God, don't let it be Abby! Perhaps it wasn't, he tried to convince himself. Perhaps her family had lied to her.

He laughed at the madness of it, but even as he did, he recalled the secrets she'd almost exposed, like the name of her home. What was it? Ah, yes, Camlochlin. She'd begged him, after that name slipped from her lips, not to use anything she told him against her family. Did the true heir to the throne live at Camlochlin?

And when she was half asleep and told him her mother didn't want to be queen. He'd thought she was dreaming. Why would her mother ever consider being or not being queen?

Hell.

He recalled how she'd grown so stiff and tense in his arms when he'd asked her about her maternal grandfather. Was that because her grandfather was King James II?

No.

His gut twisted into a knot that produced a bitter taste in his mouth. He shook his head, trying again to clear his thoughts. She'd lied to him.

That's why she was so adamant about knowing James Francis Stuart was the king's true son. Did her family know him personally?

No. It would all mean that Anne wasn't...

What if Rob MacGregor wrote to Anne claiming he was wed to her long-lost sister and Anne had fallen for it and sent for her? What if it was all a plan to plant a spy in the queen's midst? The Jacobites would have succeeded.

He turned around and looked back up the stairs.

Was Abby sent to get close to the queen and perhaps... kill Anne? The MacGregors were, after all, likely in England already, just waiting...

He bolted up the staircase, taking the steps three at a time. It was a brilliant plan and it could be taking place this very moment while Abby was alone with the queen, trusted and unguarded.

He sprinted to the solar door and pushed it open when he reached it. He didn't know what he expected when he plunged inside. He was relieved to see the queen sitting where he'd left her, alive and scowling at him.

He let his gaze slide to Abigail, his sour insides showing in his expression. "Get up. You're coming with me."

"Where?"

"To prison if I had any sense!"

She blinked at him, then glanced at the queen, who immediately took up for her.

"Daniel, why are you talking about prison with Miss MacGregor? She couldn't tell you who she was."

He stopped and turned to her. His queen. "And you couldn't tell me either."

"I did tonight," Anne defended herself.

Daniel wanted to shout at her. He wanted to demand an explanation about his own genealogy. But the truth about him would have to wait. First, he wanted the truth about Abby.

"I wish to question Miss MacGregor about why she's really here."

"Then go right ahead," the queen allowed.

"Alone."

"Yer Majesty," Abby beseeched. "Let me go with him and explain before he believes me to be yer enemy."

"Nonsense." Anne threw up her hands. "Daniel, leave my niece to me."

He laughed without any mirth and shook his head. "No one in this woman's family shares your blood."

Abby finally rose from her chair, her eyes cooling to a frosty blue. "Why are ye so sure aboot that, General?"

Odd that she didn't ask him *how* he was sure. But then he understood her question when she spoke again.

"We're outlaws and outcasts with no right to a place close to the throne. Is that not correct?"

"It may be," he told her, unfazed by her unforgiving tone. "You're also a supporter of James Francis Stuart. Killing the queen would make room for him—or for your mother, who claims to be the rightful heir."

He should have expected Abby to react poorly to his words. It was a hurtful thing to say, but possibly true. Still, he hadn't quite expected the strike of her palm to sting so sharply and split his lip.

He also should have known that Anne wouldn't tolerate it. Immediately, she shouted for the guards and ordered them to escort Miss Campbell to her room. She cut him off when Daniel protested, ready to dismiss his men and escort Abby himself.

"You will remain here with me, Daniel," she demanded. "Judith will see to your lip. There are things I would have you know."

Now? he thought angrily. What would she explain? Abby's secret or her own? Whatever it was could wait. What was another day or two?

He moved to go toward Abby, but she stopped him, her gaze hard and shadowed by hurt and insult. He met her angry glare with one of his own. She was the queen's niece! Her mother was King James's true firstborn! A thought flashed across his mind and made him break out in a cold sweat. If all this was true it would mean his loyalties had been given to the wrong person.

What would he do?

"I want an explanation!" he demanded, taking Abby's arm.

She settled her murderous glance on his fingers holding her, and then yanked away from him. "Unless ye want me to smash something over yer head on the way to my room—and get me hanged—'tis safer fer both of us if Captain Lewis accompanies me from now on."

Damn her for being angry with him when he was angry with her. He wanted answers, but he would let her go and wait. Perhaps he should return to Spain and forget this lifetime.

He couldn't.

He was in love with a fiery Jacobite princess who was in more danger now than ever before.

He wiped the blood from his mouth and released her. For now.

"Sit down," Anne said when they were alone.

He flicked his gaze to her, then returned to his cup. "I'd rather not."

"I could command it," the queen threatened haughtily.

"Yes, you could," he said, pouring himself another drink. "You could also have told me the truth about many things, one being this drivel, when the MacGregors first contacted you. I could have ended this earlier."

"They didn't contact me. It was I who found them."

She told him everything then, from hearing her father's confession to a MacGregor, who later became her father's closest friend, to tracking her sister down through various, unsuspecting sources, like her cousin Admiral

Connor Stuart. She didn't know where exactly on Skye her sister lived. The MacGregors kept to themselves and preferred to keep it that way.

Daniel knew where exactly.

"This is difficult to believe." What else could he say but the truth? "You say Davina was raised in a Catholic abbey, so she's no threat to the throne."

The queen worried her brow and shook her head. "I would agree if I had an heir. But like my sister Mary, I am going to die without a child. Miss MacGregor assures me that my sister wants no part of the throne. She claims her mother is very happy with her husband on Skye, but what am I to believe?"

For a moment, Daniel imagined what it would be like to be wed to a woman who would give up the throne for him. No wonder Rob MacGregor fought death for his wife and won. A love so true and loyal was not easy to find, and was something Daniel highly valued.

"I believe the MacGregor chief and his wife still share much love," he said. "But what if he wants to rule with his wife? If they succeed in a Jacobite revolution, the Act of Settlement will mean nothing."

Anne smiled at him. "That's what I have you for, Daniel. You won't let the Jacobites have their revolution."

He didn't return her smile but looked away, into the fire. "It would be easy for her to kill you."

"Do you honestly think she would try?"

He drew in a gusty breath, then guzzled his drink. "No, but I've learned that even the ones we think we know the best are capable of deceiving us."

She caught his meaning that he meant her. Would she finally tell him? "Oh, so you think I deceived you because I didn't tell you who she was?" She didn't wait for him to answer. "Why do you feel entitled to know the truth about her? Has she become more meaningful to you?"

He looked toward the door, then pinned Anne with a hard look. "What she means to me is not a topic for concern. What is, though, is why you think it's all right to keep the truth from me? You're supposed to trust me, Anne... with your life."

"I do," she insisted, sounding insulted. And no matter what Anne Stuart had gone through in her life, she wouldn't be insulted. "But that doesn't mean I have to tell you everything," she told him haughtily.

"You're quite correct, it doesn't." He rose from his seat and smoothed the wrinkles from his uniform. He bowed and the headed for the door. When he reached it, he turned to her again. "But you should have told me that your husband, the prince, was also my father."

He left her and shut the door behind him. He hoped Anne would consider telling him everything after having a few hours to think it over. Right now, he was eager to speak with Abigail and headed for her room. What was he going to say to her? She was a princess! She'd known it all along. Every time he called her an outlaw, she knew. When he refused to sleep in a barn and she was perfectly happy to do so, she knew. Everything she accused him of before she left the solar with Captain Lewis tonight was true. He'd looked down on her and on her family as if they were truly the savages they were rumored to be. He was angry with himself because of it, but he was angry with her too for deceiving him.

What would he do if she had come here to hurt Anne and make room for her mother? Would he throw her in prison? Could he? He needed to talk to her and find out her purpose. He would decide what to do later.

When he reached her door, he knocked and waited to hear her quiet voice before he entered.

She was sitting on her bed, alone in her room, with her pillow clutched in her arms. When she saw him, she shoved it away and sprang to her feet.

"If ye're not here to beg my forgiveness, get out."

He ignored her outburst and stepped inside, closing the door behind him. He wasn't going anywhere until he found out the truth.

But hell, she looked so damned beautiful standing there, her pale tresses falling over her shoulders, loose tendrils eclipsing eyes as welcoming as glaciers, ready to go toe-to-toe with him in battle.

"Why did you come here?" he asked her in a wooden tone and with a cold look to match hers.

"I was invited."

"What's your purpose in befriending Anne?"

She raised a sharp brow. "Should I consider her my enemy?"

"Abby," he said, sounding annoyed. She didn't blink. "What did you hope to gain by answering her invitation?"

Instead of answering his question, she folded her arms across her chest and continued to stare at him with fury in her eyes. "That doesna' concern ye. I dinna' know why the queen told ye aboot my mother. Her identity has nothing to do with ye."

"It has everything to do with me," he argued. "I'm to keep the queen safe—"

"From Jacobites!"

"From whoever poses a threat to her well-being!"

"That isna' me." She glared at him.

He noted a sheen of moisture making her eyes sparkle like jewels. Damn it all to hell, were those . . . tears? He'd made her cry? He wasn't a fool. He knew some women and the wily tactics they used to get what they wanted, but Abby wasn't one of them—and knowing it made him feel worse.

"I came here to protect my mother," she told him defiantly.

"Protect her from what?"

Finally a tear slipped down her face. She swiped it away angrily. "From men like ye."

✢✣✢

Chapter Thirty-Three

What the hell is that supposed to mean?" Daniel demanded, looking more shocked and stung than Abby had ever seen him.

She turned away from him and looked into the fire. She didn't want to be having this conversation with him. Mayhap ever. She was furious with the queen for telling him. She had no right to put Davina in such danger! No one knew how a fiercely loyal general of the queen's entire army would react to such news.

And Daniel hadn't reacted well.

Part of Abby understood his shock and dismay at discovering such a secret, but that gave him no right to insult her kin, especially her mother.

Was he a danger to Davina MacGregor now?

His voice broke through her thoughts and dragged her back to the present. "Why does your mother need protection from me?"

"Ye're a soldier."

"I wouldn't hurt her."

She turned again to look at him, hating herself for

becoming such a quivering, tearful mess. "Soldiers killed her entire family before my faither brought her to Skye."

"I thought her family was the Stuarts."

She shook her head. "They were the nuns her faither, the king, left her with when she was an infant. Nuns who raised her and loved her like their own child." She'd never told anyone what she was telling him. Only a few in Camlochlin knew Davina's true identity. It felt good to get it all out, to stop living in fear of the world finding out. "There were twenty-six of them," she went on, not caring about the stray tears spilling from her eyes. Daniel knew the truth and if he was going to do anything about it, she wanted to know now rather than later. "They were all killed by soldiers just like ye, loyal to their duty to rid the world of a Catholic monarch. But they didna' have to kill all her sisters because she didna' want the crown then and she doesna' want it now! She wants a quiet life with my faither and me and my brothers. Why can ye all not understand that?"

Daniel didn't answer her but kept his gaze on the ground while she continued.

She told him how the queen had invited her mother to England and how her father wouldn't let her go. None of them trusted the English. "They feared the invitation might be a ruse to get my mother here and kill her, but—"

"And yet they let you come in her place?"

"I insisted. My mother and I believed the queen just wanted assurances that no one was interested in deposing her. My plan was to come here and convince my aunt of the truth. Besides, the queen threatened to send her armies to Skye if we refused her. I couldn't let my kin die because I was a coward."

She wanted him to believe her. If he didn't, she would never forgive him. Why wasn't he saying anything?

"What is it, Daniel?" she asked softly, in a shaky voice. "Are ye angry to discover that the peasant is truly a princess?"

He shook his head, offering her a look so replete of yearning she closed her eyes to keep from flinging herself into his arms and forgiving him anything.

"I thought of you as a princess from the first time I laid eyes on you. Abigail . . ."

"And you, Daniel? Are you a prince?"

When he didn't answer her, she waved him away. "Please, just go." She turned away, not wanting to see him or think about what he meant to her, and how there could never be anything between them. "Ye delivered me safely to the queen, Daniel. Yer duty is done. There's nothing more fer us to discuss anymore."

"Like hell there isn't," he argued. "I understand that you thought I might harm your mother. But you know me now, Abby. You know me better now. Why did you keep this from me even after we—"

"Cease!" she cried out. His words were painful to her. She loved him too much for them not to be.

"No!" He came to her and took her by the arms. "Look at me, Abigail!"

She did, and was sorry she obeyed. His glorious eyes spoke to her. Even if he never uttered another word to her, she would have known she broke his heart just by gazing into his eyes.

"I kept a truth from you, Abigail. One I haven't yet confirmed. You, on the other hand, are James the Second's granddaughter. I've spent years fighting men who believe Anne is not the true queen. I've killed hundreds! How am I not supposed to be angry with you for not telling me?"

Aye, she'd lied to him. She hadn't trusted him. But

how could she? How could she trust an English soldier—a general bound to protect his queen—with the truth about her mother? She'd kept the truth from him and her secret was too big. Already he believed her motives were corrupt.

"This never had anything to do with ye," she told him softly, honestly. "I came here to help my mother and my kin. I came to keep them safe, not to care for the queen's right-hand man."

"Is that all I am?"

"Aye." She nodded, doing her best not to fall apart and weep like a sick fool. "Yer duty is yer life. 'Tis one of the first things I learned aboot ye, General. But ye're correct, I do know ye better now. I know that the queen is yer beloved friend, even more, I suspect. If she decides that my mother is her rival, ye will do all ye can to keep her from being deposed."

When he didn't answer she pushed away from him, breaking his hold on her, and went to stand by the door. She opened it and waited for him to leave.

He turned to watch her and simply stared at her as one moment blended into the next, tearing her heart from its place.

"Just go."

He came toward her and paused in front of her. He said nothing, but his breath echoed through her ears—ragged, short, painful.

They'd been fools, living in the false confidence of love and passion, not thinking clearly about the future.

A future that, for them, did not exist.

The queen woke early the next morning and refused to see anyone but Daniel. She'd lain awake all night thinking about what he said before he'd left her. He knew. He knew that George was his father. Charlotte must have told him.

Anne should have been the one to do it. He had a right to know, but she dreaded the task. He would leave, go off to Denmark to meet his royal relatives. Every year that she didn't tell him made doing so even harder. She had to tell him now.

Unfortunately, he had left the palace before the sun rose and hadn't yet returned. She thought of sending for Abigail, then decided against it. How much could she trust her niece? Not much, if the girl was anything like the hundreds of others who'd served Anne over the years. They all wanted something from her. None of them could be trusted. Charlotte was the best example of this. A friend for more than a decade, closer than a sister, and in the end, even Charlotte had her own agenda. To bear Daniel's child and claim that the babe was royal.

Heavens, Davina Stuart was wise if she truly wanted no part of the monarchy. Why in blazes did Anne cling to it?

It was all she had left. What would she do if she were deposed and cast off to France? She supposed she could return to her childhood home, the Château de Colombes near Paris. Perhaps she could even reunite with her cousin Connor Stuart, who still resided in France. He'd always been kind to her, and Lord help her, but the last time she saw him, she decided he was quite possibly the most handsome man in the country. But what would he want with her? She couldn't walk. She couldn't bear any children, and she had lost her looks years ago. Not that she was ever a beauty like her niece, and probably her sister.

No. The throne was all she had. She had to protect it from Catholics. Hadn't she forsaken her own father and stepmother because they clung to their outlawed religion? She'd given up so much. She couldn't give up anything else.

With nothing else to do with her morning, and with no one she wanted to spend it with, she ordered her one-horse chaise be prepared for her. The single carriage gave her the freedom she so desired to move about without anyone's aid. She often rode like one escaping the chasm of hell, speeding toward the light of something unseen— something that gave her what little joy she had left.

She waited quite patiently while her sedan chair was prepared and four of her servants carried her outside to her beloved chaise.

On the way out she saw Charlotte, but ignored her when the duchess offered her company. Her chaise was built for one. She was going to ask Lady Blackburn to leave the palace for good. But not now. Now, she wanted to run.

She wondered, while she was being secured into her cushioned seat and wrapping the reins tightly in her hands, where was her niece? Were Abigail and Daniel together? Something most surely had passed between them on their journey to England. Did Daniel care for Abigail MacGregor—a Jacobite? Finding out the truth about her last night had certainly sent him into a tail-spin. Anne guessed it would have for anyone, but there was something else. They looked at each other like they shared deeper things than Daniel shared even with her, his queen. What if he had lost his heart to her? And what if losing his heart to Abigail took him from his duty? From her?

With the thought of her only true friend leaving her, Anne Stuart cracked her whip against her horse's flank and took off in a flurry of curses and dust.

Usually, Anne stayed on her estates, but this morning she was especially reckless and careless, and after evading her guards, she rode off into the countryside to try to enjoy the day by herself.

She rode hard for over a quarter of an hour. The wind in her hair felt glorious and pulled tears from her eyes. It was the closest she had come to running in the last twelve years. She urged her horse to go faster, and leaving her troubles behind, she gave a shout and began to laugh.

Her delight quickly turned to terror when her horse collapsed suddenly and her chaise flew in midair over the fallen mount. She didn't have time to scream as her body left her seat and landed with a sickening crunch on the ground. She didn't stop rolling until she'd turned over six times, bones cracking beneath her. Finally she came to a complete stop and lay in the dirt for what seemed an eternity, until she heard another horse galloping toward her.

Help had arrived. Thank God, she managed a quick prayer and promised to pay whoever had come to her aid handsomely. She tried to move, but it was no use. So she waited, listening to her rescuer dismount.

"Yer Majesty," came a lilting male voice. "So sorry I had to shoot yer horse, but I was aiming fer ye. Damn ye fer riding so swiftly."

Anne swallowed back the sheer panic rising up in her throat. Who was it? She didn't recognize the voice. Why? Why would he try to kill her?

She tried to ask him, but she couldn't form the words. Her thoughts began to fade.

But not before he knelt down in front of her face and smiled. Beneath his leather tricorn hat, his dark eyes penetrated her very soul.

"Cameron MacPherson, Yer Majesty," he introduced himself. "And this"—he grinned and pulled a pistol from his belt and pointed it at her face—"is only slightly personal."

Chapter Thirty-Four

I think she's comin' to."

"We should keep her asleep. We're running oot of herbs."

"What would ye have me do, Tristan? Hit her over the head with the back of m' sword?"

"Nae, Will, though a hilt to *yer* temple would give me great pleasure."

Asleep. Then she wasn't dead. Anne tried to open her eyes but it was no use. She could move nothing. Perhaps she was dead and in hell. Some would say she deserved to be in that fiery place, but hell didn't smell like leather and peat, did it?

She tried to remember what had happened to her. Most of it was a blur but...her horse. Someone had killed her horse. Someone had tried to kill her.

Flashes of a man's face flitted across her mind. Dark eyes shadowed beneath the brim of a hat.

A lilting voice.

The barrel of a pistol.

She moaned. It sounded terrified, even to her own ears.

"There now, Yer Majesty," a voice said above her. Was it the voice of the man who had been about to shoot her in the face earlier? "Ye're safe now."

Safe? Where was she? The ground beneath her felt unusually soft. Was she in a bed? Who moved her inside? Why couldn't she feel anything? She wanted to lift her hand to her face to know if she still had a face, but she couldn't move her arms.

"My faither said we should no' speak to her, Uncle."

"Adam," replied his uncle, "one day ye'll have to make decisions fer yerself or yer sister will surely take yer birthright."

Someone laughed, then swore, and finally went silent when the one called Tristan admonished him.

Who were they? Why did they want her dead? She thought about weeping but then decided against it. She was the queen. She didn't weep in front of her enemies.

She thought about Daniel as she drifted off. He would find her and he would kill these bastards and then bring her home.

She didn't wake up until some time later. By then, whatever herbs her captors had given her had worn off, leaving every bone in her body in terrible pain.

She hated herself for doing it, but she wept. She just couldn't help it. She was certain she was dying, or going to die at the hands of these men.

"Why?" she whispered, barley managing that.

At first, no one answered her. But then, someone moved closer to her. Warmth from his body seeped into her and for a moment she welcomed his presence.

"Drink this," his deep voice commanded softly.

She moved her head away and tried to shake it. Was it poison? Would they stop at nothing?

"Come now, Yer Majesty," the voice said, sounding strangely comforting. Like a sorcerer's whisper it made her want to obey. "'Tis whisky and 'twill help yer pain."

Oh, she needed something to help with the pain. She tried to lift her head and then flinched when his big, rough hand slipped beneath her nape. He lifted her just a bit and she parted her lips and drank from his cup. While she did, she lifted her lids and got a good look at him.

She'd never seen him before. She would have remembered if she had. His chestnut hair was lightly dusted at the temples with gray. A little longer than shoulder length, it was tied neatly back at his nape. He looked to be about her age, in his mid-forties, give or take, with a very slightly crooked nose and extraordinarily beautiful eyes painted in shades of green and gold. She remembered eyes like his from somewhere, but she couldn't place them. He smiled and a single dimple in his cheek beguiled her senseless.

"A bit more then, aye?"

His voice was so tender that it almost made her weep again. No one had been this nice to her in years, save Daniel.

Where was Daniel?

"Who are you?" she asked in weak whisper.

"I'm called Tristan."

Another man spoke his name in a warning above them. This one was more commanding, not as friendly. Anne glanced up at him standing a few inches away. My, but he was huge. A Highlander, judging by his size and the great belted plaid he wore...they all wore plaids, draped around their bodies.

"Easy, Rob," Tristan said. "I'm no' a fool."

"She's been through much. Let her rest fer now," the one called Rob said.

"Why...are you trying...to kill me?" she managed. Whatever was in that whisky worked quickly at numbing her pain. Her spirits actually felt a bit better as well.

Rob yanked a chair away from the wall and set it down beside Tristan. He stared at her with eyes the same shade of blue as a painting she'd seen once of the Mediterranean. His hair was shorter than Tristan's and darker, almost black but for streaks of silver shot through.

"This is Rob." Tristan introduced him with a dashing smile Anne would have found most enthralling if she weren't their captive. "My brother."

Yes, she saw the resemblance. What did they want with her? Should she ask? Did she want to know?

"Why have you kidnapped me? My general will—"

"We havena' kidnapped ye," Rob advised. "We saved yer life from Cameron MacPherson, who was aboot to shoot ye in the head."

Cameron MacPherson. She remembered now. He'd killed her horse. "His name is familiar to me."

"It should be." Again it was Rob who spoke. "He's the leader of the largest Jacobite rebellion in Scotland."

Anne closed her eyes. The Jacobites. Would they never cease tormenting her?

"She's fallen back to sleep. Poor lady has been through much with all her broken bones."

She opened her eyes and was tempted to smile at Tristan. He was kind and confident and he reminded her of Daniel.

She couldn't be certain, thanks to the thick fog filling her head from their potent whisky, but did he say all her broken bones? How many were there? She began to ask when a large, wet tongue licked her from her jaw to her temple. Hot breath descended on her next and she turned slightly to the panting jowls of an enormous dog—at least, she thought it was a dog. It could have been a misshapen lion with all its thick, golden fur.

"Ettarre, dinna' bother the queen." Tristan pushed the beast away. The hound hardly moved and whined as though she'd been struck.

"She may stay," Anne said and closed her eyes again. It was amazing how calm and relaxed she felt. Why, she hadn't felt this serene in years. "I think she likes me."

"I think she does too," Anne heard one of the men say. It could have been Tristan, or his brother Rob...or Daniel.

Robert MacGregor stood over the queen of Great Britain and rubbed his jaw. He hadn't planned on this happening. That bastard MacPherson would have killed her if they hadn't been watching him for the past day and a half.

Aye, it was true, Rob and his kin were Jacobites. They would have gladly fought a battle to bring King James's son to the throne, but they would not attempt to murder the queen. Hell, she was Rob's sister by marriage. That made her kin, whether he liked it or not.

He didn't like it at all.

He let his eyes move over her, taking in her broken body. What the hell were they going to do with her? Both of her legs were broken. Her left shoulder had been dislocated until Will, cold bastard that he was, set it back in place while she was unconscious. Her right wrist was broken, along with two ribs. They'd bound her up tightly to keep her from moving and thanks to Tristan's wife, Isobel—who knew more about injuries and illnesses than a physician—Rob's brother knew what herbs to give her and how to set her bones. Bruises covered over half her body from her terrific fall. She was fortunate to be alive.

Aye, fortunate for her. As Jacobites, it would have been easier for them all if she hadn't made it. But hell, he hadn't been about to let MacPherson shoot her in cold blood. Davina would never have forgiven him, and neither would Tristan.

He turned to have a look at the knight who called himself a Highlander and shook his head at how easy it still was for Tristan to melt a woman's resolve.

"What are we goin' to do wi' MacPherson?" Will appeared at Rob's side, a thin twig of straw dangling between his lips. "Darach's havin' too much sport wi' him in the stable."

Damned hellion, Rob thought, thinking of his bard's only son. Darach Grant was nothing like his father when it came to mercy.

"Did he at least discover why MacPherson tried to shoot the queen?"

"Other than the fact that he's a Jacobite and she's sitting on a throne that belongs to her brother, ye mean?"

Rob angled his head and gave Will the dark scowl his comment deserved. "Aye, other than that."

Will shrugged. "'Twas as Colin suspected. Richard Montagu wants her dead and paid MacPherson to do it. He also promised him a stretch of the most fertile land in Scotland once the deed was done."

"Montagu isna' doin' this to aid the Jacobites," Rob said out loud. "Colin's correct. The Earl of Manchester wants to be king. He could be more dangerous to Davina than anyone else in England."

"Aye, I agree," Will said,

"We need to tell her."

"Aye, she should know her cousin plans her demise," Will looked at Anne in the bed where she was sleeping. Uncharacteristically, his gray eyes softened just a bit. "'Tis a difficult thing to hear aboot yer kin."

Rob nodded. He wondered what kind of life the queen had led and if his beloved Davina could have lived it. The thought of men trying to kill his delicate wisp of a wife enraged him.

"Are we goin' to tell the queen who we are?"

"Nae," Rob answered. "She found Davina on Skye. She's clever. If she discovers that I'm Davina's husband 'twill only be a matter of time before she finds out aboot Camlochlin."

"We should bring her back to St. James's then. Let her own physicians tend to her."

"Look at her, Will. The instant her captain general gets one look at her, he'll seek revenge. My daughter is in his care, lest ye ferget. Who will prove to him that we were no' a part of Montagu's plan?"

Will thought about it for a moment then nodded his head. He turned at the sound of his dog, Ula, and her brother Goliath fighting over a scrap of meat Adam had tossed their way.

Ethan Headly, the proprietor of the brothel they were staying in, stopped in his tracks upon entering the room and paled at the long, snapping teeth of the hounds blocking his path.

Headly knew Rob's nephews, including Edmund and Malcolm, who sat at a table by the hearth with Gaza, mother to all the hounds, sleeping quietly at their feet. Rob didn't care to know what the lads had done here in years past. Edmund was married now, as were almost all the rest of them. None of them gave the prostitutes any attention or coin while they stayed there, which wouldn't be much longer if the dogs weren't controlled.

There was only one thing to do. Rob strode toward the snarling beasts. He didn't have to bend down to grab each one by the scruff of the neck. "Enough!" he shouted with such authority both beasts whined and sank to the ground.

Rob turned to his son next and peered at him with sharp eyes. "Take them to the barn and sleep with them there tonight."

Adam didn't argue, most likely because he'd find himself a warm lass to sleep with.

Damn it. Rob missed Davina. He missed her so much he was tempted to ride into the queen's palace, snatch back his daughter, and get the hell out of England once and for all.

✣

Chapter Thirty-Five

The sun was beginning to set, much to Daniel's frustration. He looked toward the streets and narrow courts in the distance and cursed under his breath. Someone had to have seen the queen. Someone had to know her whereabouts! A royal chaise and horse don't simply disappear into thin air.

It had been two days now with no sign of her. Panic had settled on Daniel like a cold, wet blanket. He was angry with her. He still loved her, though. He'd never forgive himself if harm had come to her. He had to find her. He knew that Montagu somehow had a hand in her disappearance, since he was gone, as well.

Daniel vowed to kill him the instant he found him. If Richard hurt her in any way...

He searched for another three hours, questioning every soul he came across. He had more than two hundred men searching for her, as well. They would find her. They had to.

When he returned to the palace, Charlotte was there waiting for him. Seeing her, he drew in a deep breath. He wasn't in the frame of mind to speak to her. He would much rather be with Abby, but since the queen had disappeared, she spent much of her time in the chapel praying for her aunt's safe return.

Her aunt. Hell, he still couldn't believe it.

"Any news?" Charlotte asked, reaching him first and doing her best to sound concerned.

"No. Nothing yet." Even if there were more to say, Daniel wouldn't have told her. He didn't believe she was directly involved in any scheme to do away with the queen, but he didn't trust her.

"Come to the Banqueting Hall with me, Daniel," she purred, looping her arm through his. "You hardly eat anything anymore and you need your strength to continue your search."

It was quite late and he was hungry, but he wanted to check in on Abby before he ate. "I'll be along shortly," he told her, offering her a warm smile to soften his rejection.

She returned his smile and clung to him even tighter. "Whatever it is can wait. Come now, let me feed you."

He agreed when his belly rumbled and let her lead him down the corridor. They nearly collided with Abby when she exited the entryway leading to the kitchen and beyond, to her room.

Her eyes fell immediately to the duchess's hold on him. "General, have ye found the queen?" she asked him, raising her clear, cool gaze to his.

"Not yet, my lady, but I will."

"I've nae doubt aboot that." She offered him and the duchess a stiff smile and then moved to pass them.

"Where are you off to?"

She paused in her steps and turned to look at him. "I

couldna' sleep so I thought I'd take a walk in the gardens. Captain Lewis assured me that 'tis safe."

Daniel felt his flesh grow hot. "Captain Lewis is not assigned to your safety, Miss Campbell. I am."

Her eyes dipped once again to Charlotte's arm entangled with his. He had the urge to separate them, but sparking the duchess's jealousy toward Abby would be unwise.

"Thank ye fer yer concern, General," she said, looking anything but grateful. "But I need some fresh air. Ye are welcome to follow behind me if ye think there is peril lurking in the shadows."

"The queen has disappeared, Miss Campbell," Daniel reminded her, ignoring Charlotte's fingernails digging into his arm. "I'll not have you go missing, as well."

"For heaven's sakes, Daniel, why would she?" the duchess asked with impatience hardening her tone. "Let her go for her walk. No one wants to kidnap her!"

"Aye, General," Abby agreed with a tight smile. "Go finish whatever it is ye are aboot to do with the duchess. I shall see ye in the morning."

Before he said another word, Abby rushed away, leaving him there to watch, trying to decide the best way to break away from Lady Blackburn.

"Come now, Daniel." His unwanted companion tugged at his arm. "Everyone is not your responsibility."

Abby was, and so was the queen. He'd failed one of them. He wouldn't fail the other.

Abby hurried through the long corridors of St. James's Palace and did her best not to think about Daniel and the duchess attached at the elbow. She refused to think about whether her knight was going to take Charlotte Adler to his bed tonight. Daniel was no fool, and any man who took that viper to his bed was indeed a fool.

Besides, she had other pressing matters to think about. Namely, Nora MacPherson, and why the lass had contacted her, begging her to meet in the gardens tonight.

What was Nora doing in England? Did this have something to do with the queen's disappearance? She doubted it. She wanted to tell Daniel, but he hated Jacobites and might accuse Nora falsely. She would wait until she found out what this was all about. After all, they were friends, weren't they? Nora had stayed awake with her all night when Abby needed someone to talk to at Tarveness Keep. She knew about Abby's feelings toward Daniel and had vowed never to speak of them, lest rumor get back to Lady Blackburn. They'd parted on good terms. What danger was there in trying to help her?

The crisp night air sent a bracing chill through Abby's bones and she pulled her shawl tighter around her shoulders. She missed her wool earasaid. She missed home.

"Abby?" someone whispered from within the shadows. It sounded like Nora, but Abby squinted in the darkness, trying to see better.

Nora was difficult to see at first, with her tresses as dark as a starless sky and her black cloak to match. If not for her pale skin beneath the full moon, Abby would have missed her altogether.

They clasped each other's hands when they met on the stone path between a fountain and a row of fruit trees.

Nora looked around nervously and Abby assured her that they were alone. Still, it took a few moments for Nora's nerves to settle enough for her to begin speaking.

"Abigail, ye said if I needed anything..."

"Of course, Nora! What is it? What has ye so troubled?"

"'Tis my brother, Cam. He's gone!"

Abby wasn't sure she'd heard her right, so she repeated it. "Gone? Gone where?"

"No one knows. He never returned from Edinburgh and his meeting with Richard Montagu. The men at Tarveness are ready to attack."

"Attack who?" Abby asked, trying to keep her voice to a whisper when what she really wanted to do was run for Daniel. What the hell was going on? First the queen. Now Cam MacPherson?

"They want to attack the queen and Marlow, Abigail. They think yer general arrested him and has thrown him into prison. They want Montagu as well, and dinna' care if they have to go through the entire army to get him."

"But he isn't here. He hasna' been arrested! We havena' seen him since he left fer Edinburgh! And Montagu isna' here either!" Abby told her. "He was on his way back but when he found oot that General Marlow was still alive and waiting here fer him, he went into hiding."

Did Nora know about the queen? Should Abby tell her?

"Do ye think the general knows Cam's whereaboots? Mayhap he had him taken somewhere else. Ye know he didna' like Cam fer being a Jacobite."

Abby shook her head. "Daniel would have told me if he'd arrested yer brother." She thought about everything for a moment. Someone had informed Montagu that Daniel was alive. Had it been Cameron MacPherson? "D'ye think mayhap Montagu and Cam are together?" She had to ask, despite possibly insulting Nora.

"Nae, Cam doesna' care fer Montagu. That's why he showed General Marlow the letter the earl penned."

Nora had a valid point. Also, MacPherson would have

told Montagu about Daniel in Edinburgh. Montagu would never have returned to the palace if he'd been warned before leaving Edinburgh. Och, but she wished Daniel were here. He'd know what to do. What did all these disappearances have to do with one another? There had to be a connection.

"Nora, there is something I must tell ye, but ye must swear not to tell another soul."

"What is it?" Nora's cold hands squeezed hers tighter. "Is it aboot Cam?"

"Nae, 'tis aboot the queen. She is missing too." Abby told her everything in the hopes that they could figure something out together.

"I can only hope that yer brother is not involved with Montagu in any way to try to usurp the queen. Daniel will kill him."

"I can assure ye, he's not involved."

"How do you know that with certainty?"

They both spun around, startled by Daniel's voice as he stepped out of the shadows.

"Daniel," Abby began. "I—"

He held up his hand to stop her. "Miss Campbell, if you mean to tell me anything other than admit that you've deceived me yet again, then please spare me." He turned back to Nora without giving Abby a chance to reply.

"As for you, Miss MacPherson, you're going to tell me everything and leave nothing out. Do you understand?" When she didn't answer right away, he took a step closer to her. "Trust me, you have no choice. If you know something and you don't tell me, I'll find your brother and have him hanged for treason with you beside him."

"Daniel!" Abby exclaimed. "Ye canna' be in earnest! She's done nothing!"

He said nothing but glared at her in the moonlight until she bristled in her gown.

"What?" she demanded. "Will ye hang me too fer lying to ye?"

He looked like he wanted to say something but then thought better of it and turned away from them both.

"Captain Waverly," he called out into the darkness. When the young captain appeared, Daniel ordered him to escort Nora to a room and bolt the door. He would speak to her in the morning.

Abby couldn't believe he was being so unfeeling. "Daniel, I know ye havena' slept much, and I know ye're upset about the queen, but Nora has done nothing wrong!"

He stopped on their way to Abby's room and stared at her. "You don't know that for certain. You only know what she's told you."

"There comes a time when ye must trust others, Daniel."

"Truly?" He laughed but it sounded cold and joyless. "And when might you begin being honest with me so that I may trust you?"

Abby didn't know whether to slap him or ask for his forgiveness. It was true, she had lied to him about things but she'd felt she had no other choice. Was she supposed to trust him with her mother's life? With the lives of everyone in Camlochlin? She wanted to lead her clan someday. Didn't she have an obligation to keep them safe?

She didn't answer Daniel's question. She couldn't, because if she loved him, shouldn't she trust him? How could she give her heart to a man she didn't trust?

She walked away from him and headed toward her room alone. When she reached her chamber and stepped inside, he followed her, shutting the door behind him.

Abby watched him, horrified. "What if Lady Blackburn sees?"

"What else do you keep from me, Abigail?" he asked, ignoring everything else. "Why are your father and the rest of his warriors here?"

"I told ye already, to watch over me." She stared at him while he stood by her door. "Why else do ye think?"

He shook his head and rubbed his eyes. "I don't know," he said on a gusty sigh.

She went to him, unable to do anything else. "I understand that ye've been deceived aboot yer faither, yer entire life." She kept her tone soft, knowing now why he didn't trust her. "I'm sorry Anne lied to ye. I'm sorry I lied to ye, as well. But know this now, Daniel. My kin mean nae harm."

He looked bone weary and the urge to smooth the frown from his forehead stole over her. She wanted him to trust her, but truly, she'd given him no reason to do so. She wasn't fool enough to believe he should blindly trust her, despite the secrets she kept from him, because he cared for her, and she did believe that he cared for her. She was angry with him, but in truth, he had every right not to trust her.

"Ye need sleep, Daniel," she told him. "Ye have enough on yer mind with the queen's disappearance withoot troubling yerself with thoughts of me too." She placed her hand on his arm. She shouldn't have. She liked the way his muscles trembled when she touched him. "I know I havena' been honest with ye, but I wouldna' do anything to hurt ye. Please let that be enough."

His gaze penetrated her flesh, her soul, and made her very spirit quake. She couldn't remember what she was angry about. She loved him—and it ate away at her. What would she ever do without him? How could she remain with him?

"You are never out of my thoughts," he told her, bringing her knuckles to his lips. His handsome face was a mask of both sorrow and longing. "Wherever I am, whatever I'm doing, you haunt me. You will always haunt me."

Damn the world, and responsibilities, and fears about tomorrow. Throwing it all to the wind, Abby coiled her arms around his neck and drew him closer.

❊

Chapter Thirty-Six

She'd missed him. Oh, how she'd missed him. She kissed his face while he carried her to her bed. She refused to waste another moment worrying about the future with or without him. This was a moment they had together and she wouldn't let it pass. They'd wasted too much time already.

They undressed each other with eager hands and heavy breath, pulling and tugging on fabric, almost tearing it away to expose skin they longed to kiss.

Poised atop her on the bed, his mouth covered hers, caressing her, molding to her. He filled her with his tongue, stroking her with deep, erotic possession while his hands freed her from the last of her clothes. She cried out at the caress of his masterful touch and trembled in his arms, ready and willing to give him whatever he asked.

He asked for her body, freely given, and she gave it, coiling her legs around his waist while he guided himself into her. She held him close, relishing the intimacy of his breath on her chin, her cheek, as he thrust himself deep inside her. He moved slowly, savoring the feel of her. His whispers along her throat and jaw thrilled her and brought tears to her eyes, for he told her what she meant to him.

"Everything. You are everything to me, my life, my joy, my pain."

She took his face in her hands while he filled her and stretched her to her limit. She kissed every inch of his face, wetting him with her tears.

"And ye are the passion that warms my blood, my dreams come to life. I love ye. I love ye."

The smile he gave her melted her to her core. He moved like they had the rest of their lives together, with long, titillating strokes, every touch a caress. She outlined the muscles of his chest with her fingertips, her lips, tempting him to suckle her in return. He withdrew, then sank deep into her again and again, as careless as she of the consequences.

Let the Duchess of Blackburn find out about them, Abby could protect herself, and if the wench tried to hurt Daniel, Abby would kill her. Her clan had been in trouble with the English before and made it through. They would again.

She clung to him while they both climaxed. If she carried his seed, so be it. She would have a part of him with her no matter what happened.

He didn't try to pull away but held her and watched her while she gritted her teeth, trying not to cry out too loudly in ecstasy.

A little while later she lay in his arms, her breath short against his chest. She wanted to die here, just like this. Could she leave everything behind for this man? Her clan, her dreams and desires of being chief—for him?

Aye, she could.

She thought she wasn't sure. But she knew she could.

She would. She would do anything for him. Her heart was utterly lost to him, no matter how she tried to deny it. Leading her clan would mean nothing if he wasn't in her life. Hadn't her own mother given up the throne for her father?

She felt bad for Nora but Cameron MacPherson led a dangerous life by his own choice. Why should Abby fight with Daniel over him?

"D'ye think Cameron MacPherson has something to do with the queen's disappearance?"

Because her ear was pressed against Daniel's chest, she heard his heart accelerate again. He loved Anne.

"If he does, he won't live long."

Abby closed her eyes. He would never leave Anne's side, even if he believed James Stuart's claim to the throne. Abby would expect nothing less from him.

"D'ye think the queen lives, Daniel?" Abby hoped she did.

"Yes. I think someone holds her for ransom and we will hear from him or her soon. Whoever it is will regret ever laying a hand on her."

Abby nodded and closed her eyes to sleep. Daniel would save the queen. God help whoever had her.

The queen sat propped up against four thick pillows in her bed at the brothel. A brothel! *That* truth still stunned her each time she thought about it. She'd never been in a brothel before and she wasn't sure she wanted to be in one now, especially when she shared the room with seven Highlanders. And it wasn't like these were straggly, toothless brutes who spent too much time with their whisky and sweet cakes. No, these men, three of whom were closer to her own age, were in magnificent physical condition. She could tell by their muscular legs below their plaids and the way their shirts pulled across their chests and thick upper arms. Three of them had to duck every time they entered the room.

They were nothing like what she'd been told about men of the North. They barely raised their voices, and when they did it was at one another, not at her.

They did everything in their power to make her comfortable, including feeding her and paying two of the girls who lived here to change her bedpans and see to her feminine needs.

She still didn't know who they were or why they were helping her, but she was beginning not to care. Their good-natured bickering made her smile more times than she had since her dear husband died. They were all kind and respectful to her. Tristan seemed to have mastered the art of charm and since she knew much about honor from Daniel, she recognized the same from Tristan. Odd to think of a Jacobite Highlander practicing honor, but lord, he did. Still, it was Rob who sat by her bed every night and talked to her about her life, curious to know the details of it and if she was happy or not.

She lay in a bed inside a brothel. (Tristan swore to her that the bed linens were the cleanest in the place.) At night she shared her bed with a 150-pound dog that smelled like earth and something else less pleasant, but bearable. Her broken bones were wrapped and set and the rest of her bruises were healing nicely, thanks to the care of Jacobites, and the food they fed her wasn't as terrible as she would have imagined—if she'd ever imagined herself held captive in a brothel.

She expected to wake up any moment now.

The door opened and at the foot of her bed, Ettarre

growled from deep in her throat as Rob entered the room with another man she'd never seen before.

No. She was wrong. She had seen him once before... when he was pointing a pistol at her face.

He was almost unrecognizable, with eyelids swollen shut and torn lips. He'd been beaten, likely by the one they called Darach, his angelic features belied only by the feral glint in his emerald eyes.

"Cameron MacPherson, Yer Majesty," Rob introduced him, then pulled him closer.

Anne shrank back in her bed and Tristan appeared and took her hand.

"Dinna' be afraid of him any longer, aye?"

She nodded, but kept her eyes on the man who caused her injuries. "Why have you brought him to me?"

"Tell her!" Rob gave him a hard shake. "Tell her or I'll cut ye in half and feed ye to my dogs."

Ettarre growled again and Goliath, the biggest and the blackest of the four, sat up and barked, as if begging for the promised treat.

"He offered me land and a title and—"

"Tell her!" Rob held his blade to MacPherson's throat. "Tell her who offered ye land and a title and coin!"

"The Earl of Manchester. Yer very own cousin." He grinned down at the queen, exposing two lost teeth. "He supports James Stuart, the true king. Not a usurper who gained the throne by—"

He slammed his mouth shut when the edge of Rob's blade pierced his skin and drew blood.

"Take him back to the stables, Darach."

Anne watched them leave, then looked away from the others staring at her. Richard. Her cousin. She wasn't shocked, but it still stung.

"Yer Majesty?"

She lifted her glossy eyes to Rob and saw compassion and anger for her. She shrugged one shoulder and managed a smile. She was the queen, after all. She couldn't fall apart every time someone betrayed her.

"General Marlow had informed me of Richard's treachery, but I imagine I needed to hear it with my own ears. Now I have. It's one thing to know you mean little to your family and another to discover that they tried to have you killed."

The Highlanders were all quiet, but they nodded in agreement. Rob sat in his chair—the one between her bedside and the hearth. He waited while Tristan fed her some medicine that tasted like sweet mint and spirits.

She knew by now that Rob was the leader among these men. He spoke with authority and all the others obeyed him. She recognized his command and thought he would make an excellent general under Daniel.

"Why are you helping me?" she asked him when he motioned to his brother and Tristan left them alone and rejoined the others playing a game of chess. "You're all Jacobites. So why? Why didn't you let MacPherson finish what he came to do?"

"Ye're the queen," Rob said simply. Anne didn't believe it was as simple as that.

"A queen you don't support."

He smiled slightly and she thought he was quite possibly the most handsome man she knew...besides Daniel.

"While 'tis true we support James Stuart's claim to the throne, I dinna' believe killin' ye is the right way to get him there. Besides that, my wife and mother would kill me fer harming a woman."

His smile softened and for some mad reason it made her want to weep all the more. She decided to ask him the question that had been burning a hole in her mind.

"What do you plan on doing with me?"

"To begin," he told her, "I'm goin' to make certain ye're well before I return ye to St. James's Palace."

A flood of relief washed over her upon hearing that she would be returned, but it made no sense why they would help her. "Are you going to hold me for ransom in an attempt to sit my stepbrother on the throne?"

He shook his head. "Though 'twould be a good plan, I think this is one dispute over the monarchy that my kin will stay oot of."

"In truth," she said, trying not to sound as dejected as she felt. She failed. "I don't know that it would be that big of a dispute. I have very few true friends."

He lifted a raven brow at her. "What about General Marlow? Everyone in Great Britain knows of his dedication to ye."

She nodded and let her eyes fill with tears. "Yes, he is loyal to me. But I kept the truth of his birth hidden from him his whole life and now someone else has told him."

Rob turned to share a look with Tristan and Will, but he said nothing to her about his decision. Instead, he asked her more questions.

"Ye've nae other family who care aboot ye?"

She thought about telling him about Davina. She'd never told a soul, not even Daniel. What would this Highlander say about it? "I've recently taken a distant relative into my house as a handmaiden. But she also supports James."

He sat up straighter in his chair when she spoke about Abigail. "Has she been treated well?" he asked. "Mayhap ye could change her mind aboot where her loyalties lie."

"She's been treated very well by me, and by General Marlow, who I think may have feelings for her. She's kind-hearted and quite beautiful, but I don't think there is room for trust on either side."

"Why not?"

"She believes I wish her family harm and I'm not certain her family doesn't want me dead and out of the way."

"D'ye? Wish her family harm?"

"No. I simply fear even more people in my life wanting to depose or kill me for my title. Wouldn't you be a bit afraid?" She eyed the span of his shoulders and smiled. "Or at least uneasy?"

He smiled with her and nodded. Hell, it was good to hear her speak so. If she had admitted to wanting Davina dead, he would leave her to her enemies. But he was beginning to think all Anne wanted was people in her life whom she could trust.

They spoke for another hour, mostly about the people in her life, and she shared with him her love for her country and her desire to see it prosper. They also spoke of Richard and what his plans were. The Highlanders had cleverly planted a few of their own men into his company. That was how they had known what MacPherson was up to.

That night, Anne slept soundly, safely surrounded by a band of warriors who had saved her life.

Chapter Thirty-Seven

*R*ob woke to an ache in his back and a crick in his neck. He hadn't slept in a chair since Davina fell ill last winter. He'd kept a vigil for his wife every night for weeks. He never imagined he'd be doing the same for his wife's sister.

He looked at the queen sleeping in her bed with Tristan's giant dog snoring beside her, and drew out a long sigh. He didn't want to like her. He was never one for giving his loyalty to the monarchy, like Colin had when James II was king, and while he supported James Francis, Rob had never met him. But he liked Anne, damn it, and he suspected Davina would like her too.

But they couldn't keep her here much longer. Abby was in the palace with General Marlow and his damn army, not to mention the Duchess of Blackburn, whom Anne herself called a viperous snake ready to plunge a dagger into her back. He had to get Abby the hell out of there and back home. She was doing no good with the queen here with him! He hadn't agreed with this plan in the first place. He had to have been stark-raving mad to let his daughter come to England—and to travel with the leader of the queen's army.

Anne thought Marlow had feelings for his daughter! Rob would kill him! But another thought, even worse, made his stomach sink. What if Abby was losing her heart as well? The general claimed to be a knight, and damn it all if his only daughter had grown up with knights on her mind. Damn all the talk of honor and gallantry in Camlochlin! It would do them no good if an army attacked, which was exactly what would happen if any more harm came to the queen. They had to get rid of her. Rob wanted to go home to his wife, his clan, and his castle.

And what about Montagu? He wondered if Colin had found out anything more while staying in Edinburgh with him. Leave it to his youngest brother to want to be in the midst of the action. Damn him for insisting on staying with only a few Buchanans to fight on his side should the need for bloodshed arise. Colin had refused his son Edmund's aid, or anyone else's. Rob wanted them all home, where it was safe.

He rose from his chair and stretched his long body. When he turned to examine the bodies asleep on the floor, he discovered a few of them gone. He stepped over the rest and had almost reached the door when it opened and his youngest brother, Colin, appeared. They embraced, glad to see each other alive. Then Rob walked him back to the bed.

"So, obviously, ye were correct," he told Colin in a soft whisper over the sleeping queen. "Montagu bribed MacPherson to kill the queen."

"Aye, but I dinna' recall suggestin' that we keep her in our care and nurse her back to health."

"Should I have left her to die on the road?"

Colin shook his head. "She needs to be sent back though,

brother. Accordin' to Montagu, General Marlow will hunt down and decimate anyone who threatens her well-being. We dinna' have enough men to fight his army."

"We didna' threaten her well-being, MacPherson did," Rob reminded him.

"D'ye want to explain that to him while he's fightin' us?"

"Nae," Rob admitted. He'd fought the general already and knew the man was a master with his sword. He looked around at his nephews and his brother. He didn't want to lose even one of his men. "But we canna' send her back in her condition. She's badly broken and I dinna' think Marlow will care who is responsible."

Colin agreed and they decided to send Tristan, since he was the most diplomatic.

By the time the queen awoke, the men had decided on a plan of action.

"Robert," the queen called out, smiling at one of the brothel wenches who'd entered the room with Anne's food. "Tell the proprietor that I want Lynette here to return to St. James with me."

"Now, Your Majesty." Lynette giggled and patted the queen's hand. "You don't want a prostitute to wait on you in your palace. 'Twould be the talk of the whole country!"

"What do I care?" Anne smiled. "I enjoy our conversa—"

Her words ended abruptly when she looked toward the table at Colin sitting with the rest of them.

Rob realized an instant too late what had happened. He should have told her the truth from the beginning. Now it was too late. He motioned to Will to escort Lynette out.

"Colin MacGregor," she said softly, backing up a bit in her bed. "General of my father's army and close friend of the king." She shifted her gaze to Rob, and then to Tristan, seeing their resemblance.

"You're her husband," she said to Rob. Her eyes grew large and wet and her cheeks burned with fire before she looked away. "I've been a fool. I hope you all enjoyed my mortification."

"Nae, Ma'am," Tristan was the first to go to her. "No one here has thought ye the fool."

"Go on, then," she cried, not listening to what Tristan told her. "Do what you mean to do."

"We mean to do exactly what we've been doin'," Rob promised her. "Seein' to ye. We're not—"

"It all makes sense now," she cut him off. "You are with MacPherson—"

"Hell," Darach stepped forward, no less brazen with the queen of Great Britain than he was with any other soul. "Did MacPherson's face look like we're on his side? I broke two bones in m' fingers from hitting his hard face. If we were with him, one of his blasted teeth wouldna' have been imbedded in m' knuckle!"

"Yer Majesty," Rob went to her and sat at the edge of her bed. "'Tis true, I'm Rob MacGregor, Davina's husband and Abigail's father. We came here to protect my daughter, not to harm ye. If we wanted ye dead, we would have let MacPherson shoot ye. Ye're my sister by marriage, whether ye like it or not, and as my kin, 'tis my duty to protect ye."

He was pleased to see that she stopped looking so damn sad. In truth, she wiped her eyes and may have even smiled at him. "Do you really think of me as family?"

"Of course," he said. "And MacGregors dinna' betray their kin."

"Speakin' of betrayin' kin." Colin stepped forward and peered down at her in her bed. "Richard Montagu is enlisting men to kill ye. He docsna' support yer step-brother but plans on havin' ye both murdered so he can take over the throne."

"What do you suggest I do, General?"

Rob saw Colin examining the bruises on her face, her wrapped limbs. He watched his brother's expression go harder than he'd seen it in years.

"Let me kill him," Colin said stiffly, "and MacPherson with him."

She shook her head. "I'm sorry," she said softly. "But Richard's life is Daniel's to take if he wishes it. Young MacPherson will hang in Edinburgh, where others can witness what becomes of a man who tries to kill his queen."

Colin bowed. "As ye wish, Yer Majesty."

"You are still as handsome as you were when you served my father, Colin MacGregor."

"Thank ye, Ma'am."

"He loved you, you know."

"I know."

"Why did you abandon him to William?"

"He tried to have my future wife and son killed. He was fortunate I didna' kill him."

That seemed to mollify her. Either that, or she was afraid to ask anything else, knowing she would get the truth. Colin didn't coat his words with honey, not even for the queen.

They made plans for Tristan to return to St. James's Palace and inform General Marlow that they had the queen. And then they broke fast.

Rob enjoyed eating and drinking with his family whether in the Great Hall of Camlochlin or in a brothel in England. They shared laughter and a cup of whisky and drank to Connor Grant, who'd stayed behind to watch over their home in the mountains.

Rob caught the queen watching them more than once, a whimsical light shining in her dark eyes.

"Tell me about my sister," she asked him when they were done eating.

"She is kind-hearted and gentle to all," Rob said, missing his wife. "She was taught much at the abbey where she grew up. She can read and play half a dozen instruments. She loves fiercely and she loves silliness."

"Silliness?" Anne lifted her brow and her mouth, enjoying hearing about her.

"Aye. She wasn't allowed to play with other children when she was little. She was verra' lonely."

"As was I."

Rob covered her hand with his. "'Tis a pity ye were separated. It seems ye needed each other then. Mayhap ye still do."

She looked away, trying to keep him from seeing more moisture in her eyes. Hell, he had to do something about all these tears.

"We shall never meet," she told him quietly. "It's too dangerous for her to come here."

"Well, Yer Majesty, ye never know what the future may bring."

Rob thought it quite extraordinary that Davina and her sister looked nothing alike save when Anne smiled. They both shared an inner joy that no amount of sorrow or loss could overcome.

"Your daughter told me I would understand why Davina would always choose to remain with you and your family if I met you. Well, I've met you, and I do understand."

Rob smiled and lifted his cup to her.

Chapter Thirty-Eight

$\mathcal{D}$aniel sat on the edge of Abby's bed and tugged his leather boot up over his calf. When she moved on the mattress behind him, flashes of their night together invaded his memory. He smiled and reached for his other boot while she draped herself over his back and caressed him to her. He covered her much smaller hand where it rested on his belly.

He hated having to leave her bed, but with the queen missing and him gone from the palace so often, searching for her, he didn't want Charlotte to discover them now.

"I've been thinking," she purred against his ear.

"About what?" Hell, he couldn't let himself go hard for her now.

"Nora."

Well, that helped. He smiled, and then laughed at himself. An instant later he groaned when she moved her naked body along his back.

"If Nora knows anything, she willna' tell ye. I know because if 'twere my brother, I would say nothing, no matter what it cost me."

He grew serious and held her hand at his chest. "What would you have me do?" he asked her quietly. "If she knows where the queen is, should I not use any means to get that information from her?"

She didn't answer him, but pressed a kiss between his shoulders, and then moved away.

"D'ye believe that her brother's men are coming here to attack?" she asked him, sounding curious and a little anxious, but not angry with him for his honesty about Nora.

"They're fools if they do. They won't live a full day."

He stood up and turned to her. She was sitting up, slipping her wondrous body into her shift. He wanted to stay and peel her out of it again.

"But what reason does she have to be untruthful?"

This was a serious conversation, but that didn't stop Daniel from wanting to smile. Abby was an intelligent woman. She thought like a leader, but she was also delightfully innocent about certain things...like people. A condition, he suspected, that came from living secluded away in the Highlands. As long as that was where she stayed, she would do well to see the best in others.

But he didn't want her to remain in Skye, away from him.

"Mayhap," she suggested while she left the bed and began to dress, "she is unaware of her brother's treachery, if he is indeed involved in the queen's disappearance."

Daniel eyed his beloved from the corner of his eye and pushed his arm through his military coat. "He must be involved, Abby. It's not by chance that she came here now. She wanted to get inside the palace. Why would she risk her life coming here in the night on the pretense of seeking your help?"

"Because she has no one else?" she insisted.

"She has her brother's garrison. She could have gone to Edinburgh, where her brother was allegedly last seen. No, she came here to find out if I had taken him prisoner."

"But," Abby argued, "ye promised him at Tarveness that ye would leave him alone fer a few months as payment fer helping us."

"Precisely," he said. "Why would I arrest him unless he had done something worthy of the noose?"

She mulled it over for a moment, and then went to him. "Mayhap ye're correct. But she was kind to me, Daniel." She reached up and took his face in her palms. "Go, my love, before the palace and Charlotte awaken. I shall be safe. Go."

"Whatever happens," he told her before he left her room, "I'll take her kindness toward you into consideration."

"General!" Captain Lewis appeared on the other side of the door.

Hell, it didn't bode well that Lewis knew where to find him.

"There's a man outside the palace seeking an audience with you. He says he has information about the queen!"

"Did he give his name?" Daniel opened the door fully and stepped into the hall.

"He did, my lord. He said he is called Tristan. Tristan MacGregor."

Abby sprang from the room and appeared at Daniel's side, ready to go with him.

"Stay here."

"Nae. He's my uncle!" She raced along beside him. "If he has information about my aunt, I want to hear it."

He would talk to her later about her inability to obey

the simplest of commands. Right now, though, he wanted to know what the hell the MacGregors had to do with this! He no longer believed they meant to hurt Anne. Abby had been forced to come here upon threat of the army entering Skye. Davina MacGregor might be the true heir, but she wanted nothing to do with the throne. Daniel believed it.

He had his men escort the MacGregor into Anne's private solar. He remembered this one from Tarveness Keep and their discussion about sleeping in stables. He was only slightly smaller than the rest of the brawny Highlanders who had accompanied him that day. Why, Daniel wondered, while he waited for his guest to finish embracing Abby, was he alone now?

Abby put the question to him soon enough when she asked where her father was.

"He is well and safe," he assured his niece, "as are the rest of us." He turned to Daniel. "As is the queen."

Daniel bolted from the chair he was sitting in. "Where?"

"In a brothel six leagues west of here."

"A brothel?" Daniel wanted to start removing some heads. He held his patience in check to hear more. "What the hell is she doing in a brothel?"

"MacPherson tried to kill her." Tristan told them what happened and how they had stopped MacPherson from shooting Anne. Daniel listened, his rage seething closer to the surface.

He couldn't listen any more without doing something. He dragged his sword free with a grinding swoosh and pointed it at Abby's uncle. "Bring me to her now."

"Daniel, please," Abby begged. "Put doun yer sword. Are ye not listening? They saved her!"

"She's safe, General," her uncle told him calmly and walked over to the wine decanter set on the table. "The men guarding her will let nae harm come to her. They will keep her safe just as ye kept our Abigail safe. May I? Just a quick refreshment before we're off again?" When Daniel nodded, still holding his sword, the Highlander poured himself a drink. He took a swig, then set down his cup. "Please, General, put yer sword away. I'd hate to be forced to remove it from ye myself. I dinna' like having a blade aimed in my direction when I'm innocent."

Daniel wasn't in the frame of mind for this man's arrogance. No one had ever unarmed him, and he was sure no one ever would. Still, he did as he was asked, preferring to get the hell out of there.

"I want to see her," Daniel demanded. "You'll tell me the rest on the way."

"That's why I'm here, to bring ye to her," Tristan said, smiling amiably. Daniel understood why the chief had sent him and not any of the others. This MacGregor wasn't as quick to draw his weapon as another Highlander would be.

"I'm coming along." Abby moved forward but was stopped when her uncle spoke again.

"Ye wilna' be coming back here again, lass."

"What d'ye mean?"

"Yer faither has decided that ye're coming home with us. We've convinced Anne that yer mother has nae interest in the throne and she's already agreed to go before Parliament and do all she can to end the proscription. There's nae longer a reason fer ye to stay."

Abby fell back into her chair like she never wanted to leave it and looked up to find Daniel's gaze on her.

He'd thought about this day for weeks. The day it all ended between them. The day she returned to Skye. It had come too soon. He wanted to tell her not to go. He wanted to beg her not to leave him. He opened his mouth but only a garbled groan escaped him. He hadn't loved before her. Not like this. Damn it, he loved her so much it made him hurt worse than any wound he'd received in battle. He wouldn't love again after her. He didn't care about monarchies, British or Danish, when it came to her. But she dreamed of becoming chief of her clan.

This glorious Highland woman belonged on windswept moors, free of the encumbrances of England's stuffy courts. Her mother had rejected it, and so had Abby. How could he ask her to give up her dreams, her home, and her family?

But he wanted to. He wanted to beg her to stay.

"Ah." Her uncle poured himself another drink. "We suspected this."

Abby sniffed and watched him with eyes that gleamed like sapphires under water. "Ye did? And my faither?" she added when he nodded.

"He was afraid of it, aye. The queen suspects feelings between the both of ye, as well."

"I don't care if they all come down together on me for it." Daniel went to her and knelt before her chair. "I'm asking ye to stay here and let's discuss this when I return, Abigail." He took her hand and kissed it. "There must be something we can do to change our fate. We've more ahead of us than secrets and sorrow."

She loved him. He could see it in her eyes. When she turned to her uncle and spoke, she spoke it with her mouth. "I'm going to wait here to hear what General Marlow wishes to say."

"Yer faither—"

"Tell my faither I refused to leave. He'll know then that there was nothing ye could do to change my mind, Uncle."

Daniel winked at her as he straightened. "Let's go," he told her uncle. "The sooner I get the queen, the quicker I can return to her." He winked at Abby. Everything would work out. They would make it work. "Keep clear of Nora MacPherson's room."

"She's here?" her uncle asked.

Daniel nodded and promised to explain on the way.

While they rode to the brothel Tristan filled Daniel in on everything they knew—thanks to Colin MacGregor—about Richard Montagu and his plot to use the Jacobites to kill the queen.

"Of course, we would have preferred a Catholic king on the throne," Tristan admitted. "But that was before we met Anne. We all agree that she is most likable. And truly, what we want is a monarch who will leave us to our ways. Anne has promised that she would."

"I'm pleased to hear it," Daniel told him honestly. "Anne has enough enemies. I didn't want to have to fight more of you."

"'Twould have been a quick fight." Tristan said, offering Daniel a bright grin before picking up speed on his mount.

They reached the brothel while the sun was still high and were met by the chief and his brother Colin. Daniel didn't waste time with pleasantries, but listened on the way to Anne's room while the chief filled him in on everything Tristan had left out, which wasn't much.

When Daniel reached the door, he pushed it open and plunged inside. What he found stunned him beyond speech. There she was, his normally morose queen, propped up in a bed with an enormous dog sprawled out beside her and four Highlanders sitting around her, her head tossed back in laughter. The sound filled the room, bringing sunshine to the gloom that had covered his heart these last few days.

There was hardly any room to walk, but that wasn't why Daniel didn't move from the doorway. He didn't want to disturb her joy. He never wanted to snatch this moment from her.

When another massive hound growled at him, the queen turned her head toward the door. "Daniel!" She gasped and tried to move in her bed.

He went to her then, brushing past the fangs of the hound without so much as a thought. "Anne! I was worried out of my mind." He practically lifted her from the bed in a great embrace that made her moan. He pulled back, sorry for hurting her, but then grinned when she laughed at him and patted his face.

"Thanks to these men, I'm fine."

Daniel looked around, not knowing what to say. Thank you didn't seem enough. They'd not only saved her life, they'd bound her bones and made her laugh like a woman who had reason to be happy.

"She's doin' well," the chief told him, coming to sit at the table. Daniel caught the wink he shot to Anne. "We weren't certain how ye would receive the news that she was with us. And she was pretty beat up."

"But now I am strong enough to return home," she told them. "And I want to bring my new family with me. Of course, we will say they are Campbells and Gordons to keep anyone from finding out about Davina. I will . . ."

Hell, Daniel thought, while she continued on. Highlanders at St. James's. The palace would never recover.

"General."

Daniel turned to Robert MacGregor and knew what

was coming by the seriousness in the chief's tone, the clarity in the cool blue eyes much like his daughter's.

"Where is Abigail and why did she not return with ye?"

Daniel looked at him and then at the rest of them, each one bigger than the next, their dogs eyeing him as if he were their worst enemy yet.

Hell.

Chapter Thirty-Nine

*I*t took four hours to get the queen home. Moving her from her bed at the brothel to a carriage big enough to hold her horizontally took time and patience. Her bones were still broken and moving her without the utmost care would have damaged her further.

The men rode on horseback surrounding the carriage while a prostitute named Lynette sat with the queen inside. Cameron MacPherson rode at the back of the procession, bound with rope and caked in dried blood.

Daniel appreciated Tristan's interruption back at the brothel when he explained to his brother that Abigail insisted on staying at the palace to properly pack for the journey home.

But now, away from Anne, for he wanted to tell her alone, he looked at Abby's father riding near him and then accepted the jug of whisky Tristan offered him.

He swigged the burning liquid and thought there was nothing like true Highland whisky.

"I love your daughter, Chief."

It was no surprise to her father. According to Tristan,

Rob had suspected it. But he still looked like he wanted to kill Daniel right there on the road to the palace.

"I learned from MacPherson that ye're the Jacobite killer. D'ye think I'd allow my daughter to wed ye?"

"I fought to defend the queen," Daniel told him. "Where would you stop if enemies sought to kill someone you loved?" He already knew the answer, and so did her father.

But he wasn't done.

"Where d'ye think ye'll be livin' with my daughter?"

Daniel didn't answer right away, mainly because he and Abby hadn't yet discussed it.

"I'll tell ye why this can never be," her father continued. "My daughter has a strong desire to be chief of Clan MacGregor."

"I know."

"And ye have asked her to give up this dream?"

"No."

"Well, English soldiers are not welcome where we live, so ye will have to bid farewell to her when we return."

"Robbie, ye'll have to make an exception." Coming to his aid once again, Tristan cantered up beside them on his mount. "Else how will the queen visit her sister?"

"The queen...a visit?" Rob uttered, going a shade whiter than his normal complexion.

Tristan nodded and cast Daniel a subtle smile. "She wants to meet Davina but she willna' travel withoot her champion."

Rob groaned toward the heavens. "Was I not patient enough when the queen's father visited a dozen times after I wed his daughter?"

"No one told ye to wed the king's firstborn daughter," Tristan pointed out, ignoring his brother's glare.

Daniel still couldn't believe what he was hearing. Would he ever get used to the fact that Abby was King James's granddaughter?

"Your wife is the rightful heir," Daniel reminded the MacGregor chief.

"Nae." Abby's father turned his darkest glare on Daniel. "My wife is a MacGregor and nothin' more. Ye'd do well to remember that."

They traveled the rest of the way in silence, with Daniel wondering how the hell he was going to ask Abby to be his wife. The obstacles seemed too big to conquer, but they had to. He didn't want to live his life without her.

By the time they reached the palace, twilight was descending on the courtyard. Half of Daniel's garrison was there to meet them and aid the queen, but they possessed the same look of terror in their gazes when they reached Daniel and his party.

Daniel was about to ask what the hell was going on when his ear caught the sound of a woman's mournful wail in the distance.

His blood went cold just as one of his lieutenants reached him.

"General."

Daniel turned to the young man's pale face and dreaded what was coming. "Lady Blackburn has killed Captain Lewis."

"What?" Daniel didn't understand. How the hell—

"He was trying to stop her from taking Miss Campbell away. Jane and her sister Judith found him dead in front of Miss Campbell's chamber door. He'd been stabbed many times."

For a moment...for one blessed ignorant moment, Daniel couldn't take it all in. Captain Lewis was dead.

Abby. Abby! Charlotte had taken Abby! God, no! His fears had come to pass.

He gripped the lieutenant's shoulders and gave him a violent shake. "Where did she take her? When did they leave?"

"We found Captain Lewis a quarter of an hour ago. Miss MacPherson is also gone."

"What's goin' on, Marlow?"

Daniel shut his eyes when he heard Abby's father behind him. He had to tell him. He didn't want to, mostly because he didn't want to hear the words coming from his mouth. This couldn't be happening.

"The Duchess of Blackburn has taken Abigail and means to harm her."

He heard the chief's sword sliding from its sheath, followed by the rest of the Highlanders' blades coming out. Pistols were also being released and aimed at his men.

He turned slowly to the chief and met the face of terror that he was certain mirrored his own. "I will find her."

"Ye're damned right, ye will. I'll kill ye if ye dinna' find her. I'll be comin' with ye."

"No, I—"

"I didna' ask, General. I'm comin' with ye. Are we leavin' now or are we goin' to waste more time standin' here?"

There was no stopping him. This was the man who refused to let death take his wife. "We're leaving now. I think I know where Charlotte took her."

They explained to the rest of the MacGregors what was going on and Daniel had to insist that the fewer men who followed, the better. But it was only after the chief ordered his family to stay at the palace that they obeyed.

Daniel and Rob didn't have far to go by horseback.

Blackburn House, though as yet unfinished and the reason Charlotte was still residing in the palace, was part of Pall Mall and only a short distance away. Charlotte knew he would come. At least, Daniel prayed she did.

"Why has she done this?" Rob asked him on the way.

"Because, Chief, I'm a prince."

Rob slowed his mount and stared at him. "Did ye just tell me that ye're a prince? Of what?" he added when Daniel nodded his head.

Daniel hadn't told anyone besides Abby about his birth. He was still a bit in shock by it himself, and he wasn't certain he even wanted to do anything about it. He didn't want to live in Denmark. He sure as hell didn't want to live with all the stuffiness and stiff rules that came with being royalty. Even if he was a bastard, he was still the only living child of Prince George. He didn't want Charlotte in his life. He wanted Abby, with her Highland Jacobite family and all.

He told Abby's father the truth, making it all the more real for him. He told him what he'd overheard Anne and Charlotte saying and that he hadn't yet confronted Anne completely on the matter.

"Ye dinna' sound pleased to be in such a position," the chief said.

"I'm not," Daniel told him. "I suspect it's the same reason your wife wants no part of the courtly life."

When they reached Blackburn House, they entered through the front garden. Neither one stopped to explain to the two guardsmen what they wanted or what they were doing there.

"Alert your lord to our arrival!" Daniel shouted. "And tell him to be swift in letting us in, else I'll return with my army!"

Daniel and Rob didn't wait long before Lord Blackburn, Charlotte's husband, met them at the large doors. He looked confused and insulted, and shocked when he saw the MacGregor chief.

"What is the meaning of this, Darlington?" he asked with an indignant pitch in his voice.

"Where's your wife, Blackburn?" Daniel asked him.

"My . . . What? Whatever—"

Refusing to waste another instant, Daniel laid his hand on Blackburn's shoulder and pushed him out of his way.

"Abby!" His voice boomed throughout the large house.

"Who is Abby?" Lord Blackburn asked.

MacGregor gripped him by his ruffled collar and growled in his face. "My daughter. And if ye dinna' tell me where she is, ye willna' draw another breath."

"Charlotte . . ." Blackburn trembled on his heels. "Charlotte came home a little while ago with two of the queen's ladies. They went toward the east wing."

Daniel yanked his dagger free and held it to Blackburn's throat while Rob held him steady. "The east wing is unfinished."

"That's where they went," Charlotte's husband insisted. "Tell me what this is about? The queen will hear of it."

"Your wife is a harlot and a murderer." Daniel removed his dagger and moved toward the east wing. "And the queen already knows."

MacGregor kept pace with him, clearing stairs two and three at a time to reach the skeletal frame of the eastern wing of the house.

Charlotte's voice found its way to them through the hollow halls. They followed it until they came upon the three women on the opposite side of a narrow walkway.

Charlotte smiled at him and then scowled in response to his reaction to her. His eyes never left Abby, who was dangling from a rope over the side, bound by her wrists over her head.

The rope looked horrifyingly meager to his eyes. If it snapped and she fell, she would fall two stories into a pile of bricks and... He didn't allow himself to think of it. The leader of the queen's armies couldn't believe in anything but victory if he was to lead his men, or his woman, out alive. Death wouldn't separate him from Abigail this day. Like her father had done for her mother, Daniel would fight death for her and win.

"I expected you a little sooner, Daniel. What have I told you about keeping me waiting?"

"Charlotte," he countered, knowing her, knowing the only way to stop her was through fear. No other emotion would move this cold witch. "What did I tell you about hurting any more women?"

She faltered for a moment, then produced an axe when Abby's father moved toward them. "One more move and I'll cut her loose." Both men stopped breathing.

"Abby!" Nora's voice pulled Daniel's gaze away from Abby for an instant. There were too many people here. "She promised Cam's life would be spared if I told her what she wanted to know."

"Yes, she did tell me everything," Charlotte agreed, while Nora moved backward unnoticed and disappeared into the shadows.

"You two and your little tryst at Tarveness Keep." She glared at Daniel and then at Abby over the edge. "You don't love this commoner, do you, Daniel?" She must have sensed the shift of control and smiled. "Oh, you don't know, do you? Poor bastard." Her green eyes twinkled in the filtered light when she laughed. "Your precious Anne never told you, so please, allow me. I think you have the right know." She paused a moment for effect. Then, "You were not born to the Marlows, but to Prince George."

"And a servant girl," Daniel added, gaining again and taking a step toward her. "Yes, I know."

He watched her resolve nearly crumble. He had to finish her to save Abby. "By the queen's authority, I'm taking you into custody until you're tried for treason."

She smiled, but fear radiated from her. "Treason? Since when is killing a Scot considered treason?"

"We have Cameron MacPherson in our custody," Daniel told her truthfully; the rest was a lie to coax information from her. "He told us that it was you who paid him to kill the queen."

"He is lying! It was Richard!"

"Let her go and I'll spare you from hanging. Refuse me and I'll fashion the noose."

She may have seen Nora sweeping across the walkway like a wraith bent on killing her. But even if she had seen her, there was nothing she could have done. For with a burst of vigor and strength in one so slight, Nora hauled the duchess over the side.

Not knowing which one fell, Abby's anguished scream filled the halls, and the hearts of the men who'd come to save her.

But Daniel saw right away that there was a horrible problem. Charlotte had managed to grasp onto Abby's skirts as she went down. Abby kicked at her but Daniel stilled her, doubtful that the rope could both of them. He bent down for her just as her father reached him and did the same, and just as one of Charlotte's guardsmen appeared out of the shadows and swung a sword at them.

The chief deflected the blow and distracted the blade away from the rope.

"Save her!" he shouted to Daniel. "I'll take care of the rest."

Daniel intended to do that very thing. Leaning over the edge, he reached down and gripped Abby's wrist. He pulled, bringing her and Charlotte up another inch. He looked down at the rope. The top layer was frayed and getting worse with every breath. He pulled again, squeezing his eyes shut. When he opened his eyes, he met Charlotte's resigned gaze.

"I'm letting go," she said as if she were telling him the season.

"No! Hold on, Charlotte!" He shouted at her. "I'll pull you both up!"

"And live to hang? I think not." She released Abby.

Daniel cursed and yanked on Abby one more time. A shot rang out and pain fired through Daniel's arm. He nearly let go of Abby as the nerves in his arm momentarily went dead, but caught himself in time and held on, despite the bleeding hole in his bicep. He held on and managed to continue to hold on while another guardsman took a swing at him. Daniel ignored the attack and instead of using the strength in his good arm to fight, he used it to haul Abby up with one fully determined groan. She was almost there.

He suffered a minor slice to his left thigh but the next blow promised to be deadly, aimed at his neck. It was stopped by a shadow bursting from the other shadows and throwing herself into the man, throwing her second victim over the side.

Daniel watched the guardsman fall and hit the rocks two stories down with Charlotte. Then he looked at Nora and found her kneeling beside him.

"I'll help!" She reached down and provided just enough strength to lift Abby over the edge.

No sooner did he get her up and on solid ground than another man appeared over him. The man yanked him up by his neck, then pushed him back, trying to make him fall off the edge. Daniel caught his balance and shouted to Abby and Nora to get to safety. He stood to face the man he'd waited to kill for months. Montagu had been hiding out here, at Blackburn House, which meant Charlotte truly was involved in the plot to kill the queen. He wouldn't tell Anne.

"I'm so sorry about the queen," Montagu said, pointing a pistol at Daniel. "But what is done is done."

"The queen lives," Daniel informed him. "You failed yet again."

"You lie!"

One corner of Daniel's mouth angled upward. "You know I never do. You can also believe me when I tell you that I'm going to kill you for my men, Hubert and Ashley."

"And Andrews," Montagu told him. "I had him killed before I left Edinburgh. A true dunce, that one."

"If he gave you his allegiance then yes, he was."

The earl fired the pistol but he was slow on the draw. Daniel had never allowed his best men to train Montagu, keeping his skills at a minimal level of mastery. Daniel leaped at him while he tried to reload and they hit the ground fighting.

Somewhere close to him, Rob MacGregor inflicted his own brand of punishment on the men Montagu had brought with him. He'd stopped at least six and was catching his breath when his eyes found Daniel.

Rather than make a show of his skill, Daniel preferred mercy and kept his promise to Montagu quickly with a dagger to the heart. To the next five he did the same until there was no one left but Nora standing with them.

Daniel didn't give a damn about bringing Nora to justice. Whatever she'd done, she made up for it by helping him save Abby.

He looked up in time to see Abby on her feet and breaking from her father's embrace when she caught his eyes on her. Daniel caught her up in his arms, so relieved that she was unharmed that he didn't feel the pain of his wounds. Nothing would stop him from being with her if she would have him, not queens or princes, or land, or politics. "Abby, I love you," he told her, turning to kiss her lobe.

"And I love you."

Hell, he'd never thought anything would sound so pleasing to his ears.

Daniel bent his head to kiss her, but stopped when her father cleared his throat. "I wish to marry your daughter, Chief."

The chief cast him a dark look, as if he'd rather be anyplace but here. Finally, he gave in. "Ye proved to me that ye can protect her, Marlow. Ye saved her life despite the odds." Rob MacGregor's smile hovered over his mouth, reluctant but genuine. "I'm willin' to put aside yer heritage, but are ye?"

"Yes. I don't want any to know that I'm a royal, bastard or not."

Abby smiled up at him.

He ached to kiss her.

"And will ye tell her that she canna' succeed me if she leaves Camlochlin?"

Camlochlin. Daniel remembered the name of their home in the Highlands. Abby had been so afraid to tell him where it was. Now he understood why. He was glad her father had no trouble telling him. He wanted to see it, to visit the place that brought joy and peace to her eyes. He wanted to meet the people of her family—her grandfathers, her mother, and the rest of her cousins.

"Why would I tell her that?" He smiled, gazing into her eyes. "She'll make a fine chief, and I'll be there beside her."

Chapter Forty

"Do you smell it, Daniel?" Queen Anne leaned out the window in her carriage and inhaled another deep breath.

"Heather, my queen?"

She opened her eyes and looked up at him. "Heaven," she corrected. "It smells like Heaven here."

Daniel agreed. It looked like Heaven too. They arrived at the crest of a heather-carpeted vale behind their escorts. He didn't think he'd ever seen grass so green or flowers painted in such vivid shades of blue and red and yellow. He understood why Abby loved it here so much.

Hell, he missed her. But could he truly give up his life in London and live here, in the mountains, with men who fought over cattle? Hell, yes, he could. He longed to flick his reins and bring his mount into a full gallop to reach her.

"I'm anxious to meet her," Anne confided, peeking her head out of her carriage.

Daniel winked at her. "I'm sure your sister is just as anxious to meet you."

She smiled. A common occurrence since she'd met the MacGregors. Daniel owed them much.

After they'd discovered that Charlotte hadn't died from her fall they decided it best that Abby return home with her kin while he remained behind to see to justice and his queen while she recovered. He and Anne had talked of many things, including his father, George of Denmark, and after he learned all Anne would have him know, she agreed never to speak of it again. He thought telling her that he loved Abby and wanted to leave court would be difficult. It was. But Anne took it well. She couldn't think of anyone more deserving of Daniel's affection than Abigail. Besides, until he trained someone else to take his place, he would stay with her and his bride at Kensington Palace for half the year and then they would all travel back to Skye in the summer so Anne could spend time with her family. It was a good arrangement, for now, at least. After that, he would remain in Skye with his wife. Eventually Anne would be fine without him, just as she'd been when he fought the Jacobites. But he would miss her and visit when he could.

Anne pardoned her old friend for plotting to kill her and sent Charlotte and her husband to their house in Wales. Lady Blackburn had done damage to her spine and a chair, much like Anne's, had to be erected for her. Her punishment was fitting since they soon discovered that once Charlotte was away from Anne, the queen not only healed faster, but she began to walk again. Her physicians suspected that Lady Blackburn had been poisoning the queen for the past decade. Still Anne pardoned her.

Daniel hadn't allowed Cam MacPherson to hang. He did owe him much, after all. But MacPherson wouldn't taste freedom for a long time to come. Nora was grateful and visited her brother often. When she wasn't cooking him fine meals and bringing them to him, she served the queen and became one of Anne's closest confidants, along with Lynette.

"They are coming."

He thought he might be more nervous about seeing Abby again than Anne was about meeting her sister for the first time.

Daniel followed Anne's gaze and spotted the small group approaching by horseback. He spotted Abby right away—or was that her mother? A total of fourteen Highland warriors had come out to meet them. A bit daunting, just like the first time he'd met her family. Daniel straightened his spine and couldn't help but smile back at Tristan as the men drew closer and finally came to a halt.

They had become friends while the MacGregors stayed in England just after everything had taken place. They had much in common.

Daniel's gaze followed the sound of galloping hooves tearing up the grass behind them. He remained in his saddle, mesmerized at the sight of Abby racing toward him, her pale blond hair snapping behind her. Before her mount came to a full stop, she leaped from her saddle. He did the same and caught her up in his arms when she launched herself into them.

He was whole. Nothing mattered but her. Being away from her for three months had been torture he never wanted to endure again. He'd thought he could never love anything more than duty, but he had been wrong.

"Hell, I missed you." He smiled into her eyes and tilted her mouth up to his. He didn't care if her father was here or not. They were going to have to kill him to keep his hands off her. He wanted to marry her here. She had already said yes in their correspondence but he would ask her again, the way a Highland lass would want to be asked—atop a windswept mountain. The one behind her looked good enough.

"Come away with me," he beckoned.

"Where?" His beloved smiled, putting the landscape to shame.

He pointed to the mountain and she blushed, knowing he wanted to be alone with her and guessing why. She was only half right. He wanted to be her husband, the father of her children, the one who protected her from everything and anything that meant her harm.

They laughed and kissed, oblivious to the others around them, until her father cleared his throat.

They gave their attention to the queen's carriage and the door opening.

Daniel saw the riders part the way for another woman, this one smaller of frame than Abby, but with the same odd pearl-colored hair and enchanting smile. This had to be Davina. It didn't escape him that this was the true queen of Great Britain.

She slipped from her mount and took a tentative step toward the carriage. Her smile widened when she met her sister's gaze.

"Anne?"

Daniel fought back a burning sensation at the sight of Anne's tears falling freely while she walked to her sister.

"Welcome to Camlochlin," Davina said softly as Anne reached her and the two queens embraced. "I've never had a sister before."

Daniel felt Abby's hand on his face and looked down at her.

"'Tis called Sgurr Na Stri. The mountain," she explained when he cast her a curious look. "If ye still want to take me there."

"I do." He turned to the Highlanders greeting the queen and he waited until he caught Tristan's attention. "Is there a priest here?"

"Now?" The chief of the MacGregors paled.

"Now?" Her mother and the queen both squealed.

"Yes." Daniel took Abby's hands and brought them to his lips. He was madly and passionately in love with a Highland Jacobite—and the granddaughter of King James and the Devil MacGregor. He was about to make her his wife on a windy mountain cloaked in a thickening mist. If he'd gone mad, he never wanted to see sanity again.

"Now."

With his reckless charm and ice-blue eyes, notorious rake Malcolm Grant has never met a woman he couldn't seduce. But when he's wounded in a fight and nursed back to health by the beautiful, blind Emmaline Grey, Malcolm is the one in danger of losing his heart...

Please see the next page for a preview of

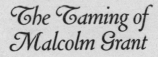

The Taming of Malcolm Grant

Chapter One

J thought travelin' with ye would be different, a bit of an adventure mayhap. But since we entered Sunderland, 'tis been nothin' but ridin' and rain."

Beneath his hood Malcolm Grant smiled at his brother, riding ahead of him. He didn't bother to look up since, in the downpour, he couldn't see an inch in front of his face anyway.

"We'll be there soon enough, Cailean," he called out, "and then ye'll thank me fer makin' haste to get here."

Malcolm had been to the Blind Mouse brothel many times in the past. It was his favorite spot to come to when he visited England. His old friend Harry Grey owned and ran it, so he always got the best room, the best girl, and the best whisky. Once in a while there was nothing better or more soothing to a man who lived in a hard world than a soft bed and a warm body to share it with. His brother was twenty and two. It was high time he lay with a lass who knew her way around a man's body. The Blind Mouse was the perfect place to go for such pleasures.

"'Tis just up ahead," he said, knowing how to get there

in the pitch-black or pouring rain. He caught up with Cailean and they followed the inviting warmth of fire-lit windows to the front of the two-story brothel. "Let me do the talkin'," he said, dismounting and handing his reins over to a stable boy. "Save fer Harry, the men are not friendly here. They'll look fer the first excuse to fight."

"So?" Cailean challenged, straightening his shoulders against the pelting rain. "Practice with our kin, nae matter how gruelin', has prepared me to stay alive against folks who might someday try to kill me." His brother slowed and waited for Malcolm to reach him. "Let them look fer a fight and I will give them one."

Malcolm shrugged, quite used to Cailean's bravado, seeing the same in almost every male—and many females—of the Grant/MacGregor ilk. He was, of course, of the same mind. He didn't mind fighting, but he'd like a damn drink first.

He pushed the door open and stepped inside. Familiar scents assailed his nostrils and he closed his eyes for a moment to savor them. The aromas of rose and wine, jasmine and whisky, sex and sweat. The only smell he loved more was early morning in Camlochlin.

Sweeping his hood back over his head, he settled his gaze on the patrons, pausing to linger over a few of the lasses who worked there. He personally didn't consider himself handsome, not with his bent nose and mostly disillusioned expression, which dulled his eyes and stiffened his grin. But he had dimples, and according to the lasses at Camlochlin, lasses liked dimples, deep ones, like his father's.

So he smiled at them, one by one, deciding which one to bed first. He turned to cast his grin on Cailean, entering behind him, but someone cursed and shouted, spoiling his good mood.

"Close the damned door before I get up and put your head through it!"

Malcolm turned to give the fool a deadly look. Truly? Was it going to begin so quickly then? Even before he wet his tongue?

What the hell else was new?

Very well then.

"Close yer mouth," Cailean called back, slamming the door, "before I walk over there and put m' fist in it."

The fool continued, as fools often do.

"I doubt you're worthy of such a boast, boy." The patron rose from his chair. "But which one of you is going to pay for letting in the rain to soak my clothes?"

Malcolm thought about it while he untied the laces of his cloak from around his neck. "I'll give ye two pence fer yer boots. The rest should have been put to the flame last month." With a flick of his wrist he freed his cloak from his broad shoulders and snapped it like a whip, showering the patron with cool droplets.

A true fight would do the youngest Grant good, Malcolm thought, stepping aside and watching the patron go barreling into Cailean. He didn't turn to see how his brother fared against the troublemaker, but turned his restored grin on a long-limbed, extremely lean man coming toward him with a cup in one hand and a bonny woman in the other.

"I wasn't sure I'd see ye pass this way again, Cal!" Harry Grey grabbed him in a tight embrace and pounded his back.

"Where would I be, Harry?" Malcolm accepted the cup and tossed his arm around his good friend. "And dinna' say wed or dead. Ye know me better than that."

They both watched Cailean make a quick end of his

opponent and toss him out the door. Malcolm motioned him over while Harry led him to a table. "I heard yer sister was kidnapped by pirates."

"She wasna' kidnapped," Malcolm corrected him, patting his brother's back when Cailean caught up.

Harry stopped and turned to him. "She went of her free will?"

"Aye," Malcolm told him, as if there were absolutely nothing wrong with it. To him, there wasn't. "She's the adventurous kind." He listened, smiling indulgently when Laurette, the lass Harry had brought to him, settled into his lap and proceeded to tell them about her adventure from Paris to England. Malcolm didn't think pointing out the difference between her journey and his sister's would do her any good.

He did suddenly feel the need to assure Harry that his sister was happy with her choice, that he or their father hadn't failed her.

They sat together for the next hour, drinking and laughing and recalling how they met.

"'Twas aboot a pair of years ago," Malcolm told them after Laurette asked. "I'd been on a bit of a drinking and whoring spree after the Union with England Act was signed. Edmund and I fought hard against it and didn't see victory."

Harry and Cailean both nodded.

"Though Harry is English," Malcolm told them, "he didn't throw me oot of his establishment on m' Highland arse."

"That's because," Harry said playfully, "you kept the thugs who would rob me away."

"Ye're hard," Laurette looked up at him with dewy blue eyes as vast and empty as the skies. "Like steel," she purred against his neck while she spread her hand over his arm and then down his chest.

Her friend Brianne joined them and sat with her foot in Harry's lap.

Cailean didn't give a rat's arse about drinking, but rather spent most of the time pursuing a bonny whore with russet curls and humble breasts. Harry explained that the gel was bought and paid for for the night by the Barristers of Newcastle. If he wanted her, he would have to wait until tomorrow. Cailean didn't want to wait, but he accepted things the way they were, as he was known to do, and set his sights on someone else—until his fiery-haired obsession was flung into a chair by one of the Barristers.

Malcolm would have let his brother fight alone for the girl, but when four Englishmen rose to their feet to go after him, Malcolm lent his arm. He didn't expect Harry to fight with them—he was the proprietor, after all—but Malcolm would have to speak to him about hiring a few strong-arms around the brothel to keep the shyt out, the way he used to.

The fight got a wee bit violent but it was over quickly, with the four Barristers dumped outside where the rain washed the blood from their wounds.

Four fewer Englishmen in their presence was a good thing. With the place less rowdy, Malcolm and Cailean returned to their table, Cailean with Sybil, his russet-haired prize, and toasted the sound of cracking bones.

Harry paled visibly while he told them about the Barristers. He was afraid of them. Most people were. Not because of any great fighting skills the Barristers possessed, but because of their sheer number. They had kin everywhere in England, with a good number of them right here in Newcastle.

What did Malcolm care about a bunch of gangly English who collapsed to the ground after three punches? Why, his sister could have taken them on two at a time. He did all to reassure Harry that the Barristers were nothing to fear.

"Drink with us, friend." He pushed another round at Harry and laughed when his friend accepted. "Laurette!" he called out to the bonny brunette who'd scurried off during the fight. "Come back to me!" He offered her his lap when she returned to him and she fell into it, dousing the blood in his veins with the sound of her laughter.

Now, here's what he had come for, he thought while he buried his face in Laurette's neck, warm flesh that tasted like summer honey, the touch of soft, eager fingers, a groan—

"Pardon my intrusion."

Malcolm opened his eyes. That wasn't Cailean's voice he was hearing. He doubted it was a voice he'd heard before. Light and flimsy, like a veil settling over him. He lifted his face from Laurette and turned to have a look at a lass he'd never seen here before. Then again, would he have remembered her? There was nothing remarkable about her appearance. Her gown was neither colorful nor cut to show off her curves, like the girls' gowns around her. She was rather pale, with large, dark eyes and long, yellow waves. She stood facing Harry, her delicate hand resting in the crook of a brawny arm.

So, Malcolm thought, glancing at the owner of the arm, here was the seemingly only guard in the brothel and he was too busy rutting to see to his duty.

"I was wondering if I might bring Hector inside for the night. It is still raining—"

"Now Emmaline." Harry sighed, sounding sincerely

regretful. "Haven't we discussed this over and over? Dogs don't belong inside, getting everything muddy and wet."

Malcolm laughed, bringing Emmaline's attention to him. "Then ye would hate my home," he told Harry. "We have five wolfhounds, or whatever in blazes they are, roamin' the halls right along with everyone else."

"You're correct," his friend agreed. "I would hate it."

Malcolm thought he caught the escorted lass's slight smile beyond the tilt of her head. She kept her gaze lowered.

By now, Malcolm was beginning to wonder who she was and why she needed an escort. The brute had no interest in her but to keep her attached to his arm. If he did care for her, he would be trying to comfort her from her obvious distress.

"'Tis a heavy downpour out there," Malcolm gave it a try, looking toward the door. He might be the worst rogue in Scotland, England, and France, but he had a heart. And he liked dogs. He knew firsthand that they perished, just like anything else, when exposed to the elements. He looked at his brother, remembering Sage, Cailean's faithful hound.

He wouldn't see it happen again.

Turning back to Harry, he said more seriously, "Come now, friend. I'll pay fer a room fer the mongrel and a lass to clean him up."

"I will do it!" Emmaline promised without haste. "And the room, too! You will not even know Hector was here when the sun comes out again."

Malcolm smiled at her. She didn't smile back, so he turned his grin on Harry, who didn't look pleased at all. "I'll count it as a favor," he told his good friend, "if ye dinna' let a dog hunker doun in the rain, aye?"

"And," Cailean added, "we willna' remain here if ye leave him ootside."

Malcolm didn't argue with his brother. Not about this. When Harry cast him a questioning look, he said nothing to refute Cailean's vow. They would leave. Malcolm would return at a later time, without his brother.

"Put your coin away." Harry held up his palms and released a long, defeated sigh. "Go, Emmaline. Fetch your dog from the rain."

He smiled and blushed a tinge of claret when she pulled her hand free of her escort and practically leaped into Harry's arms and hugged him. "Thank you."

She turned in a half circle and smiled at the wall to Malcolm's left. "Thank you, my lord." Without waiting for his reply, she turned again and hurried toward the door.

Malcolm watched her, his smile fading from his lips altogether when she banged into the table in front of her.

"Emmaline!" Harry said harshly. "Wait for Gunter!"

Gunter with the brawny arms hurried after her and returned her hand to his elbow once again. Harry shook his head, turning back to Malcolm.

"She'll want the beast inside every night now."

"She's blind." It became even more apparent while Malcolm watched her wait for Gunter, who had run out into the rain. She didn't move. She didn't watch the door, but inclined her ear toward it instead.

"Almost completely," Harry confirmed.

Hence her need for Gunter, Malcolm thought as her escort returned, soaking wet and not alone.

Hector galloped into the foyer and sprayed water and drool everywhere. When he saw Emmaline he immediately sat on his haunches, reaching her waist and still dripping all over the floor. The dog's reward for his good behavior was a hug from its mistress.

"Someone's going to have to clean that up!" Harry called out.

The lass nodded, then grasped Hector by the scruff of his neck and, abandoning Gunter altogether, let the dog lead her away. A dog that helped her see.

Fascinating, Malcolm thought. He wanted to know where Harry found her. "Who is she?"

"My sister," Harry told him, reaching for another cup of wine.

"Yer sister?" Malcolm laughed and shook his head when Laurette held a cup to his lips. "Ye never mentioned her before."

"I did tell you of her last year, but you likely weren't listening. I recently found her and I must warn you to forget her, Cal. I know you and love you like a brother. You saved my life many times."

"As ye saved mine," Malcolm reminded him.

Harry smiled. "Once."

"Once is all it takes to die, Harry."

"Like I said," Harry went on. "I love you like a brother. But if you use your devilish charms on her our friendship will end."

That sounded rather serious. Malcolm pulled him under his arm and patted his back to reassure his friend of his sincerity. "Ye've nothin' to fret aboot, Harry. I did this fer the dog. Not fer her."

Fall in Love with Forever Romance

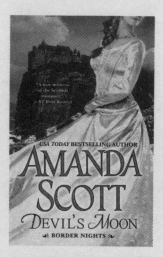
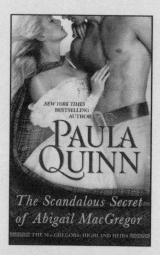

Fall in Love with Forever Romance

A KISS TO BUILD A DREAM ON
by Kim Amos

Spoiled and headstrong, Willa Masterson left her hometown—and her first love, Burk Olmstead—in the rearview twelve years ago. But the woman who returns is determined to rebuild: first her family house, then her relationships with everyone in town...starting with a certain tall, dark, and sexy contractor. Fans of Kristan Higgins, Jill Shalvis, and Lori Wilde will flip for Kim Amos's Forever debut!

IT'S ALWAYS BEEN YOU
by Jessica Scott

Captain Ben Teague is mad as hell when his trusted mentor is brought up on charges that can't possibly be true. And the lawyer leading the charge, Major Olivia Hale, drives him crazy. But something is simmering beneath her icy reserve—and Ben can't resist turning up the heat! Fans of Robyn Carr and JoAnn Ross will love this poignant and emotional military romance.

Fall in Love with Forever Romance

TOTAL SURRENDER
by Rebecca Zanetti

Piper Oliver knows she can't trust tall, dark, and sexy black-ops soldier
Jory Dean. All she has to do, though, is save his life and he'll be gone
for good. But something isn't adding up...and she won't rest until
she uncovers the truth—even if it's buried in his dangerous kiss. Fans
of Maya Banks and Lora Leigh will love this last book in Rebecca
Zanetti's Sin Brothers series!